SECRET TWINS FOR THE TEXAN

KAREN BOOTH

THE FORBIDDEN BROTHER

JOANNE ROCK

MILLS & BOON

First Published in Great Britain 2018
by Mills & Boon, an imprint of HarperCollinsPublishers,
1 London Bridge Street, London, SE1 9GF

Secret Twins for the Texan © 2018 Harlequin Books S.A.
The Forbidden Brother © 2018 Joanne Rock

Special thanks and acknowledgements are given to Karen Booth for her contribution to the Texas Cattleman's Club: The Impostor series.

ISBN: 978-0-263-93609-4

51-0718

MIX
Paper from
responsible sources

FSC www.fsc.org **FSC™ C007454**

This book is produced from independently certified FSC™
paper to ensure responsible forest management.

For more information visit: www.harpercollins.co.uk/green

Printed and bound in Spain
by CPI, Barcelona

Karen Booth is a Midwestern girl transplanted to the South, raised on '80s music, Judy Blume and the films of John Hughes. She writes sexy big-city love stories. When she takes a break from the art of romance, she teaches her kids about good music, hones her Southern cooking skills or sweet-talks her husband into whipping up a batch of cocktails. Find out more about Karen at www.karenbooth.net.

Four-time RITA® Award nominee **Joanne Rock** has penned over seventy stories for Mills & Boon. An optimist by nature and a perpetual seeker of silver linings, Joanne finds romance fits her life outlook perfectly—love is worth fighting for. A former Golden Heart® Award recipient, she has won numerous awards for her stories. Learn more about Joanne's imaginative muse by visiting her website, www.joannerock.com, or following @joannerock6 on Twitter.

Discover more at millsandboon.co.uk

SECRET TWINS FOR THE TEXAN

KAREN BOOTH

For my Desire author sisters,
Joanne Rock and Cat Schield.
I couldn't have written this book without you!

One

More than anything, Cole Sullivan wanted some dinner. It had been a long day of juggling his two jobs—running the Sullivan Cattle Co., his family's longhorn ranch, and investigating the disappearance of Jason Phillips, which had recently become a murder case. There were not enough hours in the day to be good at one thing, so Cole felt as though he was half-assing everything, and that was not the way he liked to operate.

But before food, he needed a shower. Hours out on a horse had his back in knots, and just as much time on the phone and the computer doing investigative work had his shoulders feeling even worse. He left behind his filthy ranch clothes and walked across the cool Carrara marble floor in his luxurious master bath. This was one of his favorite places to unwind and enjoy the finer things in life. With a turn of the gleaming chrome handle, a dozen showerheads sprang to life in the generous glass enclosure. He ducked into the hot spray, adjusting a few nozzles to hit his back and shoulders in just the right spots. Drawing in a deep breath, he willed his muscles to do the unthinkable and relax. The stress he was under was not good for him. His doctors would be deeply disappointed to learn how much strain he was putting his body through every day. He was practically tempting death. But it didn't matter. Worry about his physical state wasn't going to keep the multimillion dollar family business running, and it wouldn't avenge the death of an innocent man who'd left behind a seven-year-old daughter.

"Cole? You in there?" Cole's younger brother, Sam, was yelling out in the hall. This was one of the downsides of having his two brothers living on the family ranch. Separate houses for both Sam and Kane, and even at opposite corners of the sprawling property, but still, very little privacy.

Cole shut off the water and grabbed a thick white towel from the heated chrome bar, another luxury he appreciated greatly on days like today. "Yeah. I'm in here. What's wrong?"

"Nothing. I just meant to talk to you about something today, but we haven't had a spare minute."

And this was my spare minute. "Let me throw some clothes on. Grab a beer or something and I'll join you in a few."

"Got it."

Cole ruffled his hair with the towel, then wrapped it around his waist. Padding into his walk-in closet, he grabbed clean jeans and a plaid shirt, and joined his brother. Sam was out in the kitchen, sitting on one of the eight hand-tooled leather stools at the bar overlooking the center island topped with black Ashford marble. Much like the bathroom, no expense had been spared in the kitchen, with state-of-the-art stainless appliances and—something Cole considered a necessity for his coffee habit—a commercial grade espresso machine.

"What's up?" Cole headed straight for the subzero refrigerator and pulled out the steak he'd been looking forward to all day. He set it on the counter to let it come to room temperature.

"Dani's back in town."

Cole froze for a moment, letting those words sink in. He turned around. "What did you say?"

"Danica? Your ex-girlfriend? She's back in town. I thought you'd want to know." Sam threaded his fingers through his thick brown hair, a shade or two darker than Cole's. His blue eyes were plaintive, as if he expected Cole to accept the truth, regardless of the implications. Five years younger, Sam had a way of just coming out with things. There wasn't much diplomacy.

"Of course I know who you mean." Cole strode over to his brother and folded his arms across his chest. "Back or just visiting?" He hadn't seen Dani in nearly six years. That time had helped dull some of the sting of their breakup, but he lived with the reason for it every day. It was sitting inside his brain, just waiting to kill him.

Sam took a quick swig of his beer. It was the last bottle of Cole's favorite IPA. He never should've been so generous as to offer his brother a drink. "From what I heard, she's back. She's working as head chef at the Glass House over at the Bellamy."

"Not surprising." By all accounts, Dani had been wildly successful in New York. So much so that Cole was shocked she'd ever return. What job could be so enticing as to make her step off a big stage onto the decidedly smaller one in Royal?

"I just thought you would want to know. In case you

want to look her up. Or something." Sam shrugged. "I don't know if she's still single, but you are. And I know one thing for sure—you were a hell of a lot more fun when you were with Dani."

"Hey. That's not fair."

"It's the truth."

Cole didn't bother disguising his grumble. "I know better than to go barking up that particular tree. Dani would rather choke me than talk to me."

"Can you blame her? You broke her heart, Cole."

"I had my reasons. You know that better than anyone."

"And six years later, you're still alive while the woman you used to be madly in love with has just moved back to town. Maybe I'm nudging you in the right direction."

Cole shook his head. "I don't need nudging, but thanks. I'll see you tomorrow."

"That's it?" Sam got up from his bar stool and knocked back the rest of his beer, tossing the bottle in the recycling bin.

"The Dani chapter of my life is closed. She moved on and so have I." That wasn't entirely true. He still thought about her, more than he would ever admit out loud. Sometimes he even had dreams about their immediate and sizzling connection. Visions of Dani beckoning him to bed, her silky dark hair cascading over his crisp white sheets, still haunted him. Memories of making love with her were unforgettable—her luscious curves fit too perfectly in his hands to ever erase them from his mind. But she wasn't meant for him, and there was nothing he could do about that.

"You moved on to more work than is reasonable for one person to do."

"I gotta stay busy, Sam. It's the only way I know." Cole didn't need the money he earned from having two careers. Not by a long shot. But he did need to stay occupied. It was the only thing that kept him sane.

"You don't think Dani will come looking for you?"

"Are you kidding me? The woman packed up every one of her worldly belongings and moved halfway across the country three days after I broke it off. That's how far she's willing to go to get away from me." Cole's stomach rumbled. He stalked to the far side of the kitchen and pulled out a cast-iron pan for his steak. "My guess is that Dani will avoid me like the plague while she's here."

"You think you know her that well?"

"I do."

"And you don't want to reach out to her and tell her what happened?"

"No. I don't."

Sam shot Cole that look of pity that he absolutely hated. If he didn't love his brother so much, he might be tempted to knock that look right off his face. "You are a sad case, Cole Sullivan."

"That's life. The sooner you get used to it, the better."

Whether she liked it or not—and she didn't like it at all—Danica Moore could not live in Royal, Texas, and avoid Cole Sullivan forever. She was going to run into him and his handsome face at some point, and it would be ridiculously hard not to slap him. Just imagining the sting of her palm when it struck his chiseled jaw brought a bit of satisfaction, but not enough to undo the pain Cole had caused her. A lifetime of face slaps could not erase that.

Running into Cole's parents or one of his two brothers, Sam and Kane, was just as likely. The superwealthy Sullivans were as ubiquitous in this town as the sun was fierce in July. Dani was eager to avoid any surprise run-ins—too much dredging up of painful memories. His elitist parents' persistent disapproval of her. The accident. Nursing Cole back to health. And a rejection that not only knocked her back on her heels, it left her gasping for what had felt like her last breath.

But she was back in Texas, a state that was in her blood, and there was nothing anyone was entitled to say about that. She wanted her twin sons to know the open sky and fresh air she'd lived off as a child. She wanted them to know the only living family she loved, her aunt Dot and her longtime best friend, Megan Phillips. When Megan told her that the executive chef job at the Glass House at Maverick County's crown jewel, the Bellamy, was available, Dani took her chance to return to Royal. She could keep her career as top-notch chef on track and give her boys a connection to a place she loved deeply. Couldn't do both of those things in New York. Hence, hello, Texas. Again.

But for as many problems as Royal solved, it left her with one—Cole. He was the ultimate loose end. She was already living on borrowed time. She'd been back in Royal for a few weeks. She'd have to see him eventually, so she decided she would see him on her terms. Tonight. His place. He would get no warning. He didn't deserve it.

Dani turned in the mirror, sucking in a breath so deep it was as if she believed the air was made of confidence. Her long black hair was perfect—glossy and full. Touchable. Her makeup was on point, as well. The dress was the cherry on top. Cherry red, to be exact, cut to show off her assets and hugging every curve she'd been blessed with.

She'd worked hard to get back her prepregnancy body, and she intended to let Cole get an eyeful before she informed him that she'd returned to Royal for good and he was cordially invited to leave her the hell alone. Break a woman's heart and you get the cold shoulder. Or in Cole's case, trample a woman's heart, destroy her illusions about love and leave her knocked up with twins, and you got a four-alarm fire set on showing you what's what.

Dani ducked her head into the bedroom her five-year-old twin boys, Cameron and Colin, shared. She adored this room, with its powder blue walls, the bunk beds the boys had always wanted, and plenty of floor space to play with cars and trains. It was everything they couldn't have in a New York apartment. "Everybody ready for bed?"

Elena, Dani's faithful nanny, looked up from the book she was reading to the boys. "You look amazing," Elena said. "You're going to knock Cole Sullivan dead."

Dani raised a finger to her lips and shook her head so quickly she nearly rattled her own brain. She wasn't ready for Cameron and Colin to know Cole's name. Not yet. They were still so little, so innocent. It wasn't their fault their daddy couldn't be counted on.

"Oh, right. Sorry." Elena's facial expression said more than her words—she understood how important it was to keep the boys a secret from Cole and vice versa. "Boys, hold on one minute. I need to talk to Mommy." Elena got up from the floor and tiptoed over to Dani. "You sure you're not going to tell him?" She didn't need to add the part about the boys. Dani knew exactly what Elena was asking.

"No way. Not today." Dani wouldn't tell Cole anything unless she was completely certain that he wouldn't reject the boys the way he'd rejected her.

"What are you going to say to him when you run into him later and he sees the boys?"

Dani patted Elena on the shoulder. "That's the least of my worries. Cole is so self-absorbed, I doubt he'll bat an eye."

Elena smiled, even though she appeared unconvinced. "I'm sure you know what you're doing." She returned to her spot on the floor to resume story time.

"You boys be good for Elena, okay?" Dani reminded them.

"Where are you going, Mommy?" Cameron asked, ever the chatty and curious one. He looked most like Dani, with dark brown hair and hazel eyes. Colin, her quiet observer, more closely resembled Cole. Lighter hair. Soulful blue eyes.

"I have an old friend I need to go see."

"Why can't we go with you?"

"Because this is going to be boring grown-up talk and I know you'll have much more fun with Elena. Plus, it's nearly your bedtime. Growing boys need their sleep." She knelt down onto the carpet and collected her hugs and kisses. "I love you both very much. See you in the morning."

"Good luck," Elena mouthed.

Dani marched down the hall, snapped up her car keys and slipped through the kitchen to her three-car garage. She'd had nearly six years to stress and worry about the first time she would see Cole again. If she stopped to think about it for too long, she'd put it off, and she didn't want to do that. She knew the exact message she wanted to send tonight, which meant leaving the minivan parked right where it was and choosing to climb into her latest purchase, a treat for herself, a silver Porsche convertible.

Dani had always loved cars. She got it from her dad, who had been a police officer. Ten years gone and Dani still missed him like crazy, but zipping around in this little sports car made her feel closer to his memory. He'd taught her to drive stick. He'd taught her to be a great driver. All those years in New York had meant too many taxis and subway rides. Dani liked to think that her new car was a perfect metaphor for her new life. She was in control now. Completely.

She pulled out of the circular flagstone driveway, the engine purring. The Texas ash and bur oak trees dotting the perimeter of her two-acre property were lit up by the landscape lighting below. The night air was warm, but she could tell that fall was on the way. The days were getting shorter and the mornings a tiny bit cooler. As she drove away from her house, Dani still couldn't believe it was hers—six bedrooms and a nanny suite, tall leaded-glass windows and yellow jessamine vines climbing the trellises next to the arched front door. There was a big pool for the boys out back, and she was having a play structure put in next week. It was perfect, and she'd earned it all on her own.

As she pulled past the guard gate at the entrance to her neighborhood, she couldn't quite believe that, either. Pine Valley was an ultra-upscale gated golf community, the exact opposite of the neighborhood she'd grown up in. Having had a dad in law enforcement and a mother who struggled to keep a job, Dani grew up modestly. They weren't poor, but they weren't well-off by any stretch. Dani still naturally gravitated toward the clearance section in a department store if that was any indication. Even now, when she had money.

The drive out to Cole's ranch gave Dani the perfect opportunity to rehearse her speech, but every time she started it, she tripped over her words. The trouble was imagining what it was going to be like to finally face him. If he cracked his heartbreaker smile, or looked too closely at her with his piercing blue eyes, she could easily be a goner. If he touched her with his strong hands, she'd melt into a puddle. The love and passion she shared with Cole had once run so deep. Ignoring that would not be easy. Which meant she needed to give him the news in as direct a fashion as possible. "Cole, I'm here to tell you I'm back. And I don't care if you don't like it. If you leave me alone, I'll promise to do the same for you." That could work. Now she hoped that she could deliver it as smoothly as that.

Dani flipped on her blinker and turned on to the road out to the Sullivan family ranch. Just being on the outer edges of their massive property, miles and miles of some of the most gorgeous ranch land in this part of Texas, made her nervous. It was a big reminder of the deepest divide between her and Cole before he'd dumped her— his family was royalty here, with enough money to never think about it twice.

She came from next to nothing, and Cole's parents quite frankly had never seen the appeal of Dani. His mother had even once told her that she didn't think she was good enough for her son. Dani had kept that tidbit to herself, deciding at the time that love would conquer all and she would eventually win them over. That day never came. Cole broke up with her a mere six months later, and the memory of that interlude with his mom became fuel for Dani's quick exodus from Royal. She knew when she wasn't wanted and always acted accordingly.

Dani passed the opulent main gates to the Sullivan Cattle Co. property and instead drove around to the smaller access point used by the ranch hands and delivery people. She would've preferred to make a grander entrance, but she remembered the code for the side gate, not for the others. That was how far she'd been pulled into Cole's life, and just how far she'd been flung out. Still, her heart was pounding when she pulled up to the keypad and pressed the square silver buttons. Knowing her luck, Cole had changed the code.

Wouldn't you know, the iron gate creaked and rolled across the driveway. Dani decided to take this as a final sign. Today was the day she was meant to do this. The sun was still setting as she approached the house, leaving behind gorgeous wisps of red and orange set against that vast black Texas sky. Dani had always loved this house, even if it was a bit over-the-top. There were nearly a dozen peaks in the roofline, too many windows to count, and a wide porch suitable for your fifty closest friends to pull up a rocking chair and sit a spell. It wasn't even the best view on the property, either. The vista out behind the house was even better—with a sprawling flagstone patio and pool and the perfect sight lines to enjoy the gorgeous pastoral scene.

Dani pulled up in front of the main house and parked. She checked her hair and lipstick, then flipped up the visor. She'd better get going before she chickened out. She marched straight up the porch steps and on to the front door. As nervous as she'd been to punch in the code at the gate, ringing the doorbell felt one hundred times more harrowing. The chime was so loud, she could hear it clearly right through the door. She turned away and stepped to the edge of the porch, surveying the crushed-stone drive that carved its way through the grass for a mile down to the main road. Up here on this hill, tucked away from the rest of the world, she couldn't deny she was happy to be back in Royal. Even with everything waiting for her on the other side of that front door.

She turned back and took another try at getting someone to answer, this time jabbing the doorbell twice. She stood up on her tiptoes and looked through the glass at the top of the heavy wood door. In that instant, her eyes met Cole's as he strode through the front hall.

Shoot.

She dropped down to her heels. Her heart was hammering like she'd just run to the house instead of driving. She pressed her hand to her heaving chest and backed up to the middle of the porch to give herself some space. *Short and sweet. Keep it simple and get the heck out of Dodge.*

She forced a smile as he opened the door but quickly realized just how pointless her preparations in the car had been. She was in no way ready to be in the company of tempting and towering Cole Sullivan. Not his muscular shoulders or broad chest. Not his haywire brown hair, so thick it had no choice but to stand nearly straight. And good God, it was damp. Had he just taken a shower? She was not ready for those ice-blue eyes or his tanned skin or the way his lips were slack and questioning right now. She was not yet ready to handle the way he was blinking at her, in utter shock. How could anyone make confusion so sexy?

"Well, well. If it isn't Dani Moore. I heard you were back in town." His voice was all swagger and ego, and that just made her mad. Of course he already knew she was back. How could she have been so stupid to have thought any less of him? Cole stepped over the threshold, leaving him a single stride away.

Instinctively, she took another step back. She could feel exactly how drawn she was to him. Her body wanted nothing more than to press against the hard planes of his body and kiss him. Her brain was well aware of how foolish that idea was, and it was prepared to do anything to protect her. "Yes. I'm back."

"Six years and you just show up on my front porch?" He shook his head and laughed mockingly.

Dani failed to see what was so damn funny. "Hell, yes, six years and I just show up on your front porch. I was afraid that if I called, you'd lock up the whole ranch so tight no one would ever get in." She sucked in a deep breath to quiet her thumping heart. She could do this. Even if seeing him had her ready to abandon common sense and fling herself into his arms. No wonder she'd been so hung up on him for years. Seeing Cole Sullivan was like coming home.

"So this is a permanent change?" His thick eyebrows drew together, making it hard to answer in a timely fashion.

"I'm the new executive chef at the Glass House."

"That's a pretty fancy gig." Cole leaned against the door frame, crossing his arms over his broad chest. "Of course it'd have to be to pry you away from the glamour of New York."

She pursed her lips. How dare he take that tone? "It wasn't about the glamour. Going to New York was about putting myself on the map in the culinary world. And it was about getting as far away from you as possible."

He smiled wide, and damn if it didn't make the desire to kiss him that much stronger. "Gotta love that trademark honesty of yours. It's refreshing."

"I'm not here to entertain you. I don't want things to be awkward or uncomfortable if we run into each other, and you know how this town is. We'll definitely cross paths. I just don't want any trouble."

"If you don't want things to be awkward, come and have a drink." He gave a nod inside.

"This isn't social hour, Cole. This was supposed to be a quick visit."

He cocked an arrogant eyebrow at her. "If it's not social, why are you wearing a dress designed for stopping traffic?" He looked her up and down, his determined gaze making it feel as though she was wearing nothing at all. "Not that I'm complaining. I've always loved this particular view, and I have to say, it's improved with time."

Heat bloomed in her chest and ran the length of her body. Damn the more girlish parts of her. Why did they have to be so thrilled by the revelation that he thought she looked good? Oh, right, because that had been part of her plan. She'd wanted to mow him over with her assets. Well, good. She'd accomplished that much. "This old thing? I'm still unpacking, and it was the first thing hanging in my closet."

The skepticism was all over his face. "Uh-huh. Well, it seems a shame to put that old thing to waste. Come in and have a glass of scotch"

"No, thank you."

"I have a bottle of twelve-year Johnnie Walker Black from the '70s. My dad had it in his cellar. I know you love your scotch."

Shoot. She *did* love scotch, and being around Cole had her needing to soothe her ragged nerves. Plus that bottle of water she drank in the car on the way over? It had been a bad idea. She needed to use the ladies' room, pronto. Even so, it didn't matter. This was Cole Sullivan. He hadn't just trampled her heart, he'd driven over it with his big old pickup. She would never forgive him for that.

Anger rose in her like floodwaters. "I told you, no. Don't think that you can just sweet-talk me and I'll be nice to you." She whipped around so fast her skirt twirled. That hadn't been her aim, but it did make for good drama. "See ya around, Cole." She waved, not looking at him, thundering down the stairs.

"Dani. Come back. Stop being ridiculous."

She stopped dead in her tracks. "Ridiculous? What exactly about this is ridiculous? You treated me like crap, Cole. I nursed you back to health after your accident and how did you reward my undying devotion? You broke up with me." With every word out of her mouth, she was only getting more and more infuriated. She planted a finger dead in the center of his chest. "You are a jerk. And I don't have drinks with jerks. End of story."

She reached for her car door handle, but the next thing she knew, Cole had his hand on her arm. His touch was tentative, but it was enough to make her shudder. Her heart fluttered. White hot desire coursed through her veins. He sent a tidal wave of recognition through her, something for which she'd been wholly unprepared.

Two

Cole acted out of pure instinct, tearing down his driveway after Dani. Damn, the woman could run in heels. Luckily, his long legs carried him fast enough to give him an edge and he caught her, wrapping his hand around her arm before she could open the car.

The instant he touched her, he knew he'd made a colossal mistake. He knew it all the way down to the soles of his feet. There was too much fire between them. Always had been and probably always would be. Sure, that had been years ago, and a lot had changed since then, but he should have known better. Still, he couldn't let her run off like this.

"Dani, don't. Please don't leave. It's okay to still be mad."

She whipped around, sending a trail of her sweet perfume straight to his nose. How could he have forgotten how beautiful she was? Glossy black hair, fiery brown eyes and red lips that could make a man forget what exactly he'd come for. "I do not need your permission to be mad. I'll be mad for the rest of my life if I feel like it."

One thing was for sure—Cole was sorely out of practice in the art of taming Dani. "I know. I'm sorry. You're right."

She tried to wrestle her arm from his grip, but that bit of friction between them—warm skin against warm skin—sent a flood of memories through his brain. Dani had always done this to him. She'd always brought everything back to life. He'd just forgotten how good it felt to have a taste of it.

"Let me go."

He did as she requested, but she didn't move. She didn't immediately reach for the handle on the car door, and Cole decided to take that as a good sign. She wasn't running again. Not yet, at least. "Please come in and have one drink. I want to hear about New York. I want to know what's going on in your life."

"Maybe I don't feel like telling you."

"Good God, you are stubborn." He shook his head. "Probably why I could never quite get you out of my system."

"Yeah, right."

"I'm dead serious. I wasn't kidding about the scotch, either."

She looked away, and the moonlight caught her profile—an adorable nose that turned up slightly at the end, dark hair blowing in the breeze across her creamy skin. For what felt like the millionth time, he wished he hadn't had to push her away nearly six years ago, but he'd had no choice. Life and death had been hanging in the balance. Her whole future opened wide, and his narrowed to a narrow and finite point.

"I do need to use the restroom," she muttered, seeming embarrassed.

"Perfect. Come on in."

He tentatively placed his hand at the small of her back to usher her up the driveway, but she was walking a pace faster. "I wasn't kidding. I drank an entire bottle of water on the way over here."

Cole laughed and jogged ahead, taking the porch steps in two long strides and opening the door for her. "You know where it is."

She cocked an eyebrow at him. "I do."

He watched her as she walked down the hall, wondering once again if he was seeing things. Dani was in his house. Wearing a dress that hugged every glorious inch of her, especially his favorite parts—her hips, her butt, her breasts. Basically, everything that was lush and round and good for sinking his fingers into. When Sam had told him a half hour ago that she was back in town, he certainly hadn't thought she'd turn up on his front porch. It was like fate was delivering him a gift he had no idea what to do with.

There was no telling how long Dani or her lovely dress were going to stick around. His gut told him he'd better make this good. He hustled into his grand but comfortable living room, with high wood-beamed ceilings and seating for at least twenty people for the rare times when he decided to entertain. He turned off the flat-screen TV above the stacked stone fireplace and switched on an antique bronze craftsman lamp to cast a warm glow, making the room feel cozier. More intimate. He put on some soft music and lit a candle. Hopefully Dani wouldn't use that open flame to set his house on fire. He was straightening the throw pillows on one of the leather sofas when she appeared.

"Company coming over?"

"What kind of gentleman would I be if I didn't make the place presentable?"

"I don't know. What kind of gentleman would you be?"

The question was so heavy with innuendo it could've broken a bone if dropped on his foot. "On the rocks, right?"

"Good memory." She breezed past him and took a seat.

"I only poured you one of these at least a hundred times."

"Probably more like twice that."

"Sometimes we drank beer. Or wine. There was a lot of wine." The undercurrent was that there had been an awful lot of good times between them. Fun times. Celebratory, joyous times. Birthdays. A few anniversaries, even.

There was a lot of history between them, and he knew he had no business dredging it up. Not tonight. Possibly not ever. Especially not about the reasons he'd had to break up with her. Still, she'd always been his biggest weakness. A drink for old times' sake wouldn't hurt.

He walked over and handed her the drink. She took it from him, their fingertips brushing just enough to send a jolt of electricity zipping up along his arm. She was as sexy as ever, even when she was mad. Maybe *especially* when she was mad.

"Tell me about New York." He took the seat right next to her on the couch. Some habits were impossible to break. Sitting with her like this made him want to put his arm around her, pull her close and kiss her. He needed to feel her soft lips against his and taste everything he'd missed over their years apart. The realization made it nearly impossible to sit still, let alone seem relaxed.

She sat a little straighter. "It was great. I did well for myself. Well enough to buy a house out in Pine Valley."

"Did you take up golf? That's a neighborhood for hitting the links or raising a family. That doesn't really seem like your speed." Maybe she'd changed more than he'd bargained on.

"It's beautiful out there, and it's a gated community. I like feeling safe. Is there anything wrong with that?"

He shook his head. "Nope. Nothing at all." He took a long sip of his drink. "I guess your success explains the zippy little death trap you pulled up in."

"A woman is entitled to buy a sports car."

"Absolutely. Just be careful. One run-in with a semi and you'll end up in traction. Or worse."

"You're one to be giving lectures on driving. I seem to remember you wrapping your squad car around a tree and nearly killing yourself." A dark shadow fell across her face as she turned to look at him. "That's what started the trouble between us, remember?"

He'd walked right into that one. He needed to avoid subjects that could eventually lead to the stupid things he'd done. "I'm not talking about me. And you don't see me driving around in a roller skate."

"It's a Porsche. And it's fun to drive. You should try it some time." She shot him an all-knowing look that made his pants feel a little too tight. "So, she probably shouldn't have said anything, but Megan told me that you're working on the investigation into her brother's murder."

He nodded. "You know, Megan's been through the wringer. It's hard for me to blame your best friend for wanting to tell you everything. But yes, we are keeping a very tight lid on things until we can catch Rich."

"So you think he's still here in Royal? Hiding out? Lurking in the shadows?"

"I do. There's a lot of money that's gone unaccounted for and we know he's not about to walk away from that. The man has no fear. He's proven that he will do anything."

"I still can't believe he stole Will's identity, embezzled all of that money, and then went and married Megan." She shuddered. "It's so scary. I can't imagine what she's going through. I just wish there was something I could do to make it better."

"That's my job. But don't worry. We will catch him."

"Good." She knocked back the rest of her drink and gently set the glass on the table.

"One more?"

"I shouldn't." She looked right at him, her tempting lips within striking distance. He couldn't think of a time he'd wanted to kiss her more, not even the very first time he'd done it, when he was a young Texas Ranger and she was a brand-new chef. Back when their whole lives were stretching out before them and the future seemed ripe with possibilities. "But it's just too delicious to say no."

"That's my girl." He berated himself as soon as the words came out of his mouth. That's what the old Cole would've said. The Cole who'd broken her heart to save her. He got up from the couch and poured them both another drink before sitting back down. Hopefully she hadn't noticed what he'd said.

"It's been a long time since you called me that."

"I'm sorry. I shouldn't have said it."

She took the glass when he offered it to her. "It's okay. It was actually sort of nice to hear." She laughed quietly. "I don't know exactly how pathetic that sounded, but I'm guessing pretty darn pathetic. That's what happens when you go for years being single. You end up a total sucker for sweet things guys say."

His ears perked up at that. Not only was she still single, she'd been that way for a while. He knew he shouldn't take any encouragement, but now that he had a drink under his belt and she was softening her hard exterior, it was impossible not to want her and feel as though he had a chance. "Apparently the men of New York don't know a good thing when they see it."

Her eyes raked over his face. That hot, seductive look made him want to dig his hands into her hair and taste her lips. He wanted to unzip that dress, touch every inch of her silky skin, and get lost in her for hours. "A few have a clue. They just don't manage to have a clue for very long. That's the problem."

"Anybody serious?"

She arched an elegant brow. "You really want to know?"

"I really want to know." Except he didn't. The thought of her with another guy made him want to put his fist through a wall, even when he'd willingly given her up.

She took another sip of the amber scotch and cradled the glass in her hand. "One guy lasted a year. Another chef. Celebrity chef, actually. I doubt you watch the Food Network, but he has a bunch of shows. Taylor Blake."

Cole didn't watch the Food Network, but he'd have to be living under a rock to not know Mr. Blake. He was a big figure in the world of barbecue championships, handsome as a male model and knew his way around the kitchen. He also happened to look quite a lot like Cole. Apparently Dani had a type. "I know exactly who that is."

"Oh. Well, it was a long time ago now. He came close to popping the question, I think, but it didn't happen. Too many career aspirations between the two of us."

Dani had always had big dreams. She'd come from

very little and had always been determined that wouldn't define her. Her lofty goals were part of what had made Cole end things with her, even though they were also much of what had attracted him to her. He couldn't guarantee her he'd be around long enough, and he never wanted to hold her back. "I'd say I'm sorry, but I'm not really."

"I'm not sure what that means."

"It means I'm not sorry you're single." The words escaped his mouth before he realized what he was saying. He needed to ride the brakes right now, not rev the engine, even if Dani did make his heart pound in his chest and everything below his waist flicker back to life. He was in the middle of a case, back to putting himself in danger. She'd hated it when he was a Texas Ranger, running around and catching criminals. Now he was back at it as a private investigator.

But that was part of who he was—he'd always had a strong sense of right and wrong and a fierce desire to set things straight. This thirst for justice was fed when Cole was twelve and his parents had some trouble with several ranch hands that were not only stealing from them, they were committing robberies in Royal. The Texas Rangers had solved the case and recovered his parents' losses. In their cowboy hats and holsters, Cole had thought the Rangers were everything he wanted to be—strong, resourceful, and dedicated to seeing that justice was served.

"You're drunk," she said.

"No. I'm not."

She laughed that breathy Dani laugh. "I sometimes think you like to argue as much as I do." She angled herself toward him and flashed her big brown eyes, biting her lower lip. It felt like an invitation, but he wanted a little more. One more sign. "I sort of missed it. I have yet to meet another man who will stand up to me."

"Is that what you want? Is that what you need?" His pulse was thundering in his ears as he waited to hear her response. He was really hoping for *I need you. Right now. Right here.*

"Now where's the fun in telling you what I need, mister? I'd rather keep you guessing. I think I've earned the right to do that."

But he did know what she needed, and what she wanted, at least when it came to the physical. That part had never been a problem between them. In fact, it had always been perfect. Consequences be damned, he decided to dip his toes in this hot water, even if he might end up getting scalded. He lowered his head, eyes open to watch for punches launched, but all Dani did was shake her head.

"You're going to kiss me?"

"Right now." He moved a little closer.

"Right here?"

"Unless you tell me to stop." He was inches away, so close that he felt her warm breath on his lips. Her beautiful skin was calling to him, begging for his touch.

"I suppose one time couldn't hurt."

Dani sealed the deal before he could do it. Cole clamped his eyes shut and wrapped his arms around her, pulling her tight against him. It only took a second until she was bending into him, angling her neck for a deeper kiss. Her lips parted and her tongue sought his. That was all the encouragement he needed. He leaned back on the couch, pulling her with him, until her beautiful body was stretched out over the length of his.

She pulled away for an instant, breathless. "What are we doing?"

"I think you know exactly what we're doing." He hoped like hell she wasn't about to change her mind. He never knew with Dani. He kissed her neck, which was a bit of a low blow. He knew exactly how much she loved it.

Dani groaned her approval. "If this happens, it doesn't mean anything. Not a damn thing, okay?"

Maybe Dani really was a gift delivered by the universe. If he could have her one more time and go back to his miserable life later, it would be the best of both worlds. For both of them.

"I promise. This doesn't mean a thing."

The heat from Cole's body was making it impossible to think straight, but Dani did manage one salient thought: if she was going to have a meaningless hookup with some guy, Cole was her best choice. There was nothing to lose. Everything had already been lost.

He dug his fingers into her hair, deepening their kiss. Of course she was going to respond in kind. He tasted of her favorite scotch. She'd forgotten how good he was with his tongue. He was bringing to life parts of her that had practically closed up shop. He drew a line down her spine but kept going, tugging up the hem of her dress, dragging his knuckles along the backs of her thighs. The air was cool against her skin when he had the fabric up around her waist, but then his fingers slipped into the back of her panties and the heat spiked again.

He was hard between her legs. Even through his jeans she could feel how badly he wanted her. It felt like some small measure of revenge to grind against him, knowing she was frustrating him. Unfortunately, her own dissatisfaction was gaining speed.

Cole shifted up onto his elbows, and Dani reared back her head.

"Let's sit up," he said, his voice a sexy rumble. "I want to get to the rest of you."

"Of course." She hopped up and Cole straightened to sitting.

He curled his finger. "Come here." His voice was low and rough.

It sent a thrill right through her, but she shook her head. "Not yet."

"Don't tease me, Dani. You'll kill me."

"As appealing as you make that sound, I want what I can get out of this, too." She planted her hands on his thighs, leaning forward and letting him get an eyeful of her cleavage. Then she lowered herself to her knees.

Cole untucked his soft, plaid shirt and tore it open. Thank goodness for pearl buttons. Dani sucked in a gasp when he rolled himself out of the sleeves. How she'd missed his broad chest and the patch of sandy-brown hair. She spread her hands across his firm pecs, loving the way his chest rose beneath her palms. She trailed a finger down his centerline, stopping to trace the contours of his abs. A woman could get lost following those lines. Dani had, many, many times.

When she reached his belt buckle, the metal clattered. She unbuttoned his jeans and drew down the zipper. Cole raised his hips and let her tug his pants down his legs. She placed her elbows on his thighs again, leaning forward and touching him through the fabric of his black boxer briefs. He closed his eyes halfway and dropped his chin to his chest, a deep groan escaping his throat. She loved feeling how hard he was from her touch. She loved knowing that she could still do this to him after all this time.

She pulled the waistband down and took him in her hand, lowering her head and drawing only the tip into her mouth. She stroked and sucked, swirling her tongue round and round. He dug the fingers of both hands into her hair, curling them into her head, raking them through her tresses. She wasn't about to let him reach his peak this way. She just wanted a reminder that she could drive him crazy if she wanted to.

She gently released the suction of her lips. His eyes opened only partway as he looked at her. "You are wearing entirely too many clothes."

She stood and Cole scooted to the front edge of the couch, bracketing her legs with his knees. She looked down at him, watching as he untied the bow at the side of her wrap dress. The reaction he had when the dress fell open was so good she almost wished she had a camera to capture the moment. The lust in his eyes? The craving? It was off the charts. The bra and panties she'd opted for, made of the finest French lace, were clearly adding to the appeal. Dani loosened the other tie and let the dress fall to the floor.

Cole rose from the couch and stepped out of his boxers. He was towering over her, even when she was still wearing heels. All that hard manly muscle pressed against her was enough to send her over the edge. She'd forgotten just how easy it was to want Cole Sullivan.

He wasted no time reaching around and unhooking her bra and dragging it down her shoulders. He gripped her rib cage with both of his hands and rubbed her nipples with his thumbs, sending a ribbon of pleasure shooting down her torso and into her thighs. He lowered his head and drew one firm bud into his mouth, swirling his tongue in circles. She watched him as he nearly sent her over the edge with the simplest touch.

She placed her hands on his waist and felt the raised skin of the scar along his right flank. He jumped a bit and so did she. They looked at each other and she saw it in his eyes—an unspoken acknowledgment of their traumatic past. The accident. The breakup. Everything that ushered in the last five years, one of the most difficult periods of her life, despite the beauty of becoming a mother. This was a mistake. She could not let Cole in. Not like this.

She pushed away from his chest and scrambled around, plucking her clothes from the floor as humiliation washed over her.

"What are you doing? Do you have some place you need to be?" he asked gruffly.

"This is a mistake, Cole. A huge, massive mistake."

"You need to work on your pillow talk." He was just standing in front of the couch—completely naked, no less.

She was not going to let visions of his physique get in the way of her quick escape. She grabbed her fancy undergarments from the floor. What had she been thinking putting these on when she got dressed? She knew where she was going. Cole didn't deserve French lace. He didn't deserve to see her in a potato sack, as far as she was concerned. She gave him everything once—her heart, body, and devotion. He threw it all away.

A bundle of clothes in her arms, she tore off down the hall to the powder room she'd used when she first arrived. She couldn't even look at her own reflection in the mirror. She was too embarrassed and furious with herself. She'd probably spit right into the glass. She sat down on the toilet to pee and stepped into her panties. So much for telling Cole to stay away—she'd swung in the opposite direction, let him take off her clothes and climbed right onto his lap. How dumb could she possibly be?

A knock came at the door. "Dani. Come on. Stop being so dramatic."

Speaking of dumb, what was Cole thinking, accusing her of being dramatic? "Go away. Go upstairs to your room or something. I don't want to see you again." She flushed the toilet to drown out anything he might say in response. Unfortunately it didn't work.

"I want to make love to you, Dani." His voice was louder now, like his forehead was pressed against the door.

"No. You want sex. It was supposed to be a meaning-less hookup. Remember? You promised me this would mean nothing." Now that her bra was hooked, she made quick work of wrapping herself up in that stupid, stupid dress. She was going to have to throw it away or drop it at the dry cleaner's and never pick it up.

"Come on. Are you just going to leave me like this?"

Dani grumbled and made a cursory glance in the mirror, just to remove the smudges of mascara from beneath her eyes. She didn't want him to see her looking like a raccoon. "I'm coming out."

"Good."

She stormed right past him, down the hall and back into the living room to locate her shoes. "This was wrong…coming here was a huge mistake. I don't ever want to see you again. I don't want to talk to you. Noth-ing." She worked her feet into her pumps and made the mistake of looking at him. He was standing there in noth-ing more than his boxers, still sporting the erection that she was not going to make go away.

He flinched at her words, but they were the only thing that made sense to her right now. "That's a tall order. You just moved back to town. We're bound to run into each other."

Of course that had been exactly Dani's thinking when she'd come over here. Now it didn't seem like such a convenient argument. "You do your Cole Sullivan things, running around catching bad guys and raising cattle with your big perfect family, and I'll do my thing. Hopefully we won't see each other at all."

She marched to the front door and breezed right through. She would've closed it right behind her if Cole hadn't stuck his leg in there and muscled it open. Down the driveway she raced, but she could sense Cole behind her. *Get to the car. Just get to the car.*

She opened the door and climbed into the driver's seat, but this was one hell of a time to have long legs and be driving a convertible. She had to contort her body to get into it.

"Dani, stop."

"Cole, have you lost your mind? You're out here in your underwear."

"Do you honestly think I care about that right now? You come to my house all hellfire and brimstone, and I kiss you and you melt right into my arms. What is going on? I thought this could just be two friends having fun. Getting reacquainted. Apparently not."

"You act like you did nothing wrong, Cole. You broke up with me, remember?"

"You don't know everything."

She turned the key and revved her engine. "I know enough. Good night, Cole." The car jerked ahead a few feet when she let go of the clutch, but then it stalled out. "Dammit," she mumbled under her breath. So much for her dramatic exit.

"Guess I'll see you around town."

"I hope not." She turned the key and the engine purred back to life.

"It's a small town, Dani. You can't hide from me forever."

His voice faded into the black night as Dani sped away, cursing herself for coming out here. Kissing Cole Sullivan and letting him take off her clothes had been a mistake. Granted, loving him had been a bigger one. With two little boys at home relying on her to have her act together and give them a stable life, it was a mistake she couldn't afford to repeat.

Three

Cole loved downtown Royal, but especially when there was a party. The Labor Day celebration, with its food vendors, hay rides and carnival games, was a favorite. It heralded the end of the brutal Texas summer and the start of what he hoped would be a beautiful fall. But first, he and the team had to track down Rich. They had to make him pay for his litany of crimes—Jason's murder, stealing Will's identity, and siphoning off millions of dollars from Will's company and the Texas Cattleman's Club. If he was sent away for all of that, everything would be right with Cole's world. Well, almost everything. Dani coming back into town had turned a few things upside down, namely his ability to think about anything else.

He strolled through the main block, which had been closed off to traffic. He was willing to admit to himself that he was hoping to run into Dani; he just wasn't prepared to say it out loud. She'd consumed his thoughts since the other night, and not just because clothes had come off and she'd left him as sexually frustrated as he'd ever been. Six years had numbed him to the memory of what Dani did to him. She made him feel alive. She might have a terrible attitude 50 percent of the time, but he knew that wasn't what was in her heart. Her exterior was nut-hard, but on the inside, Dani Moore was as soft and tender as could be.

He'd seen that caring side after his accident six years ago, when he was still a Texas Ranger. He'd narrowly survived colliding with a guardrail during a high-speed pursuit. Cole had been carried off in a stretcher with broken bones, lacerations and contusions. After his more urgent injuries had been tended to and he was finally stable, the doctors ordered an MRI. That was when they'd discovered the tumor, an inoperable glioma, square in the middle of his brain.

Luckily, Cole had sent Dani home to get some sleep, so only his brother Sam had been there when he got the news. She wasn't there to hear the words no one ever wanted to hear, especially not from an oncologist. They couldn't remove it. Radiation was unlikely to make a difference. It was likely going to be the thing that killed him, but there was no way to know how long he had. Could be days, weeks, months, years or decades. Plenty of people walked around not even knowing they had one, the doctor had said, which had been of zero comfort to Cole.

Cole swore Sam to secrecy, although Sam had begged him to talk to Dani about it. He knew that Cole had been getting ready to ask Dani to marry him. He'd bought a ring. He'd been about to ask her to build a future with him.

Cole wouldn't hear any of it. That doctor had signed his death warrant. He'd already seen what worry did to

Dani. Hell, every time he went out on a call or worked on an investigation, she was a ball of stress. She always hugged him and kissed him fiercely when he made it home safe. Cole understood why. Dani's dad had been in law enforcement and he'd died in the line of duty. She'd had to watch the way her mother fell apart afterward, drinking and aiming all kinds of verbal abuse at Dani. Emancipated at seventeen, Dani eventually ended up with her aunt Dot in Royal. Dani's toughness came from loss. Cole would not let that happen again.

So he'd done the only thing he could think to do. As soon as he was back at home, he'd broken it off. Oh, the anger and fury unleashed that day was brutal. But Cole had taken it. Yes, she'd spent countless hours with him in the hospital, and yes, they'd been together for three years. He'd had to lie and tell her that none of that mattered anymore. He didn't love her. Those were the words that had been the hardest to say.

Of course, Dani had refused to believe him. She'd flat out called him a liar. She'd thrown things at the wall—pillows and books and magazines. So he'd had to double down on his fabrication and tell her there was another woman. That was the beginning of the end. She'd become impossibly quiet. Tears rolled down her cheeks, and she'd called him a cheating bastard. He hated to hurt her that way, but it was the only way to cut things off for good.

Three days later, Dani left for New York. By all accounts from the other night, she'd done well for herself. His plan had worked perfectly. Except he was still waiting for the day this stupid tumor might take his life. And he'd never bargained on Dani ever returning to Royal.

The late-morning sun beat down on Cole's back as he continued his survey of town for Dani. When he rounded the corner near Miss Mac's Pie Shack, he nearly ran square into Vaughn McCoy and Abigail Stewart. They both were grinning ear to ear, Vaughn's service dog, Ruby, between them.

"How are you two doing today?" Cole asked.

Abigail smiled even wider, a feat Cole did not think was possible. She pulled Vaughn closer and gazed up into his face. "We're perfect. Absolutely perfect."

Vaughn took Abigail's left hand and presented it to Cole. "Newlyweds, to be exact." The ring sparkled in the sun as she wagged her fingers.

"Oh, wow. Congratulations! When did this happen?"

"Just now," Abigail said. "We got Judge Miller to perform the ceremony in our backyard." She smoothed her hand over her protruding belly. "We wanted to get it done before this little one decides to make his or her presence known."

Cole wasn't the envious type, but he could feel the jealousy rising up inside him. Vaughn and Abigail had the life he'd always wanted, the one he'd once thought was a done deal for Dani and him. Why did some people get their happy ending while others didn't? He didn't know the answer.

He shook Vaughn's hand. "Well done. I'm very happy for you both."

"When are you going to get around to settling down? Or are the Sullivan boys all committed to being bachelors for life?" Abigail asked.

It would've taken Cole an hour to give the real answer. Instead, he laughed. "If you ask my mother, we're all running on borrowed time. She wants grandchildren yesterday."

"Good to see you, Cole. I'd better get my bride down to the diner. She's already reminded me a dozen times how hungry she is," Vaughn said.

Abigail shrugged adorably. "I'm dying for pancakes and bacon."

Cole clapped Vaughn on the shoulder. "You heard her. Get to it."

Just as the happy couple walked away, Cole spotted Dani across the street. Unless his eyes were playing tricks on him, she was with two small boys. The street was packed now, and he had to wind his way through the crowd, past folks saying hello or wanting to talk to him.

I'm so sorry. I'm supposed to be meeting someone.

Yeah, hi. I'll see you later?

Dani and the two boys were turning and walking away from him. He had to hurry. Or maybe just lunge for Dani. Without thinking, he reached past several people and grabbed her arm. The crowd parted and she whirled around.

"Cole? What in the world?" She tore off her sunglasses and nearly pierced his very being with her blazing brown eyes.

His heart was about to pound its way out of his chest. "I'm sorry. I just…" *You just what? Saw her and thought you'd wrap your hand around her?* "I wanted to say hello."

"Oh, well, hi." Dani looked down at the two boys who were right at her hips. One was clutching the skirt of her light blue sundress, the other holding on to her hand.

"Can we talk? Over here?" With a nod, he suggested a bench in front of the Royal Diner.

She pursed her lips tightly. "We said all we needed to say the other night."

He should've known he'd have to put some elbow grease into this. "It's a hot day. Probably not a bad idea to sit and take a break."

"I'm fine. Really."

He pointed down at one of the two boys. "I think he could use some time out of the sun. His cheeks are pretty pink."

Horror crossed Dani's face and she leaned down to check on the boy. "Are you okay, honey?"

He nodded. "Just hot. And thirsty."

"Fine, Cole. But just for a minute." She took the boys' hands and led them over to the bench. They both climbed up and sat, swinging their legs. Dani pulled a bottle of water from her bag and offered it to them.

"Who's this you have with you?" Cole asked.

She hesitated for a moment. "These are my sons. Cameron and Colin."

Her what? Cole nearly had to pick his jaw up off the sidewalk He was as confused as could be right now. Dani had painted herself as a single woman without a care in the world aside from her career. One would have thought the topic of having two children might have come up while they'd talked the other night. Was this why she'd glossed over part of her time in New York? And if so, what was she hiding? He crouched down in front of the boys, knowing he had to play it cool. Dani had little patience for him right now. "Hi, guys. I'm Cole. Now which one of you is Cameron and which one is Colin?"

The boy in the red-and-white-striped shirt thrust his hand up into the air. "I'm Cameron."

"So you must be Colin."

In a blue-and-white-striped shirt, Colin seemed more reticent than his brother. He nodded. "Yes, sir."

Cole peered up at Dani, who was beaming at the boys. "I guess there were a few things we didn't have a chance to talk about the other night."

She cleared her throat. "A few things."

Cole straightened to his full height. Dani was flat-out

stunning today, but he couldn't allow himself to be distracted by the way she looked in that sundress with the skinny straps, all glowing skin and luscious lips. "How old are the boys?"

She took a step away from her sons. "Uh. Four. About to turn five."

Cole turned and looked at them again, doing the math in his head. Like most brothers, they were horsing around, poking and prodding each other. Cole was no expert, but they looked ready to go to school. He wasn't buying the idea that they were four, but he couldn't ask them in front of their mom. "You putting them in kindergarten this year?"

"No. One more year of preschool. They're not quite ready yet."

"I see." He took another glance at them. Their coloring was just like his own. Hair color? Remarkably similar. It was even thick like his, not fine like most young children's. "Your relationship with Taylor Blake must've been a lot more serious than you let on."

"I don't really want to talk about it, Cole."

If he wasn't standing in the middle of a packed sidewalk, Cole would ask Dani all sorts of questions. He might even ask for a paternity test. But he had to be glad that she wasn't kicking him in the shins right now or calling him names. After the other night, he did not think a calm conversation with Dani would be possible, but here they were. He was prepared to do anything to preserve the peace.

But were these boys his? Was it possible that Dani had been pregnant when she packed up and left for New York? They'd had no contact whatsoever, except for a letter Dani sent six months after she left, asking if he wanted to talk. Unable to open that door and wanting to protect her, he hadn't responded.

He looked at the boys again. There was a feeling deep in his gut that was saying they could be his. Even if that might not be the case, he had to have the chance to get to know them better. They were one half a woman he still cared for very much.

He crouched down one more time. "Do you boys like horses?"

Colin, the quieter of the two, jumped right off the bench, nearly knocking Cole back onto his butt. "I do."

Cameron nodded eagerly. "I do, too. Do you have horses?"

"I do. I have longhorns, too. I even have chickens and goats."

"Do you have a real farm, Mr. Cole?" Cameron asked. It was incredibly adorable how polite these two boys were. Dani had done a good job.

"It's a ranch. A big one. Would you like to come see it some time? Maybe tomorrow?"

Dani stepped forward and placed her hand on Cole's shoulder, digging her fingertips into his skin. If she thought it would dissuade him, she was sorely mistaken. Her touch made his pulse quicken and filled his head with ideas of taking off the dress she was wearing today. "Surely you're busy, Mr. Cole."

He shook his head. "Nope. Not at all. I always have time for some aspiring young ranchers."

"Can we, Mommy? Can we?" Colin was jumping up and down, tugging on Dani's hand.

Cameron got off the bench and joined in. "We never got to see horses in New York."

"We did when we went to Central Park," Dani countered. She was so good at digging in her heels.

"That's not the same. We couldn't ride those horses." Cameron turned to Cole. "Can we ride your horses?"

"A few of them you can." Cole had to disguise his smile. The boys were doing his arguing for him.

Dani dropped her shoulders and sighed. "It'll have to be Thursday. I need to be at the restaurant tomorrow, and I have plans with Megan on Wednesday."

Cameron and Colin began jumping up and down again, squealing with delight.

"What time do you want us?" Dani asked.

I want you any time I can get you. Again, Cole's mind flashed to the other night and how amazing it felt to touch her velvety bare skin. "Nine? Before it gets too hot? We can have lunch. Hungry cowboys need their food."

She rolled her eyes and shook her head.

"What?" Cole asked.

"I'm just trying to figure out how you're so good at talking me into things I don't want to do."

"You don't want your boys to have a fun morning enjoying some of the finest things Royal, Texas, has to offer?"

The smile that spread across her face held a familiar edge. It was as if she was whispering, *Damn you, Cole Sullivan.* Good God, how he'd missed that sight. "No. You're right. It'll be fun."

He reached out and grasped her elbow, trailing his fingers down the underside of her arm. "I promise I'll make it worth your while."

She cocked both eyebrows. "I have two young boys to keep an eye on, Mr. Cole. May I present a prime example of how much supervision they need?" Dani pointed down the sidewalk. The boys had found an older man with a dog several storefronts away. They were gleefully petting it, oblivious to how far they'd wandered.

"I was talking about ice cream. I was thinking we could go out for some after lunch."

Dani pressed a finger, hard, right in the center of his chest. "Don't push your luck."

Cole put his sunglasses back on, feeling as happy as he'd felt in a long time. "I won't need luck. The minute I mention ice cream to those two boys, it'll be all over."

Dani just shook her head and hitched her purse onto her shoulder. "Boys, we should go now," she called.

"Oh, and bring your swimsuits Thursday. I have a slide at my pool."

Dani cast him an incredibly hot look of disapproval. "You're terrible."

"I try."

Four

The day after Labor Day, Cole pulled up outside the Texas Cattleman's Club. This visit was no social call, nor was he here to talk ranching or catch up on the latest gossip in Royal. Cole was here to propose a plan to his team, involving going undercover and hopefully catching Billy Orson, the crooked sheriff who had helped Richard Lowell by falsifying death records and saying that Rich had died in the plane crash that claimed Jason Phillips's life. Orson had received several large influxes of cash since then, which they were certain had come from Rich. It was a bit crazy, but Cole was prepared to do anything to catch Sheriff Orson.

After speaking with Aaron Phillips the other day and then receiving the results of the DNA testing of the ashes in the urn that were once believed to belong to Will Sanders, they knew for certain that it was Aaron and Megan's brother, Jason, who had died in that plane crash. This was a murder investigation. There was a lot on the line, and time was not on their side. Rich was on the run, and it was only a matter of time before he fled the country with the money he'd siphoned off from Will's personal and business accounts, as well as the TCC. They had to catch him. And fast.

But as he strode into the TCC, Cole's run-in with Dani and the revelation that she had twin sons wouldn't stop running laps in his mind. Had his eyes played tricks on him? His gut was telling him no. His gut was telling him that those boys might look like Taylor Blake, but they looked even more like him. And the timeline—especially if Dani was lying—worked. Had she gone to New York and discovered she was pregnant? Was that what the letter she'd sent six months after she'd left was really about? Had it been a call for help?

If any of this was true, he and Dani had a holy mess between them, one that would demand untangling. But for the next hour or so, Cole needed to focus on work. He had to set aside one potential headache for an entirely different one.

He entered a small meeting room down one of the long halls at the back of the building. They were keeping a tight lid on the investigation, but this was the best central meeting place. Too many flapping mouths at the sheriff's office.

Will Sanders was speaking to Sheriff Battle and his deputy, Jeff Baker. Several other deputies were on hand as well, in addition to new full-time members of the task force, courtesy of the FBI—Special Agents Thomas Bird and Marjorie Stanton. Cole had pulled some strings to bring these two on board, but the new DNA evidence had helped convinced the bureau that he needed the extra hands. Bird and Stanton were a crucial part of cracking this case.

Thomas Bird, a reedy man with a thick mustache, was an expert in money laundering, having made his name working on cases involving organized crime. He fully understood the intricacies of the money trail Rich had left behind, especially everything uncovered by Luke Weston's financial tracking software. Marjorie Stanton, a poker-faced redhead, was a tactical expert specializing in sting operations and undercover work. She was also expecting her first child in three months. Her pregnancy had left her doing investigative work and less of the hands-on work she loved. She wasn't happy about it, or so she had mentioned to Cole several times when they'd talked.

Sheriff Battle gave Cole the high sign and informally called the meeting to order. "Now that we have Cole Sullivan on hand, we can get down to business. Cole, why don't you brief everyone on where we stand?"

Cole stood at the front of the room while everyone took a seat. "Sure thing. I believe Deputy Baker has given out the latest brief, but DNA tests have confirmed that Jason Phillips was killed in the plane crash in Durango City, California. We believe Richard Lowell was on that plane and managed to escape. We also believe that he bribed Sheriff Billy Orson to have Phillips's body cremated before it could be identified. Orson identified the body as Will Sanders. Of course, we all know that Will Sanders is alive and well. Shortly before the plane crash, we got an eyewitness report from Abigail Stewart of an argument between Jason Phillips and Richard Lowell posing as Will Sanders. That was the last time Jason Phillips was seen alive. We believe now that Jason was confronting Rich, and that's what got him killed. Although we don't have direct evidence linking Sheriff Orson to the cover-up, it seems pretty clear that he did it. The information given to us by his deputy was invaluable and all pointed to him."

Stanton raised her hand. "This deputy. Is she a credible source? How do we know she isn't trying to lead us on a wild goose chase?"

"Her father was the sheriff before Orson. He was a good man, and she hates seeing her father's legacy ruined like this. She actually put herself in great danger by going to Aaron in the first place. Orson has eyes and ears all over that county."

Stanton nodded and scribbled down a few notes while her partner, Bird, raised his hand. "We're still tracing the payoffs from Lowell to Orson. There's a chance that some of it was cash, but I have to think for this big of a cover-up, it would've been too much money to go that route."

"Orson is a greedy man," Cole said. "He has a massive house up in the hills. He's got his fingers in everything within his jurisdiction. The more I dig, the more dirt I find. All kinds of shady dealings and a lot of evidence of bribes and kickbacks. I'm sure Rich had to make a substantial payoff."

"Everything hinges on Orson right now," Sheriff Battle said. "If we can find a way to get him to talk and admit that Rich bribed him to have Jason's body cremated and falsely identify the body as Will, we could blow the case wide-open."

"And find the money," Bird added. "We still have to find where Lowell has stashed the small fortune he stole. That's crucial to our case against him. A big part of his apparent motive for impersonating Will Sanders was to siphon cash from his personal and business accounts.

My search for offshore and shell accounts has turned up nothing. I think we're looking for a physical stash, and my gut is telling me we're looking for gold."

"Really?" Deputy Baker asked. "Isn't that a little impractical? How do you skip the country with gold?"

"It's not about the how. It's about the why. It's the one currency that works anywhere. The disclosure laws are easy to work around, especially if you know what you're doing, and gold is untraceable by electronic means."

This really got Cole's mind going. Did Rich have a stash somewhere in or around Royal? That might explain why they were still sporadic Rich sightings, most recently when Aaron thought he saw Will at the Glass House, when the real Will was miles away at the Ace in the Hole. Was Rich still trying to hide in plain sight, waiting for the perfect time to get to his money? If so, they had to act quickly.

Cole cleared his throat. Time to make his pitch. "Orson is hosting a cocktail party in a few days for potential investors in a pipeline project he's trying to get in his county. It just reeks of more kickbacks and skimming. What if I posed as a bigwig money guy and wore a wire and tried to get him to say something stupid?"

"Yes. That's an amazing idea. I could go with you," Bird offered.

Stanton cast him a doubtful glance. "At a cocktail party for rich people? You're too socially awkward. You'll stick out like a sore thumb."

Bird pressed his lips into a thin line. "Thanks for that."

"Hey. I call 'em like I see 'em." Stanton tapped her pen against her pad of paper. "You need bait. You need a lure. You're a handsome guy, but something tells me you aren't Sheriff Orson's idea of a good time."

Cole leaned back against the wall and crossed his legs at the ankle. "What'd you have in mind?"

"If you do an internet image search for the guy, you get a lot of pictures of him with women, and they are never the same. We're talking a real revolving cast of characters. I think we need to send you with a female. A damn good-looking one." Stanton rubbed her round belly. "I'd do it myself if I wasn't carrying around a baby disguised as a bowling ball."

For a split second, Cole had an idea, but it was crazy. Maybe it was the mention of a "damn good-looking" woman that had him thinking of Dani. But she was a mom with two small kids. That was too crazy to make any sense. He couldn't put her in that kind of danger.

"Sheriff, you have any female deputies right now?"

Sheriff Battle shook his head. "Unfortunately, no. We had one last year but she moved away."

Stanton eyed Cole, but he could see that the gears in her head were churning. "I doubt the bureau will let me steal an extra agent right now. But I can look into it. Otherwise, you might have to find someone, Sullivan."

"You really think it's necessary?" Cole was truly drawing a blank on who he should ask. His brain just wanted to circle back to Dani.

"Honestly? I think it's essential. I don't see you catching this guy without a beautiful woman on your arm."

Dani had really been looking forward to going out to lunch with Megan. Between getting settled in the new house and navigating the landscape of her new job at the Glass House, Dani hadn't had nearly enough time for her best friend. They were supposed to meet up at the Labor Day celebration, but Megan had decided she couldn't deal with questions from well-meaning folks about her husband, the man she'd *thought* was Will Sanders but turned out to be Richard Lowell. Dani still couldn't comprehend the betrayal Megan must be feeling, having built a life with a man who had been lying to her all along. As bad as that was, the death of her brother Jason was worse. Megan knew that he was dead, but most residents of Royal had no idea. Because of the investigation, it had to stay a secret.

Dani pulled into the circular drive in front of Megan's gorgeous French chateau–style home on the edge of town. There had been a time when Dani might've been a little envious of her friend, living in a big beautiful house like this, from the lush landscaping softening the hard edges of the stone facade, all the way up to its grand arched windows peeking out from beneath the roofline. But Dani had made her own strides since she'd first moved to Royal as a teen, and Megan, the beautiful spark plug with deep roots in town, had inexplicably befriended the girl who'd had almost nothing.

Megan came outside, wearing curve-hugging jeans, cowboy boots and a cute black-and-white gingham blouse, along with oversize sunglasses. She had her black designer handbag in the crook of her arm and carried a small soft-sided case in the other hand. "Nice," Megan called out as she approached the car. "You not only brought the convertible, the top's down."

"The minivan makes it hard to pick up guys."

Megan laughed. "Maybe we just keep it to the two of us today. Men are not my favorite people in the world right now." She leaned over and gave Dani a big hug. "I'm so damn happy to see you."

"Me, too. This was half of the reason to move to Royal—to be able to hang out."

"Not that I didn't enjoy coming to visit you in New York every now and then. That was fun, too."

"What's in the bag?" Dani asked as she pulled out of the driveway.

"You up for a little shooting before we go to lunch? I bought a .380 and I could use some practice. I just joined the Royal Gun Club."

Dani hadn't been to a firing range since her dad had taken her when she was a teenager. "Yeah, sure. Just tell me which way to go."

Dani followed Megan's direction, taking back roads. "The boys and I missed seeing you on Labor Day." Dani raised her voice a bit since the top was down.

"I missed seeing you, too. I ended up holing up in my office and working on new shoe designs. Did I miss any excitement?"

"I ran into Cole. With the boys."

"It was going to happen. I told you."

"I know you did. I just didn't think it was going to happen so soon."

"What happened?"

What *had* happened? Everything had whizzed by so fast, Dani was hardly able to keep up. She'd known that day would come, but just like she hadn't been fully prepared to deal with Cole on her own, she hadn't been ready to see him with the boys. "He's suspicious. I could see it in his eyes." She stopped at a red light. "He asked the boys if they like horses, which of course got them all riled up. I'm supposed to take them out to the ranch tomorrow."

"Great idea. Since your last visit to the ranch went so well." Megan knew that Dani had nearly ended up in Cole's bed the other night and did not hold back on the sarcasm.

"What was I supposed to say to them when Cole offered? I'd already gone and filled their little heads with how much fun we were going to have when we moved to Texas. Getting to ride horses and spend time on a ranch are high on the list of things they want to do." The light turned green, and Dani shifted and sped away. Talking about the visit to see Cole tomorrow had her all tied up in knots. She hated the way she acted around him, almost like she was a different person, casting aside her normally rational thoughts.

"What's your plan then?"

"Honestly, I have no idea. I made a plan for the other night, and it was a disaster. I'm thinking this time, I just go with it."

"Do you plan on telling him someday?"

Deep in her heart, Dani knew she would have to tell Cole, but her protective instinct with her boys was impossible to ignore. Could she trust Cole? She wanted to think she could, but she needed to *know* it. He'd lied when he broke up with her—Megan had snooped and there had been no other woman. Then he'd quit his Texas Ranger job a few months after she went to New York. She'd begged him to do that after the accident, but he'd refused. And of course there was the letter she'd sent about a week before the boys were born, asking him to call her so they could talk about what had happened. She'd meant that as an open door. All he would've needed to do was walk through it. But he hadn't. He'd simply left it to close on its own.

"When I tell him, it'll be for the boys' benefit, not his. I gave Cole plenty of chances, and he hasn't done much good with any of them."

"But he did kiss you. Does that make you think he wants to get back together?"

"No. It makes me think he enjoys kissing me, which does nothing to fix the past."

As Dani pulled into the drive at the Royal Gun Club, she realized she'd managed to avoid the topic of Rich, but she knew she was going to have to bring it up at some point. She couldn't ignore the elephant in the room forever. Megan didn't always like to talk about the things that made her vulnerable, but how could she not be feeling that way? She'd married a man who was assuming someone else's identity, and that man had, in turn, killed her brother. Every nerve in her body had to be raw right now. She was hiding it well, too, which only made Dani worry more.

"I sort of hate to ask this, but did the Rich situation precipitate the gun purchase?" Dani asked as she and Megan walked through the parking lot toward the sprawling one-story cedar-clad building housing the firing range.

"I need to protect myself. It's most likely that he killed my brother. There's no telling what he's going to do next, or who he might go after just to get what he wants."

"That's some scary stuff." Dani could only imagine what Megan was enduring. Dani might've felt betrayed by Cole, but what she'd gone through didn't come close to this. "Are you going to keep the house?" Add that to the list of nightmares Megan was currently living—sleeping in the same house where she and her lying "husband" had once lived as a happy couple.

"Will thinks I should move to the ranch for my personal safety. I don't want to move. I'll feel like I'm letting Rich win if I do that."

Just outside the main entrance to the building, Dani put her arm around Megan and pulled her close. "I'm so sorry."

"It's okay. I'll feel better once I pull the trigger." Megan patted Dani on the back and stepped back. "Plus. I'll be honest. Will's a little too tempting and I'm not ready to go there. The last thing I need is romance."

Dani wasn't surprised. How could Megan not be attracted to the real version of the man she thought was her husband? "You do what's best for you."

Dani and Megan walked inside and made their way to the reception desk for the indoor firing range. As a member, Megan had already completed the necessary paperwork, but Dani was asked to sign a waiver and present identification. She decided to rent a gun so she could shoot as well, choosing the same model Megan had bought, minus the pink pearl handle.

"Are you two sisters?" the man behind the counter asked.

Dani and Megan looked at each other, each trying hard not to roll their eyes. They used to get this all the time in high school. Even though Megan had blue eyes and Dani's were brown, they were nearly the same height, both with long dark hair. "We're not, but people ask us that all time."

"We might as well be sisters," Megan said. "We tell each other everything."

The man behind the counter simply nodded. "You're free to go through the airlock. You have lanes five and six."

They put on their ear and eye protection and headed in. There was only one other person in the range and it appeared as though they were packing up. Dani got settled in her lane, arranging her ammunition to one side, placing the gun on the ledge pointing downrange and carefully loading the magazine just as her father had taught her years ago. As a police officer, he'd been thorough about gun safety, drilling it into her head. She'd found it a bit annoying as a teenager, but she could appreciate it now.

Both women sent their targets downrange and began shooting. Dani was impressed with this little gun. It fit perfectly into her hand and had very little kickback. She had to admit that she was proud of her aim, too. She hadn't lost it after all these years. Between reloads, she watched to see how Megan was doing. Shot after shot, she hit close to dead center of the target, the usual outline of a faceless man. Wherever Richard Lowell was lurking these days, he'd better give her a wide berth.

Dani used up her practice ammunition and stood back, watching Megan as she kept going. She waited for Megan to quit, or even just notice her, but she didn't. She kept reloading round after round. Megan's shoulders were tense. Her jaw was set with determination. After about ten minutes of this, Dani noticed that Megan was trembling as she went to reload. Dani stepped forward and placed a hand on her shoulder.

Megan jumped and pulled off her earmuffs. "What's wrong? Is something wrong?"

"No, honey. Everything is just fine, I hope. But if you don't slow down, you're going to cut that target clean in two."

Megan's brow was glistening with sweat. Her eyes were wild. She sucked in a deep breath and blew it from her lips. "I think I need to get out of here."

"Good idea. Let's scoot." Dani gathered her things and met Megan at the door. She turned in the gun she'd rented, and they made their way outside.

As soon as they were back in fresh air, Megan leaned over and rested her hands on her knees, like she was exhausted. "I feel like I'm losing it. Some times it feels like somebody is trying to squeeze the life out of me."

Dani again went to comfort her. "You're grieving, honey. You lost your brother. Your marriage isn't what you thought it was. Honestly, I'm surprised you're even able to get out of bed in the morning and go to work. I don't know if I could do that."

Megan straightened and held her hand to her chest, taking more deep breaths. "It's not so much what he did to me. It's Jason. My brother is gone. My sweet, amazing brother. He had his whole life ahead of him and he's gone. And my niece, Savannah, not only had to lose her mom, she's lost her daddy, as well. It's just not fair, Dani. It's not fair." The tears rolled down Megan's cheeks and Dani knew that her best friend was in agony. Megan never cried. She was always tough about everything.

"You're absolutely right. It's not fair at all."

"I would kill him if he was here. I'd just kill him. I'd shoot him dead and the police could come and cart me off and I wouldn't care."

"Let's not think about that right now. I don't want my best friend to go to jail." She took Megan's hand and led her back to the car. They both climbed in. "Cole is on the case, and I know he's determined to catch him."

Megan shook her head and stared down into her lap, picking at her fingernail. "I hope to hell he does. If he doesn't, I'm going to have to do it myself."

Dani wished at that moment that she could do something to help. Anything. Maybe keeping her distance from Cole was the best course of action. She didn't want to be a distraction. That being said, she couldn't exactly go back on her promise to bring the boys to his ranch to-morrow. They were already so excited about it.

"I think you need some closure," Dani said. "I mean,

you're caught in this impossible situation—you can't even talk about Jason or Rich because of the investigation. But maybe it would be helpful if you had a small memorial for Jason. Something private where you and Aaron and Savannah can say goodbye."

Megan hung her head, the tears falling onto her lap. "You're right. Maybe I just need to say goodbye."

"I think you'll feel better. You can't keep everything bottled up inside forever. And until Rich is caught, you know that's going to be the way things have to be."

Megan sat a little straighter and dabbed at her eyes with a tissue she'd pulled from her handbag. "Maybe we could have it at Aaron's house. Savannah is living there full-time now. I don't want it to be too much of a disruption for her. She's still so little."

"I think it sounds wonderful. I'm happy to help in any way I can."

"I'd want Will to be there, too. He's been so great to me since this happened. He's the one who brought Cole on board with the investigation in the first place. I'd like to invite Cole, too, but only if it's okay with you."

Dani had to think about that for a minute. "This isn't a ploy, is it?"

"I tend to think of situations that are a bit more romantic than a memorial service if I'm trying to set up a couple." Megan looked up and flashed her trademark smile, making Dani feel one hundred times better.

"Perfect. Just name the day and I'll be there."

"I'll talk to Aaron, but I'd like to do it sooner rather than later. Maybe Saturday."

"I'll keep it open."

Megan reached for Dani's hand. "Thank you. For everything. I don't know what I would do without you."

"You're welcome, and I feel the exact same way. Now, let's go get some lunch. I'm buying."

"Cocktails, too?"

Dani turned on the ignition and shifted the car into gear. "Of course. I think we both could use one."

Five

Cole didn't get a wink of sleep on Wednesday night. Between the investigation, the upcoming sting operation and knowing Dani and the boys were coming to the ranch, there was too much rattling around in his head.

The topic that really wouldn't go away, no matter how hard he tried to focus on other things, was that of Colin and Cameron. Could they be his sons? The fact that he couldn't let it go when he had so much on his professional plate said a lot. Cole was frequently guilty of putting career before anything else. He just couldn't walk away from the immense satisfaction of it. It all led back to Cole's childhood fascination with the Rangers and their ability to solve tough cases. No matter what it was, Cole had to find the truth and get to the heart of what was right.

Cole had to find out the truth about Colin and Cameron. Had he and Dani conceived twin boys? Or had

Taylor Blake been not only lucky enough to have been with Dani, but to have fathered her children? He cringed at the thought, but the alternative wasn't much better. If Colin and Cameron were his sons, Dani had kept a massive secret from him for more than five years. Of course, he'd stomped on her heart, so maybe in her mind, they were even.

Cole was out in the yard talking to one of his ranch hands. He'd been working on the investigation all morning and was sorely out of the loop with the state of the ranch. One of the mares had given birth to a healthy foal that morning. The boys were in for a real treat. In the middle of their conversation, a minivan came up the driveway. Dani was in the passenger seat, and a woman Cole didn't recognize was driving. When it came to a stop, the side doors opened on their own, and the boys unbuckled their seat belts and ran up to him. Cole waved to Dani as the boys nearly tackled him in the driveway.

"Mr. Cole, we're here!" Cameron exclaimed while Colin nodded in agreement.

"Hi, guys. I'm happy to see you."

"Hey, Cole," Dani said, walking toward him. Her perfume got to him first, then the gorgeous skin of her shoulders, left bare by her white tank top. And to think he'd had his hands all over her the other night...the very idea made his whole body come alive with electricity. "I need to ask you a favor."

"Yes. Of course." *Anything.*

"That's my nanny, Elena. She wants to check out the antiques at Priceless. I told her she could take the minivan since not much can fit in the back of my convertible. Do you think you could give us a ride home when we're done?"

"I'm happy to do it." He'd never before felt that the

chance to give someone a ride was a prize, but he sure felt that way right now.

"Great. As long as you don't get any ideas about what this means. We're just in need of a ride. That's it."

Cole fought the sigh that wanted to leave his lips. "Don't worry. You'll get no ideas from me."

"Good. Thank you. I appreciate it. Let me get their boosters." Dani headed over to the minivan, where Elena was a step ahead, pulling out the boys' car seats. Dani waved goodbye to Elena, who drove off a moment later.

"What do you boys want to see first?" Cole asked.

"Horses!" Cameron didn't hesitate with his answer.

"How about you, Colin?" Cole asked.

"That sounds fun. As long as it's okay with you."

Cole arched his eyebrows at Dani and put on his sunglasses. "Horses it is."

The boys tore off, Cameron leading the way down to the stables.

"I noticed you can tell the boys apart." Dani was right at his side as they strolled along.

"It's more from the way they talk than their appearance. Colin hangs back a little bit. Cameron's more outgoing."

"Ever the detective, huh? Always observing."

"I couldn't stop if I wanted to." What he really wanted to say was that Colin looked and acted a lot like him—same faint freckles, same need to observe before speaking. But again, he had to wonder if his mind was playing tricks on him, if this was all just projection because a part of him wanted a connection to Dani. Even if they couldn't be together as a couple, perhaps they could be close again. As intense and passionate as their relationship had once been, they'd always been great friends.

He'd have been lying if he'd said he didn't want at least that much again.

When they got to the barn, Cole quietly let Colin and Cameron know what was in store. "Boys, we have a brand-new foal in the barn. A baby horse. She was just born this morning, so we have to be real quiet around her. We don't want to spook her or her mama, okay?"

"Can you do that?" Dani asked.

Mouths zipped tight, both boys nodded in agreement, their eyes wide as saucers. Cole adored their sweet innocence. It was such a wonderful change of pace from the usual things he dealt with—grueling ranch work and chasing evil men.

"Okay, then. Let's go." Cole led them over to the far end of the barn. One of the ranch hands was watching closely, arms resting on the gate to the stall. Cole realized then that they'd have to pick up the boys for them to see. He wanted to give Peanut and her new baby all the privacy they deserved.

Dani scooped up Cameron, and with a nod, let Cole know it was okay for him to do the same with Colin. Cole held on tight to the boy, struggling a bit with how to best hold him. He didn't want to drop him. Dani demonstrated, putting Cameron on her hip. Cole followed her lead, and that made things much better. They crept toward the stall and there was the mama horse, eating away while the foal suckled. The boys were both completely still and silent, just watching. Peanut pulled away from her food and let out a blow, probably curious about her visitors. The foal unlatched from the teat and took a few unsteady steps around the stall, shaking and hobbling. Cole watched in awe, just as he had a hundred times before. This was one of Cole's favorite parts of being a rancher—new life. He loved it when the animals gave birth and there were babies around to care for.

"Wow," Colin whispered right into Cole's ear. "She can walk already?"

Cole grinned. "She can."

Dani and Cole put the boys back down on the ground and led them out of the barn. As soon as they were out of earshot of Peanut, the boys were full of questions.

"Why was the baby sucking on the mama's belly?" Cameron asked.

"That's where she gets the milk," Cole answered.

"I don't understand how a horse can walk right after being born. Doesn't she need to learn how to do that?" Colin asked.

Cole was ready to give him the nickname of Mr. Professor. "They're just born knowing how to do it. Pretty cool, huh?"

"I've seen pictures of us when we were first born, and we were very small and wrapped up in blankets. I don't think we were able to do much more than cry," Colin said.

Cole swallowed hard as that picture popped up in his head. If these were his boys, he'd missed out on a lot. First steps, first words and—certainly from Colin—first questions. At some point, he was going to have to just come out and ask Dani the hard question, but not in front of the boys. It wasn't right. And if he was being honest with himself, the answer scared him. If she'd kept this from him, she'd had her reasons. Dani didn't do anything without good cause.

"Would you boys like to get up on a horse? Go for a ride around the pen?" Cole asked.

"Yes, please," Cameron said.

"Just nothing dangerous, please," Dani interjected.

"I promise they'll get nothing but the oldest, kindest horse. That would be Gentry. She's out in the pasture right now, but she'll come if I whistle. We'll have to get her saddled up, but she loves kids."

They strolled out past the barn to a small pasture for the horses. The longhorns were kept farther away from the main house. Gentry was easily found with her chestnut-and-white coloring. She was a pretty horse now, but she'd been stunning in her prime.

Cole placed his thumb and middle finger between his lips and whistled. Gentry looked up and, seeming resigned, made her way to the gate. Cole unhooked the latch and started to walk right up to her, but the boys and Dani hung back. "It's okay, boys. Come on. She won't hurt you."

Cameron sprinted into action, and Colin followed. Gentry dropped her head when she got close to Cole and he gave her exactly what she wanted—scratches behind both ears.

Cole took the boys and Gentry down to the small corral next to the barn, saddled up the horse and let them take turns riding her. They took to it easily. These boys were born ranchers—one more reason for him to wonder if they might be his. Dani leaned against the fence, her long hair flowing over her shoulder in the breeze. She kept watch over her boys, but Cole also caught her keeping an eye on him once or twice. When that happened, their gazes locked for a heartbeat or two, making Cole's pulse thunder in his ears. Then Dani would drop her head or look away, and he'd be plunged right back into self-doubt.

He tried not to think too much about the tension between them, the unfinished business, but it was next to impossible. It was all around him. An indelible force.

He'd love it if she'd let down her guard and talk to him about the boys. But how could he expect her to open up about anything when it was his secret that kept them apart in the first place? Especially since his was a secret he refused to share. He didn't want anyone's pity because of the tumor.

Just then a familiar, gleaming RV pulled up in front of the house. Cole's stomach sank. His parents. Those two and Dani did not have a good history. If he was trying to smooth things over with her, his mom and dad were going to stand in the way. No question about that.

"Come on, boys, we're going to let Gentry have a rest," Cole said. He waved over one of the ranch hands to have him take care of the horse.

"We were having fun," Cameron said, seeming disappointed.

Dani strolled over. "Who's that in the big RV?"

It wasn't merely big, it was massive. A top-of-the-line Prevost, with a king-size bed in the master suite, hardwood floors, and marble tables. His parents had spared no expense. Cole smiled, as if that was going to make this any easier. "That would be my parents."

"Your parents are here?" Dani muttered with a biting edge to her voice. "Why didn't you tell me they were coming over?"

Cole was already on edge. His parents had not been particularly kind to Dani when he and Dani were together. "I didn't know they were going to. They're retired now and living out of that thing most of the year." He pointed in the direction of the RV, just as his parents climbed out. Of course, they managed to spot Cole, Dani and the boys right away. "But they drop in unannounced every now and then to check in on things with the ranch. I'm so sorry. I know they're not your favorite people."

"Great. And I have no car. I really don't think this is a good idea."

Cole couldn't help but notice the panic in Dani's voice. This was a big deal for her. "Don't worry. I won't let anything bad happen." If only he could be so certain that he could keep that promise.

"I swear to God, Cole. If they say one thing to me, I'm leaving. I will call Elena and get her to pick us up."

Cole rested his hand on her shoulder, trying to ignore how good it felt to have his fingers on her bare skin. "I will drive you myself if something happens. Or better yet, I'll tell them to leave. Just give them a chance, Dani. They've both mellowed out a bit with retirement."

Dani pressed her lips together tightly. "Hmm." She did not seem convinced.

"Come on. Let's just say hello." The four of them made the trek up to the driveway. Cole's mom, Bonnie, approached them, her curly blond hair up in a ponytail. Always impeccably dressed, she was wearing a sleeveless black blouse and white Capris, her trademark diamond stud earrings glinting in the sunlight. Mom spread her arms wide, but to Cole's great surprise, that embrace was not meant for him—it was for Dani.

"Dani Moore. I can't believe you're here. It's so nice to see you." She gave Dani a pat on the back and stepped back. "You look just as gorgeous as always." She turned to Cole's dad. "Gus, doesn't she look amazing?"

"She does. She does." Dad was looking especially tan, and dressed like he was ready to go golfing, in khakis and a blue polo. Now that he was retired, he always looked more at ease than he had when he was still running the ranch. He hugged Dani, too, then shook Cole's hand. "Son. Good to see you."

"Nice to see you guys. I wish I would've known you

were coming." *Seriously. Maybe give a guy a phone call next time?*

"And who do we have here?" Cole's mom asked.

Colin and Cameron introduced themselves. Cole was impressed.

"Would you boys like some cookies? And to check out our RV? If it's okay with your mother, of course."

Dani crossed her arms. "Oh, sure. Go right ahead."

As soon as his parents walked off with the boys, Cole had to check in and see how Dani was feeling. "That wasn't so bad. I mean, considering how you feel about them."

"Anything I feel about them is because of things that they said. I never wanted anything but to be accepted, Cole."

"I talked to them about it that one time, and they got better, didn't they?"

"And then the accident happened and it got ugly. You weren't there in that hospital waiting room. It was awful."

Cole sighed. Everything came back to the accident. "I'm so sorry. I don't know what to say. If I had been there, I would've told them to stop. I would've told them it wasn't right."

Dani shrugged and looked off in the distance, shaking her head. "I guess I just need to get over it, but it's hard."

"I understand. I'd appreciate your willingness to put up with them for a little while today."

"I'll do my best." She started to walk toward the RV. "Plus, there's no way I'm getting the boys out of here until they've had a chance to swim in your pool."

After spending several hours with Cole's parents, anybody could've knocked Dani over with a feather. Bonnie and Gus hadn't just been nice or pleasant. They'd gone out of their way to be kind. Dani almost asked Cole if his parents had been abducted by aliens.

They'd spent a few hours sitting out by the pool while Cole swam with the boys. Cole had bought the fixings for sandwiches and a fruit salad for lunch, and Bonnie not only deferred to Dani's expertise in the kitchen, she applauded it, declaring the herb aioli she made "divine." Now that it was getting to be late afternoon, Dani was ready to head home. The boys were tired and she was, too, even though she'd had an incredible day.

"Cole, do you mind taking the boys and me home?"

Cole hopped up from the couch, where he was sitting with the boys and his dad. "Yeah. Absolutely. I'll grab my keys."

Bonnie pulled Dani aside. "It was really nice to see you today, Dani. I just want to tell you that I'm sorry for the way I acted with you when you and Cole were together. And especially for the things I said after the accident." She placed her hand on Dani's shoulder. "I hope that maybe now that you're a mom you can understand a bit of what makes you feel protective. That's all it was. Me going overboard with being a mama bear. I'm not proud of it. And I do regret it. Please accept my apology."

Dani could hardly believe what she was saying. And, she had to admit, she did understand what Bonnie was saying. She had her hyperprotective moments, too. "Thank you, Bonnie. I appreciate that. I really do."

"Now that you're back in town, I hope that you and Cole can spend some more time together."

"We'll see. We're getting reacquainted right now." Dani didn't want to say any more.

"Ready?" Cole asked.

"Yeah. I think the boys already ran outside."

"Of course they did."

Cole got the boys, the booster seats and everything else loaded into the truck, and off they went to Dani's house. Despite their busy day, the boys were a flurry of conversation. Cole stayed quiet, so Dani did, too. She needed time to think about today. She'd had a good time, even with his parents, which she had not thought was possible. And to think, just that morning she'd been dreading seeing Cole. She still didn't like the way she behaved around him, acting as if she had no common sense. She didn't like that he still had that kind of control over her, whether he realized it or not.

When they got to the house, Cole asked if he could come in and see her new place. It was against Dani's better judgment, but it was so hard to say no to Cole, especially after he'd gone out of his way to make their day so special.

Of course, once the boys realized Cole was coming in, they weren't about to let him leave.

"Can he stay for story time?" Cameron asked.

Dani had very little resolve at this point. "Sure. But you both need a bath first. I don't care how much time you spent in that pool, you're both filthy."

Just then, Cole received a phone call from one of the FBI agents, and excused himself, walking into the kitchen. He'd gone for hours without working, so that was no big surprise. He was front and center for story time, though, listening to Dani read one of the boys' favorite books about trains that could talk. She glanced over at him at one point while she was reading and couldn't help but notice the way the boys wanted to be near him. It created the strangest feeling in her chest—both happy and sad. That was the way things should've been. The way they could've been.

"Can Mr. Cole read us a book now?"

Dani wasn't sure she could take any more sweet and tender moments between the boys and Cole. It was too strong a reminder of how the life they could've had together never materialized.

"Maybe some other time, honey. It's late. You both need to get some sleep."

Dani closed the door on the boys' room after tucking them in. Cole was still by her side. It had been the most incredible day—the horses, the time spent laughing in his kitchen and watching the boys swim in Cole's enormous, over-the-top pool. She'd certainly had her pangs of guilt over not telling him about the boys all these years, but that was a scenario of Cole's design. She'd never wanted to break up. She hadn't wanted to leave Royal, that was for sure.

"Heading home?" Dani half hoped he wasn't, even when she knew what a bad idea it was for him to stay. She had so little willpower when it came to him.

"I'd love a glass of wine if you're offering."

She owed him that much for such a wonderful day. "Absolutely. Let's go downstairs." They descended her sweeping staircase and trailed into the kitchen, where Dani pulled out a bottle of cabernet and opened it. She sniffed the cork and handed it to Cole. Working at the Glass House gave her access to some incredible wines, most of which were private reserve and difficult to find.

He took a whiff and shrugged. "Smells like wine to me."

"You are a true connoisseur."

He winked and tossed the cork in the trash. Dani didn't want to admit it, but she liked that he was so comfortable in her house already. He looked good here. Too good. Good enough that all she wanted was for him to take his shirt off. How could she have let herself forget until the other night exactly how much she loved his chest and shoulders? She would've been lying if she said that she didn't long to touch him again, to have him pressed up against her. Being this close to him was only making her lips twitch with the memory of his kiss.

Cole raised his glass and clinked it against Dani's. "To a great day."

"To a great day." Dani sipped her wine, trying to keep her eyes off Cole, but it was impossible. Part of it was just general admiration. He'd been in the sun most of the day and had that glow that took her breath away. The way it played off his icy blue eyes just wasn't fair. No woman should have to withstand the pressure of being in the same room with that, knowing that it was best if she walked away. It was so impossible it should be an Olympic event. *And now, with the bronze medal in Resisting Cole Sullivan, is Danica Moore of the USA. She could've taken the silver if she hadn't allowed him to kiss her the other night and let it snowball from there.*

Cole was staring off into space, absentmindedly gnawing on his lower lip, which was ridiculously sexy.

"You seem preoccupied. Everything okay?" Was he thinking what she was? That a kiss might be a bad idea, but a whole lot of fun?

"I'm fine. I was just so distracted by you and the boys today that I stopped thinking about the investigation into Jason's murder. Now that things have quieted down, I guess my mind naturally wants to go there."

"I'm sure it's hard to keep your mind off it. Spending time with Megan yesterday really put everything into perspective. She's struggling. She's sad and mad and I think she's even a little scared, not knowing what Rich might do."

"I know. The whole thing is a nightmare, especially

for her." The crease between his eyebrows got deeper. Dani knew that meant he was stressed. "After spending time with the boys today, I realize just how much this is going to impact Jason's daughter, Savannah. She's not that much older than them."

"What's the next step? With the investigation?"

"You know I shouldn't talk about it."

"I know, but it's my best friend we're talking about. And you know you can trust me to keep my lips shut. I know exactly how dangerous things can get if someone goes around flapping their mouth." Dani's dad had worked in law enforcement. She knew not to talk.

"I'm coordinating a sting in the Sierra Nevadas near the location where the plane carrying Jason and Rich went down. There's a sheriff up there who is a real slimeball. Everybody says he's crooked, but nobody's caught him. We got a tip that he took a bribe to lie about who died in that plane crash and have the body cremated before anyone could identify it."

"That's horrible. Did you say the Sierra Nevadas? Whereabouts?"

"Durango City. It's a real mess. The sheriff is pretty slick, but we're worried about him getting skittish. He doesn't trust anyone. And it's my job to figure out how we get him to confess on tape to everything that happened."

Dani couldn't believe what she was hearing. "What's this sheriff's name?"

"Billy Orson. Real son of a bitch."

She'd heard Cole correctly. The sound of that name made the hair on the back of her neck stand up. "I've cooked for him before. In his home."

"What? Are you serious?" Cole set down his wineglass.

"Yes. Remember when I got my first job out of culinary school working for that catering company? We got hired by the sheriff to cater this very extravagant party he threw. I guess he had the hots for my boss. They'd met in Vegas on vacation. As near as I could tell, he was just trying to get her into bed."

"And what happened?"

"We were flown out there. Just the two of us. I was the sous-chef. He hired servers, but we did all of the food. I remember thinking that it made no sense that a sheriff would have a house that big and fancy. And he paid for us to fly out there, first class. Anyway, he was a total creep. Kept hitting on me all night."

"Do you think he would recognize you?"

"Probably not. It was seven years ago. My hair was shorter and much lighter."

"Do you remember the house well?"

"Yeah. We spent an entire day there and stayed overnight."

Cole leaned against the kitchen counter, rubbing his forehead.

"Are you okay?"

He looked up at her, nearly knocking her over with the intensity in his eyes. "Yeah. Just got a lot of stupid ideas going through my head."

"Like what?"

He straightened and waved it off, stuffing his hands into his back pockets. "It's crazy."

"Just tell me." She topped off her glass and his, as well. Judging by the tone of Cole's voice, they both might need it.

"So I'm running a sting to catch the sheriff. I got myself a spot at a cocktail party he's hosting to court investors in a pipeline project up in the mountains. I'll be posing as a hotshot money guy from Houston. But one of the FBI agents helping us on the case is convinced I won't be able to get him to confess anything. She says I need a woman with me."

Dani put two and two together so fast her head was spinning. This was perfect. She could finally help Megan in some real way. And all she had to do was go to a cock-tail party and talk to an overly flirtatious scumbag? She'd done that so many times in her life, she could practically do it in her sleep.

But she also had to think about the boys. "Are we talk-ing a dangerous situation? I mean, it's a cocktail party. How dangerous could it possibly be?"

"The FBI will be on-site that night. So not super dan-gerous. But still." He pressed his lips together and looked right at her, shaking his head. "I know what you're think-ing, Dani. What about the boys?"

"Precisely why I asked if it was going to be danger-ous. I know the house. That's got to count for something, doesn't it?"

"It does. Still doesn't mean I think it's our best shot. I need a woman who can persuade him to talk."

"Like a woman who's been around law enforcement her whole life? A woman who is smart and, most impor-tant, knows how this guy operates? I am not afraid of him. If he was standing in front of me right now, I know I could get him to talk."

Cole drew a breath through his nose. "I'll think about it. And I'll talk to Agent Stanton about it. See what she says."

Dani had to admit she was a bit disappointed. "Okay. I understand if I might not be the right person to do it."

A quiet laugh left Cole's lips. She loved that sound. She loved hearing it in the middle of the night, his mouth near her ear, his body warm against her. "You're perfect for this. You're beautiful and smart and sexy. What more could I possibly want?"

"I don't know, Cole. What more could you want?" She hated the way her voice cracked, but this was clawing at the essence of what had hurt most about their breakup. She hadn't been enough for him. And she still didn't understand why.

"Nothing. Nothing at all."

She wasn't sure if they were talking about the investigation or their past, but she had to make her case one more time. "Then let me go to this party with you. Let me help you get some justice for a little girl who doesn't have her daddy anymore."

That idea really hit home with her. Her dad had protected her so fiercely when she was growing up, buffering her from her troubled mother. It nearly killed Dani when that was all taken away from her. She hated the thought that Savannah was having to go through the same thing.

"I promise I will think about it." He reached out for her shoulder. His touch brought up every conflicted feeling, her heart and her body at war with each other. "You're so amazing for even offering to do it. Thank you." He squeezed her bare shoulder then trailed his fingers down the back of her arm. His touch was impossibly light, but there was no mistaking what it was saying. It left a white-hot path in its wake, warming Dani's face and chest. "I'm only considering it because I would die before I let anyone so much as lay a hand on you. I would never let anything bad happen to you. Never."

"That's good to know." Cole did not throw those words around lightly, but the reality of their past was that he had not only let something bad happen to her, he'd done it. "It's getting late."

"It's been a long day. We're both tired." He nestled

his fingers in the palm of her hand, then began to journey back up the length of her arm. He stepped closer to her, until they were toe-to-toe. He dropped his head. At that scant distance, it made his shoulders that much more deliciously imposing. She watched as his chest rose and fell with every breath, hypnotizing her with its steady rhythm.

She couldn't help the way she was drawn to him. When his hand reached the tender underside of her upper arm and his fingertips grazed the side of her breast, she sucked in a sharp breath. She dared to look up into his face, just as a self-satisfied smile crossed his lips.

"I'd forgotten how much I love it when you make that noise."

Before Dani knew what was happening, she was kissing him, if only to get him to not talk about her weakness for him. She flattened a hand against his solid chest, curling her fingers to feel the flex of his muscles, while her other hand grabbed his neck and tugged him in closer. Taking what she wanted was so liberating, she didn't know which way was up. His arms snaked around her waist, his hands smoothing over the small of her back and trailing down until he squeezed her bottom. Dani bowed into him. Memories of the other night swirled in her consciousness. Had it really felt that good to take off his clothes, or was she making too much of it because she wanted to end the longest drought of her adult life? Maybe this required further investigation.

Cole angled his head and took the kiss even deeper. He'd always known how to make her feel desired. "I want you, Dani," Cole muttered between kisses. As if his words weren't quite enough, he grabbed her thigh and hitched her leg up on his hip.

"I want you, too." She couldn't lie. She pressed her

center against his hipbone, creating heat and friction that left her dizzy.

They kissed again, Cole's lips so firm and insistent, his tongue quickly seeking hers. He cupped her breast with his hand, brushing against her nipple with his thumb. Through the thin cotton of her dress and her silky bra, it was almost as good as if he'd touched her skin. But she wanted more. She wanted the real thing.

She pulled the strap of her dress off her shoulder, and tugged down the front of her dress. "Touch me, Cole. Please." She was breathless, her chest heaving.

Cole looked at her, slack-jawed and his eyes heavy with lust. She could see his internal struggle, the way his eyes stormed. She would've been mad at his hesitancy if she hadn't endured so much of it herself the other night at his house.

"I want to Dani. I do. But maybe you were right the other night. Maybe it's a mistake if you and I give in to this."

The reality of her situation slammed into her. Where would she be after a casual tryst with Cole? It would be that much harder to stay away from him. Once she had a real taste of him, she knew she'd only want more. And she had other people to worry about—Cameron and Colin, to be exact. She sighed heavily. "I understand. It was a great day, but you should probably go."

Cole gently let her leg go and stepped back. He drew in a deep breath through his nose and neatened his hair with his hand. "Okay, then."

"Sorry." It had to be physically difficult for him, but she was just as raring to go as he was.

"Don't apologize, Dani. It was my idea." Cole snapped up his keys from the kitchen counter. "I don't think my ego can take you calling me a mistake again."

Six

Dani's biggest worry about Jason's memorial was how Megan was going to handle it. After their time at the firing range the other day, Dani knew pretty well how much all of this was eating her up inside. But she also knew that Megan needed today. She couldn't move forward with her life until she said goodbye to her brother, as sad as that was.

Cole had called that morning and asked if Dani wanted a ride, and Dani had said yes, mostly because she still felt bad about the way things had ended the other night. He'd put a stop to things, but he'd made it clear it was because of the precedent she'd set with that word—*mistake*. It didn't mean that she hadn't gone to sleep that night, immensely frustrated, thinking about how Cole could've been in her bed, weighing her down with his solid frame and sending to her peak over and over again.

He picked her up at her house, and Dani hurried outside as soon as he arrived.

"I was hoping to see the boys today," Cole said. The disappointment in his voice was heavy, which worried Dani. Did he suspect they were his? She shuttered aside her paranoia by focusing instead on how incredibly hot he looked in a charcoal-gray suit and his black Stetson.

"Oh. I'm sorry. Elena took them to see Aunt Dot." Cole was getting attached to them and she knew they were getting attached to him. It was dangerous territory that made her wonder about the wisdom of spending more time with him. Still, looking at his face and his soft and tender eyes, she couldn't deny that there was this pull deep inside her that made her want to be with him.

"Okay then. I guess I'll see them some other time."

Dani got settled in the truck and decided she should change the subject. "You're looking sharp, Sullivan."

He smiled and pulled out of the driveway. "Thanks. You aren't looking too shabby yourself. Although I like seeing you in brighter colors. Like red." He cleared his throat and cast a quick glance at her.

"Yeah. I noticed."

"Can you blame me?"

Dani just stared out the window, not knowing how to answer. She'd known exactly what she was doing when she went to his house that night. There was just some part of her that wasn't willing to admit it. At least not out loud.

"Are you going to respond?" Will asked.

"I don't know what you want me to say, Cole. Did I wear the dress to get your attention? Yes. Absolutely. Did I wear it so you would kiss me? No. That was not the point."

"Then what was the point?" Cole took the turn into Aaron's neighborhood.

Dani looked down at her hands, which were folded

neatly in her lap. Could she own up to this? Now seemed as good a time as any. "I wanted you to see what you were missing."

"Well, mission accomplished."

Dani was ready to put this subject to rest. She had nothing else to add, and she'd already come clean. "Is Will going to be there today?"

"I'm sure he will be. He and Megan have been spending so much time together."

"They're in such a weird predicament. Technically still married, needing to pretend like everything is fine."

"Definitely makes for a situation only the two of them can understand."

Dani sighed, just thinking about Megan's lot in life. "I'm glad we're doing this. I think it will be good for everyone."

"It was sweet of you to suggest it." Cole pulled into the driveway on Aaron Phillips's impressive estate and stopped before the brick mansion standing sentry on the manicured grounds.

They made their way to the grand arched front door, greeted by Kasey Monroe, Aaron's executive assistant turned nanny, and now, his fiancé. "Thanks you two for coming. Everyone is out back. Savannah is chasing the puppies so she can put them in the mudroom."

Cole and Dani walked inside. Savannah was indeed running around with one dog tucked under her arm and in hot pursuit of the other, all while wearing a lavender dress with a full skirt and Mary Janes.

"Does she need help?" Cole asked.

"No. She's the dog whisperer. I just try to not get mad when they eat my shoes."

They followed Kasey out to the backyard, which was just as stunning as the one at Cole's house. "Megan, Will and Aaron are over by the koi pond under the tree. We're going to do everything over there. I'll go get Savannah."

Dani and Cole wound their way past the pool to the serene setting.

Megan pulled Dani into a hug right away. "I'm so glad you're here."

"Of course. You know I wouldn't miss this for anything."

"You, too, Cole," Megan added. "It means a lot that you came. I know it was important to Will that you were here."

Dani looked over at Will and Aaron, who were immersed in what appeared to be an intense conversation. That was the nature of Aaron, though. Everything about him was strong and at full force.

Kasey appeared, holding Savannah's hand. Savannah was really starting to shoot up. It wouldn't be long until the little girl was as tall as Kasey. "I think we're all ready. The puppies have been secured."

Aaron and Will broke up their conversation and acknowledged Cole and Dani with a nod. Aaron stepped closer to Megan and whispered in her ear before scooping Savannah up into his massive arms and taking a spot right next to Kasey.

Megan removed her sunglasses and made eye contact with everyone in attendance. "Aaron and I have asked Will to deliver the eulogy today." She cast an adoring look at Aaron. "My brother and I aren't quite ready to talk about it yet. We just want the chance to honor Jason and the life he shared with us."

Megan stepped back and made room for Will to stand in front of the koi pond. The sunshine filtered through the leaves of the trees overhead, casting beautiful dappled light onto the stone patio.

Will cleared his throat, and Dani could see the pain in his eyes. "We're here today to honor the life of Jason Phillips, a brother, a father and an incredible friend. I will keep this short, because I know that words won't bring him back. I didn't write any of this down, but Jason always spoke from the heart, and I want to do the same for him." Will stood a little straighter. "This has been hard for all of us. The loss we have experienced is great. But we still have today. And we still have each other. Jason would've wanted us to cling to what we have, not think about what we have lost."

Will looked at each one of them. "What's keeping me going right now is being able to see Savannah, Aaron and Megan. I see Jason in all of you. Aaron, I see your brother's strength and intensity. That tenacity has shown in the investigation into his death. You uncovered details that have helped Cole and the entire team."

Aaron's jaw quivered, and Kasey leaned in to him.

"Savannah, I look at you, and I see the hope and youthful spirit that your dad always had. He and I were only a little older than you when we met. I will never forget that day." Will's voice faltered, in a way that made Dani wonder if he could continue, but he collected himself. "We were the very best of friends. We both loved horses, and we loved living in Texas. We'd get in some trouble from time to time. But your dad wasn't afraid to admit it if he'd made a mistake. That's an important life lesson. You have to own your mistakes and move on."

Dani swallowed hard and looked over at Cole. Had she made a mistake with keeping the boys from him? She'd been so certain when she was in New York that she hadn't, but as she spent more and more time with him, that certainty was giving way to questions.

Will turned to Megan and reached out for her hand. "Megan…"

"Don't you dare make me cry, Will," Megan said. "I did not put on waterproof mascara today." Everyone laughed quietly.

He stepped closer to her and put his arm around her shoulders. "It's okay to cry. It only means that you loved him."

Megan looked into Will's eyes and shook her head. "I did love him. I loved him so much."

Will set a finger under her chin and kept her face tilted upward. "That love is still here, Megan. It lives inside you. I see it every time I talk to you. I see it when you laugh. Don't ever let go of that. Hold on to it forever. For Aaron. For Savannah. For me." Will broke down and pulled Megan into his arms.

Dani leaned into Cole, and he tugged her closer. The entire scene was so overwhelming, reminding Dani just how precious loved ones were. Will and Megan had lost so much because of Rich. Will had his identity stolen. Megan had a sham marriage. They had to continue living a lie until Rich was caught. But losing Jason was obviously the breaking point for both of them.

It made Dani realize how lucky she was to have Cole to lean on right now. She closed her eyes and inhaled his warm and manly scent, allowing herself to be comforted as he trailed his warm hand up and down her arm. It felt so good when he was being protective. It felt so right in his arms. He could be her rock when he wanted to be. But did he want that? Was it possible for them to work out their differences?

Megan sniffed and wrenched herself from Will's arms. They were holding hands, still standing close. "Okay, everyone. If Jason was here, he'd tell us that this was enough sadness for one day and we should go inside, toast to him and eat."

"It's probably time to let the dogs out of the mud-room, too," Kasey added. "There's no telling what they got into."

"Free the puppies!" Savannah wiggled out of Aaron's arms and bolted inside the house.

"You okay?" Cole asked Dani, pulling her aside.

She nodded. She wasn't really okay, but she had to be for Megan. "I'm good."

Dani and Cole went inside and had a quick bite to eat and a glass of iced tea with everyone. The mood was sub-dued, although Savannah kept things lighter, playing with the Newfoundland puppies on the floor. Dani couldn't take her eyes off the young girl, only two years older than Colin and Cameron. Clearly, Savannah was in a good situ-ation, living with her uncle and Kasey, who were engaged to be married. But it still made Dani's blood boil to think about what Rich had done. And for what? Money? Was any amount of money worth taking a parent away from a child? It wasn't right. In fact, it was unthinkable.

Cole leaned closer to Dani. "You sure you're okay?"

"I am. I'm just ready to get back."

"You guys taking off?" Megan had apparently heard Dani's answer.

Dani produced a sheepish smile. "We are. Is that okay? Do you need us for anything?"

Megan got up from her seat. "I'm as good as I'm going to get at this point. Thank you for suggesting this. It was nice. Now we just need to catch that bastard Rich. I need to put this all behind me."

Dani hugged Megan, and they said their goodbyes, but Dani was haunted by what her best friend had said. *I need to put this all behind me.*

* * *

"Ready?" Cole asked after Megan walked away.

"Yes. I'm wiped out," Dani said.

"Me, too." This small gathering for Jason made Cole's charge feel all the more urgent. He had to get this case resolved as quickly as possible. Everyone had suffered too much at the hands of Rich, and every day that went by was another chance for Rich to get away.

They headed into the foyer. Will was on the phone. He held up his finger, presumably to asking them to wait.

"Well, Case, don't worry too much about me," Will said. He had to be speaking to TCC president, Case Baxter. "I've just been busy with work. You know how it goes. I appreciate the call, though. Thanks." He hung up his phone and cast Cole a look. "That was Case Baxter asking if I was okay. He said I seemed out of sorts when he saw me leaving my office at the TCC. Less than an hour ago."

The blood in Cole's veins went to ice. "Rich."

"It has to be."

Dani covered her mouth. "Oh my God."

"You didn't tip Case off that it might be Rich, did you?"

Will shook his head. "No. I think I covered pretty well."

"Good. I guess I'm glad that he's still around, because that means his stash is likely still somewhere in the county. We just need to find it. That's the key to catching him. And I need to get my hands on the security tape from the TCC. Maybe it'll tell me something about what he's up to."

"Do you think I should tell Megan?" Will asked.

Cole thought on that. Sheriff Battle had a deputy regularly patrolling her street, making sure she was safe. Plus, Megan was so independent and pissed off, knowing her, she'd probably go looking for Rich herself. "Let's keep this between us for now."

Will nodded, seeming distracted. "I don't like knowing that Rich is around. I worry for Megan's safety." He looked off toward the other room. "I just want to protect her."

"Of course you do," Dani said. "You said some lovely things about Jason today. I know it meant a lot to her."

"It's literally the least I can do," Will said. "I'm sure you've struggled with wanting to help, too."

Dani nodded. "I absolutely know what you mean."

Cole could see how much this was weighing on Will. "Okay, buddy. I'll catch up with you tomorrow, okay? And don't worry. We'll get him. I promise."

"I know we will. I know."

Dani and Cole said their goodbyes and headed outside. Cole was trying to tamp down his frustration over not having caught Rich yet. He really wanted to think about something fun like spending time with Dani, although he was fairly sure she'd turn him down. After all, he'd been the one to stop things the other night.

"Cole." Dani stopped with a hand on his shoulder just as they got to the car. "Slow down a second. You're walking a million miles a minute."

"I am?"

She cocked both eyebrows at him. "You are. Which means that you're just as worked up about all this as I am."

"Well, of course I'm worked up about it. This case means a lot to a lot of people."

"It does. Including my best friend. Megan needs justice, Cole. You have to let me do it. You have to let me go with you on the sting."

"Dani, we've talked about this. I'm not sure it's a good idea." He turned and rounded to his side of the car.

Dani climbed inside. "Just hear me out. After sitting in that room and thinking about how much Jason is missed, seeing that little girl and knowing she doesn't have her daddy anymore? You know I lost my dad. No girl should have to grow up without a father. It's not right."

"I hear what you're saying, but I'm still not sure."

"Look. You know me. I am cool as a cucumber under pressure. And going to a party and trying to lure a man into saying something he shouldn't? I'm practically built for this job. I'm very good at getting men to do things they shouldn't."

Cole laughed quietly. "Yes. I'm aware of your superpower."

"And I know you'd never let anything happen to me." She took his hand. That one touch sent a jolt of electricity right through him.

"Is now the part where you get a man to do something he shouldn't?"

Dani smiled, which only made him do the same. He couldn't help it. "I don't know. You tell me."

She was right. She was perfect for this job. And in theory, it was a simple one. Plus, he knew Bird and Stanton. They would never let anything happen to a civilian. Even more so, he would never let anything happen to Dani. He would stand in front of a barrage of bullets for her. He did want the chance to live up to his promises to her. He knew he'd let her down all those years ago. "I won't let anything happen to you. I promise."

"Is that a yes?" Her voice was bubbly and excited.

"Yes. That's a yes."

She clapped her hands and rubbed them together. "Awesome. Tell me everything I need to know."

Cole started the car. It felt good to know she still had

confidence in him. "We leave Tuesday afternoon. I have a private plane chartered."

"Fancy. Is that really necessary?"

"Yes. Sheriff Orson knows everything that happens within a hundred-mile radius of his county. He thinks I'm a major big hitter. He has to know that we're flying into that tiny airstrip in our own plane."

"Will he be able to trace where the plane came from?"

"The FBI is taking care of that. They've set up a false identity for me, and the plane is registered to that name."

"Sounds like you have it all figured out. What else is left to do before we go?"

Cole and the FBI had indeed gone over every contingency. He certainly felt prepared. Still, he'd have to be at the absolute top of his game. There was no room for mistakes. "I'll brief you on everything on the plane. But we are going to have to go dress shopping. You'll need something suitable for catching the eye of a very bad man."

"I have dresses. No need to go shopping. I attended several black-tie events in New York."

"Well, then, maybe we just need to go through your closet." Visions of Dani filling out slinky dresses popped into his head—the pleasing contours of her hips, the swell of her breasts, the sexy bow of her lower back as it led to her butt. His body was buzzing just thinking about it.

"You don't trust me to pick out my own dress?"

He did trust her to choose a gown, absolutely. Still didn't mean he didn't want to be there for it. "I need to make sure that it passes muster on the sexy scale. It needs to be really sexy."

"How sexy?" Dani's voice was soft and husky.

"Super sexy." Cole glanced at Dani just as she ran her tongue over her plump lower lip. Cole thought he might fall over.

"We could go look now if you want. Elena won't be back with the boys for a few hours."

"So that big, beautiful house of yours is empty right now?" A few hours…the idea was exhilarating. It was terrifying, too. They'd both demonstrated their ability to stomp on the brakes when clothes started to come off. They'd both shown their hesitation with letting the other in. Trust was a funny thing, fleeting and so easily broken.

"It is. What are you implying?" The flirtation in her voice was sending electricity straight to his groin. She knew damn well what he was suggesting.

"Just want to know whether or not I'll be able to get a parking spot in your driveway. That's all."

"Oh, okay." Her voice dripped with sarcasm. She slapped his thigh with the back of her hand. "Drive the car, Sullivan. We've got dresses to pick out."

Seven

Dani glanced over at Cole as he pulled into her driveway. She loved him in jeans, but damn, the man looked good in a suit. The cut of his black jacket accentuated the strong line of his shoulders. All she wanted to do was spread her hands across his chest—under the guise of admiring what he was wearing, of course.

Cole put the car in Park and turned off the ignition. Dani's pulse couldn't settle on one speed, so it was doing crazy chaotic things in her throat right now. Cole had stated the obvious—they were about to have her big beautiful house to themselves. Did that mean they were about to put the memory of their two false starts to rest? And if so, how did she feel about that? There was so much unfinished business between them, things that had to be said, but she still wasn't sure she could trust him to truly let her in. She couldn't trust him not to hurt her again.

Inside, Dani set her purse on the kitchen counter, unsure what her next step was. "Do you want a drink?"

"I wouldn't mind a little bourbon to take the edge off. That memorial and knowing that Rich was at the TCC has my mind going about a hundred miles an hour right now."

"Sounds like a plan." Dani headed into the living room, and Cole followed. Her bar, a stunning handcrafted piece made with dark wood and glass, was in the corner near one of the front windows. Pouring the drinks, she reminded herself that she needed to keep her wits about her, but she, too, needed to soothe her ragged nerves. She was feeling jumpy and anxious, too fixated on the freedom they had right now. If he was on board, they could tear each other's clothes off right there in the living room. Maybe that was all she needed—to get Cole out of her system once and for all.

"Cheers," he said when she handed him his glass.

"What are we toasting?"

"How about just that we're here, together? Nothing like a memorial service to put life into perspective."

"Hear, hear," she replied, clinking her glass with his. The bourbon went down like warm silk, leaving behind a pleasant tingle in her throat and a rush of warmth in her chest.

"Ooh. That's smooth." Cole tilted the glass and shook his head before taking another sip.

"Nothing but the best. I learned that in culinary school. It's just that I can actually afford it now."

Cole surveyed the room. "You really have done well for yourself. The house is beautiful."

"It's amazing what celebrities will pay for you to cook for them. The investments I made with the life insurance money from my father have done very well, too."

"But that's you. Standing on your own two feet. You don't need anyone else."

"I've always been that way. Never had a choice. You

know that." Dani choked back the words she wanted to say. She hadn't been *exactly* like that when they had been together. She'd leaned on him, especially when she was in the stressful home stretch of culinary school. They had been a team once, and she missed that more than anything. The loss became especially apparent when she found herself with two newborns. She would've done anything to have had Cole by her side at that time. But he'd made that an impossibility.

"It's always been one of the things I admired most about you." He took the last sip of his drink and set the glass on top of the bar. His voice was as warm and smooth as the bourbon, sending ripples of recognition through Dani. She knew what that particular tone meant. He was standing only a few inches away now, his smell so sexy and inviting. "Although you have lots of things to admire." He gripped her elbow and looked down into her eyes. "Can I kiss you, Dani?"

A breathy laugh rushed past her lips. "Do you realize you have never asked me that question before?"

He was already coming in for what he'd asked for, a clever smile tugging at the corners of his enticing lips. "I never had you turn me down before the other night, either. I'm not taking any chances."

"Yes, Cole. You can kiss me."

He cupped her shoulders with his strong hands and planted a soft and sensuous, unmistakable kiss on her lips. A little tongue. Leaving her wanting more. She was dizzy from it.

"No more surprises between us, okay?" he asked.

That question was dripping with serious consequences. She sighed. Nothing between them was strictly fun and carefree, however much she wanted it to be that way, if only for an afternoon. She couldn't promise no more surprises, so she kissed him, popping up on to her tiptoes. She dug her fingers into his thick hair. He tugged her closer, giving her bottom a squeeze. Dani gasped. "Didn't you come over so we could figure out what I'm wearing to my first-ever sting operation?"

"Why do I feel like I'm being punished for stopping things the last time we kissed?"

"No punishment. Come on." Dani made her way up the stairs, Cole behind her. She was definitely aware of the sway of her own hips as she climbed those stairs. Let him get an eyeful of everything he'd been missing out on all these years.

She traipsed down the hall and into her bedroom. "Have a seat in the chair and I'll bring out a few options."

Cole marched over to the chair, but only to remove his suit coat and drape it across the back. Dani wasn't about to argue with the idea of him undressing. He sat on the bed instead, giving it a bounce. "Nice." He cocked an eyebrow at her while loosening his tie. Dani was about to be the next thing in the room to come undone.

"This will just take a minute." She retreated to her closet, mumbling to herself, "What are you doing? Do you really want to sleep with him? Won't that make things so much more complicated?"

"What was that?" Cole called from the other room. "Did you say something?"

"No. Just deciding what to show you." She rushed over to the far corner, where the full-length gowns she owned were hanging. She chose her three favorites— dark blue beaded, slinky black satin, and a red crepe mermaid gown.

She took all three dresses to Cole. "Well? Thoughts?"

He leaned back on the bed, placing his hands on the mattress and scrutinizing. "I need to see them on."

She smiled. This was definitely a fun form of seduction.

"Of course." She marched back to the closet and took off her clothes—every stitch. All three of these dresses required a strapless bra, and two required a thong or no panties at all.

She tried the blue one first. "Well?" She twirled, loving Cole's eyes on her. All of this silky fabric against her naked body was nice, but she wished he had his hands all over her.

He bit down on his lower lip as his gazed traveled up and down her body. Her heart was thumping in anticipation. She didn't care about the dress right now. She wanted him.

"I don't think it's quite sexy enough." He shook his head. "The black one next."

Disappointed, she headed back into the closet and changed. This one was even more torturous. The soft satin skimmed her breasts as she threaded the dress over her head, causing her nipples to come to attention. Mr. Tall, Dark and Dreamy being in the other room was not helping.

"Well? Thoughts?" This time she walked right up to him, turning once and looking down at him, trying her damnedest to send him psychic messages. Even if this dress wasn't the one, it was an excellent choice for ending up in a puddle on the floor.

He reached out and touched her hip lightly. "I don't love it."

"What don't you like?" Dani looked down at herself. She loved the way this dress hugged her curves.

"I just don't think it's the one."

A frustrated grumble left her throat. "Okay, then. One more. Otherwise you're taking me shopping, and I'm telling you right now that it's not going to be cheap." She returned to the closet once more.

"Something tells me I'd live."

"Damn you, Cole Sullivan," she muttered.

"I heard you that time."

"Good." She pulled the flame-red dress from the hanger and unzipped it. It was a mermaid-style gown made of fine jersey crepe, with impossibly skinny straps and a plunging back. The skirt followed every contour of her body and then flared out at the knee, making it deliciously swishy when she walked.

She was ready for another ego-crushing comment, but this time, Cole's eyes gave it away. The smoldering flash across his face made heat plume in her chest, down her belly, and straight to her thighs. "Well?" she asked. "Thoughts?" This time she gave him no buffer, stepping so close she was between his knees. She turned slowly, letting him drink in the vision.

"Wow. Just wow."

"You're just saying that because you have a weakness for red dresses."

He shook his head. "I have a weakness for *you* in a red dress. Every other woman is on her own."

She fought a smile. Why was a compliment from Cole so much better than a kind word from another man? She had no idea. "So you approve?"

He sat straighter, bringing himself closer. His eyes were about even with her chest. "Can you move well in it?"

She leaned forward at the waist and gave him an eyeful. "I can. It's nice and stretchy. It's actually surprisingly comfortable."

He drew in a deep breath through his nose, seeming to be grappling with a few urges. Good. She'd been fighting a few of her own. He must have unbuttoned his shirt when she was in the closet the last time. There were three undone now, giving her a view of his sexy chest and the tiny patch of hair in the center of it. She wanted to tangle her fingers in it. She wanted to get lost in him.

"Good. I want you to be comfortable," he said.

"So that's that, then." She turned her back to him and cast her sights over her shoulder. "I'm going to need help with the zipper, though. It's a little sticky."

Now Cole was sitting up pin straight, his eyes plaintive. "No games, Dani."

"No games."

"Good. You knock me down a peg every time you stomp on the brakes."

Dani hated the way the past crept into these conversations, intentional or not on either of their parts. It was omnipresent—the hurt, the transgressions, the untruths. She needed a break from all of it. She wanted to disappear into the one place she'd ever truly felt safe—Cole's arms. She wanted him to make her feel good. She wanted him to make the rest of the world go away.

Which meant she had to face this head-on. She turned and looked him square in the eye. "I brought you up to my bedroom, Sullivan. I'm trying on dresses that leave very little to the imagination, and I'm doing my best to make you want me the way I want you."

His trademark cocky smile made an appearance— the one that said the universe was particularly good at glossing over his mistakes. He was too handsome. Too likable. The irresistible golden boy, like dessert for breakfast, lunch and dinner. "You want me to show you my intentions?"

Her breath hitched in her throat. "I do."

He placed his hands on her hips, the heat from his palms nearly searing her through the dress. He curled his fingertips into her flesh and tugged her closer. Her knees were flat against the side of the mattress, his face

close enough to her breasts that her nipples drew hot and
tight. He trailed one hand to the small of her back and
dragged the zipper down. Electricity danced along her
spine as his fingertips grazed her skin along the way.

"Does this help?"

She nodded. "It does." With one hand, she slipped
both dress straps from her shoulders, clutching the gown
to her bosom with her other arm. "Does this help you?"

Their gazes connected. Cole's eyelids were heavy with
desire, making her want to give in to this right here and
now. "I want it all," he said. "Everything."

Dani let the dress drop to the floor, placed her hand
on Cole's shoulder and pushed him back on the bed. She
planted one knee on the mattress between his legs, unable
not to notice the bulging ridge in his pants. Any doubts
she'd had about whether or not he wanted her had been
a waste of time and energy.

She leaned down and yanked his shirt out of the waistband of his pants, then made quick work of the buttons,
traveling north as she went. As soon as his chest was
bare, she stretched out along his side and let her fingers
roam, threading them through the hair she'd been dying
to touch mere minutes ago.

Cole rolled to his side and cupped the side of Dani's
neck, his fingers warm and craving at her nape. They
kissed like their lives depended on it, mouths eager and
open, tongues wet and hot. Cole rolled her to her back,
his thigh firmly rocking against her center, making heat
flame between her legs. She couldn't remember ever
wanting him more. Maybe because she knew what was in
store for her and she'd gone so long without him. Too long.

"You're wearing too many clothes," she said.

He shifted to his knees and tore his shirt from his
body, tossing it to the floor with her dress. She unbuck-

led his belt, then unhooked his pants and drew down the zipper. She could already feel the tension coming from his hips. It radiated from him like the sun off a tin roof. He pushed his trousers past his hips, leaving them bunched at his upper thighs. Dani couldn't wait anymore. She sat up and tugged down his boxer briefs and took him in her hand, stroking lightly, letting her palm roll over the smooth skin with every pass. He moaned so deeply that the bed nearly shook. Her other hand trailed down his firm belly, her fingers knowing every hard contour, remembering every luscious dip and bulge of his body.

Cole stood and shucked his remaining clothes, then climbed back onto the bed. He pulled her into his arms, kissing her softly as their legs tangled and hands roamed everywhere—hers down his back and his to her hip, then up to cup her breast. He pushed her to her back and their gazes connected as he drew delicate circles around her nipple. She felt like she was floating as the need built inside her. She loved it when he took things slow and drew out the pleasure, but there was a lot of want bubbling to the surface. She needed him.

"I'm on the pill, but do we need a condom?" She'd been in near zero danger of getting pregnant in New York, having had only one boyfriend, who hadn't lasted long. She'd only kept her prescription to regulate her cycle. Still, she knew very little about Cole's personal life while she'd been gone.

"You tell me, Dani. There's been no one since you left. No one."

She kissed him softly, to give her a second to think. "Nobody? Not a single girl you picked up at a bar or anything?"

He shook his head. "You say it like it's a bad thing."

"I just…" She searched for the right words. "I'm surprised, that's all."

"Well, do you want to be surprised, or do you want me to set your world on fire?" He pushed up on his arms, towering over her. His chest was heaving. So was hers. She hooked her leg over his hip and grabbed both of his strong shoulders.

The muscles twitched beneath her touch. "I want the fire."

As much as Cole wanted to soak up the stunning sights of Dani, he had to close his eyes as he sank down into her. The warmth and pleasant tug of her body was so familiar and yet had been out of reach for so long. It was as if he'd gone without her forever. She wrapped her legs around him, caressing the backs of his thighs with her ankles. He planted both elbows on the bed and combed his fingers into her hair, kissing her unforgettable mouth. She tasted so sweet, even when her tongue did things that made him feel like he'd been a very bad boy.

Dani tilted her hips, allowing him to thrust even deeper. He pressed his lips against her cheek, along her jaw and down her neck. They moved together in that rhythm he knew so well, one that belonged to only them. He hadn't merely missed Dani, he'd missed this closeness with her—where nothing else mattered and the rest of the world could be forgotten. He'd lost his shield when he lost her—or, to be more accurate, when he pushed her away.

Dani's breaths were short and ragged now. The motion of her hips was more insistent, and that only made Cole want to try harder. He pushed up from the bed, holding his torso tight, trying to keep it together while he made his thrusts longer and deeper. His legs were on fire, the pressure coiling in his hips, gathering in his belly. He listened carefully to Dani, watched for clues as she closed her eyes and bit her lower lip, looking so impossibly beautiful and sexy. She turned her head to one side and he kissed her neck, knowing how much she loved that. She arched into him, muscling him closer with her heels.

She didn't have to tell him that she was close. He could feel the tension inside her. He stayed focused, not ready to give way until she did, even when his mind was fuzzy and the pleasure was knocking at the gates, threatening to barrel through him. He had a hell of a lot to make up for. His performance needed to be spectacular—enough fireworks for a hundred Fourths of July.

Her mouth was slack now, her breaths halting and choppy. She dug her fingers into his shoulders and tightened the grip of her legs. The next thing he knew, she was unraveling, falling apart at the seams in the most stunning way. He watched her, transfixed by the vision, until his climax ran through his body like a freight train headed straight down a mountain. He pressed his hips into her one more time and dropped his head, nestling his face in her neck.

Dani wrapped her arms and legs around him even tighter, humming softly, a habit of hers he'd nearly forgotten about. She hummed after sex. He still had no idea why and she could never explain it, either, beyond the fact that she was happy.

"That was incredible," she muttered into his chest.

Yeah, well, remind me to go without sex for nearly six years. That'll do that to a guy. "It was, Dani. It really was."

He eased to his side and she hopped up from the bed, flitting into the bathroom. How he loved watching her lovely rear end bouncing along in close proximity. He hadn't merely missed Dani. He'd been starved for her.

She made him feel more than alive. She made him feel invincible. This high was something he hadn't felt in six years. He hadn't felt this good for even one minute since she left.

That meant he needed to get his priorities straight and figure out what he wanted from her. They couldn't just sleep with each other and walk away—there was too much between them. Too many secrets. But then again, would he ever get her to tell him the truth about her sons? She'd kept things hush-hush for so long.

Dani stopped in the doorway of her bathroom and leaned against it, trailing her finger up and down the jamb. "I almost hate to say this, because I don't want to feed your ego, but you look spectacular in my bed."

"Consider my ego fed. That's the best thing anyone has ever said to me." Laughing, Cole peeled the covers back, offering them in invitation. "Please. Join me in looking spectacular."

Dani climbed into bed and placed a soft and delicate kiss on his lips. Her breasts pressed against his chest, sent the all-hands-on-deck signal straight to his groin. No question this would be his shortest recovery ever. And damn, he wanted another chance at everything they'd just done together. He couldn't wait for more.

Dani slipped her leg between his, rocking her thigh against him. "Ooh. Again?"

He was so hard it nearly made him dizzy. "Yes. And maybe again after that."

Dani didn't hesitate to straddle his hips and take his erection in her hand, guiding him inside her. She sank down onto him, and his eyes drifted shut as her warmth enveloped him. She dropped down and kissed him hard, bouncing her hips in a rhythm that had his head spinning. He curled his fingers into the velvety flesh of her bottom. Tension coiled tightly in his groin and hips. He needed the release again. He thrust more forcefully, lifting her off the bed. She was grinding her hips into his and he could tell from her breaths that he was hitting the right spot. Just when he thought he couldn't take it much longer, Dani called his name and buried her face in his neck. The pleasure rocketed right out of him in waves while Dani let her full bodyweight rest on his, a feeling he'd always loved.

She rolled to his side and curled into him. "So was that a line about not being with any other woman since me?" she asked, still a bit breathless.

Cole pulled her closer, loving the feel of her silky skin against his. "What if it was? Would you be mad?" If only it *was* a line.

"No. I mean, I've fallen for worse, for sure. And you certainly made it worth my while."

"But? I'm sensing a but here."

"But nothing. I'm just surprised. I don't know how often you look in the mirror, but I'm trying to figure out how you stayed out of the beds of every last woman in Royal during that time."

He placed a kiss on her forehead. "Thank you. That's sweet." If he looked back, it seemed impossible, but at the time, he hadn't seen any other way but to stay single. He wasn't about to pull another woman into his orbit. He was damaged goods. Had he looked at women and wanted them? Sure. But his heart hadn't been in it. He didn't see the point. But things were different with Dani, and not just because they had a past. Not because it took no effort at all to want her. She knew the Cole he had been before the glioma was discovered. She knew the old him, the person he wished he could be again.

Trouble was, that was the guy she'd loved, too. And that guy no longer walked the earth.

"I wasn't trying to be sweet. And I already knew there was no other woman when you broke up with me. Megan told me."

He lifted a brow. "How does Megan know the details of my personal life?"

"You've said it yourself a thousand times. This is a small town. People talk."

Cole sucked in a deep breath. Maybe it was time to come clean on this one point. "Yes, I lied about there being someone else. And I'm sorry about that, but I had my reasons."

She shook her head in disbelief. "Just like you had your reasons for waiting until after I left town to quit the Rangers, even when I'd begged you to quit?"

"Would you quit your job if I begged you? That wasn't fair, Dani. I would never ask you to leave behind something you loved."

Dani sat up and cast a look of deep anger at him. "I was trying to guarantee our future together. A long life. I was hoping to grow old with you, Cole. But you threw all of that away."

That stopped him dead. How could he tell her that the thing she'd once hoped for was something he could never give her? Not even now. "Can't we take a break from the past? Just for one day?"

"I don't see how we can, especially when you don't want to talk about it."

From downstairs, the sound of children's voices filtered into the room. Dani slapped the bed and gathered a chunk of the comforter in her hand, narrowly missing Cole's thigh. "The boys are home. You have to get out of here right now." She flew out from under the sheets and began flinging his clothes at him. His shirt hit him square in the face.

"Slow down a minute." He scrambled out from under the covers and started putting on his boxers, hopping on one leg to do it. "I have a good reason for being here."

"Not in my bed, you don't. They're little boys, Cole. They ask lots of questions. You need to put your clothes on right now." Dani was furiously making the bed. Naked. It was the best view ever, but he had zero time to enjoy it.

Dammit.

Cole was turning his shirtsleeves inside out when the boys' voices grew louder. The door was closed, but who knew who long it would be before they burst through it.

Dani raked her dress from the floor and scampered into the bathroom. "Get in here," she whispered to him, loudly.

He followed orders and Dani closed the door behind him. She was still naked, clutching that man-killer dress to her chest. Cole buttoned up his shirt and gave himself a tour. It was like a spa—white marble and sleek fixtures, fluffy white towels, and a shower that might even be bigger than his.

"How many people does this accommodate?" he asked with a leading inflection, pointing to the spacious enclosure wrapped in clear glass.

Dani smacked him on the arm. "There's no time to talk about that. Just finish getting dressed." She pulled a robe from a hook on the wall, and he took his chance to drink in her luscious curves before she wrapped them up in terry cloth and cinched the belt tight.

Cole tucked his dress shirt into his pants, zipped them up and buckled his belt. "Is it okay for me to go out there? I can't spend the whole day in your bathroom. Unless we get to use the shower. For that, I will rearrange my schedule."

"Why are you being so cavalier about all of this?"

He didn't want to tell her the truth—this was a good diversion from the stupid way he'd put his foot in his mouth a few minutes ago. Why he'd walked into the trap of discussing his departure from the Texas Rangers, he had no idea. He made a mental note to avoid the topic at all costs in the future. "It's a little funny, don't you think? Sneaking around and whispering in your bathroom? We're adults."

"And you know absolutely nothing about parenting. It's my job to shield them from stuff like this." Dani cracked the bathroom door and leaned out. Cole leaned against her, and they both craned their necks.

"Mommy? Is Mr. Sullivan here?"

"We saw his truck outside." About a million tiny knocks accompanied the boys' questions.

Dani closed the bathroom door. "See what you did?"

"What? I gave you a ride home. Last time I checked, that was not a federal offense."

"I have to go answer them. You stay here. I'll let you know when you can come out."

Dani disappeared through the door, shutting it behind her. Cole finished putting his suit back on and neatened his hair, which was wonderfully disheveled after his afternoon delights with Dani. He fetched his shoes from her bedroom floor and was putting them on when Dani returned.

"Okay. The boys are out playing in the backyard with Elena. You can go now." She'd changed into her bathing suit and was wearing a cover-up over it. "I'm going to go join them."

"Maybe I can have them over to swim in my pool again?"

"We'll talk about it."

"Okay, then. I guess I'll go." Cole followed her out of her room and headed downstairs. He hated the cool turn things had taken, but thus was the state of their friendship, or relationship or whatever anyone wanted to call it right now. There were problems lurking in every corner of their past. Dare to poke at one issue and the rest would likely rush out for their hiding place.

"Cole," Dani called from the top of the stairs. He turned and looked up at her, wondering if there was any way they'd ever get their act together. "I'll see you on Tuesday? For the trip to Durango City?"

For once, the investigation had been the absolute last thing on his mind. "Yeah. I'll pick you up at four."

"Perfect."

Cole merely nodded and walked away. *Perfect* was about the last word he would've used to describe the current state of affairs.

Eight

Cole would've been lying if he said that he was feeling completely certain the sting would go off as planned. All of this effort—an entire team of people, a private jet, countless hours and resources, bringing Dani into it—it had to add up to something. If it didn't, there would be no justice for Will or Megan or Jason. Cole couldn't let this operation fail.

"Folks, we'll be landing in a few minutes," the pilot said.

Cole took Dani's hand. "You got everything straight?"

"Yes. You're Chet Pearson, one of the largest private investors in crude oil and natural gas in the US. I'm Melanie Skye, aspiring actress and your girlfriend of six months. I really wish I could've been a chef."

"Too dangerous. We don't want to remind him that he's met you."

"It was a lifetime ago. I mean, I'm memorable, but not that memorable."

Cole managed a nervous grin. "Just stick to the plan, okay? You'll give me a heart attack otherwise."

She slipped her hand from his and picked a tiny piece of lint from her dress. "It's pretty straightforward, isn't it? I do everything I can to ingratiate myself to Sheriff Orson and try to get him to brag to me about how powerful he is and the sneaky things he's done."

"And what else?"

"I don't let you leave my side." She was definitely taking this seriously. She was throwing his exact wording back at him.

"Right. I don't trust that mic they put in your handbag. It's not as reliable as a wire."

"You should've let me pick a dress that would've accommodated one. Then we wouldn't have to worry about that part."

He glanced over at her, memories of the other afternoon threatening to overtake what should've been an entirely professional train of thoughts going through his head. The dress was perfect. Dani was perfect. He loved seeing her in it, and he knew exactly how lucky he was to have had the privilege of taking it off her the other afternoon. It had been such an incredible physical reunion, but could they get on the same page with their other issues? Could he finally just tell her his secret? It had felt good to come out with one untruth the other day, but she hadn't taken it well. There was no telling how she'd react if he finally told her everything.

"You look very handsome in that tux," Dani said.

Cole had gone all out with the Armani, his most expensive pair of cuff links, and his Rolex. No detail was too small for tonight. "Thank you. You look even more amazing now in that dress than you did the other day."

Dani reached out and touched his arm. "Thank you."

Cole stole another eyeful of Dani, but now he was second-guessing the dress. Did it make her too much of a sitting duck? Too enticing? There was no way this sheriff, with a known weakness for beautiful women, didn't glom on to her right away. It was the perfect plan. And that scared the hell out of him.

"Honestly, I'm glad you aren't wearing a wire. I don't want you thinking about being alone with him for even an instant."

"Look. I've been around this guy before. I can handle him. Plus, I won't put myself in danger. The boys need me."

Don't remind me. The plane dipped down, and Cole saw the small airstrip below. "There's still time to back out. You're not obligated to me or this investigation."

She turned and gave him a look of admonishment. "I have to do this for Megan. And for Savannah. I *was* that little girl. The little girl without the family she should have had. I can't let her down. We have to catch the men responsible for Jason's death."

"Okay then, Melanie. It's showtime."

The plane landed safely and taxied down the short runway. After a few moments, the pilot stepped out of the cockpit. "Your car is waiting for you at the bottom of the stairs. He'll bring you right back when you decide to fly home. Enjoy your evening." He winked at Cole but otherwise kept a straight face. The pilot worked for the FBI and would be on hand to leave at a moment's notice if needed.

Cole squeezed Dani's hand three times as a reminder that they were officially in sting mode. From this moment on, they were Chet and Melanie. Eyes could be watching and ears could be listening. Sheriff Orson's influence was all over this damn county. His deputy wouldn't have been so nervous about offering information if that wasn't the case.

As they rode up into the mountains along a winding road, Cole reminded himself that this was for Jason. It was for Savannah and Will and Megan. Rich belonged behind bars for the rest of his life.

Miles away from the landing strip, the car pulled up to an ornately scrolled iron gate. It was flanked by massive stone pillars and tall walls that trailed off into the dense woods on both sides. As the driver buzzed the intercom and requested entry, Cole noticed a security camera panning the length of the car. They drove onto the property, which was sprawling and immaculately landscaped, lit up with dramatic lighting. At the top of the hill—the highest point, as near as Cole could tell—the house sat waiting. It, too, was lit up, glowing in the inky blackness of the night.

"I remember this place," Dani muttered under her breath, referring to the time she'd done a catering job out here years ago. "He made it sound like he was a businessman who just happened to be sheriff."

"No. He's a sheriff involved in business he shouldn't be. That's the reality."

"How are the citizens here not completely up in arms about this place? The man is clearly abusing his power."

"He's greased a lot of palms along the way. Only trouble with that is people will only stay quiet for so long, especially when your misdeeds keep getting worse."

Dani wrapped her arms around herself and nodded. "We need to get this guy good."

They came to a stop, and the driver opened the door on Dani's side. She slid across the seat and climbed out. Cole followed. Now that they were out of the confines of the car, things were about to get that much more real.

"I'll be waiting for you, Mr. Pearson," the driver said to Cole. He, too, was one more agent on-site. That definitely gave Cole a sense of security.

"Thank you. We might be late."

He nodded. "Take as long as you need, sir."

Two armed security guards were waiting outside the front door. "We need to check you for a weapon, sir," one of them said, patting down Cole with little warning. "He's good."

Dani smiled and held up her hands in mock surrender. "I'm sorry, gentlemen, but I can assure you I couldn't hide a gun in this dress if I wanted to."

"Yes, ma'am." The guard seemed embarrassed. "But we need to check your handbag, as well."

With no hesitation, Dani handed it over. "Oh, sure. Just a bunch of tampons in there."

Just as Cole was wondering why in the hell she was choosing to share that bit of information, the guard returned her bag without looking. "I'll take your word for it, ma'am."

Cole grinned and snuggled Dani closer as she hooked her arm in his and they made their way up the stairs to the front door.

A tuxedoed waiter with a silver tray of champagne was waiting inside the door. A young woman with a clipboard was checking names. "You must be Mr. Pearson and Ms. Skye. Sheriff Orson is eager to meet you both."

Dani smiled and said, "We're eager to meet him, too."

As soon as the words came out of her mouth, Cole caught sight of their target, Sheriff Orson. A trim and fit man, he was well groomed, wearing a fitted dark suit and crisp white shirt.

The sheriff noticed them and came right over, introducing himself. "Sheriff Billy Orson. You must be Mr. Pearson and Ms. Skye. Pleased to meet you both." He turned to Cole. "Mr. Pearson, I hope you're going to write me a big fat check this evening. It won't be much fun if you don't."

This guy does not mess around. Cole couldn't believe he'd hardly been through the door before he was the recipient of a thinly veiled threat. "I assure you, I've come here tonight with only the best intentions."

"Glad to hear it." He then turned to Dani. "As for you, Ms. Skye, I hope you will join me for a drink. I'll be sorely disappointed if you say no." The man had the nerve to reach out and take her hand, looping her arm around his and leading her to the far side of the room, where a long line of bar stools sat along a counter with a view of the gourmet kitchen.

It took every ounce of control Cole had in his body not to pounce on the guy. He followed them closely, watching every move. Orson asked Dani to sit at the bar but didn't offer Cole a seat. He did, however, pour them both a drink. He and Dani had agreed ahead of time that they would fake their way through drinking this evening. They needed to be on top of their game.

"Could I get some extra ice?" Dani asked, her voice dripping with sweetness.

"Why of course, you can, beautiful," the sheriff replied. Cole wanted to strangle him.

The sheriff downed his drink in a single gulp and poured them another, then proceeded to go into his sales pitch to Cole about the pipeline investment. He said everything a wealthy man who wanted to get wealthier could want to hear—that it was not just a gold mine ripe for the taking, but that he was the only person who could get the pipeline approved. He had the contacts with all local authorities. They would do whatever he wanted. He also knew how to put the thumbscrews to what he called "the do-gooder environmental groups." He claimed that he would have no problem rushing through the project and getting the oil flowing, and the money would start rolling in. Sheriff Orson would simply be receiving a generous cut of the deal for his expertise and connections.

Dani hung on every word, and there were a lot of them. The guy would not stop talking. Every time another high-roller guest walked by, the sheriff would pull them into the conversation and start the sales pitch all over again. Cole and Dani endured hours of the sheriff bragging about his power and unfortunately witnessed his inappropriate flirtation and not-so-subtle innuendo with the women at the party. By the end of it, Cole felt like he needed to take a shower.

The sheriff was very good at closing the deal, though. He got signed investment agreements from every guest at the party.

"Are you ready to sign on the dotted line, Mr. Pearson?" Orson asked now that Cole was the sole remaining holdout.

"What do you think, Melanie?" Cole asked Dani the question as if it actually mattered. Chet Pearson's signature meant nothing.

"I think you should do it. Then we can have a drink to celebrate."

The sheriff squared his sights on Dani. "I'm not sure which is better, hearing those words or hearing them come out of your gorgeous mouth."

Cole glanced at her as she smiled through what had to be unimaginable disgust. All he could think was that they had to steer this conversation in the right direction, or Sheriff Orson was going to be dead. A few more comments like that about Dani, and Cole would have to kill him with his bare hands.

* * *

The other guests had departed, meaning Dani's determination to nail Sheriff Orson to the wall was as strong as ever. After hours of watching him be inappropriate with women and boastful with men, he'd proven himself to be exactly what Dani had thought the first time she'd met him—scum of the highest order. Knowing that he'd played the pivotal role in the cover-up of Jason's death made it that much more certain. Now they just needed to get him to talk.

"Sheriff, now that Mr. Pearson has signed your agreement and we've had our celebratory drink, I think we should go. I'm afraid we've overstayed our welcome." She had no intention of leaving. She just wanted to threaten him with it.

"Little lady, as long as you're wearing that dress, you can stay as long as you like." Sheriff Orson was slurring his words now. All the drinks he'd had were taking effect. Little did the sheriff know that Cole and Dani had been dumping their drinks into a nearby potted plant all night.

Dani really hated being called *little lady*. "Sheriff, I have to say that you have quite an impressive home. I don't know that I've ever seen a public servant with such a grand setup."

Cole took a sip of his drink but stayed otherwise quiet, letting her take the reins.

"Public servant? Is that what you think of me? The people of this county are damn lucky to have me. I work hard."

Judging by the way he was raising his voice, Dani knew this was the right approach. Men like Sheriff Orson felt that they weren't like everyone else. They were above the law and the rules simply didn't apply to them. "I'm not saying you don't work hard. I'm sure you do. I just wasn't aware that driving around in a car with a shotgun all day was so lucrative."

"I have business interests on the side. A man is entitled to augment his salary."

"Of course. Like your little pipeline, which sounds like such a neat project." Dani was sure to lend extra emphasis to *little* and *neat*. She knew how much egotistical men hated to be dismissed like that.

"It's not a little pipeline. It's a massive project. We're talking millions of dollars on the line."

"Million with an *M*, right? Not billions, like they would have in Alaska or the Dakotas."

"Excuse me?" The sheriff's eyes blazed with an anger that made Dani distinctly uncomfortable. She had to calm him down a bit.

She reached out and touched his arm. "I'm not trying to disparage your hard work. I'm guessing you're by far the most powerful man in this corner of the world."

His shoulders visibly relaxed, and Dani felt as though she could breathe again.

"Oh, absolutely," Cole chimed in.

The sheriff glanced over at him, and Dani had the distinct impression that she wasn't going to get anywhere with Cole in the room. His role as protector was getting in the way.

"If you'll excuse me, I need to visit the little cowboys' room," the sheriff said.

Dani smiled, thinking that only a complete buffoon of a grown man would refer to it as that. As soon as he was out of sight, she grabbed Cole's arm.

"You have to leave me alone with him. Just for a few minutes. I think I can get him to say it."

Cole shook his head. "No way, Dani. It's too dangerous." His jaw was firmly set and he stood a little straighter. He was determined to keep her safe. It was so damn sexy, even if it was giving her problems.

"My purse is sitting right there. Just go to the bathroom when he's done and listen. If I'm not getting anywhere after five minutes, come back and we'll try something new."

He grasped her bare shoulder with his warm hand, his thumb landing on her clavicle, sending a zip of electricity through her. "I don't like this."

From the hall, she heard the sound of a toilet flushing and water running. "I can do it. Just give me a chance."

"Can I pour y'all another drink?" Sheriff Orson asked, returning to the room, his presence making Dani's skin crawl.

"Oh, sure," Dani answered. "How about you, Chet? Another drink?" She stared him down as subtly as she could.

Cole swallowed hard enough that she could see his Adam's apple bob up and down. "That sounds great. But I think I need to use the washroom, as well. I'll be back in a few."

Bingo.

As soon as Cole disappeared down the hall, the sheriff made his move, as she'd been certain he would. "What's the deal with you and Chet there? He doesn't really seem like your type."

"You've only known me for a few hours. How did you deduce that?"

"Gorgeous woman like you deserves a man with money and power. Chet seems to have the first, but that's about it."

She took a calm breath, even though her stomach was churning. "I appreciate the gesture, Sheriff, but I'm not sure you wield the kind of power that really turns a woman on." She bit her lower lip, looking into his eyes and seeing nothing but pure evil. In her head, she repeated the reasons she was here. *Do this for Megan. Do it for Savannah.*

"I have more power than you could imagine." He leaned against the kitchen counter, narrowing his sights on her cleavage.

Dani had no choice but to sit a little straighter and employ her assets. "Somehow I doubt that."

"Oh, yeah?"

She nodded confidently, feeling nothing of the sort on the inside. "Sorry, but yeah."

He moved in on her, coming closer until he was only inches away. With him standing and her sitting on the bar stool, she felt overpowered. Overmatched. "I can make a person disappear."

Dani laughed, but it was out of sheer nervousness. *Oh my God. He's going to say it.* "Like a magician? Or for real?"

"For real. I've done it many times. Did it to a man just a few weeks ago."

She dared to look up at his face, stretching her neck and making herself more vulnerable to him, knowing she only had a few more seconds until Cole would be back. "You were daring enough to do that? Aren't you afraid of getting caught?"

Sheriff Orson shrugged it off. "I told you, darling. I'm in charge here. A man showed up and told me he needed a body cremated, ASAP. I took his money, put a phony name on the coroner's report and told them to flick the switch."

Before Dani knew what was happening, the front door burst open and a stream of men wearing navy jackets emblazoned with FBI stormed inside. They were all over

Sheriff Orson, bringing his hands behind his back, reading him his rights and slapping handcuffs on him.

The sheriff stared her down. "You bitch."

Dani didn't know what else to do other than smile. She watched as he was led away, overcome with the most intense rush of relief and accomplishment she'd felt in her entire life. Well, aside from when the twins had been born. That was no small feat, either.

She was still standing there in a daze when she felt Cole's presence and he wrapped his arm around her shoulder. "You were unbelievable. I'm so impressed."

She turned to him and looked up into his gorgeous blue eyes, feeling almost as if she was living outside her body. Everything was surreal right now. "You are?"

"Are you kidding? I heard every word. I never went to the bathroom. I was standing right around the corner, ready to pounce. I couldn't have done this without you. I hope you know that."

It meant so much to hear him say that. Having Cole's approval and appreciation felt so good. Six years ago, she'd lived for it. Now that she had a taste of it again, it brought back a flood of the best feelings between them. They'd been as rock solid as a couple could be. Could they have that again? "I couldn't have done it without *you*. You believed in me. You believed I could do it. And you let me run with it, even when things were getting a little hairy."

Cole laughed. "You definitely waded into some waters I wasn't quite sure of."

"And you trusted me." She didn't take having Cole's trust lightly. That made her extra appreciative of it now, and that much more scared of losing it. Would he forgive her when she told him about the boys? She knew now that no matter what Cole's secret was, even if he never told her, she had to tell him about the boys. And if that killed the trust, she'd just have to rebuild it, brick by brick.

"Of course I did, Dani. I never doubted you could pull this off. I was just waiting to see how you were going to do it."

Just then a tall redheaded woman with a pretty sizable baby bump strolled over, wearing the same jacket the other agents were. She held out her hand for Dani. "Special Agent Marjorie Stanton. I've conducted an awful lot of sting operations in my day, and I have to tell you that was a top-notch performance."

"You were listening, too?"

"Down the street in a van. I heard every word. If you ever decide to give up your culinary career, give me a call." A walkie-talkie at her hip buzzed. "I'm sorry. I need to grab this. Cole, I'll talk to you tomorrow when we're all back in Royal. Bird is closing in on Richard Lowell's stash. We're getting close to catching him and putting him away."

"Great news. I'll get the update tomorrow." Cole took Dani's hand. "I know this is an awful lot of excitement, but are you ready to get out of here?"

"Are you kidding? I never want to come back. What a slimeball."

"A slimeball who's about to go away for a very long time. Right after he gives up Richard Lowell."

"Music to my ears. Now let's get back to the plane." All Dani wanted right now, was for the world to go away so she could be alone with Cole.

Nine

As soon as the plane was up in the air, Cole felt true relief. They'd accomplished what they came to do. He and the team were a monumental step closer to putting Rich away. He'd been working so hard for a major break-through like this, that he hadn't had the chance to consider how incredible it would feel to be closer to this goal. And he couldn't have done it without Dani.

He looked over at her, still so stunning in that dress, except now she was even more desirable. They were a team tonight and a damn good one. There was just some-thing about their connection that brought out the best in each of them. Could they be a team again? He'd been ask-ing himself that question non-stop since they'd made love at her house. She made him feel so alive. She made him a better version of himself. He couldn't imagine going back to the way he'd been for the last six years. That ver-sion of Cole Sullivan was sleepwalking through life. He couldn't do that to himself anymore.

"Can I just tell you that the way you handled yourself tonight was so damn sexy?" he asked.

She blushed and smiled. "You know what was really sexy? Having you there to protect me." She reached down and took his hand in hers, rubbing her thumb along his knuckles. "It made me do and say things I never thought I could."

The darkened airplane cabin was romantic and even felt private, with the captain up in the cockpit and he and Dani alone in the last row. All Cole could think about was kissing her supple mouth. He moved in, and just like a wish granted, Dani raised her lips to him. They fell into a kiss that was immediately passionate. Maybe it was the thrill of what they'd just been through, but it was clear they were both turned on. Dani dug her fingers into his scalp, and her tongue teased his. Cole tried to get his arms around her, but the stupid armrest was in the way.

"Come here," he said.

Dani looked at him, her lips full, her mouth slack with surprise. "Come here?"

"Yes. Come and get in my lap. I need you in my arms. I need to kiss you for real."

A mischievous smile tugged at her lips. "Are you serious?"

Cole groaned. "I have never been more serious in my entire life. Get over here."

"Okay." Dani unlatched her seat belt and stood, then sat across his lap and put her arm around his neck.

"I thought I'd died and gone to heaven the other day when I got to take this dress off you," Cole muttered against the soft skin of her neck. "I just want to do it again."

"I don't think you can really take it all the way off

me this time," Dani countered. "If the pilot looks back here, I'd like at least a slight chance of saving my pride."

Cole unzipped her dress and dragged the straps down her arms. Her breasts were bare to him, her nipples standing at attention in the cool air of the plane. He lowered his lips and drew one into his mouth. Dani responded by moving her bottom in circles against his crotch. She was so sexy it boggled the mind, but knowing that they could get caught added a whole new level of sexiness to this.

Dani dug her fingers into his hair and kissed him deeply, rotating her hips in maddening circles. He planted a hand on her ass and pulled her even closer, wanting no distance between them. The heat was building fast, but they were still wearing too many clothes. "I need to be inside you, Dani."

She reared back her head, and her eyes popped wide. "What if we get caught?"

"Then we get caught. No jury in the world would convict me if they saw you in this dress."

"You're a bad boy, Cole Sullivan." She eased off his lap, hunching down behind the seats, and reached under her dress, shimmying her panties past her hips and leaving them on the floor.

"Plus, I probably won't last very long."

"You're not exactly selling it." She cocked an eyebrow at him.

"Don't worry. I'll be sure you reach your final destination." Cole had unbuttoned his pants and tugged them and his boxer briefs past his hips. Perched on the edge of his seat, he reclined back.

Dani lifted her dress to the middle of her thighs and, one at a time, bracketed his hips with her knees. Her breasts were bare to him, her nipples tight and hard, her hair slightly mussed. He wasn't sure he'd ever seen a hotter sight in all his life.

He took himself in hand and slipped inside Dani's body. He grappled with the incredible sensation as she sank down onto him, her slick heat molding around him, holding on to him tight. It felt unimaginably good, just as it had the other day. Dammit, he and Dani were just right. Everything today had proven that. It made him want to work that much harder for what had once seemed completely out of reach—a future. With her.

Dani rotated her hips in near-perfect figure-eights. It was enough to make Cole rocket into space, but he had to do better than a teenaged boy. Dani changed her motion, rocking forward and back against him. "I need to see your chest," she murmured, unbuttoning his shirt. She spread her hands across his skin and then kissed him as the pleasure began coiling tightly in his belly.

"Well, folks, looks like we've got a bit of turbulence ahead," the captain said over the PA.

Dani and Cole both froze. Her chest was heaving, she was breathing so hard.

"Just hold on tight back there and I'll get you out of this as soon as I can," the captain said.

Dani giggled, then went back to kissing him, back to moving her hips in those mind-bending rotations. The plane dropped a few feet and they both sucked in a breath, but neither broke the kiss. Right now, even gravity was not a concern.

Dani's breaths were getting choppy, but Cole could tell she wasn't quite getting what she wanted. She was fitful in his arms, now kissing his neck and burying her forehead into the seat back behind him. He shifted one of his hands under her dress and, using his thumb, found her center. His other hand was at the small of her back, pushing her against his hand.

"Yes," Dani gasped. "Right there."

The plane bounced and pitched. Cole blocked it out. He had Dani in his arms, and that was all that mattered right now. He hadn't felt so aligned with her in a long time, between their amazing teamwork at the party tonight and now, handing their fate over to gravity and turbulence and Mother Nature. As ecstasy flamed in his belly and Dani muttered in his ear for more, he was hit again by the realization this was the way things should be. As crazy and dangerous as ever, he and Dani should always be like this. Together.

Dani muffled her voice in Cole's shoulder when she reached her peak, and he pulled her tight against his chest as the pleasure charged through him.

She settled her head against his chest. "Tonight meant a lot to me, Cole. That you were proud of me."

That struck him as a bit amazing. Most of the time, Dani seemed like she didn't need anyone's approval. "It did?"

She slowly raised her head and nodded. Her eyes were misty.

"You okay, Dani?" He reached up and cupped her cheek.

She turned into his touch immediately, pressing her lips to the inside of his hand. "I am. I just didn't want to let it go unsaid."

He pulled her close again, kissing the top of her head while her words cycled through his head. Leaving things gone unsaid had torn them apart. He simply hadn't been able to utter the words. He hadn't had the courage to say that he was a man with a ticking time bomb in his head. That was only one big secret between them now, though.

Cameron and Colin had to be his. His gut was telling him they were. All of this needed to come to light. All of it. And with the sting behind them, that was the most pressing issue he and Dani faced. Once that dirty laundry was aired, would they still be okay? And what did "okay" even entail? His glioma was never going away. That much would never, ever change.

A still quiet Dani carefully climbed off Cole's lap and sat down in her seat, replacing the straps of her dress and turning so Cole could help her zip up the back. She smoothed her hair while peering over the tops of the seats in front of them.

"You don't think he heard us, do you?"

Cole shrugged. "Not much we can do about it now." He'd gotten his pants sorted out by that point. Now to finish buttoning his shirt.

Dani leaned across the armrest and gave him a kiss. "Never a dull moment with you, is there?"

"You know me. Total adrenaline junkie."

"I'd better sneak into the bathroom and tidy up. God only knows how bad my makeup looks right now." She bent down and plucked her panties from the floor. "Yikes. Can't forget these." She scooted past him.

Cole's mind started making plans as soon as Dani was gone. Would she be up for coming out to the ranch with him tonight? Or would she invite him over to her house? He couldn't stand the thought of putting off his admission or his questions about the boys any longer. It had to happen tonight. He decided he would ask her as soon as they were back in his truck and leaving the airfield.

Dani returned and Cole took his chance to use the restroom and put his clothes back together in a way that made it look at least slightly less obvious that he and

Dani had just had sex on the plane. As he strolled back down the aisle, he was struck by a sharp pain at his temple. He grabbed the seat back and clamped his eyes shut. He couldn't see past the pain. It was like a thunderbolt of white, like someone was shining a searchlight square in his eyes.

"Cole. Are you okay?" Dani asked.

His eyes were still shut. The instant he tried to open them, he regretted it. The flash of agony that ripped through his head was unlike anything he'd ever experienced. And he'd been through a lot of pain in his life. The plane was dipping and pitching again. He found it hard to stand up straight. Somewhere he could hear Dani's voice, but it was coming in and out, like someone was turning the dial on a radio.

He could feel her touch, though, her insistent hands on his biceps pulling him down. The next thing he knew he was sitting.

"Cole Sullivan, talk to me right now or I will never speak to you again."

There was her voice. He heard it clear as a whistle now. It made him smile, but only slightly. Just moving his lips made his head hurt more.

"Headache," he managed to say. "Bad headache."

"Like a migraine?"

Cole nodded. He'd never had a migraine before, but his mother suffered from them and he knew that they often involved extreme reactions to light and they could came on very suddenly. He hoped to hell a migraine was all it was.

"What can I do?"

He shook his head as slightly as possible. What could she do? Nothing right now. "Hold my hand."

She wrapped her fingers around his. That prompted

another smile from him, one that hurt less than the last one. Maybe this wasn't a big deal. He really hoped that was the case.

"Cole, you're worrying me."

"I'll be fine." His words were raspy and dry. He almost didn't recognize his own voice.

"We're supposed to land in ten minutes. We can take you straight to the hospital."

Cole shook his head. He didn't even care how much it hurt. He did not want to go there. Bad things happened there. Bad news. Life-altering news. He couldn't live with that. Not when he had a chance to have Dani again.

Aside from the time the boys got strep throat, Dani had never been so worried in her whole life. She held on to Cole's hand, studying every movement of his face since he wasn't saying much. His eyes were closed, but the muscles of his forehead and around his eyes twitched from time to time. He was in immense pain. She could see the way he flinched from nothing at all.

"Folks, we're making our final approach into Royal," the captain said.

As the nose of the plane dipped down, Dani wrapped her other hand around Cole's, not wanting to let go. Worry was consuming her. Cole was tough as nails. Almost too tough. He did not like for people to see him in a compromised state—he saw it as weakness. Dani only saw how human he was. Which meant whatever was going on right now was bad. How could she go from the high of the sting to the slow burn of making love on the plane to being worried sick about Cole? It was a miracle she could manage a single coherent thought right now.

Luckily, the landing was smooth as silk. Dani didn't want anything jostling Cole too much. "You stay right here. I'll go get the car and bring it around. Then I'll get the pilot to help me get you off this plane."

Cole shook his head and opened one eye. "I'm fine."

"You are not fine. Keep your butt in this seat and I'll be right back."

As if Dani needed confirmation that Cole was indeed hurting badly, he nodded and slumped back in the chair. He almost never listened to her. Again, the worry ate at her. What in the world was going on?

She got the pilot up to speed and he sat with Cole while Dani ran—in heels and her mermaid dress, no less—to get Cole's car. Thank goodness they'd been able to fly in a private plane in and out of Royal. She never would've been able to get him through the airport terminal in Houston. She would've needed a wheelchair, and if she knew one thing about Cole, it was that he would not put up with that. The amount of negotiating she and the head nurse at Royal Memorial had had to do after his big accident six years ago was ridiculous. Cole was as stubborn as a mule.

She tore up the stairs to the plane. Cole was in the same spot, but his eyes were open and he was talking to the pilot. Dani had to wonder if he was actually feeling better or if he was just putting on a show because there was another man present.

"How are we doing?" she asked.

"Better," Cole replied, getting out of his seat a bit more easily than he'd been moving before she'd gone to get the car.

"Well, good. Thank you," she said to the pilot. "I really appreciate your help."

"No problem."

Dani took Cole's hand and they walked off the plane, Dani going first down the stairs. She got him into the passenger seat, but he was already grumbling. He really was the worst patient.

"You know, most people say they have a headache before sex, not after," she said when she got into the driver's seat.

Cole clicked his seat belt. "Very funny. You know I would never turn down sex. Not even right now."

Dani started his truck and put it into gear. "Somehow I doubt that." She pulled past the security gate. "I know the hospital isn't your favorite place, and I know you already said you don't want to go, but I really think I should take you."

"I really don't want to go tonight. I'm sure it's nothing. Probably just the stress of the sting. I can go see the doctor in the morning if I'm still in pain."

"Well, I don't feel comfortable with the idea of you being alone tonight. And I'd rather not stay out at the ranch. I don't like being away when the boys get up in the morning, and we'll be closer to the hospital at my house."

"Are you inviting me to sleep over?"

"Yes. But there will be no sex. Just resting. And if you aren't feeling completely better in the morning, I'm taking you to the doctor."

"But—"

Dani held up a finger. "No buts. My rules."

"Yes, ma'am."

"And who's your doctor? I need to know who to call."

"Dr. Lee. Royal Memorial," he muttered.

"Good."

The drive to her place was thankfully short, especially this late. It was nearly 2:00 a.m. by the time they got to the house. Between the adrenaline rush of the sting and sex on an airplane, Dani was exhausted, but she managed to help Cole upstairs to her room.

"We need to get you out of that suit," she said.

He grinned, but she could see a wince around his eyes. He was still in a lot of pain.

"Get your mind out of the gutter. You're going straight to bed. To sleep."

With some rambling commentary from him about how she was being a stick in the mud, Dani was able to help him take his pants and shirt off and got him into bed.

She sat on the edge of the mattress right next to him. It was impossible to not think about the last time she'd taken care of Cole, in the weeks after the accident. She'd always worried so much about his job, and then the near worst had happened. At least she hadn't lost him, she'd told herself over and over again. That would've been an unbearable loss. He was her everything then—her sun and moon, the reason for getting out of bed in the morning. Her career was important to her and she loved to cook, but that didn't take up space in her heart the way Cole did.

When someone you cared about that much had a brush with death, it made you realize exactly how much you loved them. Honestly, it scared her at first, walking into that hospital and understanding exactly how much was on the line. It was overwhelming—creating a burning pit in her belly, making her feel cold and helpless at the same time.

One of the worst parts was the scene that unfolded in the waiting room while he underwent surgery. Cole's family had been there, and his mother got downright territorial about it, trying to send Dani home. "We only need family here right now," she'd said. Dani would've been hurt if she wasn't so damn mad about that. His parents had never approved of her, the kid from the wrong side of the tracks, no impressive family lineage to back her up. "We can call you when he wakes up," she'd said. Dani's only response to that had been to grit her teeth and politely reply, "I love your son, Mrs. Sullivan. So, no, I will not be going home."

Dani had loved Cole deeply before that day, but it was a young love built on invincibility. She'd worried about his job, but the reality of her worst nightmare was almost more than she could bear. She threw herself into his recovery, doting on him, making sure he had everything he needed. And, impossibly, her love for him only grew. It reached depths she had never imagined. It was impossible during those moments not to think about the what-ifs. *What if he'd been paralyzed? What if he'd been burned?* Or even worse, *What if he hadn't made it out alive?* Thoughts like that made her cry her eyes out when she was alone. She was so thankful. He was so lucky. They were incredibly fortunate to have each other and to have found each other. She had to hold on to Cole's love forever. She'd never, ever known a love like the one she had with Cole at that time. Not even close.

Which made the breakup not only more crushing, it had made it impossible to believe. Of course you wouldn't break up with the person who had just nursed you back to health and shown you unconditional love in the face of dire circumstances, ones you were facing because you had refused to do the one thing your loved one had begged you to do—quit your job. Who would do that? Who would take that kind of love and devotion and throw it away?

Cole Sullivan, that was who. And she was still desperate for the answer to one question—why?

He settled back in bed and closed his eyes. "Thank

you," he said. "I think I just need to get some sleep. I'm sure I'll be feeling much better in the morning."

Dani snugged the covers up around his shoulders, even when it denied her one of her favorite views—his glorious chest. "I'm sure you will be, too." She then did the one thing she probably shouldn't have—she leaned forward and placed a single, tender kiss on his temple. Tears misted her eyes the instant she did it. She couldn't deny what was in her heart now. She loved Cole just as much as she'd ever loved him. Possibly more. She'd spent every day of the last six years caring for the most beautiful extension of him—his two sons. It was a perpetual reminder of how much good there was in him, despite the things he'd done to hurt her.

But that realization also sent the guilt crushing down. If Cole had done the unimaginable when he'd ended their relationship, Dani had done something far worse. She'd kept his own children from him. She'd had every good reason in the world when they were thousands of miles away from each other, but now that they were in the same place again, she couldn't help but feel sick about it. Even when she'd given him a second chance and sent him that letter right before the boys were born. No, he hadn't replied, but she also hadn't told him what was *really* going on.

Cole's breaths grew more even, and Dani got up to change her clothes and wash her face. Looking into the bathroom mirror, she had to wonder what was going to become of her. Was Cole just enjoying their undeniable physical attraction? Or was he serious about her? Did he want a second chance? She didn't want to admit to herself just how badly she wanted it. Right now, it felt like she might not be able to live through it if the answer was no. But she'd told herself that she would never again put that much stock in Cole, and here she was, pinning a bunch of hope on what he wanted. What about what she wanted? Didn't that count just as much?

What do you want? Dani could hear the question crystal clear in her head, but the answer wasn't quite so quick to come. It was complicated. The minute she'd become a mother, the boys became an inextricable part of this equation. What they wanted and needed was equally important, possibly more so. She wanted stability for them. She wanted a good life where they could count on everything and everyone around them. She wanted green grass, clean air and laughter in the backyard, giggles at the dinner table, and bedtime stories that went on too long. *Just one more, Mommy.* And after the boys gave in to sleep each night, she wanted someone to talk it all over with. She wanted a partner, someone to share all this good she'd managed to build. She wanted everything she'd thought was possible before Cole ended it with her.

She flipped off the bathroom light and leaned against the door frame, watching Cole sleep in the soft glow of the lamp on her side of the bed. What in the world had happened on that day nearly six years ago? What had gone through that head of his that made him want to throw away what they had? Her gut was telling her that he'd left out some key piece of information. He was hiding something from her. If they had any chance of moving forward, he was going to have to come clean. Yes, she had her own secrets to confess, but he'd set them on this path. And there was no going back.

She walked around to the far side of the room and turned off the light, climbing into bed. She didn't want to disturb his sleep, but she wanted to be close to him. She couldn't help it. She scooted closer, wrapping her hand around his arm and stretching out beside him. Closing her eyes, she drew in his smell—warm cedar and soap. She knew she had to get some sleep. She and Cole had a lot to talk about in the morning. She couldn't endure another day of not knowing what he wanted from her. And that was going to involve her own confession, one that had been waiting too long.

Ten

Cole hadn't slept. He'd only slipped in and out of consciousness. During the moments when he came to, the pain reminded him to keep his eyes closed and his body still and to try to claim real slumber. It was his only escape from the agony and the worry.

And now that the Texas sun was peeking through his eyelids, he was going to have to face reality. His headache had not improved—it had only settled in. The doctors had warned him, told him to watch out for events like this. They'd told him he needed to come in right away when it happened. He'd already ignored those orders by coming to Dani's last night. But the truth was that he was scared. He'd seen a glimmer of what his future could hold and just like that, his body was trying to take it away. There was some part of him that had hoped the headache would simply go away. Unfortunately, it hadn't. He couldn't ignore what he needed to do anymore.

"Morning." Dani's sweet voice was a brief respite from the chaos in his head. "How are you doing?"

He still hadn't fully committed to opening his eyes, so he rolled to his side to put the window behind him. Light was not his friend right now. He went slowly, and he couldn't have had a lovelier vision to wake up to— Dani with her hair up in a high ponytail, wearing light pink pajamas and offering him a cup of coffee. Still, it took more effort to keep his eyes open than could ever be considered normal.

"I gotta be honest. I'm feeling pretty rough."

She caressed his arm. "Headache's no better?"

"No."

"Okay. Well, I looked up the number for Dr. Lee's office and called them. They said they want to see you as soon as we can get there."

Panic coursed through Cole's body. What if the doctor's office slipped and told her about his condition? "You called Dr. Lee? What did he say?"

"I only spoke to the nurse. She just said you should come in. That was all. He's doing rounds at the hospital this morning and will see you as soon as we get there."

He sighed and resigned himself to the fact that even though it was the last thing he wanted to do today, he was going to have to see the doctor. "I guess I should get dressed."

"You want to wear a suit to the doctor's office? I could call one of your brothers and ask them to bring you some different clothes."

"I have a pair of jeans and a T-shirt in a duffel in the truck."

"Oh, right. A rancher never knows when he's going to get dirty."

He forced a smile. "Exactly."

"I'll get it. You stay put."

Dani was back a few minutes later with his things, and Cole did his best to soldier through the most mundane of tasks—going to the bathroom, putting on clean clothes.

"Is it okay if we take my car? I'll leave the minivan for Elena and the boys." she asked. "No offense, but I hate driving your truck."

As if he was in any position to argue with her. "Yeah. No problem." He tried to look on the bright side. With his car there, he'd have an excuse to come back to Dani's house as soon as the doctor gave him some real pain-killers and sent him on his way. Then they could have their talk.

Dani took charge when they arrived at Royal Memorial, getting them right into a triage room. The nurse took his vitals and got him settled on the exam table, but the minute they were left waiting, the bad memories started to come back, and that made his head pound even worse. The fluorescent lights overhead were nightmarishly bright, and that hospital smell was everywhere. Cole couldn't escape it.

"You doing okay?" Dani asked.

It took a ridiculous amount of effort to nod. "Yep." He hadn't realized until then that she was holding his hand. Had it become that comfortable? Or was he that out of tune with what was going on around him right now? Too stuck in his own body? That had been a huge symptom of the last six years—feeling trapped. How else was a man to feel when he was saddled with a condition from which he could never escape?

The telltale sound of the exam room curtain sliding on its rails came. "I spoke to Dr. Lee," a voice said. "He wants to go ahead and do an MRI first, and then he'll see you after that."

Cole broke out into a cold sweat. "I just need some painkillers." He didn't want to know if this was all because the tumor had grown. He didn't want to know if this was the beginning of the end. Plus, he hadn't had a chance to talk to Dani yet and he couldn't see straight right now, let alone think straight.

"Isn't that a little excessive?" Dani asked. "He just has a migraine."

"Given his history, Dr. Lee felt it was not only the most logical step, it was the only course of action right now."

"His history?" Dani's voice was nothing if not incredulous. She was mystified by what was going on. If only she knew. "What history? His accident? Is there something I don't know?"

"I'm sorry, but are you family?" The nurse had taken a tone that he knew Dani would hate.

Cole's mind raced. He would have done anything to put this conversation on pause, but his thoughts weren't merely jumbled, they were fighting each other. He wanted Dani there, but he wanted to be able to break this news to her the right way. Not in the hospital. Not when he was in so much pain. "She's my girlfriend." The words just came out. They were the only thing that made sense. Cole forced his eyes open, only to see a truly surprised Dani standing next to him.

"I'm sorry, but I can only discuss the patient's history with a spouse or next of kin. Mr. Sullivan, I'm going to check in with the radiologist to find out how long before we can get you in."

As soon as the nurse left, Dani whipped around and looked Cole square in the eye. "What does she mean when she says your history?"

Cole dug as deep as he ever had for strength. He needed the presence of mind to say this clearly. He needed the stamina to fight through the pain and look Dani in the eye. He needed the courage to tell her the most difficult and damning detail of his life.

"When the doctors did the MRI the day after my accident, they discovered a glioma. It's a small tumor in a part of my brain they can't reach. It's inoperable. It's not going away. It might get bigger. It could very well be the thing that kills me."

"Oh my God." Dani clamped her hand over her mouth. Her eyes were hurt. She was starting to cry. Was she devastated to hear the news? Or was it because he'd kept it from her all this time?

"That's my secret, Dani. I never told you because I wanted you to live a long life with someone who could be there for the whole thing." Cole could hear his own voice starting to fall apart.

"Cole. No," Dani said.

The nurse returned, and Cole could see the gurney coming for him. "Mr. Sullivan, we need to get you in right now. Dr. Lee wants these results as soon as possible."

The nurse helped him up from the exam table and onto the gurney. He could hardly look at Dani, fearing her reaction. She'd said so little. Too little. He felt even more nauseous now than he had when he'd first gotten this headache. Or the day he'd gotten the worst news.

The orderly began pushing Cole out of the room.

"No. Wait. Stop," Dani said. Her voice was nothing but desperation. Cole had no idea if it was because she was worried or if it was because she was trying to understand his betrayal.

The nurse grasped both of her arms. "Ma'am. You need to stay here. He needs to go in for that test right away."

The orderly kept going, down the hall, away from Dani. It was such a metaphor for everything that had happened between them, and the way things had gone so haywire. Just when he was ready to tell her his secret, the headache stopped him in his tracks. Just when he was ready to ask her if they had a future together, this thing in his head was stepping in and saying, *Not so fast, buddy.*

They wheeled Cole into the MRI room, where the hum of the machine was deafening and everything around him was cold and white and sterile. This was the room where he got the worst news of his life. This where he'd started to lose everything.

Was that going to happen all over again? Would Dani ever forgive him for the things he hadn't said? Or was this MRI about to tell him that none of it mattered, anyway?

Dani stood in Cole's room, frozen.

A tumor. *Cole has a tumor.* She couldn't believe this was happening. Just when she'd learned to trust him again, the truth threw her for far more than a loop. She couldn't even be mad at him right now. All she could do was worry. What were the doctors going to say? And would she and Cole ever be able to move beyond whatever that news was?

Dani's phone rang and it rattled her back to the here-and-now. She dug in her bag, fumbling past her wallet, keys, lipstick, and a million other things. When she finally found her phone, Elena's name was on the caller ID.

"Hello," Dani said.

"Oh, thank God you answered. I'm super sick, Dani. It just hit me like a ton of bricks."

Dani's first instinct was to start walking to her car. She could not believe this day. She didn't think it was possible for her to worry any more than she already was. "What's wrong?"

"I think I've come down with a stomach virus or maybe food poisoning. I can't keep any food down. Or anything at all, actually. I can't watch the boys the way they need to be watched. I'm running to the bathroom every ten minutes. And I don't want them to catch this if it's contagious."

"I'm on my way. I'll get there as fast as I can. Can I pick you anything up on my way home?"

"No, thank you. I just need a break."

Dani ended her call with Elena and quickly scrolled through her contacts for Cole's brother Sam's number. As soon as she had the number ringing on speakerphone, Dani climbed into her car, jammed the ignition button and sped out of the parking lot.

"Dani Moore," Sam answered. "This is a surprise."

"Hey Sam. Do you have a second to talk?"

"For you? Always." Sam was such a charmer.

"I'm calling to let you know that Cole's in the hospital because of a bad headache. They're doing an MRI right now, but I had to leave to tend to something at home. Can you go and make sure he's not alone? I don't want him coming back to an empty room if he doesn't have to."

"Is he okay? Did something happen after the sting?"

"He got a blistering headache pretty soon after. I tried to get him to see a doctor last night, but he wanted to try and sleep it off. That didn't work."

"Sounds like Cole. You know how he feels about doctors."

Dani choked back a sigh. "So do you know about his condition?" Dani wasn't sure who knew what anymore. Thus was the problem with secrets. All the more reason to come out with hers, if she got the chance.

"Did he tell you?"

Dani felt like she and Sam were talking in code, tiptoeing around the truth. "If you're talking about what they discovered in that MRI six years ago, yes."

Sam blew out a breath. "I'm glad to hear he told you."

"Me, too. I just wish I'd had the chance to talk to him about it before they wheeled him down the hall. I'm sick with worry. Someone should be there."

"Don't worry. I'll get over there right now."

"Will you let him know that I'm thinking about him? And let him know I'm ready to talk whenever he wants to. His truck is at my house, but we can sort that out later. It's not a problem for it to stay here as long as possible."

"Thank you for being there for my brother, Dani. You've always been a rock for him."

"Maybe on the outside. On the inside, I'm tied up in knots." Dani turned into her neighborhood and pulled past the security gate.

"That's what you get with my brother." Sam cleared his throat. "I know this is none of my business, and you can tell me to take a hike, but are you two back together?"

Dani shook her head when she caught sight of Cole's truck in her driveway. It was not only a visual of what could be, it was a reminder of everything that was wrong. What was he going through right now? What was happening? Was he okay? "I don't know yet. We've got some things we need to work out." That felt like the understatement of the century, but at least she knew a little bit of what was behind their breakup. "Hey, Sam. I just got home, so I need to run."

"Oh, yeah. Sure. I need to get my butt to the hospital. Thanks so much for keeping me in the loop."

Dani hung up and rushed inside. "Elena?" she called.

Cameron and Colin came running around a corner and nearly plowed right into her.

"Elena's sick, Mommy," Cameron blurted.

"Where is she?"

"In the kitchen." Colin took her hand and led her as if she didn't know the way.

Elena was sitting at the kitchen table with her head in her hands. She turned as Dani approached. She was extremely pale and there were dark circles under her eyes. "I'm so sorry."

"Please don't be sorry. These things happen. We just need to get you feeling better. Can I get you anything?"

Elena shook her head. "No. We had some ginger ale in the fridge. I'm just going to climb into bed and hope it goes away quickly."

"Yes. Of course. I have the boys. Just promise me that you'll buzz me if you need anything at all."

Elena slowly rose from the table, seeming unsteady. "I will."

Dani watched as Elena walked down the hall to the nanny suite and disappeared into her bedroom. Dani dropped down to a crouch to talk to the boys. "What do you guys want to do for the rest of the day?" Between the sting, the hospital, and Cole's big news, Dani was quite frankly exhausted, but there would be no rest for the weary.

"We saw Mr. Cole's truck in the driveway. Is he here?" Cole asked, seeming terribly excited by the prospect.

"We looked everywhere," Cameron added.

"Is he coming over? Please say he's coming over."

Dani laughed quietly, but this was merely confirmation that she couldn't let Cole slip away this time. These boys loved him, and she did, too. She had to fight for him. She hadn't done that the first time, and perhaps that had been her biggest mistake. Everything might've been different now if she'd fought for him.

"No, Mr. Cole isn't here right now, but hopefully he'll come to get his truck in the next day or so. He's very busy right now." Dani didn't want the boys to worry, so she didn't mention that Cole was in the hospital. Dani still had no idea exactly how serious the news would be. She prayed that whatever it was, that she had the strength to help Cole with everything he was facing. Of course, she had no idea if he would even speak to her after she finally told him that the sweet boys standing before her were his sons.

Both boys' faces dropped in disappointment at the news that Cole was not around for fun. Dani felt the same way.

"We wanted him to see the swings and the monkey bars," Colin said.

"We were hoping he'd come play with us," Cameron added.

"Well, how about this? It's a beautiful day today. Why don't we do whatever Mr. Cole would want to do if he was here with us?"

"Swimming!" the boys proclaimed in unison.

Dani had little doubt that fun-loving, full-of-life Cole Sullivan would want to do exactly that. She choked back a few tears at how sad it was that he wasn't here. Making her all the more determined to finally come clean.

Eleven

Cole arrived back at his hospital room, only to learn that Dani was gone. His disappointment was immense. That was it. She'd taken off. She wanted no more of Cole Sullivan. Everything he'd feared as they wheeled him into that MRI room was right on the money. Well, maybe not everything. He still hadn't received his news from the doctor.

He got settled in his bed and took the pain medication the nurse offered. The headache had inexplicably gotten better during his test, but this stuff was fast acting and his agony was quickly fading. His physical misery might be disappearing quickly, but it was being upstaged by his state of mind—a harrowing mix of sadness, trepidation, and plain old worry. Between waiting for the doctor and wondering if Dani would ever speak to him again, things couldn't get any worse.

Out of nowhere, his brother Sam burst into his room.

He was wearing his clothes from the ranch, cowboy hat and all. "I got here as fast as I could."

Cole sat up, wondering who in the hell thought up the design for hospital gowns. "How did you know I was here?"

"Dani called me." Sam sidled up to the bed and took a full survey of Cole. "She was worried. She didn't want you to be alone. But she had to leave. I think she needed to get to her boys."

Cole let out a deep sigh. Dani was clearly juggling a lot today and he'd had to go and heap one more thing on the pile by telling her about the glioma. At least she knew now. Come what may, the truth was out. "I'll have to thank her for that."

"Of course, it would've been nice if you'd called me or one of your other family members yourself. Were you just going to sit here and stew?"

Cole pressed his lips together tightly. "I'm thinking. And I needed to do it by myself."

"Thinking? Or worrying?" Sam reached for a small side chair and pulled it closer to Cole's bedside.

"At this point, I'm not sure I can separate the two. Every thought seems to come with a worry by default." Cole looked all around the room, hoping to hell this was not about to become his future. The doctor still hadn't come in to talk to him, and it was making him crazy. If he was dying, he just wanted to know so he could put his jeans and boots on and head back to the ranch, where he could at least keel over with a glass of bourbon in his hand while he sat out on the back terrace and watched the sun set. That was the way to go, not sitting in a mechanical bed wearing a sheet that opened in the back.

"Dani seems really worried, too."

"She does?" Cole couldn't decide if that was a good thing or a bad thing. "Tell me what she said."

Sam reared his head back and bugged his eyes. "I already told you. She didn't want you to be by yourself."

That wasn't enough to keep Cole going. That concern could certainly come accompanied with the sentiment that she never wanted to see him again. "Did she say what was going on with the boys? Are they okay?"

Sam shook his head. "She didn't say. And that was actually just a guess on my part. I think she said she needed to get home."

Now Cole felt even worse. Maybe Dani had simply wanted to get as far away from him as possible.

Just then there was a knock at the door and Dr. Lee came in with an entire team of people in white coats. Cole's stomach felt like it was down at his feet. Why would he need an army of doctors except to tell Cole that he was a goner?

"Mr. Sullivan, I brought a few of the residents with me today. I hope that's okay. If you prefer, they can wait out in the hall, but this is a teaching hospital. It's part of what we do."

Great. Cole had spent six years not wanting to share this with the woman he loved. Now he had to share it with strangers. It didn't really matter, though. He'd already lost all sense of privacy, courtesy of the hospital gown. "Yeah. It's fine. Just tell me how long I have so I can get out of here. No offense, but I'm not a huge fan of this place."

Dr. Lee raised both eyebrows at Cole. "I hate to disappoint you, but you have exactly as long today as you did the day we last ran a scan. The glioma hasn't changed. At all."

Cole sat there for at least fifteen seconds, staring.

Blinking. "Then why did I get that headache?" It had been the worst pain he'd ever endured, far more excruciating than broken ribs.

"I don't know. Could be any number of things. Stress is the most likely. You'd said you were on an airplane when it started, so the change in altitude could've built up pressure."

"So now what? More tests?"

"I'm on the fence, to be honest. It wouldn't be unreasonable to formally admit you and monitor you until tomorrow morning."

"What would that entail?"

"You sitting in that bed and the nurse checking on you every two hours."

Cole threw back the covers. "How about I just call you if the headache comes back?"

Dr. Lee stepped forward and held up a hand. "Hold on a minute. Are you really that anxious to get out of here?"

Cole nearly laughed. "Yes. I am." *I've got a woman I need to talk to.*

Dr. Lee pressed his lips into a thin line. "Okay. We will release you. Plus you have to promise me you will call me the instant you get a headache this bad again."

Cole held up his hand. "I promise."

"You're still going to need to wait for the paperwork to clear. Which could take a few hours."

Hospital bureaucracy—Cole hated it. But he did need to look on the bright side. The glioma hadn't changed. It hadn't grown. In six years, nothing inside his head had changed. But in less than two weeks, Dani had not only turned around his thinking, she'd gotten his heart beating again. She'd reminded him just how badly he wanted to be here. She'd shown him how good it was to be alive. Especially when you have someone to love.

"I'll have the nurses get your paperwork going. Plan on coming to see me during clinic hours in six months or so. I'll have them send you an appointment reminder. And call me if anything changes."

With that, the doctor and crew left, meaning Sam and Cole were now alone.

"That's good news, buddy," Sam declared, rising up out of his seat. "Now you just need to get the rest of your life straightened out."

"What exactly is that supposed to mean?"

"I asked Dani if you two were back together."

Cole sometimes couldn't believe his brother's willingness to say or ask anything, but today, he was glad for it. "And what did she say?"

"She said she wasn't sure. She said you had some things to work out."

A heavy sigh left Cole's lips. "I need to finish telling her everything about our breakup. What I was thinking. I need to explain myself. I hardly got it out of my mouth before they whisked me out the door."

"Only she can say what her reaction will be, but judging by my conversation with her, I'd say she'll definitely listen."

"Well, that's something." Cole sat back, trying not to play out the conversation in his head. These things weren't always predictable with Dani.

"I'm sensing there's something else that's still bothering you."

Cole didn't know how to bring up this subject with Sam, so he certainly wasn't ready to do so with Dani. Maybe simply talking about it would help him sort this out a bit in his head. "I want to talk to her about her boys. Cameron and Colin." Just saying their names made for this tug right in the center of his chest.

"What about them, exactly?"

Cole realized how crazy this was going to sound. "Have you noticed how much they look like me? Especially Colin."

"I've only seen them for a few minutes the day you had them over to swim in the pool. But yes, it did make me wonder. She hasn't told you who their father is?"

"No. And I haven't asked. She's a single mom. It's incredibly insensitive."

"Of course. There's no good way to bring it up."

"Exactly." At least Sam seemed to understand how he was feeling. "But there's this feeling in my gut that says they're my boys. I have to know. I just need to know if I'm off base."

"Will that change the way you feel about Dani? Could you forgive a woman for keeping your children a secret for that long?"

Cole ran his hands through his hair and looked his brother square in the eye. "I don't want to waste any more time in my life, Sam. I have to forgive her. My heart won't survive it if we can't find a way to make it work. One half of that job is mine, which means I have to forgive."

"And how will you feel if they aren't yours?"

Cole shrugged. "Honestly? I don't know if it would make a lick of difference. I'd still adore them. I'd still want to be in their lives."

Sam grinned sideways. "You know, I watched you that day in the pool with the boys. You were having so much fun. And I've seen you with Dani, It's like you didn't skip a beat. If ever there was a family just waiting to be put together, it's the four of you."

Cole smiled and nodded slowly, looking out the window of his room. Another beautiful, sunny day in Royal—clear blue sky and a few fluffy clouds. It was the perfect day for turning life around. And now that he'd had the chance to talk out his feelings with Sam, he felt all the more ready to do the same with Dani. Everything else he'd have to put in her hands.

Cole changed into his regular clothes while Sam went outside to make a phone call. Once the paperwork was complete and Cole got the all clear, Sam insisted on driving him straight out to the ranch. "I don't feel great about you driving yet. We can get your truck from Dani's later," he'd said. As soon as he dropped Cole off at the main house, he left. "I need to check on some things in the barn. I'll see you later."

Cole headed straight upstairs and immediately climbed into the shower to wash off that hospital smell and hopefully start to feel a bit more human. With a clean pair of jeans and T-shirt, and his mind mostly straight, he knew he had to reach out to Dani. Maybe she could come over tonight so they could talk. It might take hours, but they had to arrive at some understanding. He hoped like hell that at the end of all of it, they concluded that they should be together. He wasn't sure he could handle the heartbreak of the alternative.

He bounded downstairs in search of his cell phone, which he'd left on the kitchen counter. As soon as he pressed Dani's number, he could've sworn he heard laughter, and not just any laughter. Kids. *The boys.* He walked into the living room with the phone pressed to his ear. The call was still ringing as he opened the front door. The boys made a beeline for his front steps. He hadn't imagined this. This was real.

"Hello?" Dani said into the phone, a tentative grin on her face as she climbed out of the minivan. "I was hoping we could talk."

"Good. Me, too," he answered.

"I'll hang up now." She closed the driver's side door and started heading for him, but he couldn't get a handle on what she was thinking. There was part of him that still worried she was here to tell him she just couldn't get past everything he'd kept from her. "How are you feeling?"

"A lot better now that you're here." Cole was slow to tuck his phone into his pocket, even after she'd hung up. He didn't want to risk wasting a second of their conversation, even when the boys were now hanging on him, tugging on his shirt and begging to go see Gentry.

Dani arrived at the base of the staircase. The late-afternoon sun lit up the side of her face, making her somehow even more beautiful than usual. "Do you have some time for me?"

"Always." Out of the corner of his eye, Cole saw Sam walking out of the stable and heading for the house. Cole crouched down. "Hey, Colin and Cameron, your mom and I have something to talk about. Do you want to spend some time with Sam and see how the new foal is doing? She still doesn't have a name yet. I was hoping you two could think of one."

The boys turned and saw Sam, then tore off down the stairs. Cole followed them. "I'll be right back," he said to Dani, then caught up with his brother. "Do you mind taking the boys to see the foal? I was thinking that they might be able to give her a name."

Sam swiped his sunglasses from his face. "Time to straighten things out with their mom?"

"You know it. This could take a while. I've got a lot to apologize for."

Sam clapped his brother on the back. "You need to stop being so hard on yourself."

"A man messes up, he needs to take responsibility."

"True. You did mess up." Sam glanced behind him.

The boys were waiting patiently at the stable doors. "I'd better go catch up with those two."

"Thank you." Cole watched as his brother sidled down to Cameron and Colin. He felt a tug on his heart just looking at those boys. They were his. He knew it. But he sure as heck wanted to hear Dani say it.

He turned back to the house and there Dani was, sitting on the top step of the porch. The breeze blew her glossy dark hair from her shoulders, and the sun was now lighting up the other side of her beautiful face. He'd be lying if he said he didn't want this to be his entire life— Dani and the boys, on the ranch. It was all he wanted.

Dani stood when she spotted him heading back. She spoke as soon as he was within spitting distance. "I don't care what you're facing, Cole. I don't care what's going on. I'm here for you."

He climbed the stairs, stopping on the step below her. "I appreciate that. A lot." Even though that made him feel a bit better, his heart was still pounding in his chest.

"I won't let you push me away again. No matter what the doctor told you today."

He managed a bit of a smile. In the midst of all this turmoil, he'd gotten good news. "The glioma hasn't changed. They think the headache was brought on by stress and the pressure changes in the plane."

Dani let out a huge exhale and pressed her hand to her chest. "Oh, thank God. I'm so relieved to hear that."

She peered up into his eyes and took his hand. "And I have something that I need to tell you. Something I should have told you a long time ago that I don't want to keep inside anymore. Colin and Cameron are your sons."

He scanned her face as she waited for his response. She was so nervous and uncertain it nearly broke his heart. "They're mine? Really?" He couldn't have disguised the excitement in his voice if he'd wanted to. He'd been unprepared for how good it was going to feel to get this news.

She unleashed a relieved smile. "I never should've kept that from you, and I'm sorry. But I was sure you wanted nothing to do with me, ever."

Cole let her words wash over him, soaking them up. This was confirmation that he had no more time to waste. There was a whole lot of life waiting for him, and he didn't want to spend another minute of it worrying about what might be. "The glioma is why I ended things. Every minute you spent taking care of me felt like confirmation that you deserved a long life with someone who could give that to you. I couldn't promise you that I would be around."

Dani's eyes were so soft and caring. It was like he could see how big her heart was. "So what's the prognosis now?" She sat back down on the top step and Cole joined her, taking her hand.

He launched into the technical side of his condition, or at least the parts he could remember. "I still feel a little bit like a ticking time bomb, but Sam and I had a good talk at the hospital. I'm sorry I didn't have the chance to tell you more before they whisked me off for my MRI. Everything happened so fast."

"It's okay. I understand so much more now. You were in an incredibly tight spot." There were tears in her eyes when she looked at him. "And I'm so sorry you didn't feel like you could tell me. That's why you told me there was another woman, isn't it? That's why you didn't answer my letter."

He squeezed her hand tightly. "I need you to know that both of those things were hard for me. Very hard. I thought it was for your own good."

"You can do some really stupid things, Cole Sullivan." She added a sweet smile, just to let him know she was giving him a hard time for fun.

"Yeah. I realize that now. Being protective isn't always my best quality."

"No. I think it's one of your best." Dani cast her sights off in the distance, holding on to his hand just as tightly he was holding on to hers. In that single touch he knew exactly how badly they needed each other. "I came close to telling you about the boys when I wrote that letter. That might've changed everything."

"It absolutely would've changed everything. Why didn't you?"

"Because I wanted you to want to be with me out of love, not because you felt obligated."

"I never stopped loving you, Dani. And it would've been impossible for me to not feel obligated. Even if we didn't work out, I still would've been their daddy."

She nodded. "I can see now that it wasn't the right call, but at the time, I couldn't see another way. Those boys are the best thing that has ever happened to me, but they've also been my greatest trial."

The thought of Dani doing the work of both parents for all these years made it hard for Cole to get past the lump in his throat. Talk about his male ego getting in the way—he really hated the thought of not living up to his responsibilities, even if he hadn't known they'd existed. Regardless of how things played out with Dani, he had a lot to make up for. "Because you were raising them on your own."

"Well, there's that, but that's not the real reason. It's been hard because I had to look into their eyes every day and see the face of the man I loved. It was like being haunted by the ghost of Cole Sullivan."

Cole had to laugh, but it wasn't funny. This was something born out of deep frustration with himself. "I think I've been living with that same ghost. I was so sure I was going to die that I think I stopped living. But that all changed the night you showed up on this porch in that ridiculously sexy red dress. It was like you brought me back to life that night."

"I turned you down that night. And I called you a mistake."

"Sometimes it's the cruelest things that remind you you're alive." He turned to her, studying her sweet face and those tempting lips. He couldn't wait another second to kiss her. He wanted to start their new chapter right here and right now. "But for right now, I'd like to go for a good reminder that I'm still here."

Twelve

Sitting there on Cole's font porch, Dani's mind was running a million miles a minute, thinking about the suffering he'd done all alone, when they could have been together. A less charitable woman might be berating him right now, but Dani was done with being mad. She just wanted to move on with the man she loved.

He pulled her into his arms and placed the softest kiss on her lips. It felt like a new beginning, a hello, a beautiful fresh start. It was exactly what they both needed so badly. It left her heart pulsing like crazy, full of good feelings that had been gone for far too long.

Cole gently pulled his lips away and rested his forehead against hers, but he was still holding on tight. "I never stopped loving you, Dani. Not even for a minute. I just had to protect you. Now I can see how foolish that was."

She gripped both sides of his face and looked up into

his incredible blue eyes. For as tough as Cole was, his eyes had always revealed kindness. They were the way in. "I'm ready to put that all behind us. I think we could both use a fresh start."

"As long as you understand there are no guarantees."

She could hardly believe he was still couching this. "I hate to break this to you, but there are no guarantees with any man, especially not one foolish enough to want to run around and chase bad guys like Richard Lowell."

Cole laughed quietly and smiled. "I'm sorry, but I don't know any other way. There's just this part of me that will always want to find justice."

She turned her hand and tenderly brushed the side of his face with the backs of her fingers. "I know. That's part of what I've always loved about you. Just like my daddy."

"I wish I could've known him."

Dani choked back the weight of Cole's statement. "He would've loved you. I think the boys got that same justice-seeking bug. You already saw how riled up they get if one of them gets more ice cream than the other."

"Ice cream is serious stuff." His head moved slow as molasses as he nodded, like it was all sinking in. "Wow. Is this real? Am I really a daddy?"

She clapped him on the thigh. "It's really real. And I think it's time that we tell them. If you're ready."

"I think we both know I'm done with waiting."

If only Cole knew what a big leap that was for Dani. She'd spent the years trying to teach the boys that it didn't matter who their daddy was, that they had her and that was all that was important. But the reality was it did matter—Cole was a good man and he wanted a relationship with his boys. He wanted to be a part of their lives, she wanted the same, and she already knew they would welcome him.

Sam and the boys were heading up from the stables, Colin and Cameron running so fast that they were kicking up dirt. They ran Dani ragged some days. Now they could start spending time with their father, and hopefully he could help to wear them out a little bit. Sam waved at Dani and Cole, then headed off behind the house. He must have sensed that they would need their time together.

As the boys ran up the stairs, they were a flurry of news and announcements.

"We gave the foal a name," Cameron said.

"What did you decide on?"

"Dottie. After Great-Aunt Dot," Colin explained, as if the name required clarification.

Dani smiled wide. They were so impossibly sweet. "I think that sounds like a wonderful name."

"Is that okay with you, Mr. Cole?" Cameron asked.

"Absolutely. I approve."

"Oh, good." Colin seemed legitimately worried.

"There's only one thing," Cole added. "I'd like it if you boys started calling me something other than Mr. Cole."

Dani's gaze connected with Cole's, and she knew the moment had arrived. She pulled both boys close. "I have something important to tell you. Do you remember when we talked about how one day you might meet your father?"

Colin was busy putting two and two together, but Cameron seemed to catch on right away. His mouth flew open and he looked back and forth between Cole and Dani. "Is he?"

Dani nodded. "Yes, honey. Mr. Sullivan and I were in love a long time ago. And that's when you two came along. Mr. Sullivan is your daddy."

"You are?" Colin, ever the skeptic, stepped up to Cole

and placed his hands on his knee, scrutinizing his face. "Are you spoofing us?"

"I would never spoof you about something so important. You boys have the same freckles as Mr. Sullivan and everything. You don't get those from me," Dani said.

"Actually," Cole interjected, "I have some photos inside the house of me as a little boy. Maybe we can get a drink of water and take a look at those."

"I think that sounds like a wonderful idea," Dani said, amazed how the boys were taking this all in stride, although she probably shouldn't be surprised. They'd loved Cole from the moment they met him, and they were both so sweet natured and accepting, it only made sense that this news would be well received.

That said, she knew they'd have hurdles to jump at some point. Undoubtedly, both boys would have questions about the future, about what would happen and how this all might shake out. She had to prepare for that, which meant another big discussion with Cole.

She followed Cole and the boys inside, and they settled in the living room with a photo album and ice water, while Dani decided to make a pitcher of lemonade. When she returned to the living room, the vision took her breath away—Cole sitting on that big leather sofa of his, Colin on one side and Cameron on the other. The boys were still so small, their feet hardly reached the edge of those deep seat cushions. They were looking through a photo album.

"Now, this is me and Sam at one of our first state fairs, showing goats. I'm guessing I was eight and he was five," Cole said.

"Did you win?" Colin asked.

Cole shook his head. "Nope. Competition was steep. But we learned a lot. I guess that's the most important part."

"I made lemonade," Dani said, setting down the pitcher and glasses on the coffee table. The boys practically leaped off the sofa to get theirs.

Cole scooted to the edge of his seat, and took a sip, breaking down Dani's defenses with a single smoldering gaze. Not that she had any need for defenses right now.

"Mommy, why didn't you tell us about Mr. Cole earlier?" Colin asked.

"Hold on one second, because I do want to hear Mommy's answer, but I think the foal isn't the only one on the ranch who could use a new name." The boys turned to him, their eyes wide with curiosity. "I realize this is all brand-new, and you don't have to call me anything you aren't comfortable with, but if you don't want to call me Dad or Daddy, or maybe Pa, at least just call me Cole." He dropped his chin and looked at both boys, appraising their response.

Colin turned back to Dani. "Mommy, why didn't you tell us about Daddy sooner?"

A satisfied grin crossed Cole's face and he cocked both eyebrows, laughing to himself. "I guess I'm Daddy."

"Indeed you are," Dani replied. She turned her attention to the boys so she could answer Colin's question. "Grown-ups make mistakes, too. This was a big mistake I made, but your dad and I had an argument once and that was the start of it. I'm sorry about that. Truly sorry. But I hope you can both forgive me."

The boys both smiled and smothered her in hugs and kisses. It was the absolute best part of being a mom. A close second would be seeing them with Cole just now. Everything was right.

"Boys, I was a big part of this mistake, too. Your mom was doing her best to protect you."

Dani appreciated Cole's willingness to shoulder some of the blame, although she was simply tired of pointing fingers. "The important thing right now is for you two to spend some time with your daddy and get to know him even better."

"Would you like to sleep over here at the ranch to-night?" Cole asked.

The boys erupted into a chorus of affirmation.

"I mean, if it's okay with Mom," he added.

She knew exactly what he was up to with that leading inflection of his voice, and she had to say that she was board. Sharing a bed tonight would be the perfect way to top off their reconciliation. Maybe in the morning, they could begin the discussion on how to merge their lives and households.

"Of course it's okay with me. I want us to spend as much time together as possible. Elena's still resting, but I'll run back to the house and pick up some clothes."

"Mommy, can you bring our bathing suits?" Colin climbed back up on the couch and snuggled in closer to Cole.

"Does that mean you want to go swimming?" Cole asked.

Colin looked up at Cole with all earnestness. Dani could only admire them—the spitting image of each other, and they finally knew why.

"Can we? Please?" Colin asked.

Cole put his arm around his son and pulled him closer. "We can do whatever you want, buddy."

As soon as she got home, Dani went to check on Elena, rapping softly on her bedroom door.

"Come in," Elena said.

Dani stepped inside. "How's the patient?"

Elena was sitting up in bed, reading. "Much better.

I think it was something I ate. I should be back to normal tomorrow."

"Good. I'm glad to hear that."

"Where are the boys? I don't hear them, so I assume they aren't home."

"They're actually out at the ranch with Cole. We're all staying over there tonight."

"Oh, really?" Elena arched a brow and turned to Dani. "What's the latest?"

Dani told her everything about how she and Cole had both finally divulged their secrets.

"A glioma. That's serious stuff."

Dani nodded. "It is. But I told him we'll just face it together."

Elena smiled. "That's great. It seems like things have been worked out."

Now that the high of her reconciliation with Cole was starting to die down, reality was starting to settle in. Everything wasn't worked out, but Dani had to be hopeful. They had a lot to decide. Logic said that they would move in together. Blend their lives. Get married. Dani knew she needed to take this one step at a time. After all, they'd moved beyond two huge obstacles to find forgiveness. If they could do that, everything else should be a piece of cake.

"We're beginning the process of putting things back together. It's going to take some time to figure everything out."

"I don't need to worry about my job, do I? I hate asking the question. You've done so much for me." Elena's face was painted with worry, and Dani felt as though the bottom of her stomach might drop.

"There is absolutely nothing to worry about. Nothing. I need you to be there for the boys. Nothing about that has changed."

The corners of her mouth turned into a smile. "Oh, thank God. I was worried."

Dani went and sat on the edge of Elena's bed. "Are you kidding? I couldn't have gotten through the last five years without you. And the boys love you. I would never take you away from them. Now get some sleep. I'll be home in the morning. I have to go in to the Glass House tomorrow afternoon to talk menu changes with the staff, and I told them I'd be there for tomorrow night's dinner service. Between that crazy trip to California and everything with Cole, I've spent too little time in the trenches. I need to put my chef's coat back on and get to work."

"Well, just keep me posted. I'll be at the house if you need anything."

Less than an hour later, Dani returned with a duffel of clothes for her and the boys, along with toothbrushes and other essentials. Cole helped the boys change into their bathing suits while Dani left their bag in the guest room where the boys would sleep and took her own things to Cole's master suite, directly across the hall.

Dani headed back downstairs. Cole had left the French doors leading out to the backyard wide-open, ushering in warm breezes and the sound of big splashes and delighted squeals. She stepped out onto the flagstone patio, which was already darkened by plenty of water. Cole and the boys had wasted no time. He was in the shallow end with them, hoisting Colin up high and tossing him into deeper water. Colin swam to the edge and shook the water from his face while his brother took a turn. Cole waited until Cameron swam to safety, then approached her, wading to the side where she was standing. If ever a man was poetry in motion, Cole was, especially while the droplets of water on his chest and shoulders glistened in the sun and his aviator sunglasses sparkled.

"You gonna put on your bathing suit and get in with us?" He reached out and touched her ankle with the tip of his finger. How the man could turn her on with a single touch, especially when she had so much on her mind, she didn't know.

"I am. I was just enjoying the scenery."

Cole's eyebrows bounced. "Oh, yeah? Well, there's plenty of time to enjoy that later tonight."

As planned, the instant the boys were sound asleep, Dani and Cole were in his room, door locked, hands all over each other and clothes coming off faster than Dani could keep up with. It was no surprise things boiled over so quickly—they'd spent their entire evening together exchanging heated, smoldering glances while there was absolutely nothing they could do until the boys went to bed.

They kissed, tongues winding. They fell into a naked heap on the bed. Cole was quick to roll Dani to her back and start kissing her neck. She wanted him so badly she could hardly see straight.

"I'm so glad we worked everything out," Dani managed before Cole claimed her mouth with another hot, wet kiss.

"Me, too." Cole gripped her ribcage and drew her nipple between his warm lips, gently tugging.

Dani moaned softly, digging her fingertips into Cole's shoulders. "I want you, Cole. Now." She spread her legs and watched as she fell under his gaze. She'd never felt so wanted *and* loved. What a wonderful combination.

As he drove inside, Dani raised her hips to meet him. They fell into their rhythm effortlessly, just as they'd managed to fall back into sync with their lives. Cole's eyes were dark with desire, his breaths ragged. Dani's peak was approaching, so she wrapped her legs tightly around Cole's hips, muscling him closer. He got the message loud and clear, bearing down in exactly the right now. A few forceful thrusts were all it took before Dani was unraveling in his arms. Cole followed with his climax, kissing her deeply as the pleasure shuddered through his strong body.

He rolled to Dani's side, but was quick to pull her close. He tenderly brushed her messy hair from her forehead. His was lightly glistening with sweat.

"I love you so much, Dani. We can rebuild a life together."

Dani smiled and burrowed her face in Cole's chest, inhaling his warm smell. "I love you so much, too. And I know we can. We can do anything now."

After a blissful night in each other's arms, Cole and Dani awoke to the sound of tiny frantic knocks at his bedroom door. It sounded like there was a woodpecker out there. "Mommy? Can we come in?" the boys asked.

"It must be seven if they're up," she said to Cole, getting out of bed to open the door.

"How do you know it's seven?"

"The boys know not to bother me before then unless it's an emergency."

"I guess I have a lot to learn." Cole, too, got out of bed and joined Dani at the door. He crouched down for the boys. "Hey, guys. Do you remember how I showed you the other day how to feed the chickens? Do you think you could go do that for me?"

Cameron nodded so fast Dani thought his little head might pop off. "Yes, please."

"Go put some clothes on," she said. "We'll meet you downstairs for breakfast when you're done."

"Okay." With that, the boys tore off.

Cole straightened and shot Dani a quizzical look. "Was that okay? Is there some morning routine I don't know about?"

She kissed his cheek. "Not today. You did perfectly."

Cole went off to change and Dani padded downstairs to put on a pot of coffee, doing some prep for pancakes while it brewed. She took a mug into the living room and looked out over the backyard, with the miles of ranch land stretching out beyond it. She wasn't sure she could feel more fortunate than she did right now.

The front door opened, and in waltzed Cameron and Colin. "The chickens were super hungry."

"And how about my boys? You two up for pancakes and bacon?" Dani asked.

As with most things, they responded with great enthusiasm.

Dani went to work while Cole sent the boys to wash their hands and poured them some orange juice. When they returned from the bathroom, Cole got them seated at the kitchen island. He walked over as Dani was flipping the pancakes and pulling the bacon from the skillet.

"Can I help?" Cole wrapped his arms around her waist, pulling her against his long body and kissing her neck softly.

Dani nearly had to grab the kitchen counter to remain standing. "Your timing is impeccable. We're ready to eat."

They got the boys' plates ready, but Dani stopped Cole before he delivered them. "Do you have a few minutes to talk this morning? After breakfast?"

"Probably. I'm waiting for a call from the FBI agents.

They've been scouting out a location where they think Rich might have his stash hidden."

"Okay. Well, there are some things I'd like to discuss about the future."

Cole's phone rang right on cue. "I'm sorry. I have to take this." He wandered off into the living room, leaving her with the boys.

"Are we staying here again tonight?" Cameron asked before putting nearly half a pancake in his mouth.

That was exactly the sort of question she'd wanted to avoid, or at least have an answer for. "I'm not quite sure, honey. I think we might stay at our house tonight. I have to go to work and I think Daddy does, too. There's no preschool today, so I'll take you home to spend the day with Elena."

"What about tomorrow?" Colin loved to dig deeper.

"I'm not sure yet, sweetie. But don't worry. We'll get it worked out."

Cole tucked his phone into his back pocket and walked back into the kitchen. "I'm so sorry. I have to go. They need me for this."

Dani nodded. She understood the importance of it, and she wanted Rich to be caught just as badly as Cole did. "No problem."

"We can talk later. I promise." He took her hand and raised it to his lips, flashing those brilliant blue eyes of his.

Tingles raced over the surface of her skin. She knew they would work every last silly detail out. They'd come too far to accept anything less. "I love you, Cole."

Cole pulled her into his arms and placed a soft kiss on her lips. "I love you, too."

Thirteen

Based on intel gathered before and after the sting to catch Sheriff Orson, the team was racing to find Rich's stash. Or so Cole hoped. There had been so many setbacks in this investigation, it was hard to bank on much, but Cole was hopeful. Having Dani back in his life had helped him turn around his thinking. Hope had been missing for too long.

"You feeling good about this?" Will had met Cole at the TCC and jumped into his car with him. He really wanted to be there for this, and it was hard to blame him.

Special Agents Bird and Stanton were leading the way in an unmarked car, with Sheriff Battle behind them. Everyone was keeping their distance to avoid the appearance of a caravan. They didn't want to announce their arrival or risk anyone being tipped off, especially as they ventured farther into the rural reaches of the county, where traffic jams did not happen.

Cole sucked in a deep breath. "I am. I don't want to jinx it or anything, but I know we are closing in on Rich. Today we should find another piece of this puzzle. A big one."

"Well, good. That makes me glad. I just want this to be over with so I can get on with my life."

"I know. Things have been on hold for you for too long. But don't worry, Will. We'll get him. Your name will be cleared, and hopefully Rich will spend the rest of his life in a very small jail cell." Just saying those things reminded Cole that there was an awful lot on the line here and he'd better not screw any of it up. Whether or not Will could move on from this nightmare and live a normal life depended on Cole. The same went for Megan, Savannah and Aaron. A lot of people were counting on him.

"You've been a real friend to me through all of this," Will said. "I'm not sure how I could ever repay you."

"You're already paying me. I'm just doing my job."

Will laughed quietly. "I know. But when your life has been turned completely upside down, it's nice to have some help turning it right side up. You've been on my side this whole time."

Cole nodded, taking in Will's kind words and letting them tumble around in his head for a bit. If Cole were honest, he'd turned his own life upside down the day he'd banished Dani. Thank goodness she'd resurfaced and helped him see the error of his ways. "I appreciate that. Truly. I just want to get the TCC their money back and make things right for you and for Jason's family, too. They've suffered too much at Rich's hand."

"I really want that for Megan. Hell, I need it for her. She deserves a new beginning. At the very least."

Cole wasn't the type to come out and ask a guy about his love life, but there had definitely been sparks between

Megan and Will at Jason's memorial service. Judging by the passionate tone of Will's voice, there might be a real romance brewing. "Of course. She deserves that new beginning so she can move on and live a happy life."

"Yes. I want her to be happy."

Cole took a gander at the GPS on his dash. "That's our turnoff up ahead. We're almost there." The site was about fifteen miles outside town, up a long and twisting dusty road. From the information they'd been able to gather, the property had been unoccupied and unused for years, tucked away in a forgotten corner of the county. The incline was getting steeper, Cole's truck shifting into a lower gear as the tires of the car ahead of them kicked up more dirt.

Cole took the final bend, a near hairpin turn. The road narrowed and pitched sharply downward, now suspiciously covered in fresh gravel. Someone had done some work out here recently, possibly to make it easier to get a truck in and out. The hair on the back of his neck stood up straight. They were in the right place. He knew it. Ahead, down in a flat gully, sat a tired ramshackle house with a wraparound porch and faded gray clapboards. The windows were boarded up, and a rusty No Trespassing sign hung from a metal cattle gate leaning against a rotting post.

Cole parked his truck next to the FBI vehicle, and he and Will climbed out. Bird and Stanton were arguing like an old married couple, which was par for the course for them. Battle's car pulled up right behind them. Cole had considered obtaining a warrant to search the property, but Bird had done some digging and learned that this was a foreclosure that had been on the books with a bank in Albuquerque for more than ten years.

Leave it to Rich to find the one place in Royal that

neither Cole nor the sheriff knew about, a place that for all intents and purposes didn't matter to anyone. For that reason, and since this was a fact-finding mission where they intended to leave no trace that they'd been on-site, they'd decided to forgo the warrant. Rich had managed to be a step ahead of them at too many points in this investigation. They couldn't afford a single mistake now that they were closing in on him.

"Cole, you leading us in?" Sheriff Battle asked.

Cole smiled, securing his bulletproof vest, which was just a precaution at this point. Agents coordinated by Bird had had eyes on this location for more than twenty-four hours and hadn't seen anyone come or go, so they were reasonably sure it was unoccupied. "I'd be happy to." He led the way down the steep drive, his boots crunching in the gravel. They advanced on the house, and Sheriff Battle and his deputy ran around to the back. Cole stepped up on to the front porch. The decking boards were so dry and brittle it felt as if his boot might go straight through them.

He pounded on the wood door, which was far sturdier than the porch floor. In fact, Cole was pretty sure it had been reinforced. If there was something inside this house, the owner did not want it found.

No answer came. Sheriff Battle radioed that there was an unboarded window on the back and that they couldn't see anyone inside. Cole pounded one more time, then got out his kit to pick the lock. It was the best way to keep their visit a secret.

Like magic, the door popped open. Cole immediately saw that it *had* been reinforced with heavy-gauge steel. The place was empty—old wood floors, more dust and cobwebs than a bad haunted house. Cole trailed across the front room and rapped on the window glass. Thick. And hazy, although he suspected not from time or grime.

It was bulletproof. Further evidence that something was here, and whatever it was, it was big.

Stanton walked back into the room. "The house is clear."

"All right, then. Now we really look," Cole said.

The team searched every square inch, rapping on walls, listening for dead spots. It wasn't until Cole drove the heel of his boot into the floor of the kitchen pantry that he figured out there was a false panel. "Sheriff," he called, dropping down to his knees and feeling around the perimeter near the baseboards. "Bird. Stanton. I think I found something."

Sheriff Battle rushed into the room, followed closely by the FBI agents. "Let's see what we got."

With the help of a crowbar, Cole was able to lift the panel, which was cut perfectly to fit the space. What he saw under the floor was almost too much to believe— bar after bar of solid gold. "Bingo," Cole said. Vindication sure felt good.

"Hoo, doggy," Sheriff Battle said, looking over Cole's shoulder and down into the carefully constructed metal compartments hanging between the floor joists. This gold had been well hidden. Just not quite well enough.

"There's no way we can confiscate this now. It's just too much. We'd have to bring in much bigger trucks and a crew. And get that warrant." Cole's brain was in overdrive as his eyes pored over the glistening gold bars, mulling over the questions and possible answers. Was this the money missing from the TCC and Will's accounts? Was it Rich's plan to use this money after he faked his own death and killed Jason in the process? If so, Rich had to be coming back soon. What more damage could he possibly do? They not only had to catch him soon, this was the best place to do it. "We can be damn sure that Rich will come back out here for this. There's no way he's just going to leave this behind, especially if he's figured out we're on to him. It's only a matter of time before he tries to get to this and hightail it out of the country, probably back to Mexico."

"Agreed. I think that's our best course of action," Stanton said. "We'll lock everything up and request a pair of agents out here to keep an eye on it around the clock. Nobody will be able to touch this without us knowing about it."

Cole was a bit disappointed in that part of the plan, since it only meant more waiting, but he reminded himself that his patience would ultimately be rewarded. With the help of Sheriff Battle, he got the panel back into place and they left the house in the same condition as when they'd arrived.

Cole said his goodbyes to Battle, Bird and Stanton, promising that they would have a call soon to discuss their plan to get Rich out to this house to retrieve his gold. He then drove Will back to his car at the TCC.

"Thanks for letting me ride along today," Will said. "At least I know we're one step closer to catching Rich."

"Every step forward is a good one." He clapped Will on the shoulder. "I'll talk to you soon."

"Absolutely."

Cole waited until Will's car started up, then he got his own show on the road, racing back to the ranch as quickly as traffic laws allowed. He was filthy after running around at that old house, and that did not mesh with his plans for this evening. He bounded up the stairs when he got home, rushed inside and turned on the shower. It took a few minutes to wash away the grime, but he was focused.

As he looked at himself in the mirror and shaved his stubble away, he rehearsed a few things in his head. *I love you so much. I can't lose you again.* Just the thought of saying those words put a lump in his throat. He hoped to hell he could actually do this. With no time to overthink it, he dressed in a pair of jeans and a clean shirt. Before he ran out the door, he grabbed the most important piece of this puzzle—still residing in his sock drawer, at the very back, tucked away for six years. The ring. He popped open the box to make sure it was still there and indeed it was, just as sparkly and lovely as the woman he hoped would wear it. Now to get his answer.

His heart flip-flopped in his chest as he climbed into his truck and headed over to Dani's. The thought of what he was going to ask her made his hands clammy. A bit ironic considering he hadn't felt a lick of nervousness breaking into a criminal's stash of gold a few hours ago. But he hadn't waited as long to do that as he'd waited for this. Much more than the six years they'd been apart. He shouldn't be so unsure of himself, but if Dani could be relied on for anything, it was the unexpected. If she said no, he wasn't sure he could survive, but he couldn't think like that. Not now. He'd lost his precious family once, and there was no way he was going to lose them again.

Dani drove home just after 10:00 p.m., exhausted. It'd been an amazing night of business at the restaurant and everything had gone great, but she'd forgotten how hard it was on her body to be in the kitchen during the dinner rush.

She was struck by the thought that kept cycling through her head—she wished she were going home to Cole. She wanted nothing more than to share a glass of wine with him, fall into his arms, make love with him and slip into blissful sleep. That was all she needed—the simplest, but most beautiful of things in life, with Cole.

She was also listening loudly to her heart right now, which was whispering to her, pointing out that what Dani really wanted was marriage. She wanted to go home to Cole every night. Not just this one.

As she pulled into her neighborhood and turned on to her street, she smiled to herself when she realized that she could be the one to ask Cole to marry her. She could look into his beautiful blue eyes, tell him she loved him and pop the question. Would it be the craziest thing in the world? She did love the idea of catching Cole off guard. It would be an amazing story for their grandchildren.

When she approached her house, Cole's hulking truck in the driveway was unmistakable. Her already present smile grew wider. She did get to come home to Cole. Or at least see him for a little bit. Now she was feeling decidedly less exhausted.

As soon as she opened the garage door, things got confusing. The minivan was gone, which was not right for this time of night. Were the boys home? What about Elena? She parked her car and turned off the ignition, rushing into the house. It was incredibly quiet. Almost too quiet. "Hello?" Her voice echoed in the back hall off the kitchen. She got no response, so she hurried upstairs.

The boys' bedroom door was closed, and sure enough, when she opened it, they were sound asleep in their beds. Elena would never leave them alone, so what in the heck had happened to the minivan? And if Cole's truck was here, where was he? She tiptoed in and straightened their blankets, kissed them each on top of their heads, and quietly closed the door.

She headed into her bedroom and jumped when she saw what was waiting for her—Cole, asleep on her bed. He was reclining on several pillows propped up against the headboard, a book resting on his chest. The bedside table lamp was on, casting him in a warm glow. She couldn't contain her grin as she approached him. He was so handsome it nearly sucked the breath right out of her. Good God, she loved him. That much she didn't have to worry about ever again.

She perched on the edge of the bed, sitting right next to his leg. She gently picked up the book, but that was enough to get him to stir.

"Hey. You're home," he said, looking sleepy and more than a little sexy.

"I am. What are you doing here?" She rubbed his arm gently, feeling so lucky that the dream scenario she'd cooked up in the car might actually happen.

"I came over as soon as I finished up my work stuff. I wanted to spend some time with the boys. We swam for a while, and then I took them out for burgers for dinner."

"Oh, yum."

"We had french fries and shakes and everything."

Dani nodded. Cole's mischievous side was definitely one of his more appealing qualities. "Healthy."

"It wasn't. But it was delicious." He unleashed his electric grin.

"Where's the minivan?"

"I told Elena I had everything under control. She went to a movie, I think."

"So what happened after dinner?"

"We came home and I gave the boys a bath and read them stories and put them to bed."

Dani didn't cry easily, but she felt that single tear leak from the corner of her eye, and she knew it was futile to try to stop it. Another tear followed. And another.

"Why are you crying?" Cole sat up and put his hand on her shoulder, seeming truly concerned. "Oh my God. I completely forgot I was supposed to call you. I was so wrapped up in work, and then I wanted to get over here to see the boys, and I don't know what happened. Time just sort of got away from me. I'm so sorry."

She shook her head, thinking about everything tumbling around in her head, everything she wanted and everything she'd waited so long for. Everything Cole had waited for, too.

"It's not the phone call. You didn't do anything wrong. You did everything right. I love you, Cole. More than I have ever loved another man. I will never love anyone as much as I love you." She took his hand in hers. "Can we get married? Is that something you would consider?"

The corners of his mouth drew down. It was a full-on, no-doubt-about-it frown. "Dani, don't ask me that."

"What? Why not?"

He drew his legs up and swung them off the bed. "Because you're ruining my plan."

"Your plan? Why do you get to make a plan and I don't? I'm trying to make a plan for us, Cole. I thought that was what you wanted, too."

He paced over to the dresser, where his leather laptop bag was sitting. He must've been doing work at some point this evening. That was Cole. Ever the workaholic. He reached into the bag and turned around with a small gray box in his hand. "This is why you're ruining my plan." He handed her it to her and gathered his hands behind his back. "Go ahead. Open it," he said with a nod.

Certainly Dani wasn't lucky enough to have this many stars align all at once. Her heart was threatening to pound its way out of her chest as she tilted the top back. Inside, sat a beautiful, sparkly diamond solitaire.

"I don't want to sound like I'm copying you, but I love you, Dani. I don't want to waste another day not having you as my wife. We belong together. As a family."

Dani looked down at the ring. "You've been busy all day. When did you have time to buy this?"

"Is that your way of saying yes?" The expectation in Cole's eyes was enough to make her melt. He took the box from her hand and plucked the ring out of its home. "It's not hard. You just say.something like, 'Yes, Cole Sullivan, I *will* marry you. I *will* be your wife.'" He batted his lashes at her mockingly.

Dani laughed. How she loved their back-and-forth. "It is a stunning ring," she said, messing with him a little bit.

He slid the ring on to her finger. "It looks good on your hand. It fits perfectly." He then cast his mesmerizing eyes down at her with an expression she couldn't fully describe. "Here's where I make my full confession, Dani. I bought you this ring a week before my accident. Six years ago. I was all ready to ask you to marry me, and like a fool, I let our life together slip away. I'm not going to let that happen again. I can't offer you a lifetime, but I can offer you *my* lifetime. Whether I have fifty years or fifty minutes in me, I don't know. I only know that every second of it that we're not together is a second wasted."

The tears had turned to a steady stream. She'd once thought she could never get past the hurt of everything that had happened between them, but this step forward not only healed, it made them stronger. "I will marry you, Cole Sullivan. I want nothing more than to be your wife."

He pulled her close and gave her his trademark kiss— soft and sensuous and so potent she couldn't think straight. "That is music to my ears. I've never wanted to hear anything as much as I wanted to hear that."

She set her head on his shoulder and admired her ring when she flattened her hand against his chest. "I've never been happier to say something."

"So, I've been thinking since this morning. Just about everything else that we need to talk about." Cole traced his fingers up and down Dani's spine. "I want you and the boys to move out to the ranch. I know it's a lot to ask, but it's been in my family for generations and it would mean a lot to me."

How could she possibly refuse such a heartfelt request? She couldn't. She gazed up into his eyes. "Yes. Of course."

Cole rewarded her with a sensuous kiss that made her knees wobble. "I was thinking that with you, Elena and the boys living out at the ranch, there won't be nearly enough room for my parents when they come to visit. I was thinking we could have them stay here. Many miles away from the ranch."

"Good God, you're sexy when you're brilliant." Cole's parents had certainly mellowed, but that didn't mean she wanted them around all the time. Visits could be nice.

"We still need to talk about your job, Cole. I just can't deal with you doing dangerous stuff all the time. It'll kill me. I know you're not really a desk job kind of guy, but surely there's some compromise somewhere. Somehow."

He was grinning like a fool, which usually meant he had something up his sleeve. "I'm way ahead of you. I've already decided I'm just going to do the investigative part of my job as soon as this case is done. It's not good for me, anyway. The doctor wants me avoiding stress."

"You know what's good for alleviating stress?" Dani drew her finger down Cole's chest, then leaned in for another kiss.

"I feel calmer already. Just imagine how great I'll feel after you get out of that chef's coat and into something more naked."

The door behind Cole cracked open. Dani and Cole

both jumped. "Mommy?" Cameron croaked. "I woke up and I can't get back to sleep."

"It's okay, buddy. Maybe we can read one more story and then head back to bed," Cole said. "But we'd better read it in here so we don't wake up your brother. Do you think you can tiptoe into your room and get a book?"

Cameron nodded eagerly and rushed out into the hall.

"Hey. I'm sorry," Dani said. "This shouldn't ruin our plans tonight. He should go back to sleep pretty easily."

"They're our children, Dani. If you think I'm feeling put out, I'm not. I actually feel great." He smiled and pulled her into his warm embrace. "I have two sweet boys and the sexiest, most incredible woman on the planet." He punctuated his sweet statement with another soft kiss. "I can't wait to be married to you."

"I can't wait, either. I love you so much." She pulled him even closer, their gazes connected, and she reached down to grab his magnificent butt, giving it a nongentle squeeze. "And as soon as Cameron goes back to bed, I vote we start practicing for the honeymoon."

* * * * *

THE FORBIDDEN BROTHER

JOANNE ROCK

To Lisa Rivard for the friendship,
the party-bus rides and all the fun texts
that make me smile.
So glad we met!

One

Jillian Ross ordered a bottle of the house's best wine and tipped back in her chair at her table near the window. Considering that the bar, centrally located in downtown Cheyenne, Wyoming, was called the Thirsty Cow, and the best vintage available was a cabernet she could have picked up at her local grocery store, she was pleasantly surprised by how good the first sip tasted.

Maybe that was because Ordering the Best Wine Off the Menu was a line item on her list of One Hundred Life Adventures—a set of goals she'd composed during radiation treatments for breast cancer two years ago. She was determined to accomplish every single objective, and then some, now that she had a second chance at living. It felt incredibly satisfying to cross off another ambition, even if she wasn't in a five-star establishment. Just being in Cheyenne fulfilled another goal, since Seeing the Western States had also made the list.

Actually, the travel category accounted for almost a third of her line items, now that she thought about it. She'd hoped her new job as a film location scout would put her in the perfect position to see the world—or at least the United States. Too bad she was already at risk of losing this gig.

"Can I get you anything else, miss?" asked a tall, harried waiter in a T-shirt printed with the name of a local college. Balancing a trayful of beers, he set her bottle on the table.

Country music blared through the Thirsty Cow, the Friday night crush a mix of local ranchers and tourists, peppered with military personnel from the air force base. Jillian had driven in from Pasadena three days before to meet with a wealthy ranch owner—the reclusive and powerful Cody McNeill—to try to change his mind about allowing a film crew on his land. Her mission was hampered by the man's complete lack of presence online. How could she make a personal pitch if she couldn't get a direct line to him?

The formal written request she'd sent to his business manager had generated a tersely worded refusal. But Jillian's boss had fallen in love with the photos she'd taken of the Black Creek Ranch—photos she'd snapped before she'd known the land was so carefully guarded. She hadn't seen any posted signs. But now that she needed formal permissions to move ahead, the higher-ups in her organization wouldn't consider any of Jillian's plan B spots, pushing her to sign the deal and book the Black Creek Ranch. Now, she was in town to convince ranching magnate Cody McNeill to change his mind.

"I'm all set, thank you." Jillian lifted her glass to toast her retreating waiter. "This is perfect."

She would never drink the whole bottle on her own, especially since she'd carefully avoided alcohol following her initial diagnosis. But she was at the two-year mark, damn it, and she liked the idea of having it on the table to top off the glass. Besides, who was she to question the wisdom of her One Hundred Life Adventures list, since it had been dreamed up under extreme duress?

She turned her attention to the notes on her tablet, studying who owned the lands abutting the Black Creek Ranch. Cody McNeill's father, Donovan, had divvied up some parcels for his three daughters and three sons, giving the McNeill family expansive holdings in all directions. Those adjacent properties had some similar features to the Black Creek, but none possessed the iconic old barn that Jillian's boss had fallen in love with. Still, there had to be something Jillian could do. Carson McNeill, one of Cody's brothers, owned a ranch next door. She typed his name into her tablet. And...bingo.

Carson, in direct contrast to his phantom sibling, had current social media profiles like the rest of the world. His posts were mostly updates about the ranching industry, but every now and then there was a photo of the man himself. These seemed to be posted mostly by other people, female people, but in light of the man's rugged good looks that was no surprise.

In a word? *Yum.*

In Jillian's brief time working in the film industry this past year, she'd run across all manner of handsome men. Carson McNeill was every bit as attractive as any A-list star she'd spotted, but his dusty boots, perpetual five o'clock shadow and generally mussed appearance lacked Hollywood polish. Which was a plus in her book. His dark hair, strikingly blue eyes and charming grin drew attention, no question.

One photo showed him lugging a keg off the back of a pickup truck in the middle of a golden hay field, a hay baler behind him, a handful of workers surrounding him. Another image pictured Carson at a local bar, long legs sprawled out, booted feet crossed, while he slouched in his chair and grinned at the women, plural, seated beside him. There was a photo posted by the local newspaper—a throwback shot—that showed a younger Carson riding a bucking bull in a competition ring, a crowd of cheering cowboys in the background. Jillian could swear the man was grinning even then, his body arced backward, poised to slam hard on the ground.

Surely this seemingly good-natured rancher could be persuaded to help her win over his brother? Pleased with the new discovery, she took another sip of her wine and leaned back in her seat again, allowing herself a moment to daydream while the music switched to a slow country ballad. As two-stepping couples took the floor and a blue neon moon dropped from the ceiling, Jillian thought through the possibilities. If she could secure Cody McNeill's permission to film on his ranch, she would ensure future work from her boss. And since this film location manager was well-connected in the industry, she might pass along Jillian's name to her friends as someone who could find key locations and had the cinematography sensibilities to know what a director was looking for.

That meant more work. New travel. Additional items crossed off her list. Even better, that meant more ways

Jillian was kicking cancer's ass. And that was what she wanted more than anything. Triumph over the thing that had scared her—almost—to death.

She stared out the window overlooking the street, preferring not to dwell on romance and two-stepping couples while remembering a period in her life that had been frighteningly loveless. Her boyfriend at the time had bailed right after her surgery to remove a tumor. He couldn't deal with chemo, he'd said. Let alone the radiation.

That still got to her. *He* couldn't deal with it. Like he was the one having to slog through that hell and not her.

Closing her eyes to banish the old demons, Jillian took a bracing breath. When she opened them again, she had to look twice.

Because she could have sworn that out there on the street, in the rainy Cheyenne night, she saw Carson Mc-Neill. Instantly alert, she craned her neck to follow his progress up the sidewalk. Decidedly handsome from the rear, the guy looked to be the correct height and build. His worn-in jeans were a feast for the feminine eye. His boots and his Stetson were the wrong colors from what she'd seen online, but a man could own more than one hat, couldn't he?

Jillian gathered up her tablet and maps and shoved them into her homemade cloth satchel. Finding a couple bills in her wallet, she tossed them on the table beside her barely touched wine. The server was getting one heck of a tip, since she couldn't wait around for change.

After darting and weaving through the crowd toward the exit, she levered open the door and stepped out into the rain. Just in time to see the fawn-colored Stetson disappear into a building a block up the street.

She hugged her bag to her chest, wishing she'd taken the time to slip into her sweater. Cheyenne was windy on a good day, and during a rainy night, the gusts took on a brutal chill. Especially for a woman who still chilled easily. Sometimes she thought the chemo drugs would never fully leave her body.

She reached the building where Carson McNeill had disappeared and saw it was another bar. Wrangler's wasn't nearly as busy as the Thirsty Cow, so when she stumbled inside, in a rush to escape the weather, the patrons seemed to notice.

All five of them.

Hank Williams was playing on the jukebox and the dude behind the bar, with a grizzled beard halfway down his chest, was no college student. The wiry old guy gave Jillian a nod and went back to pouring a beer for the only other woman in the place—a middle-aged lady dressed like a biker in a leather vest over her long-sleeved T-shirt.

Wrangler's definitely wasn't the sort of joint where Jillian envisioned smiley, social Carson McNeill hanging out. But there could be no mistaking a man that good-looking. He was seated in a corner booth, and he'd just laid his phone on the table, flicking on the screen with his thumb before scrolling.

Jillian didn't realize she was staring until the bartender called over to her, "Have a seat anywhere you like." He gestured with a sweep of his arm to the empty tables.

Feeling silly for having been caught gawking, Jillian scooted into a booth across from her quarry. He hadn't glanced up at her since she'd first walked in and she wondered now how it would feel to have those intensely blue eyes on her. Which was peculiar, given that she'd lost all her mojo where men were concerned.

Part of that was her former boyfriend's fault, since he gave men a bad name. But the majority of the blame belonged to her disease and the treatment that had left her feeling like a dried-out husk of a woman. She'd read the brochures on what to expect after dealing with her chemo and radiation, so she knew that feeling was normal enough, and as side effects went, it wasn't the worst of them. After all, what did it matter if sex and men held no appeal when she was focused on her career and her recovery?

But right now, stealing glances at the tall, well-built cowboy two booths away, Jillian could almost forget she hadn't experienced deep physical arousal in two years. Because the man was intriguing. He wore a blue T-shirt under his gray-and-white work flannel, and she found herself fascinated by the play of muscle beneath the cotton. The edge of his jaw, shadowed with bristle, made her wonder about the texture and feel of him.

Then, to cap off a night full of surprises, Carson McNeill glanced up from his phone and stared back at her. His blue eyes narrowed. A fierce, intensely male energy vibrated all around him. She felt the electric jolt from that single look on her skin, tingling its way over her arms beneath the featherweight sleeves of her blouse. Her breath hitched in her throat with a soft, startled gasp. She couldn't seem to pull her eyes away.

A shiver traced its way down to the base of her spine. But this wasn't the kind of shiver that came with a chill. This one brought an undeniable flare of heat.

Her throat suddenly parched, she couldn't speak. Only this time, it wasn't because she felt like a dried-out husk of a woman. As she stared at a man who could hold the key to her professional future in his hands, she realized that her long slumbering libido had finally made a comeback.

For a moment, Cody McNeill wondered whether the lovely redhead seated in the booth across the way had mistaken him for his twin.

His whole life, he'd witnessed women stare at Carson in just that manner—like he was the answer to all their fantasies. It was strange, really, since he and Carson were supposedly identical. To people who knew them, they couldn't be more different. Even strangers could usually tell at a glance that Carson was the charmer and Cody was...not. It was in the way they carried themselves. The propensity to laugh. Carson's easygoing, leave-it-to-tomorrow approach was a far cry from Cody's belief that the buck stopped at his desk.

But somehow the redhead hadn't quite figured it out yet. She had been watching him since she stepped through the door of Wrangler's. The local dive suited him, since the food was good, the beer didn't require a dedicated menu and he'd bought the building a month ago to remodel for a more centrally located ranch office. Tonight, Cody needed a retreat from his family—mostly his twin. They'd been at odds for weeks over the sudden appearance of their paternal grandfather, a rich-as-Croesus hotel magnate from New York who'd disinherited their father over twenty years ago. Carson wanted to make peace with the guy, while Cody had no use for someone who'd betrayed their dad. The arrival of Malcolm McNeill in Cheyenne was tearing their already fractured family apart, and Carson had to make things worse by inviting the old man to dinner at the main house on Creek Spill Ranch. Technically, the property belonged to their father, Donovan, even though Carson oversaw the daily operations.

That latest bit of disloyalty made Cody mad as hell. His twin was too busy having fun all the time to ever think about the consequences of his actions. Which, of course, was why Carson attracted the kind of wide-eyed attention the woman in the opposite booth was currently exhibiting. Carson said yes to every entertaining opportunity that came his way, whether or not it was the right thing to do. Normally, that ticked off Cody. But at this moment, with the vivid hazel eyes of an attractive female following Cody's every move, he had to ask himself why he played it straight all the time instead of taking a page from his twin's book. If Carson was here, he'd have the decidedly sexy stranger under his arm in no time.

Between the dark mood hovering over Cody and the realization that he wouldn't mind stealing away one of his brother's admirers, he did something he hadn't done since he was a schoolkid.

He pretended to be his twin.

"Would you like some tips on what's edible around here?" He tested out the words with a smile. The expression was as fake as the pickup line, but he'd seen similar patter work for his brother a hundred times.

Hell, he ended up sounding just like him.

The grin gave the words the right amount of easy irreverence.

But the petite beauty in the booth nearby appeared to be stunned silent. Although slight in stature, she had a powerful presence. From her warm, henna-colored hair to the vivid blues and greens of her butterfly-printed blouse, and turquoise cowboy boots that had never seen a day's work, the woman stood out. She shone like a light in the darkened bar.

"Edible?" The word was a dry croak from her lips, a belated response to his question. Her cheeks flushed pink with hectic color.

"On the menu," he clarified, withdrawing his own laminated copy of Wrangler's entree choices from the metal napkin holder. "There are some good options if you'd like input."

The way she blushed, he had to wonder what she'd thought he meant.

And damned if that intriguing notion didn't distract him from his dark mood. He couldn't remember the last time he'd made a woman blush, and the telltale heat in her cheeks sent an answering warmth through his limbs.

"I, um…" She bit her lip uncertainly before seeming to collect her thoughts. "I'm not hungry, but thank you. I actually followed you in here to speak to you."

Ah, hell. He wasn't ready to end the game that had taken a turn for the interesting. But it was one thing to ride the wave of the woman's mistaken assumption. It was another to lie, and Cody's ethics weren't going to allow him to sink that low.

The smile his brother normally wore slid from Cody's face. Disappointment cooled the heat in his veins.

"Are you sure you want to do that?" It was a shot in the dark, and he was surprised to hear the words fall out of his mouth.

"Do what?" She frowned, confused.

The music in the bar switched to an old George Jones tune, a surprise choice from the jukebox, which was as ancient as the rest of the place. But the slow tempo gave him an idea to put off a conversation he didn't care to have.

"Are you sure you want to talk?" Shoving himself to his feet, he extended a hand to her. "We could dance instead."

He stared down into those green-gold eyes, willing her to say yes. He needed three more minutes to let the remnants of this hellish day slide away. Wanted an excuse to touch this pretty stranger who blushed for no reason. She took so long deciding he thought she must be debating a good way to refuse him. But then, surprise of all surprises, the sweetest smile curved her lips, transforming her face from pretty to...

Wow.

It was like someone flipped a switch inside her, making her come more fully alive.

"That sounds great," she agreed with a breathless laugh. "Thank you."

Sliding her cool fingers into his palm, she rose and let him lead her to the dance floor. It was small and a little warped on one side, but then, they were the only couple out there. Cody turned her to face him before drawing her into the circle of his arms. She fitted there perfectly, even if she was a head shorter than him. It put her at the perfect height where he could have buried his face in her hair. The glossy red curls smelled like honeysuckle.

She tipped her head up to look at him as they began an easy two-step, moving together well enough. She let him lead, her feet mirroring his as he spun them in slow circles around the floor. The full sleeves of her blouse grazed his arms, gently clinging to him.

Sensual hunger stirred with new restlessness, reminding him of every single month he'd spent alone since his last relationship. All twelve of them, in fact. And he hadn't been remotely tempted by anyone after discovering his ex-girlfriend's faithlessness, a treachery she defended by saying he was "too cold" for a woman to love.

Tonight he was anything but cold.

"I like this idea," the redhead in his arms confided, her fingers flexing ever so slightly against his shoulder where she touched him. "I can't remember the last time I danced with a stranger."

Stranger?

Cody assumed she'd mistaken him for Carson. Did she not know his twin, either? He wasn't sure how he felt about that. At first, he'd been just as glad to undermine his disloyal brother. But as his temper cooled, and the longer he held this vibrant woman in his arms, the more he appreciated the idea that Carson didn't have any kind of prior claim.

"You've improved my Friday night a whole lot, too." He liked the feel of her, his hand warming the cool skin through the thin blouse she wore. "It's been a long time since I've thought about anything outside of work."

Her eyebrows lifted. "Leading me to wonder what you could be thinking about right now." Her lips curved. "Admiring the Wrangler's decor? Or maybe remembering how much you like a good George Jones tune?"

He laughed appreciatively. "I do respect a bar that still plays a classic. But the vinyl upholstery in the booths isn't doing much for me in the decor department." His gaze skated over her features; he was looking forward to making her blush again. "And I was thinking about you more than anything else."

His directness might have caught her off guard. She nibbled her lower lip briefly before meeting his eyes. "I haven't been the center of anyone's attention in…a long time."

There was a story there. He heard it in her voice. Saw it in her eyes.

"You aren't involved with someone else?" He needed to be sure before he let this go on any longer. But his pulse was already thrumming. "I don't see a ring, but I have to ask."

"I am very much unattached." She shook her head, red curls catching the overhead light as she moved. "What about you? No one waiting at home?"

"The only ones who might be missing my presence right now are a couple of rowdy shepherds back at my ranch who would have preferred the night off." He swayed with her. Her knee brushed his now and again in a way that fired right through him. "But no girlfriend. No wife."

He respected that she asked, even though she was clearly feeling the same spark as him. And now that those formalities had been cleared away, he could simply enjoy the moment. The completely unexpected pleasure of having a beautiful stranger in his arms. He didn't want to let go of her now. He wanted to take her outside into the fresh, rain-cleaned night and kiss her. See if she tasted as good as he imagined.

"The stars are aligning for us so far, aren't they?" She peered up at him with something like wonder in her eyes.

He couldn't remember a woman ever looking at him

quite like that. As if he was the answer to a question. An answer that pleased her.

"It feels that way." He didn't want to scare her off with empty pickup lines, or come across as some low-life playing games with a woman in a bar. But as the music shifted again—this time to an even slower, modern country love song—Cody wondered if he could convince her to let the spark between them run wild. To follow the heat wherever it led. "And since the stars aligning would be a first for me, I wonder if can ask you just one thing."

He halted them in the middle of the floor, now that the two-step was done. Bringing her fractionally closer, he swayed to the slower tempo in a barely moving lovers' dance.

She followed him seamlessly, her gaze never straying from his. She was fully focused on him. Framed by dusky brown lashes, those green-gold eyes reminded him of new grass and spring.

"Sure. Ask away." Her voice had a sweet-sultry quality that made him want to listen to her speak more.

"Don't you ever wish you could forget about the expectations of the world around you and just...choose your own adventure?" He remembered books like that when he'd been a kid, where you could test out different endings to a story.

For someone who'd always taken the safe route in real life, he had liked the option of seeing how another choice played out. At least in a book. Cody couldn't do that with ranching. Or his family. But he could take a chance here. Tonight.

Her lashes swept down for a long moment, hiding

her expression. But when she tilted a glance up at him again, there was a new curiosity there.

"Are you asking to share an adventure with me?" She sounded disbelieving. But maybe a little intrigued.

"I suppose I am." He would never have made such an outrageous suggestion to a local—a woman who knew him or his family. But she had *tourist* and *temporary* written all over her. Surely there couldn't be any harm in drawing out the flirtation? "What would you say to throwing away the rule book for a little longer?"

He let go of her hand for a moment to tip her chin higher, to see her face in the dim overhead light of the dance floor. Feminine interest flickered in her eyes. He inhaled as she released a pent-up breath. He could almost taste her in the space of silence between them.

Then he leaned closer to press his cause. "Choose me tonight."

Two

It was kismet.

Normally, Jillian wasn't the kind of woman who jumped on the fairy-tale bandwagon. Cancer had shredded every last romantic notion she had about the world and her place in it. These days, she was a realist. A pragmatist.

But how else could she view this man's suggestion that she choose a new adventure with him, at a time in her life when she was desperately rewriting her personal script to embrace new challenges? She owed her sanity and maybe even her physical health to that list of life adventures she'd written.

So for Carson McNeill to somehow tap into the deepest hunger of her soul and suggest they throw out the rule book, Jillian knew there had to be some kind of cosmic destiny at work. Call it providence, or maybe luck. Surely she could table her business agenda—just for a little while—to pursue this off-the-charts attraction? Once he'd rolled out the idea of an *adventure*, her personal mantra this year, Jillian saw it as a gauntlet thrown down by the hand of fate.

She was powerless to refuse.

To say nothing of how deeply attracted she felt to the man. She hadn't experienced the shimmering warmth of desire coating her skin this way since…ever. There was no precedent for the wobbly feeling in her knees. The light-headedness and the tingle over her scalp. The rest of the barroom faded away.

Her business with the McNeills would have to wait.

And if this turned out to be a mistake, she'd have to find another way to get to Cody McNeill that didn't involve this very charismatic brother.

Simply put, if she didn't say yes to this moment, she would regret it forever.

"Yes," she answered him. Smoothing her hands over his flannel shirt, Jillian let herself inch a fraction closer. "I'm game."

It would be an adventure, but a safe one. She had her own car parked outside. She would text a friend her whereabouts. Besides, she had the reassurance that Carson McNeill was a respected member of the ranching community. A well-known, well-liked local. She'd scanned his entire social media profile just moments ago.

His masculine smile of triumph made her toes curl, sending an answering heat smoking through her.

"I can't wait to kiss you," he whispered in her ear. The brush of his mouth so close to her neck was tantalizing.

"I like where this is going." She swayed to the music there in the corner of the bar, the scents of beer and wings distracting her from the occasional hint of his aftershave when she got close enough to him. She thought about tucking her head against his chest and breathing him in, but she was already pushing the envelope. "Even though this would be the first time I've ever kissed a total stranger."

"I'm going to be heartbroken if you're backing out of this adventure already." The deep tone of his voice vibrated in her chest, making her tremble.

Another couple joined them; the woman who'd been sitting at the bar earlier tugged a rough-looking cowboy onto the floor with her. Their weaving, unsteady dance made Jillian's partner tighten his grip protectively, his hand splayed low on her spine.

Her heart rate quickened, her breasts brushing against his chest, sending an ache through her.

"Not a chance. Besides, I already know some things about you," she reasoned, recognizing that she couldn't get much nearer to this man without appearing positively indecent. Their thighs grazed together now and again, the contact reminding her how long it had been since her legs had tangled with a man's.

Too. Damn. Long.

"Is that so?"

"You like dive bars." She wondered why he'd come here alone. All his photos online showed him surrounded by friends—men, women, employees, coworkers.

"And redheads." Gently, he tugged one of her newly grown spiral curls, a hint of a grin playing at the corner of his lips. "Actually, I never knew how much I liked this fiery color of hair until tonight."

His gaze seemed to follow his fingers as he toyed with the ringlet for another moment, and her heart faltered at the sweetness of the gesture. Or maybe it was simply the affirmation that he enjoyed the crazy curls she didn't dare tame with hair product, fearful she would somehow lose the fragile regrowth.

Her throat dried up again. This night and this man were was making her feel things. Arousal. Romance. A giant dose of normal. She blinked fast to banish the sudden rush of emotion, unwilling to ruin things with an attack of weepiness. She would enjoy every second, damn it. Except the wellspring of feelings was already bubbling.

Gratitude for her new lease on life.

Joy in the simple warmth of a man's caress.

And yes, the return of physical longing, a keen hunger for more.

Unsure what to do with all that, and worried she would do something mortifying—like burst into tears on the side of the dance floor—Jillian rose on her toes and channeled all the sentimental burn into a kiss.

She could tell she'd surprised him. For a split second, he went absolutely still. Was he thinking she was crazy? Sex-starved? She closed her eyes to shut out those fears and simply let herself concentrate on the feel of his mouth on hers. The bristle of his jaw against her skin. The contrasting softness of his lips, which were full and sensual. He smelled like cedar and pine, woodsy and earthy, as if he'd been outdoors all day.

Just when she would have pulled back, however, the kiss changed. He became fully engaged, taking over her tentative efforts, which had been more about hiding her emotions. He pulled her into him, anchoring her body with his while he let his hands and tongue roam.

An onslaught of sudden, acute physical awareness put a stop to all her distracting emotions. His new command of the kiss allowed her to follow his lead, just like when they'd danced. Her head tipped back, her knees gave way. She wound her arms around his neck to hold herself steady, and to feel the full impact of his hard, muscular body.

Lost in the moment, she arched into him. Hip to hip, breast to chest. She needed full contact and she needed it now. Maybe he could tell as much, because he broke away from her suddenly, staring down at her while expelling his breath in a rush. With his hands on her shoulders, he steadied them both, since he seemed as surprised by the moment as she was.

The music had changed. A more modern country rock tune blared from the speakers and they were alone on the dance floor again. A waitress sidled past with a trayful of food; the scents of tabasco and beer were heavy in the air.

All that was secondary to the desire coursing through Jillian's body like wildfire, the red-hot sensation that was totally foreign, since her libido had been on ice for over a year.

"You see that door over there?" he asked, tipping his forehead so close to hers they almost touched.

She followed his gaze to the exit marked Private.

"Mmm." She nodded, since her voice wasn't working. Her lips were more inclined to kiss than speak.

"My offices are just through there and up a staircase."

"You work in the bar?" She didn't think that could

be true. Wasn't he a successful rancher with considerable acreage?

"I bought the building and rent the space to Wrangler's. I'm remodeling the upper floors for…my business." He hedged about his line of work.

But of course, she already knew what he did for a living.

"How convenient to work close to a bar you like," she observed, not sure what else to say. Her thoughts were muddled from the kiss.

She wanted another one.

"It is," he agreed. "But right now, I'm thinking about how much privacy we could have for another kiss, on the other side of that door."

"Oh." That was logic she could follow. "Yes. Just let me grab my purse."

He scanned the bar, his gaze halting on the table where she'd left her bag, while she reached into her pocket for her phone. She texted a quick message to a friend to let her know where she was, taking basic safety precautions.

But if there was another kiss on the table, Jillian was taking it. And if that meant entering the backroom of a dive bar in a building Carson McNeill owned, that didn't deter her in the slightest. Her whole body hummed from his touch. She felt vitally alive, and that was a gift that neither her recovery nor the group counseling sessions she'd attended afterward had given her.

"Are you sure?" He paused and frowned down at her before they reached her table.

Perhaps he'd seen her text.

"I'm positive." She craved the adrenaline high his touch inspired. Thirsted for the physical contact that ignited sensations all over her body. Even before her chemo days, she hadn't experienced the kind of tantalizing thrill that contact with him provided.

Darting toward the booth, she retrieved her satchel. "Okay." She tried to restrain herself from leaping into his arms. Plastering herself to him. "I'm ready."

She didn't want to worry about work or filming on Cody McNeill's ranch anymore tonight. She just wanted to follow this adventurous path Carson had proposed, and hope it led her back toward joy and health. Well-being and wholeness.

Taking her by the hand, he drew her with him across the bar, past the dance floor and through the exit marked Private. He flipped a switch and an overhead lamp threw the space into view. As he closed the door behind them, Jillian's gaze immediately went to the vast office, which was still under construction.

The exposed brick walls and bamboo floors had been cleaned and restored. A staircase with dark slats and a thick, Craftsman-style handrail led upward, the mirror on the landing reflecting the dull light of silver pendant lamps. The beautifully detailed hammered-tin ceiling tiles looked original.

But she didn't have a chance to compliment him on the remodeling project in progress. He stalked toward her, his intent gaze rising from her mouth to her eyes. Her pulse quickened as she remembered why they were here.

The music from the jukebox drifted in through the open door. The rest of the world was close, but not close enough to see what was happening in here. He paused near her, took off his Stetson and settled it on a wrought-iron hook beside the door. She could see his eyes better now that the brim wasn't casting a shadow. Jillian let her satchel fall to the floor with a soft thud. Her eyes remained on Carson. The stranger she knew.

Then his hand was cupping her face, tilting her chin. Her eyelids fell, the sensations coming so fast and fierce she needed to focus simply on what she was feeling.

His kiss chased off any reservations she might have had, providing instant clarity about what she wanted. Desire shot through her; it felt like going up too fast in an elevator. Her knees almost buckled, and her whole body was seized with dizzying sensations. She reached to steady herself against him and ended up molded to the hard expanse of his muscles, from her hips to her breasts.

Her instincts took over. Winding her arms around his neck, she sought a closer connection.

For a moment, he kissed her harder. Deeper. She sucked air into her lungs in hard pants when he finally angled back, breaking the kiss to study her.

"Are you okay with this?" he asked, his thumbs stroking lazy circles on her shoulders through the thin fabric of her blouse.

She wanted more than a kiss, she knew now. Much, much more.

"Better than okay." She laid her palm on his cheek. Willed him to understand what she needed.

Connection. Affirmation. Him.

His jaw flexed; his breathing was as labored as hers. Then he backed her into the wall and she vaguely registered the rough brick against her spine for a moment before he hooked an arm under her hips and hefted her higher. The action slid her along the rigid length of—

Oh. My.

She ran her fingers through his thick dark hair, clearing a path to his ear so she could whisper, "Don't stop."

Her soft plea undid him.

Up until that moment, Cody had been doing his damnedest to keep the explosive attraction in check. He'd made sure she was on board with what was happening between them. Helped her to feel safe and in control at all times. There was a bar full of people—well, a few people—just on the other side of the door.

But now?

She was like an out-of-control blaze in his arms. The chemistry was blistering. And her quiet, insistent "Don't stop" torched the last shreds of his restraint.

Cupping her sweet curves in his hands, he brought the juncture of her thighs against his rock-hard erection, feeling the heat of her right through her long skirt. With the flip of his belt buckle, he could be inside her in no time.

"Please," she murmured against his neck, kissing her way down his throat as she tugged at his T-shirt. "I have a clean bill of health. No partners since my last checkup." She stopped kissing him long enough to glance up at him.

His short bark of laughter surprised him. Hell, *she* surprised him with the glimpses of an efficient woman beneath the passionate kisses.

"Me, too." He set her back on her feet. "And thank you for that. I have protection somewhere. A bathroom upstairs, I think." He'd stocked the basics, since he'd spent a few nights here overseeing the construction work when it had run late into the night.

"I have one," she blurted, scrambling to retrieve the

patchwork bag she'd dropped on the floor. "I bought it when I—well, in a fit of optimism." She combed through the papers and electronics in her satchel. A bright pink pair of earbuds and a lipstick tube spilled out. "Here."

She stood back up and stuffed a foil packet into his right hand, then launched herself into his arms. He wanted to move them upstairs where there was a sofa, but her fingers made quick work of his belt and the button fly, scrambling the last of his good intentions as she stroked him lightly.

"Hold on to me." The words were a brusque command as he lifted her against him, a thigh in each hand as he helped her to wrap her legs around him. With her secured that way, he stepped close enough to the door to lock it.

She took the forgotten condom from him while he backed her against the door, a smoother surface than the brick wall. With her pinned there, he used a hand to tug her skirt higher. Out of the way.

She was in the process of tearing open the packet when he touched her through the silk of her panties, finding her hot and ready for him. He withdrew the condom from her, rolling it into place. His pulse pounded in his temples, the need for her an undeniable urge. A fierce ache. He wanted to take more time, touch her until an orgasm simmered through her. But her restless hands roved over him, peeling away his shirt and undershirt, tracing down his spine, spearing through his hair. Her hips bucked, and the slide of her soft, feminine center against his rigid length threatened to take his knees right out from under him.

Being inside her was his only option.

Slipping her panties aside, he entered her, slowly. Her fingers flexed against his arms, her nails gently biting into his skin as she held herself still. Head thrown back, she parted her lips on a sigh of pleasure. Her cheeks flushed deep pink, her lashes fluttering as she started to move with him.

The feel of her all around him was the sexiest high he could remember. From her boots hooked around his waist to her blouse sliding off one shoulder, she was all in. Her honeysuckle scent called to him, and he licked her tender skin while he buried himself deep inside her. Over and over again.

He held back when he could tell she was close. Her cheeks went from pink to small spots of red, her breath hitched and her hips went still. He slipped a hand down to touch her intimately, caressing tender circles right... there.

She came apart in his arms with a cry of pleasure that brought his release surging right afterward. Heat blasted his shoulders as sweat popped along his spine. The sensation went on and on, pummeling him, wringing everything from him. She clung to him, shifting against him as the aftershocks rocked her.

"Carson." She breathed the word with a sigh, her eyes closed and her head thrown back.

His brother's name on his lover's lips brought everything inside Cody grinding to a halt. His heart rate slowed. His brain ceased working, too. Nothing made sense.

"What did you just say?" His mouth formed the words even as a chill rushed over his skin. He shifted his hold on her, barely able to think.

She peered up at him through eyelids at half-mast.

Whatever she saw in his expression must have given her pause, because she tipped her head sideways and worried her lower lip with her teeth.

"Carson," she repeated, loud and clear, even though she looked abashed. "I'm sorry. I knew who you were when I walked into the bar. I was looking for you."

"Not me, sweetheart." With an effort, he straightened his shoulders. "I'm Cody McNeill. You've got the wrong twin."

Three

"You're Cody?" The color drained from the woman's face, as if that was extraordinarily unpleasant news.

Not that he was surprised. Cody did just fine with women when he chose to, but Carson had always been the ladies' man. Clearly, Carson was the guy she'd been hoping for. So yeah…he wasn't surprised, but definitely a bit disappointed given the incredible encounter they'd just shared. After his last go-round with a faithless female, Cody wasn't in the market for a woman who had her eyes on another man.

"In the flesh." He disentangled himself with an effort, setting her on her feet.

Only to realize, as he tidied up, that the condom she'd given him was now in shreds. The realization—coming hard on the heels of her mistaking him from Carson—sent him stalking to the other side of the work space and slumping down in a chair.

"Oh, no." The woman held her head in her hands. And she didn't even know the worst of it yet.

"Maybe you'd better have a seat." He used his boot to shove a second chair out from under the long, makeshift conference table that was a holdover from the retail store that had occupied the building long ago. "And tell me your name, for starters."

He'd had unprotected sex with a total stranger.

And while, yes, he'd started out wanting an adventure, he hadn't expected things to go so far. Especially not with a woman who had mistaken him for his twin.

"I'm Jillian." She lifted her chin and picked up her bag before joining him at the table. She dropped into the utilitarian chair he'd offered her, her red curls drooping as much as her shoulders. "Jillian Ross."

The name sounded vaguely familiar, but he couldn't place it.

"Well, Jillian Ross, we've got bigger problems on our hands than you mistaking me for my younger twin brother."

"A twin." She repeated the word, shaking her head like she'd never heard of such a thing.

Cody steeled himself against the surprise kick to his ego and shared his more pressing concern.

"Correct." He heard his clipped tone and couldn't help it. "But right now, I'd like to direct your attention to the fact that the condom broke."

Her head snapped up, green eyes flashing even in the dim light.

"Excuse me?"

"Equipment malfunction," he explained, trying to keep frustration out of his voice. "Maybe the condom was past the expiration date?"

"No." She shook her head and then straightened her spine, seeming to recover herself a little bit. "I'm sure that's not the case, but it doesn't matter, since I'm disease-free, like I told you." She pulled in a quick breath and tipped her chin up. "And as for the other concern, there's a high percent chance that I'm..." She closed her eyes for a moment, as if gathering strength. Or patience. When she opened them again, there was a glitter in her gaze. A hint of emotion he couldn't fathom. "I'm most likely infertile."

He hadn't expected that. He ran a hand through his hair, his brain buzzing with unanswered questions. Questions he wasn't sure he should ask.

Then again, they'd taken a big risk tonight. He needed to know.

"How high a percentage?" He leaned on the conference table, only just now realizing he wore no shirt. He'd been so distracted he forgot to retrieve the only clothing they'd discarded before having sex. He spotted his T-shirt in a heap on the floor. "And how can you be sure?"

"I'm not comfortable divulging all my unhappy health history." Her words were clipped, possibly angry. "But I'm sure."

"I'm sorry for that. But you have to admit there's a lot at stake here."

"No." She shook her head. "There probably isn't."

Her shoulders were ramrod straight. It was a defensive posture. He told himself not to pursue the subject now. Not to push when emotions were already running high.

But then some of the tension seemed to seep back out of her. A sigh slipped from her lips.

"I've had extensive chemo and radiation, okay?" She held herself differently when she said it, arms crossed protectively over her midsection. "My doctors warned me before we started that it was unlikely I'd be able to carry my own children. And not that it's any of your business, but I went so far as to freeze my eggs." Her jaw flexed. "So don't worry about it."

A stab of empathy had him reaching across the table. Touching her forearm. He hadn't meant to unearth something so personal—so huge.

"I'm sorry."

"It's fine." She swallowed with visible effort. "I'm fine now." Blinking fast, she shrugged and pulled away from his touch. "I'm alive."

The quiet fierceness in her voice told him that fight had been hard-won. He wanted to know more about her—what she'd battled, how long she'd been in remission—but he didn't want to pry on a night when they'd already gotten under one another's skin in surprising ways.

"Very much so," he agreed, humbled by the small glimpse of herself she'd given him. "I didn't mean to encroach on something so private."

A wry smile quirked her lips. "You have a right to know, given the circumstances."

"Thank you." He appreciated her honesty and hoped it would continue now that he had another sticky question to ask. "So tell me, Jillian Ross, what exactly did you want with my twin when you followed me in here tonight?"

For the sake of great sex, she'd set fire to her career. How could she have missed the fact that Cody and

Carson McNeill were twins when she'd been researching their ranches? Jillian couldn't believe her bad luck
as she stared across the table at the incredibly handsome shirtless rancher. Who'd be very angry with her
when she revealed what she'd been trying to accomplish. She shouldn't have been plotting to gain access
to one brother through the other, and she surely should
have come clean before she committed to the sensual
adventure.

Then again, why had Cody refused her request to
film on location without any explanation or opportunity to plead her case?

"I thought Carson might lead me to you," she told
him honestly. If she was going to lose the opportunity
to film on the McNeill ranch altogether—and lose her
job in the process—she would go out fighting.

"You wanted to find *me*?" He lifted a dark eyebrow,
his brooding, skeptical expression not intimidating her
so much now that he was shirtless.

She still couldn't believe she'd had sex with him. He
held her professional future in his hands.

"Yes." Lifting her satchel, she laid it on the table and
drew out the county land map. "I've been trying to contact you about this piece of property."

She pointed to the location where she'd taken pho-
tographs a few weeks ago.

"Black Creek Ranch." He spun the map to face him,
smoothing the edges where it curled. "What do you
want with—" He glanced up at her, recognition dawning on his face. "You're the location scout."

The tone of his voice made it sound like her job was
in the same category as a tax collector's. His eyes lingered on her.

"One and the same." She smiled tightly. "I sent a letter to your business manager—"

"More than one," he reminded her, shoving himself to his feet. He prowled along the perimeter of the room until he reached his discarded shirts, and punched his fists through the armholes. "You asked repeatedly. But I don't want any film crews on my property."

"So you said in your two-line refusal." She knew she should be nice. Professional. But she'd burned that bridge when she entered the door marked Private.

"You didn't leave me any opportunity to explain how quickly we could finish the shoot, or the options we have for sending as few people as possible onto your land—"

"Because I'm not interested in having anyone on my land. That's the whole point of private property, isn't it? It's private. I don't have to let strangers trample all over it."

"But we're hardly strangers now, are we?" She hadn't been able to resist saying it. Her body was still tingling from incredible feelings—feelings she probably wouldn't get to experience again with him. She also thought about her list and all the adventures she wouldn't be able to accomplish if she lost her job. Real fear for her future rattled her. "Sorry. I didn't mean to have this conversation with you tonight. I—"

"You hoped to sweet-talk my brother into convincing me on your behalf?" Cody McNeill had put all his clothes back on, and the forbidding expression on his face made it difficult to believe he'd teased the best orgasm of her life from her just moments ago.

She remained in her seat at the conference table, unwilling to get too close to him when her fingers still ached to touch him. "I looked up who owned the property neighboring yours, since you're an extremely difficult man to reach."

"My work keeps me busy."

"Since Carson McNeill was easy enough to find online—"

"No surprise there," he muttered, reaching for his Stetson and planting it on his head.

"—I thought fate must be smiling on me when he walked past the Thirsty Cow tonight." She could really use the rest of that wine she'd left behind. Her head throbbed with a mixture of embarrassment and frustration that Cody didn't seem willing to give an inch.

She drummed her fingers on the tabletop, a blond wood that looked out of place in this very Western-style remodeled space.

"Except it wasn't Carson." His smile was a poor facsimile of the one he'd given her earlier.

Because, she realized, that hadn't been his real smile.

An idea took hold. A dawning comprehension.

"You were pretending to be him, weren't you?" She realized that initial exchange—when she'd first arrived in Wrangler's—was the only time she'd seen a genuine smile from him.

Except it hadn't been genuine at all. He had been imitating his brother. She could tell she had guessed correctly when a fleeting defensive expression crossed his face.

Indignation rose in her as she got to her feet and grabbed the map and her bag. She wouldn't be a fool for any man again after the way her ex-boyfriend had walked out on her after surgery. She was smarter than that.

"You know, I can take some of the blame for not

telling you who I was tonight." She charged toward the door, ready to put this night—this obstinate man—behind her. "But it seems like you also played a role in this…misunderstanding."

"Misunderstanding?" He stood between her and the door. He didn't seem to be blocking it on purpose, he just hadn't stepped aside yet. "Is that what you're calling it? You came into town looking for a way to circumvent me."

She gestured at his imposing form with a flourish. "Sort of like I am right now, since you're still standing in my way. Apparently you take pride in being immovable."

His jaw worked silently; maybe he was chewing over the idea.

"That's not true," he said finally. "But I don't want you to storm out of here until I know you have a safe way home. And I'd also like to know where I can reach you tomorrow."

"Seriously?" She shook her head. "I'm perfectly capable of finding my own way back to the hotel. And I can't see why you'd need to reach me when you've made it clear you don't want a single soul on your *private* land."

He caught her off guard by reaching toward her and smoothing aside a curl that fell over her eyes. His touch, unexpectedly tender, reminded her of all the heat he'd roused in her before. What they'd shared had taken her breath away.

Even if he was being difficult and unreasonable now.

"First of all, I kept you out late and I want to at least walk you to your car, because that's what a gentleman does." His voice stirred memories of everything they'd shared, from a dance to so much more. "Second, I want to speak to you once the dust settles from tonight, because I owe you an explanation."

He had a point. She was dealing with too much sensory overload to wade through it all now.

"And third," he continued, opening the door that led back out to the bar, "we need to stay in touch because no matter what the doctors say about your fertility there could still be repercussions." He spoke in a low voice, his hand splayed across her back as they made their way across the dance floor toward the exit. "And I can assure you, if there are, I won't be a difficult man to reach."

Four

Cody knew he needed to head back home. He didn't usually grant himself perks like a midafternoon horse ride to clear his head—even on a mild, sunny Sunday like this one. But he didn't know how else to fix his state of mind.

His bad mood could be traced back to Friday night and the arrival of Jillian Ross in town. Then he'd spent an unproductive Saturday arguing with the company fixing the ranch's irrigation system. He'd handled it with so little diplomacy his contractor had walked off the job. Afterward, Cody had argued with Carson when his twin called to invite him to a Sunday noontime meal where Malcolm McNeill was going to be present.

As if he wanted anything to do with that branch of the family.

Giving Buxby, a retired stallion from the family's

quarter horse breeding program, a nudge to the flank, Cody steered the animal through a thicket of cotton-wood trees toward the stables at the Black Creek Ranch. He had done his damnedest to put the sexy and deceitful location scout out of his mind after he'd walked her to her car on Friday. But she'd shown up in his dreams both nights since then, and she'd barged into his waking thoughts, too.

He found himself remembering her laugh during a meeting with his ranch manager on Saturday morning. And recalling the way she'd murmured his twin's name at the peak of passion while Cody was directing the excavation for the irrigation system. He had been ornery and angry all weekend, and he blamed her.

He'd warned Carson about her presence in town when they'd spoken briefly on the phone this morning, skipping over the personal details of their encounter. Cody had thought it was important to let the family know that a Hollywood film company was angling to use McNeill land in a movie. He needed them to thwart her efforts, too. There was enough strife in the family over land rights and inheritance now that their estranged grandfather had entered the picture. Cody's dad hated Malcolm and wouldn't appreciate any of his sons or daughters breaking bread with their grandfather. But apparently, Cody was the lone holdout on that score. His half sisters had all decided Malcolm was a nice enough guy. Even Carson and their other brother, Brock, were coming around to recognize Malcolm McNeill as family.

That was fine for them.

But Cody's allegiance was to his dad, a man who'd built a ranching empire on his own, without any help from the billionaire who'd raised him. Cody not only respected that, he admired it. And if that meant missing out on a Sunday meal with his siblings, so be it.

As he cleared the cottonwood trees and came within sight of the stables, Cody recognized the familiar silhouette of one of those siblings now. Scarlett, the youngest of his three half sisters, paced circles behind the stable, her red boots kicking up dust. Her long, dark hair spilled over the shoulders of a fluttery yellow blouse tucked into a denim skirt that was too damned short. She was talking nonstop on her cell phone.

When she noticed Cody, she quit pacing and ended the call, tucking her phone in her back pocket. Her dark bangs fell in her eyes as she peered up at him. She patted Buxby's haunch when he slowed the horse to a stop near the paddock.

"Is it true?" she blurted without preamble. "Is there a film scout in town who wants to do a movie at Black Creek?"

"Hello to you, too, sis." Hauling a leg over the stallion's back, Cody swung down to stand beside Scarlett.

He took an extra moment to plant a kiss on her forehead, stalling just because she was clearly beside herself and eager for details. The least he could do was wrest a small amount of fun from tormenting his sister. His other half sisters, Maisie and Madeline, wouldn't much care about a film crew in Cheyenne. But Scarlett had been born with stars in her eyes. While she could ride and rope as well as any woman he'd ever seen, she'd made it clear from the time she could talk that ranch life wasn't for her.

"Hello." Sighing, she arched up on her toes and landed a haphazard return kiss on his jaw. "Now, spill it. Carson said you met a location scout at Wrangler's on Friday night. Is she still in town? Did you find out what movie they want to make? Or when?"

Cody passed off Buxby's reins to one of the ranch hands' kids. Thirteen-year-old Nate was as excited about working with the animals as Scarlett was about moviemaking, and Cody had given the okay for him to help out in the barns as long as his dad was overseeing him.

"Make sure you brush him down thoroughly, and water him, too." Nate nodded as Cody kept talking. "Hang all the tack back where it belongs, and put the brush away afterward."

While the kid took over the care of the horse, Cody headed toward the main house. Scarlett kept pace beside him.

"Cody? I don't respond well to silence," she said as they passed her sporty silver Jag in the driveway. "And I drove all the way over here—"

"You live here," he reminded her.

They'd all been raised on the Black Creek Ranch. Carson had moved out long ago to run another of their father's holdings, the Creek Spill Ranch. And Madeline lived on site at the White Canyon, a small guest ranch. But all their places were within a dozen miles of each other.

Scarlett had remodeled an old bunkhouse after college when their father hired her to help the farm-operations side of the business. Technically, she was an assistant to the foreman. But lately she spent more of her time at the White Canyon with Madeline now that the guest ranch enterprise had expanded.

"But I hadn't been planning to come back here, since

I'm leading a fly-fishing outing for Maddy's guests later," she argued, following him into the equipment shed.

Halting beside an old International Harvester tractor he was restoring in his spare time, Cody turned on her. "That's some outfit for fly-fishing."

She grinned. "I'm glad to see your sense of humor is still in there somewhere." She poked him on the shoulder. "Now spill it. What's the deal with the movie?"

Leaning against the wheel of the tractor, she folded her arms and waited.

Cody entered the small space that served as an office and reached for a set of truck keys. There was a weather-beaten desk and a file cabinet they used to keep records on the vehicles. He took a seat on the desk. The shed was open to the elements on one side; the big overhead door was raised. They were alone, though, since most of the staff had Sundays off.

"I can't tell you anything about the film." He'd been far more interested in flirting with the stranger than asking her name, let alone asking about her job. Truth be told, he was mad at himself for thinking he could get away with some kind of anonymous encounter with a woman.

One-night stands were for other guys. He'd never been that person.

"Why not?" Scarlett asked, hitching the heel of her boot on the chair rung. "Didn't you meet the location scout in person?"

"I did." Which was an understatement. What he'd shared with Jillian Ross would be filed away in his memory banks for the rest of his days. "When she asked about filming, I told her absolutely not. End of story."

Scarlett pursed her lips. She had a big, expressive personality. Most of the time she was a sweetheart. Kind and thoughtful. Still, she definitely had a steely side that he'd rather not tangle with.

"You're not the only member of this family. I'm not sure that's your call to make." She straightened, putting both feet on the floor.

"Honey, I know you have stars in your eyes—"

"No." She cut him off with a fierceness he had never heard from her. "Do not patronize me. Being feminine and having ambitions outside of this ranch doesn't mean I have stars in my eyes."

He drew a breath, wanting to apologize. To backtrack.

But she lit right into him again.

"Furthermore, did you ever consider how the exposure would help the White Canyon?" She planted her fists on her hips, warming up to her argument. "Madeline deserves that kind of spotlight, Cody. She's worked hard to make the guest ranch a success, and she's not the only one who would benefit from a film crew up here."

Cody cursed his twin for sharing the news with the rest of the family before he'd had the chance to. And yes, he cursed himself, too, for not making his stance clearer when he'd written to Jillian.

Although then he never would have met her. Never would have tasted her or touched her. And that he would have regretted. Even if he resented the hell out of her deceit.

"You're right. I'm sorry." He said the necessary words before his sister started in again. "I was only thinking about how Dad likes the privacy up here. You know how resistant he was to the guest ranch from the start."

Their father's fight against commercial development in the area had deep roots in his feud with his own father. When Donovan McNeill had first come to Wyoming and married Kara Calderon, they had soon run into financial trouble with her ranch, and had asked for his billionaire father's help, only to have Malcolm McNeill attempt to build a hotel on it. When Kara's father, Colt, protested, Donovan had nearly bankrupted himself hiring attorneys to untangle the mess and keep the peace. But the incident had created as many hard feelings between Donovan and his father-in-law as it had between Donovan and Malcolm.

When Kara died just a few years later, leaving behind three orphaned sons, Donovan had soon remarried, this time taking Scarlett's mother, Paige, as his bride.

And the land around the Creek Spill Ranch—land that extended all the way to the White Canyon—was still zoned to allow hospitality development, thanks to Malcolm McNeill's thwarted project. But to this day, Donovan didn't want anything to do with resort hotels. The guest ranch had come about only because he'd bought a failing bed-and-breakfast from a couple who were looking to retire and Madeline had wanted a shot at making it work.

"Dad doesn't make all the decisions for this family any more than you do," Scarlett reminded Cody. "We've diversified. Brock has the horse breeding business. Maddy has the guest ranch. Carson and you still work the cattle. But your business isn't more important than anyone else's in the family."

"Cattle brings in the bulk of the income." To an extent, each sibling's financial prospects were tied to the herd production, since all six of them owned a share. Their father had put some of his money in a trust for them, but the land and the businesses had been divvied up when the youngest—Scarlett—turned twenty-one.

"Yes, but since we each still have a stake in the Black Creek Ranch operations, we all have a voice in how it's run." Scarlett gave him an even stare.

"You've gone along with every decision I've made about purchasing bulls or negotiating prices on our calves, but now you're going to assert your authority over some film project you know nothing about?" Resentment stirred. He tightened his fist around the truck keys. He needed to move on with his day.

To put all thoughts of Jillian and her movie in the past.

"If I think the publicity could help us in the long run, you're damn right I'll assert my authority." She withdrew her phone from her pocket and passed it to him. "Now, would you like to write down the name and contact information for this location scout? Or did you want to give me the original letter she sent you and I'll track her down from that?"

If his sister were digging in her heels about anything else, he would have applauded her fierce defense of family and business. But Cody didn't appreciate her efforts when they flew in the face of what he wanted for the Black Creek Ranch.

"I don't know what I did with her letter." But he took the phone and typed Jillian's name on the notes screen. "This is her name, though. She was staying at the Cheyenne Suites last I heard."

He'd asked Jillian that when he walked her to her

car, wanting to make sure she didn't have far to drive in the rain.

Scarlett raised an eyebrow, but didn't comment as she took back the phone and jammed it in her pocket.

"Thank you. I'll get out of your way now." Turning on her heel, she flounced toward the open door and out into the afternoon sun, the wind ruffling her dark hair.

He wanted to tell her that there was no way in hell he was letting a production company onto the family land, no matter what she said. Yet sometimes these disagreements fizzled out before he had to draw a line in the sand. With five siblings, he'd learned a few things about dealing with conflict over the years.

Still, seeing the determined set to his sister's chin as they'd argued told him it might not be that easy. He could only hope Jillian wanted to get out of town—and away from him—as much as he needed her gone. Their sizzling chemistry sure didn't pave the way for a smooth working relationship. Her deceit had only made it worse.

No matter how appealing he found the sexy film scout, she had played him from the start. And no amount of cajoling from his family or his baby sister would make that okay.

How dare Cody stomp on family opportunities without consulting a single one of his siblings?

Scarlett marched out of the equipment shed, phone in hand, to follow up on the film prospect her oldest brother had tried to ruin for them all. Did he have any idea how hard she and Madeline had worked to reach an audience beyond Wyoming? Or how hard Brock had worked, for that matter, to raise awareness about his quarter horses? The exposure a film could bring would make a huge difference to them all—and they'd be paid for it into the bargain.

Not to mention her own reasons for wanting this film to happen. She'd longed to get out of this town—out of ranching—for years. She'd tried to move to the West Coast after college to pursue an acting career, but her father had applied a first-class guilt trip, convincing her that she owed the family four years of her time and talent, since they'd financed her education. Too bad he hadn't made that clear *before* she went to Purdue University, since, with her grades, she could have gone to a state school for free—which would have eliminated his leverage for making her feel indebted to him. But okay. She'd ignored her urge to pursue acting and done the family thing like a dutiful daughter. Even though her relationship with her father had always been…tense.

She was the last of six kids and—in her father's eyes—one too many. He'd never made a secret of the fact that his daughters hadn't proved as useful on the ranch as his sons, although Maisie came close. Scarlett had stayed on here to ensure she worked off the cost of her education even though her family could easily finance half the state's tuition if they chose. She refused to be a trust fund baby.

But Scarlett's four years were almost up. And she was more than ready for something different. That acting career she'd once dreamed of wasn't out of the question. She could always go to Hollywood for a year and just see what happened.

Scarlett dialed the hotel her brother had mentioned. "I'd like to speak to a guest," she said when the clerk came on the line. "Jillian Ross, please."

Scarlett slipped through the back door of the old

bunkhouse she called home. Her father had given her a generous budget to remodel it. At first she'd refused, knowing she didn't want to be stuck in Wyoming for long. But when he shot down her simple renovation plans, insisting he wanted the grounds of the ranch to have an updated look for visitors, Scarlett had thrown herself into the task.

Now the bunkhouse had higher ceilings with exposed beams. The barn-style exterior had been modernized with heavy retractable doors that could be raised on temperate days. Tall posts supported the deep, extended roof that sheltered porches on two sides of the building. Indoors, an open floor plan allowed her to see the living area, kitchen and family room from the seat she took at the breakfast bar. She grabbed a sheet of notepaper from the sleek concrete counter as the hotel representative came back on the phone.

"Ms. Ross is not currently a guest with us, ma'am," the woman informed her. "We're not allowed to give out more information than that."

Damn it. Had she left town?

Thanking the woman, Scarlett disconnected the call and opened her browser to search Jillian Ross online. She found her profile immediately. A gorgeous redhead with short auburn curls... It was easy to find the name of her production firm.

Scanning the company's list of projects, Scarlett discovered a modern Western that might be the film Jillian was working on. For the heck of it, she did a search on that, too.

And found a man's name she knew well.

Logan King.

Everything inside her went still. It couldn't be a coincidence. She'd met him—then, a small-time actor—a few months ago on a flight to Los Angeles when she'd taken a shopping trip for her mother's birthday. They'd flirted. Kissed. Had an incredible surprise night together. She had thought it was about more than lust, and grew certain the feeling was mutual when they'd messaged each other for a few weeks afterward. Then he'd mysteriously stopped texting. Had vanished. She'd been ghosted.

Since then, he'd had a big breakout movie. She'd been slammed with images of him all over social media, endless reminders of how forgettable she'd been for him. How dispensable.

Could there be a chance he might really come here? To her home turf? Anger simmered through her all over again as she remembered their night together. The hurt of the aftermath. He'd made it clear that his Hollywood career was more important than a fling with her.

Her brain raced with half-formed revenge schemes, each more outrageous than the last. What she really wanted was to tell him off to his face. But in *his* hometown, not hers. She couldn't wait around for him to show up in Cheyenne, possibly with some new actress girlfriend on his arm. Somehow, she needed to tell him exactly what she thought of him before then.

She had to hurry and change for her fly-fishing expedition back at the White Canyon Ranch. But first, she looked up Logan on one of the star-watcher sites to find out where he'd been spotted last. Just in case one of her revenge schemes came together. She also left a message for Jillian Ross at her production company.

Because Scarlett's primary concern was making sure the whole family's interests were represented. There was no reason Madeline's guest ranch shouldn't benefit from the movie exposure. And maybe Scarlett would make some valuable contacts in the business, too.

But if she could also find a way to confront Logan King and tell him he could go to the devil? So much the better.

Five

Steering her rental car down a public access road that bordered Carson McNeill's Creek Spill Ranch, Jillian tried to picture the landscape standing in for the property where she truly wanted the film to be shot—Cody's Black Creek Ranch with that gorgeous, iconic barn as a backdrop.

It was tough to imagine her original plan coming together now. Not after what had happened between them. Cody had taken her number and told her he would call the next day, but all of Saturday had passed without a word. The silence shouldn't have bothered her, since she'd wanted a simple, no-strings encounter. And yet... she couldn't deny the sting that came with not hearing from him.

She'd checked out of her hotel room in town this morning, planning to register at the White Canyon

Ranch tonight. It was yet another property owned by a McNeill sibling. The family possessed the second most acreage in the state, so they were a powerful voice in the ranching community. That could hurt Jillian's cause, of course, if they banded together and refused her request. But the McNeills were a large and disparate group of individuals with wide-ranging interests and pursuits. Surely one of them could be swayed to compromise with her. Two executives from Jillian's company had already booked flights this week to visit the location.

She couldn't give up her quest yet because this job was her means to an important end—her ticket to seeing all the places she'd promised herself she would go after her treatments. Life was too short to live in the shell she'd been stuck in before cancer struck.

Even though Cody had shut her down after their surprise encounter, she still had options. She could find a way to salvage this trip and keep her job.

Her cell phone chimed and she pulled off to one side of the road to take the call, high grass brushing the passenger door as the tires dipped onto the shoulder. She didn't recognize the number, but it was local.

"Jillian Ross," she answered, as she moved the gearshift to Park, wondering if her earlier inquiries had paid off. She'd left messages for both Carson and Madeline, hoping one of them could accommodate the film crew.

Or reason with their stubborn brother.

"Jillian." The male voice on the other end made her pulse quicken. "This is Cody."

He put the slightest emphasis on his name, giving the simple sentence a whole wealth of subtext. That subtle reminder about the identity mix-up, delivered in his sexy voice, stirred all kinds of feelings inside her.

Resentment, maybe. A little embarrassment. And, no matter that she wished otherwise, a whole boatload of attraction.

"Hello." She rolled down her window before switching off the engine, wanting to feel the Wyoming breeze on her suddenly warm face.

"I hope I didn't catch you at a bad time."

"No." She stared out over fields of golden hay waving gently under the bluest sky she'd ever seen. There wasn't another car or person in sight. "I'm just surprised to hear from you after the way we parted."

She closed her eyes, breathing in the scent of roadside wildflowers. Yarrow and daisies. Some tiny yellow blossoms she didn't recognize. She was determined to take joy in this trip, even if she failed in her quest and lost her job. Her dreams of travel and adventure had gotten her through the darkest hours of her disease.

"That's why I'm calling." He paused a beat, and she opened her eyes, surprised. "To apologize about that. No doubt I overreacted."

Hope shot through her. Maybe he was giving her a second chance to film on the ranch? Or maybe he wanted to see her again? She really shouldn't want the latter. But she couldn't deny how the idea ran through her brain, tantalizing her.

"When you didn't phone yesterday, I assumed I wouldn't hear from you again." She picked at a loose thread on the leather steering wheel cover.

"Sometimes I'm slow to think my way through things," he admitted. "But my youngest sister made a point of reminding me I don't speak for the whole family when it comes to the McNeill lands."

So he was calling about the film. Part of her rejoiced

that there was a chance he would reconsider. But she couldn't help a small twinge of regret that his call had nothing to do with what they had shared.

"Should I get in touch with your sister?" Jillian asked quickly, sweeping aside her disappointment that this wasn't a more personal conversation.

"Actually, I hoped I could give you a tour of the ranch," he offered, his voice a warm rumble in her ear. "Show you some of the drawbacks that might make you reconsider where you want to film."

She would see him again. A hidden, secret part of her feminine self stretched and preened like a satisfied cat. She closed her eyes to shut out the feeling, impatient with all the wrong-headed instincts that had landed her in his arms in the first place.

"But a tour might further convince me that the Black Creek Ranch is the ideal location." She wondered if she'd meet this sister he'd mentioned.

"I'll take the chance." He sounded sure of himself. "When would be a good time for you to come? How much longer will you be in town?"

"I'm close to the ranch right now," she admitted, knowing she could be at Cody's place in ten minutes, tops. "How's today?"

She was met with silence for a long moment.

"Today is fine," he said finally. "Drive straight to the main house. I'll meet you out front. Assuming, of course, you know the way here?"

He knew perfectly well she'd been trespassing when she had scouted the location the first time.

"I'll manage." She started the engine on the rental car, a surge of anticipation firing through her. "See you soon."

Disconnecting the call, Jillian contemplated her best approach. For starters, she'd take the scenic route to the Black Creek Ranch. No sense revealing she'd been lurking just around the corner from his property, contemplating how to get in touch with Carson.

Based on what had transpired between her and Cody Friday night, the news that she was still trying to meet with his twin wouldn't be well received.

She was excited to see him again, but she couldn't let that attraction draw her into doing something that would risk her job. And there was beginning to be hope on that front. Jillian might have allies in some of his siblings, particularly his sister. But she needed to work fast now that executives from her company were coming into Cheyenne this week.

She would be sharp, professional and keep an ear out for any way to get an agreement signed with the McNeills. And perhaps most important, keep squarely focused on business around the man who'd shown her a kind of physical pleasure she might never experience again.

Absently pulling a few weeds out of the cook's cottage garden by the main house, Cody steeled himself to see Jillian Ross again.

He'd had nearly two whole days to process what had happened between them and put it behind him. He hadn't.

If it hadn't been for Scarlett's objections, he wouldn't be seeing Jillian at all. He would have called, as he'd promised, but just to make sure their night together hadn't had consequences. He wasn't a careless man, and the way he'd lost his head with her that night didn't sit well.

Cody heard a car pulling into the driveway, followed by a sudden chorus of barking dogs. Straightening, he dusted off his hands and turned to see Jillian waving tentatively at the animals from the driver's side of her car as she parked.

Cody whistled, bringing the two border collies and the Australian shepherd to his side while Jillian got out of the vehicle and strode toward him. She was as colorful as he remembered. The red hair and bright turquoise boots were the same as the other night. But today she wore dark jeans and a tan blouse with Aztec designs embroidered in green, red and yellow beads around the tassel ties down the placket.

"Thanks for calling off the dogs." She grinned down at them. "They looked friendly, but I wasn't sure what they thought of strangers. May I pet them?"

The canine trio looked longingly at her, tails wagging. At least they minded their manners, sitting still for the moment.

"Sure. Start with Hammer." Cody pointed to the Australian shepherd. "He sets the tone for the younger two."

"As older siblings do." She met his gaze, her hazel eyes teasing. Then she turned her attention to the dog, scratching him behind one ear. "Hello, Hammer."

"How did you know I was the oldest?" He wondered how much research she'd done on the family in her quest to access his land.

"I didn't." She petted the collies as they hopped up to meet her without being asked. "I just knew you were the older twin because you mentioned it the other night."

He didn't recall that, but then, he'd been fairly pre-occupied.

"That's Gomez and Morticia, by the way." He pointed out which dog was which and she patted them briefly before they trotted off to seek shade. "The younger ones never think the rules apply to them."

"Is that so?" She tucked a springy curl behind one ear as she faced him.

Something about the gesture triggered a vivid memory of Friday night, of his face buried in that honeysuckle-scented hair, her arms twined around his neck as he kissed her deeply. Blinking, he forced aside the thought.

"Are you a younger sibling?" He waved her toward the equipment shed, where he'd gassed up one of the Gator utility vehicles to show her around.

Hammer rose, too, following Cody, as was the dog's habit.

"I'm an only child, so sibling dynamics fascinate me." She walked quickly beside him, making him realize he was burning a path to the shed like he was being chased by a grizzly.

He slowed down, leading her to the small lot beside the shed where the two-seat vehicle was parked.

"Well, I've got two younger brothers, my twin and our other brother, Brock. Then I have three half sisters from my father's second marriage—Madeline, Maisie and Scarlett." He glanced over at Jillian as she stared at the Gator. "I thought I'd drive you around the ranch. Unless you'd rather go on horseback?"

It hadn't occurred to him she might ride.

"This is fine." She nodded. "I've just never seen anything like it. Sort of a modified lawn tractor?"

He laughed. "Hardly. Hop on." He proceeded to take his own seat behind the wheel. "We use this to get around the property quickly, especially for hard-to-reach places where a truck is too heavy. It's quick and economical."

"It looks like you have your own fleet in there." She pointed to the equipment shed, where he kept the tractors and trucks.

"Most days, those are all out in the fields and pastures, but it's quiet around here on Sundays." He switched on the Gator while she fastened her seat belt. "And that brings me to the first of many dangers of ranch life I'll be pointing out on the tour today. Accidents happen all the time with heavy machinery, especially when untrained people are around. Visitors get too close, the operator can't see them and the next thing you know, there's a serious injury."

He knew too many people who'd lost fingers, toes or whole limbs to accidents. She needed to understand why filming around here could be dangerous.

"Maybe we could get most of our shots on a Sunday when it's quiet." She reached for the roll bar on the passenger side while Hammer jumped into the cargo bed behind them.

Cody stepped on the gas, holding back the argument that rose to his lips. His sister would get on his case if she found out he was being too difficult, so it wasn't wise to alienate Jillian before they even got under way. Besides, given the way they'd parted at Wrangler's the other night, he figured it made sense to smooth things over with her. He'd been speechless after what took place. And once he'd learned why she couldn't have children, he'd been so caught off guard he had forgotten to ask about taking the extra precaution of a morning-after pill. Hell, he hadn't known what to say, period.

For now, he focused on driving Jillian around the spread, pointing out some of the outlying buildings and pastures. She asked a few questions about the hay fields and the different breeds of cows, but mostly she seemed to take in the long views. Every now and then she would snap a few photos on her phone.

"It seems idyllic," she observed while they watched a herd of cows grazing on a green hill.

"It's nonstop work." He'd kept her away from most of the ranch activity today, not wanting to get in the way of the foreman and a few others who were putting in hours on the weekend. "And believe me, it's dangerous."

He couldn't give her the impression the ranch was just some scenic spot for touring around.

"You mentioned the equipment."

"Plus the weather. And the animals." He hadn't wanted to share his personal nightmare, but she still seemed convinced this place was nothing but the perfect backdrop for the movie she had in mind. "My mother grew up on a bigger spread than this. She was an experienced rancher. And that didn't save her when she tried to separate a bull from one of the cow pens."

He'd been only four years old at the time, but the memory of seeing his mother downed by that bull had been burned in his brain. He hit the gas harder, but knew he'd never outrun that memory.

"You mean…" Jillian turned her head to him. He sensed the movement even if he didn't see it.

"She died from her injuries three days later." Cody and his brothers had filed into her hospital room to say goodbye. He couldn't recall what he'd said to her. He only remembered his father sitting in the chair beside her—shell-shocked and white as a ghost as he stared at his dying wife.

"Cody, I'm so sorry." Jillian touched the back of his hand where it rested on the steering wheel. "How frightening that must have been for you and your brothers."

He ground his teeth, unwilling to accept condolences for something that should have never happened in the first place. For something preventable. "It taught me to respect the animals and the land."

He glanced at her, hoping she recognized the dangers better now. Her eyes were filled with empathy. But this wasn't about his loss. It was about safety.

Jillian's hand fell away and she nodded. "I understand."

"Good." He didn't want to dwell on the past. He just wanted her to find someplace else to shoot her movie. Somewhere that wouldn't pose risks to her film crew or to his own workers. Or his cattle, for that matter. He hoped he'd talked her out of her plans by telling her about his own tragedy.

They continued the tour. About ten minutes later, he stopped the vehicle, and she stood up and turned three hundred and sixty degrees, shielding her eyes from the sun as she drew deep breaths. He couldn't help but be drawn to her.

"What do you think?" he asked. They were near a shallow creek between grazing fields. He was resting this pasture now, giving the plants time to regenerate. There wasn't much to see.

She stood tall beside him, resting her elbows on the high roll bar as she looked out over the hills.

"I know it's a dangerous place, but I still think it's

incredibly beautiful." The warm sincerity in her words stirred something in him. Sunlight turned the tips of her hair yellow, giving her a special glow. "I've never seen so much nature. So few people." She tipped her head sideways and glanced down at him. "I'm used to crowds everywhere, and this is just so peaceful."

He nodded, understanding. And he was grateful to have moved the conversation away from his past. "Whenever I go to Denver or Dallas—any of the bigger cities where we have business—I think about that. How there are too many people and not enough of this."

They shared a moment of common ground, soaking in the serenity of the ranch. This was why he was determined not to unleash a film crew on this quiet land. Not to trample the beauty.

Beside him, Jillian let go of the roll bar and lowered herself back into the seat. Hammer jumped down from the cargo bed to sniff around in the weeds.

"I took this job to travel. To see things like this." Her hazel eyes, more green than gold in the sunlight, remained fixed on the horizon. "I realized last year that travel is really important to me."

The sense of kinship with her faded as Cody realized she wasn't taken by *this* land so much as seeing new places. Jillian Ross wouldn't be sticking around Cheyenne, no matter how beautiful she might think it was.

"Because of your illness?" he asked, remembering what she'd said about the radiation and chemo. He'd been curious Friday night, but it hadn't been the right time to ask.

Was now the right time? He wasn't sure where any of this would lead with her, but if there was any chance she carried his child, he would need to get to know her much better. And even if she didn't, he at least wanted to stay in touch with her for the next few weeks—until she knew for sure one way or another. He couldn't afford to alienate her.

She nodded once. A quick affirmative. "I made a list of life adventures." He recognized the defensive stance as she folded her arms around herself. He'd seen it that night in his office when she'd admitted she couldn't have children. "It seemed like a productive thing to think about during my treatments. A way to focus on something positive."

He couldn't imagine what that must have been like for her. And she had no siblings. Had her parents been with her? A partner? If she'd had one then, he obviously hadn't stuck around long afterward. A surge of defensiveness on her behalf moved him to place a hand on her shoulder, offering whatever comfort he could for a memory that must be painful.

"I'm sorry you had to go through that." He wasn't sure how much to ask about it. "Have you been in remission long?"

A sad smile pulled at her lips while she watched Hammer take a half-hearted nip at a butterfly. She shook her head. "I won't be considered in remission for three more years, so I've got a long road ahead of me yet."

"Ah, hell." He squeezed her shoulder through the thin blouse. It didn't compute that this vibrant woman could be so vulnerable. "I didn't realize..."

"Of course not." Her smile, though still sad, was more genuine this time. Her hand landed on his knee. "You couldn't possibly know. It's awkward for people to talk about, but I appreciate you acknowledging my journey. Breast cancer—any cancer—is scary."

No wonder she hadn't been worried about pregnancy. Her body had been through hell, and not all that long ago. He regretted raising a topic that had to be difficult for her. For a moment, the only sound was a plane far overhead and the snuffle of the dog as he searched the grass.

"So you fought back by plotting your life's adventures." Cody's fingers stroked the nape of her neck, the skin barely covered by her red curls. New hair, he guessed. Regrowth after her treatments.

All of her seemed suddenly more fragile, even though he guessed she would hate that description. Her eyes mesmerized him. Her lips parted for a moment when he caressed the side of her throat, trailing a knuckle behind one ear. The touch that began as comfort had become something else entirely.

"It started out as me daydreaming about things I wanted to do. I'd gone to school for accounting and I'm good at it. But I did it because it was reliable—good job security and a decent living." Her fingers curled on his knee, squeezing lightly through the denim. "Once I got cancer, though, I asked myself if that was enough reason to do something I didn't really enjoy for one third of the hours in my day."

"And you decided it wasn't." A gust of wind slanted the grass in the pasture. Hammer sniffed the air before returning to nosing the ground.

"Not at first. It took weeks of me thinking about all the other things I wanted to do with my life if I had the chance to do it over again." She stared down at her hand where it rested on his knee. "Then, one day when

I was sick out of my mind and miserable—my personal cancer rock bottom—I decided I owed myself that do-over. If it was in my power to make it happen, I would."

He couldn't possibly know how hard that battle had been for her. But he admired her strength and conviction.

She straightened in her seat, her hand sliding away from his knee, the moment of connection broken. Or maybe she simply didn't want to share any more with him. They'd had a sizzling encounter together, but they sure didn't know each other well.

Against his better judgment, however, Cody found himself wanting to know more about Jillian Ross. He couldn't seem to force himself to pull his fingers from her neck. His hand lingered the same way his thoughts did—on her.

"And here you are." He watched the way the sunlight played on her pale skin. "Living your adventure on a ranch in Cheyenne."

"It's a long way from Reseda, the Los Angeles neighborhood I grew up in." She pointed toward a pronghorn buck emerging from a thicket at the edge of a field. "I need a photo of that."

Digging in her leather handbag, she came up with her phone. Cody forced himself to slide his hand away from her while she lined up the image she wanted on the view screen. After she snapped a few pictures, she tucked the phone away and they watched the buck stalk across the field. Cody saw all kinds of deer and elk around the ranch frequently enough, but it had been a long time since he'd simply sat and watched something like that. Her breathless appreciation made him see the common sight with new eyes.

He whistled for Hammer, putting the utility vehicle in motion again after the dog hopped in back.

"Can I ask what other adventures are on that list of yours?" Cody asked as they headed back toward the main house. He hadn't gotten to all of his concerns about the dangers of ranch life during this tour, but now wasn't the right time.

His sister's concerns that he'd shut down the film crew without consulting anyone else had resonated. He wanted to at least be able to tell Scarlett that he'd taken the time to show Jillian around without scaring her off completely.

That didn't mean he'd changed his mind about hosting a movie production at the ranch. Still, even if she was sure that pregnancy wasn't a possibility for her, he planned to keep her close for the next few days. Just until he could convince her to get a blood test and rule out the chance of a baby.

Besides, he couldn't deny an interest in the film scout. Spending more time with her wasn't going to be a hardship.

"Mostly travel, but there are some other experiences I've never had that are on the list." She began counting things off on her fingers. "Hear a world-renowned symphony orchestra in concert. Take a ballet class. Study Italian. Bungee jump. See a rodeo—"

"A rodeo?"

"I've never been to one." She shrugged. "It sounds fun."

"You know Wyoming is the called the Cowboy State for a reason." He pushed the gas pedal harder as they got back onto well-traveled roads closer to the house. Hammer stuck his nose between them for a better view ahead.

"I've seen a wealth of Stetsons since I stepped off the plane." She reached over to stroke the dog's head.

"And they're converging on Cheyenne for Frontier Days. The bull-riding finals are in town this week, the biggest rodeo of all."

"Really?" She peeked at him around Hammer's head. "I saw some signs about that, but guess I didn't look too carefully at when it took place."

"Maybe you should stick around town a little longer so you can cross another adventure off that list." He drew to a stop in front of the equipment shed not far from her car. The shepherd jumped down from the cargo bed, leaving the two of them alone.

Jillian's eyes veered to his, her windblown curls teasing her cheeks as she seemed to weigh the idea. "That sounds fun. And I was thinking about checking out your sister's guest ranch, anyhow."

So she'd been planning to stick around. Of course she had. She wasn't giving up so easily on her plan to talk him into hosting the film crew. Although she would go home disappointed on that score, maybe they could make a few other pleasurable memories. The attraction between them sure hadn't dimmed.

"Tuesday night, then." He skimmed a touch over her cheek, just enough to brush away a curl. He liked seeing the way her pupils dilated and her lips parted slightly. "It's a date."

Six

In her bathroom at the White Canyon guest ranch two days later, Jillian brushed her hair carefully, a habit she'd developed in the early stages of regrowth. Cody would arrive to pick her up shortly and she was excited about seeing the rodeo together. Excited to see him— far more than she should have been, given their stand-off over his granting permission to film on his lands.

Jillian forced herself to set down the hairbrush and quit primping. As much as she admired cancer patients who could bare their bald heads in defiance of the disease, she'd developed a tingling sensitivity in her scalp that had persisted for months. She'd felt cold and naked in so many ways during her treatments, and the lack of hair only added to her sense of being exposed. She'd worn head scarves with abandon, taking inspiration from women of other cultures who kept their heads wrapped. Now, even with the wild curls that covered her skull, she sometimes missed the warmth of the scarves.

Today, however, she would have Cody beside her and that would keep her plenty warm. He wasn't due to arrive for another ten minutes, but as she slid her phone in her purse, she heard the familiar rumble of his voice downstairs.

Was he laughing?

Curious, Jillian slipped from her room and stood beside the heavy wooden railing overlooking the huge foyer below. Madeline McNeill, the proprietor of the White Canyon, sat on the long leather bench in front of the huge windows near the front door. Two other women flanked her; the three of them shared enough physical similarities that they had to be related. They were gathered around an open box full of snowshoes, as the one who seemed the youngest attempted to withdraw her expensive-looking high heel from its snowshoe clamps.

Cody stood with his back to Jillian, facing the women, his good-natured chuckle surprising her.

Until she realized it wasn't Cody at all.

She saw her chance to speak to Carson McNeill personally and hurried downstairs to join them.

"Jillian," Madeline called to her as she entered the foyer. "Do you have a minute? I would like to introduce you to some of the family."

"I'd like that." Her gaze went to Carson first, and it surprised her that a man who looked the same as Cody could be so different.

This one didn't have the same physical effect on her. No warmth, no spark. But his smile was the kind that made you want to smile back, and she did.

"This is my mother," Madeline began, pointing to the older woman in the corner of the window seat. "Paige McNeill."

"Nice to meet you." Jillian stepped forward, dodging the obstacle course of snowshoes, and squeezed the woman's hand. She couldn't be much older than her midforties, slim and beautiful, with medium honey-colored hair and light green eyes.

"You, too, Jillian." Her gaze skittered away, though her brief smile seemed genuine.

Jillian didn't have long to puzzle over the half-hearted reception before the younger woman sidled up to her. She shared Madeline's long dark hair and blue eyes, but her bangs and curls gave her more of an ingenue look.

"I'm Scarlett, Maddy's sister, and I'm excited to have a movie filmed on McNeill land." She extended her hand, and Jillian saw that her pink-manicured nails were decorated with palm trees. She wore a blue-and-white-polka-dot scarf around her head, a big bow tied behind her hair with the ribbon's ends trailing over one shoulder. "I've already talked Carson into letting a film crew stay at his ranch if Cody doesn't come through for you."

Jillian thought she noticed Paige McNeill frown before she turned to gaze out the front window. "Cody won't like that," the older woman murmured, mostly to herself, while Scarlett slid a hand around Jillian's elbow and turned her toward Cody's twin.

"This is Carson, the most reasonable of my half brothers."

Jillian reached to shake his hand, but he was holding the aqua-colored high heel shoe he'd helped Scarlett with earlier. He thrust it at his sister and wiped his palm on his jeans before taking Jillian's hand and squeezing it.

"Welcome to Cheyenne, Ms. Jillian. My ranch is all yours whenever you need it."

Jillian thought back to the photos she'd seen of Carson McNeill online and realized she would never confuse him for Cody again. There was a charm about him, for sure—in his pleasing voice and warm smile. Yet having gone through a painful journey herself, she recognized a person battling a deeper hurt, and saw that same starkness in Carson's eyes.

"Thank you. The executives at my company are really sold on the Black Creek for our project, but if I can persuade them to use your ranch instead, I will gladly do so." She'd need to make the decision soon. The shooting location manager and the film's director would touch down in Cheyenne tomorrow.

"No luck convincing my brother to let you on his land yet?" Carson asked, while Madeline stacked up the snowshoes and returned them to their box.

"No." Jillian felt oddly disloyal talking about Cody with his family when he wasn't there. "I understand he has concerns about the potential dangers."

The room went quiet for an instant. Even Madeline paused briefly in packing up the snowshoes. Jillian thought she saw a flash of anger, or maybe hurt, in Carson's gaze. And then it was gone.

"The oldest son is always the responsible one," he said drily. "Looks like my twin is here now." He nodded toward the window. Cody's pickup truck was pulling into the driveway. "Just keep in mind my offer. I know the exposure a film could bring would mean a lot to the rest of the family."

He tipped his dark Stetson ever so subtly before stalking toward the kitchen—which was the opposite direction from where his brother was about to enter the room.

Scarlett picked up the theme of the conversation. "We're all really excited about it and flattered you like the area. I read online a little about your company's films. Are you scouting for *Winning the West*?"

"I am." Impressed that Cody's sister had researched the project, Jillian had new appreciation for how valuable an ally the woman might be.

From the window seat, Paige leaned toward them, her honey-colored ponytail falling forward over one shoulder. "You know, Scarlett, not everyone wants to be stuck on a movie set in the middle of nowhere. The actors might be happier if the filming took place in Colorado or someplace closer to LA." She looked to Jillian for support. "I'm sure it must make it easier on the talent to be closer to home. And cheaper."

She seemed so hopeful that Jillian would agree with her; it was obvious Paige wasn't wild about the idea of having a movie crew on her doorstep. Because of the potential dangers Cody had mentioned? Or was there another reason?

Madeline was currently busy taking a phone call, and Scarlett didn't seem to notice her mother's reservations as she scrolled through pages on her phone. "I'm sure they don't care where it's filmed, Mom," she said distractedly. "And it looks like I can get Gramps's pilot to fly me to LA tomorrow, after all, so I'm going to need the day off." Scarlett shot to her feet, her floral skirt swinging around her knees as she headed toward the door.

Cody entered the foyer then, tipping his hat to Scarlett and her mother, who was following fast on her daughter's heels.

"Isn't that kind of sudden?" Paige was saying as they walked away. "If you want to shop, I can go to New York with you..."

The sound of their voices faded as they slipped outside.

Jillian turned her attention to Cody. His broad shoulders filled out his gray Western-cut shirt, and his dark jeans were an upgrade from the work denim she had seen him in last time. His blue eyes lasered in on her and a familiar warmth made her skin tingle.

"Are you ready to rodeo?" he asked, holding out his hand.

The flutter in her belly was an indication of just how ready she was. Now that Carson had offered his ranch for filming, some of the pressure was off. Except the unforgettable views she wanted were still on Cody's land, not his brother's.

And she had the feeling that housing her crew on his twin's property would seem like a betrayal. Maybe tonight, she could change Cody's mind.

"I'm ready." Taking his hand, she gave herself over to at least one more adventure with the rancher who was filling her dreams lately.

Seeing the worry in her eyes, Cody wrapped an arm around Jillian during the last ride of the night. Taking her to the bull-riding finals was sort of like bringing a first date to a scary movie. She gripped his arm every time the chute opened to release another rider into the arena, her fingers squeezing tight while she cheered for every single one of them.

"Did he win?" she asked, when the crowd erupted in cheers after the reigning champ held on for all eight seconds.

Cody chuckled. "It's always a win when you don't end up being dragged by your boot through the dirt. But they're just cheering for his good ride, and because he gets to compete again in the second round of the finals tomorrow."

The dust and the noise rose as the cowboy pumped his fist and the rodeo clowns worked to distract the bull.

"Tomorrow?" She shook her head. "I would think one ride like that in a lifetime was enough." Smiling, she patted her chest. "I don't think I could take the adrenaline spike every day."

"They train hard for this, though. No one ends up riding a bull unless they love the sport." Cody led her out of their row of seats, wanting to show her more of Frontier Days than just the rodeo. There was a whole carnival waiting outside, with live music and plenty of attractions. "Carson competed for a long time until he broke so many bones our father threatened to give Creek Spill to someone else unless Carson quit the sport."

"And that worked?" Jillian frowned, glancing up at Cody. "I only met him briefly, but he didn't strike me as the kind of man who would respond well to an ultimatum."

"He didn't. But by the time he was healed up and ready to start training again, his fiancée left him for another guy on the tour. Carson decided it wasn't worth circulating in that world again."

"How awful." She took Cody's hand as they wound

their way out of the arena. The temperature outside had dropped, but was still mild.

Midway lights flashed red, green and blue in every direction and a big wooden ride on a pendulum swooshed past them overhead. The scents of funnel cakes and hot turkey legs was heavy in the air.

"Though it may have saved Carson from hurting himself even more. I think he's got screws holding him together."

"Still, it has to hurt to see a dream die like that." She wrapped her arms around herself.

"Sooner or later, he would have had to come home and face the reality of running the family business anyhow." Cody had pulled his brother's weight for too long as it was. He rubbed a hand along Jillian's back, feeling the delicate curve at the base of her spine. "Are you warm enough?"

"I'm fine." She nodded, but she looked chilled. "I don't think that pursuing a dream means you're not facing reality. Some people might argue that our dreams are the most important reality we have. They anchor us and make life worth living."

He'd touched a nerve. "It's different for Carson."

"Because he's not a cancer survivor?" she quickly retorted. "That doesn't make his dreams any less important."

"Wait." Cody drew a deep breath and hoped she would, too. "I didn't mean to suggest that. Selfishly, I'm glad Carson's focus is back on our business. And for his sake, I'm relieved he's still in one piece, because you saw how dangerous bull riding can be."

She nodded stiffly, accepting his answer.

"I know my parents aren't supportive of my new direction in life, because they perceive it as irresponsible. So I can't help but empathize with your brother." She rubbed a hand along her arm again. "And I am getting a little chilly."

He nodded, looking up and down the midway at the shops, grateful for the change of subject. "Let's keep walking." He picked up the pace.

"Sometimes I think being cold is psychosomatic. You know what it's like when you wake up from surgery and the drugs are making you cold?" She glanced up at him as they neared the vendors showing their wares. "They slow your heart rate or something? It's like that, where I feel like I'm chilled on the inside."

He imagined that her surgeries to remove tumors had been scarier than most, especially with the added fear that they might not be able to excise all the cancer. He hated that she'd been through that. Hated that he couldn't do anything to change the past for her. But he could do one thing for her now, at least. Looking around the carnival, Cody spotted what he needed. He led her toward a big, well-lit display from a local Western clothing supplier. He brought her to the women's flannel shirts and held up a red one.

Smiling, she looked down at herself with the shirt in front of her. "Doesn't it clash with my hair?"

"I like you in bright colors." He enjoyed seeing the vivid splash of hues all around this vibrant woman. He grabbed another one, which was purple and blue. "How about this?"

He could tell by her expression she liked it. There was a little flicker of interest in her eyes, maybe. He wondered when he'd started to notice those small details about her.

"Purple is more me," she admitted, unbuttoning it to try it on. She went to a full-length mirror hanging on one of the posts holding up the display and slid her arms into the sleeves. The shirt fit perfectly.

Cody popped off the tag and gave it to a hovering saleswoman in a crisp white Stetson.

"I can get it," Jillian protested. "I want to pay my own way."

"Not a chance. You're my guest." He passed over the cash and told the woman to keep the change. Then he returned to Jillian's side and watched as she buttoned up the shirt. "If you want the full rodeo experience, you need a souvenir."

"The full rodeo experience?" Smoothing the collar down to her satisfaction, she turned from the mirror and faced him. "In that case, thank you."

Her hazel eyes were more gold tonight, reflecting the lights of the carnival midway. He couldn't deny the pull of attraction, the desire to get closer to her. Their fast and furious time together in his office Friday night hadn't eased his need for her in the least. Now there was a new element to his feelings for her, too. The urge to protect her.

"We're not done yet." His gaze dipped to her lips, and he remembered how she tasted.

"We're not?" Her voice softened as her eyes locked on his.

Even more than he wanted to kiss her, he wanted to shield her from any more blows life tried to deal her. To make her smile.

"Not by half." He lowered his head to speak into her ear, inhaling the scent of her hair. "It's not a rodeo without a turkey leg."

* * *

Two hours later, Jillian looked out the passenger-side window of Cody's pickup truck, warmed by her new flannel shirt and the cowboy in the driver's seat. She hadn't necessarily expected to share the adventures from her list with another person, but she had to admit that attending the rodeo with Cody McNeill had been fun. She'd tasted the funnel cake, a turkey leg and even a few bites of a caramel apple that had been out of this world.

Or maybe everything had tasted delectable because of the company she kept. Because she'd been thinking about kissing him every time he offered her a bite.

Now, as the truck rumbled up the long driveway of the White Canyon guest ranch, she wondered how the night would end. She knew they couldn't take things any further than the front seat of his truck would allow. Not with his half sister watching over the foyer.

Of course, Jillian couldn't allow their attraction to sway her into making another bad decision, anyhow. She had thought a night with him sounded sexy and exciting when she was thinking solely of her life adventures and how much this man reawakened her senses. But that had been before she knew him better. Before she realized how much "adventure" was out of character for this fiercely practical, responsible rancher.

He wouldn't be kissing her senseless again anytime soon. Not when he viewed their encounter at Wrangler's as a deception on her part. After all, he'd accused her of trying to circumvent him by seducing his "twin."

"Everything okay?" he asked her as he pulled up to the White Canyon. "You've been quiet the whole ride home."

He parked the truck and pocketed the keys. Landscaping lights around a few prominent cottonwoods illuminated the walkway to the wide front stairs of the guest ranch.

"Just thinking about what's next," she admitted, shifting to see him better as she slid off her seat belt. "Debating if I should give up asking you to film at the Black Creek or—"

"Yes," he told her flatly. "That's not happening."

Frustration that he hadn't even given her a chance to get out the rest of her proposal and plead her case simmered.

"Then you should know your brother already offered to house the production crew at the Creek Spill." She didn't even realize she'd made up her mind to accept that offer until she heard the words roll off her tongue. But what choice did Cody give her?

She'd have to find a way to talk the film executives into the alternate location.

"You already spoke to Carson about this?" His blue eyes narrowed as he stared at her from across the dim truck cab. "Without telling me?"

"You knew I was interested in filming up here," she reminded him. "And that I had planned to speak to Carson at some point—"

"I remember you were plotting to intercept Carson all along. Even before I landed in your path Friday and confused things." His jaw flexed and a shadow crossed his expression. "I imagine my twin was very accommodating."

She didn't appreciate his implication or his tone, since she wasn't the kind of woman to pit brother against brother. Yet even through the crackle of frustration, she felt the pull of this man in the small, enclosed space. Remembered the way it had felt to be pressed against him, peeling off each other's clothes. To distract herself from those thoughts, she stared out at the night sky full of stars.

"Scarlett approached him before I did. Apparently, she thinks a film shot here will boost the profile of the other McNeill businesses besides ranching."

"Of course she does. She met an actor on a flight to LA a few months ago and it reignited her old hope of trying her luck in Hollywood." Cody shifted in his seat, his voice a rumble that vibrated through her. "I'm sure she sees a film in Cheyenne as a way to brighten up her otherwise boring life. She's a typical twenty-five-year-old."

Jillian told herself this wasn't her family and she had no reason to weigh in with her opinion. But in light of her own journey, she found it too hard to keep her feelings to herself. She was probably more let down than she should have been that a man who attracted her so much could feel that way.

"Maybe Scarlett's already seen the way your brother lost out on his bull-riding dream, and she doesn't want to become the next McNeill to sacrifice her future to the good of the ranch." Levering the truck door open, Jillian didn't wait for Cody to help her out. "Not everyone wants to spend their whole life playing it safe."

She shouldn't want a man like Cody—someone so bound to an idea of what was right that he couldn't appreciate the idea of being happy. Before he could argue with her anymore, she said a terse thank-you and goodnight, and exited the truck.

Only to have him catch up to her halfway up the

walkway. He matched her fast gait, opening the door to the guest ranch for her.

"Who says I want to play it safe?" He stared down at her in the porch light, his gaze intense.

Missing nothing.

She'd stopped too close to him. The nearness of his body communicated a whole different set of messages than the conversation they'd been having.

Attraction. Hunger. Desire.

"When it comes to the film—" she struggled to keep a thought in her head as she glanced up at him, breathing in the warm hint of spice from his aftershave, a scent she could almost taste on her tongue in her memories "—you won't risk anyone's safety."

"Correct." He somehow managed to hold the screen door open for her while simultaneously blocking the threshold, his broad shoulders taking up all the room. "I won't risk anyone else's safety. But that doesn't mean I won't consider a gamble of my own."

Her mouth was too dry for conversation. All she really wanted was a kiss. To lose herself in this man. It made no logical sense, since she was frustrated with him and all the ways he was thwarting her career. But she couldn't deny the heavy pulse of blood in her veins. The tingle of anticipation on her skin.

"I don't understand." She shook her head, her hair teasing her oversensitive skin as it brushed her cheek and bare collarbone. "You aren't gambling a damn thing."

Her voice sounded breathless. She felt light-headed.

He backed her up a step, letting the screen door close behind him as he slid his hands around her waist. The sensual impact of that touch flared hot inside her.

"On the contrary." He leaned closer, his lips hovering just above hers. His voice got softer as he breathed the words over her mouth. "I risk my sanity every time I'm next to you, Jillian."

Seven

You're insane.

Scarlett reread her sister Maisie's text as she packed her suitcase for the trip to Los Angeles.

Her flight had been easy to arrange on short notice. It helped that her grandfather had a private plane, a Learjet that he had made available to her, since no one else in the family needed it for the next few days. Her father had tried to warn her that Malcolm McNeill was only attempting to buy her affection, but Scarlett didn't think that was the case. She'd been spending afternoons with her grandfather and his new girlfriend, Rose, learning more about the rest of the family that her father had turned his back on before she was born. Scarlett had met a few of her cousins, including Gabe McNeill, the youngest son of Donovan's brother, Liam.

Scarlett had even flown to Martinique this winter to spend some time with Gabe and his new wife, Brianne.

That trip had brought her closer to the rest of the family, including Rose, a feisty former singer in her eighties, who was Brianne's grandmother. Malcolm treated Rose like royalty, but not just by spending money on her. Yes, he'd bought himself and Rose matching, high-end smartphones, but just so they could download all the apps their family members used and figure them out together over a pot of tea in the afternoon.

It was adorable. Unlike Maisie's texts.

Why insane?? Scarlett texted back, as she studied the contents of her wardrobe critically. Because I'm doing something I want to do instead of what the family expects??

She didn't have to wait long for Maisie's reply.

Because you're surprising him. He ghosted you last year, babe. What makes you think he's going to be happy to see you now?

Scarlett's stomach twisted. It was her own fault for sharing that private pain with her sister in a moment of weakness. She should have never confessed that story to Maisie, of all people, who'd never doubted herself for an instant.

I don't care if he's happy. I plan to tell him in no uncertain terms what I think of him.

Of course, Logan might not be pleased to see her. But even worse was the fear that he might not remember her at all. Scarlett's worst nightmare was being forgettable, a fear her older sisters would never understand. Madeline and Maisie were born secure. They were both smart and beautiful, and had received full-ride scholarships to top-tier universities. They shared the McNeill good looks. And, most important, their father acknowledged them, appreciated their contributions to the family businesses in his own gruff way.

Scarlett looked like their mother—pretty in a way that would fade over time, her beauty a fiction created by silk and bows, accessories and makeup. She was the daughter her mother had wanted and her father hadn't. The baby. The "one too many," according to whispered arguments she'd overheard as a child.

Not that it mattered anymore. Scarlett had stuck around Cheyenne after college more for her mother's sake than to honor her dad's insistence she give something back to the family. Her mom had been deeply unhappy for years, and Scarlett felt no one else noticed.

Perhaps that was why she so fully identified with her mother. No one would notice Scarlett either if she didn't make the effort every day to rise above her average looks. To paint a cat's eye on her lids and swirl glitter in the shadow she used under her brow bone.

Sifting through the outfits of every color in her wardrobe, Scarlett pulled out a dress raided from Madeline's closet long ago, a gold lace stunner from the Halloween when Maddy had dressed as a flapper. Scarlett could picture the fringed hem going well with white leather go-go boots and her dark hair piled on her head in a modified beehive.

She might not be beautiful, but she knew how to look hot.

She was packing the outfit in tissue paper for her trip when her phone chimed again.

That's more like it. Want some backup?

Scarlett felt tempted. But how much satisfaction could she take in her big moment if she needed her sister to hold her hand? No. Better to tell him off on her own.

Steeling herself, she texted back, *I've got this*, and slid her cell phone into her purse.

Scarlett swallowed her fears and zipped up her overnight bag for tomorrow's trip. She wasn't settling for being the also-ran McNeill anymore. She would go to LA and finally step out of the shadows of her successful family members.

And make Logan King eat his sorry heart out.

Kissing Jillian tonight had not been in Cody's plan.

He'd intended only to keep her close for a few more days until he could convince her to get a blood test. After the mishap with the condom, he needed to rule out any chance of pregnancy. Then she'd leave town for good, especially now that his brother had interfered and offered Creek Spill for the filming. Her work was almost done here.

But being with her made Cody want her again. Simple as that. The attraction was as automatic as breathing, happening on its own whether he willed it or not. He could tell the same was true for her, because she'd stormed out of his truck a minute ago and now here they were, inches apart on the front porch of the White Canyon Ranch, unable to keep their hands off each other.

She reached for his face, her fingers trailing down his cheek and along his jaw, her green eyes following the movement before her gaze tracked back to his.

He bent to kiss her, a barely there graze of his lips over hers. She tasted like funnel cake sugar, so sweet he wanted a lick. He took in the feel of her as she wound her arms around his neck, her whole body swaying against him.

"This is crazy," she whispered, as a night breeze blew around them and she pressed closer. "We can't get carried away out here where anyone can see us."

"You're right." Taking her hand in his, he pivoted, drawing her toward the back of the building. "I know a better place."

He didn't want to go in through the front door and risk running into Madeline or any guests who might try to draw them into conversation. He wanted Jillian all to himself. He guided her down one side of the wrap-around porch to steps that led into a rose garden.

"Wait." She halted on the flagstone path between two towering rosebushes, their scent heavy even in the cool evening air. "Why continue this madness? You can't get me out of Wyoming fast enough, but you're willing to sneak me into my hotel up the back stairs so we can…" She shook her head, unwilling to complete the thought.

Cody kept hold of her hand, feeling her pulse throb fast at the base of her palm. A soft, subtle hint of how he affected her.

"Who said I want you to leave? Just because I'm in no hurry to have a movie crew film on my ranch doesn't mean I want you to go." He liked the idea of Jillian sticking around. For one thing, he hoped she'd stay at least until he could convince her to get the blood test.

For another? He wasn't done exploring this attraction. How long could a powerful draw like this last?

He needed to know. And intended to find out with her.

Her eyes searched his. "You mean I've been misreading all your cues? Like when you accused me of plotting to intercept your brother on the night we met?" She arched an eyebrow. "I took that as a sign you weren't pleased about me being in Cheyenne."

The breeze rumpled her curls, which softened the scowl on her face.

Cody wanted to kiss them away from her mouth. To feel the strands of hair on his bare skin. For now, he skimmed them off her cheek.

"You should have read it as a sign that I don't want you to ever look at my brother the way you look at me." He could burn himself on that heated gaze of hers. "Because that's all it meant."

Her mouth worked silently for a moment, then snapped shut.

"And I'm not trying to sneak you up the back stairs to your room right now," he added, remembering the other accusation she'd lobbed at him.

"You're not?" She glanced up at the building.

"No." He leaned closer to speak into her ear. "If you're interested in a little more privacy, I thought you might like seeing The Villa."

A slow smile spread over her face. "There's a villa nearby?" She turned her head back and forth, looking in both directions. "On the grounds of a Wyoming guest ranch?"

"'The Villa' is what we call the only freestanding unit for guests. It's more of a bungalow, but in the literature for this place, my sister labeled it that." Cody led Jillian through the rose garden to the far edge of the grounds. "Apparently, the name helps communicate the level of luxury. It doesn't get rented very often."

"No one's staying there now?" Jillian asked as they arrived at the building in question and stepped onto the lit front porch. In most of its details, The Villa mirrored the look of the main house.

"I am." He took out his master key card printed with the White Canyon logo and passed it to her. "I reserved it just in case."

Her slender fingers wrapped around the key and she stared down at it.

"Just in case..." She flicked the plastic against her nails. "You thought there might be a vicious storm tonight that would prevent you from driving the rest of the way home?"

He shrugged. "That particular scenario didn't occur to me. No."

"I have a perfectly good room upstairs in the main house," she reminded him, settling the edge of the key card on his chest before lightly dragging it down the front of him. "Just in case you suddenly wanted somewhere to stay."

"I wouldn't want the rest of the ranch guests speculating about us if I followed you up those main stairs." He wanted Jillian all to himself. All night long.

He didn't want to spare an extra second of his time fielding questions about how their evening went.

"I don't care what anyone else thinks." Her eyes were serious for a moment, as her hands hovered at his waist. "I let go of worries like that two years ago."

When she'd been treated for cancer. His chest constricted as he thought about her battling for her life.

"I had another reason for wanting this space." He'd messaged the housekeeper from the rodeo to ensure the room was readied the way he wanted. "But only if you're game."

"You know I can't say no to an adventure." Jillian held up the card and moved toward the door.

She slid the plastic into the lock mechanism and the light turned green. He opened the door.

Heat rushed out from the room; the hearth glowed with a freshly laid fire. The scent of applewood and hickory filled the air.

"I thought you might appreciate the warmth of a fire," he said, following her into the room after locking the door behind them. Then he saw the expression on her face.

The naked emotion.

And—damn it to hell. The tear.

Cody McNeill was supposed to be her adventure.

Her wild fling that helped resurrect her long-snoozing sensuality.

He was not supposed to touch her heart with a tenderness that brought her to her knees.

Blinking from the brightness of the fire, Jillian tried to swallow back the sudden tide of emotions threatening to swamp her. She didn't want Cody to see how his kindness affected her. Couldn't bear to expose another piece of her soul.

But when she pivoted on her heel to face him, she could see his hesitation. His careful consideration of her reaction, as though she were a puzzle to solve rather than a sensual woman. By letting her runaway emotions intrude, she'd ruined the mood just when things were getting heated.

So, unwilling to deal with any of it, unable to let her cancer steal this from her, Jillian tossed the key card on the floor and headed toward Cody. She ignored the question in his eyes and flung her arms around his neck.

Then she kissed him like it was her last night on earth.

And his, too.

She worked the fastenings on his shirt with unsteady hands, attraction and emotion fueled by a new frenzy. She craved having his caresses all over her, hot and possessive, to see if this chemistry was as combustible as she remembered. To burn away the tangle of confused feelings until all that was left was passion.

"Jillian." Cody broke the kiss long enough to rasp her name, his chest rising and falling like he'd run a marathon.

Meeting his gaze in the glow of orange firelight, she paused long enough to see what he wanted.

"Are you sure?" His fingers traced a path down one cheek before he tipped her chin up. "About this?"

Her grip tightened on the cotton shirttails she'd dragged from his jeans, the fabric still warm in her hands. "This might be the only thing in the whole world that I'm positive about right now."

His eyes lingered on her for a moment—long enough that she wondered what he saw. A woman desperate to feel desirable? Whole? But no matter. Because a moment later, he nodded. Decision made.

"Come with me." He took her hand and led her into the darker recesses of the guesthouse.

They went through a cool kitchen, where the only light was the glint of the fire reflecting off stainless steel appliances, and past a staircase with a heavy pine banister. They finally arrived at an open door toward the back of the unit. More flickering light emanated from within.

The master bedroom, she realized. There was another fire laid in the simple black hearth. The glow illuminated a king-size sleigh bed with a simple white duvet and a mountain of white pillows in every size. A tea cart near the bed held a white ceramic pitcher, stemware and a few silver-domed platters.

A pewter cup held a bouquet of echinacea flowers in yellow, red and purple.

While she took it all in, Cody drew her forward, deeper into the room that had been so carefully prepared for them.

"You should have a bed this time," he told her simply, explaining his thoughtfulness. "Every time."

He stopped at the edge of the footboard, hooking a finger in her flannel shirt to tug her one step closer. Until there was only a breath between them.

He was so near, and yet it felt like she was standing at the edge of a cliff. Like if she moved forward that fraction of an inch, she would be in free fall, tumbling down into something deep and unknown.

"I'm so ready for this." She said it aloud. To herself. To him.

She didn't know if it was true. But she wanted to lose herself in his touch. His hands.

His answer was a kiss on her cheek. Impossibly gentle, but the start of so much more. She tipped her head back, giving him everything. All of her.

He kissed his way to her ear. Her neck. Down her throat. He undid the rest of the buttons on her shirt, sliding the flannel apart. Tugging the gauzy blouse over her head. Flicking free the clasp of a bra that hid the rumpled knot of scars on one breast.

Last time they were together had been so rushed, so hungry, that she'd never been naked. Never had to worry about the roped surgery marks where the surgeons had operated to remove her tumor, or the patches of pink, shiny skin from radiation therapy.

Threading her fingers through his, she gently steered him away from her breasts, wanting to prepare him.

"My body is…" She blinked, not ready to have this conversation. Not sure how she even felt about her scars. "I just don't want you to be surprised. I'm a little… misshapen."

She didn't feel ashamed, necessarily. She felt proud of her body for surviving. For triumphing.

But at this moment, she wished it was beautiful.

"You're exactly the right shape for a warrior. A survivor. I can't imagine anything more beautiful." His gaze was steady. "Does it bother you to be touched there?"

His words soothed her. Eased her doubts.

"No." She shook her head, a curl grazing her cheek. "It feels good."

"Then I hope you'll let me touch you more." He eased his fingers free from where she'd held him back. "But first I'm going to lay you right in the middle of all those pillows."

His hands spanned her waist and he lifted her. She held on to his shoulders until he dropped her gently in the center of the bed. The cream-colored lace of her bra still fluttered open around her chest, the straps loose on her shoulders.

Cody tugged off her boots and her jeans, setting them aside before he stripped naked. The firelight burnished his skin with a bronze glow. His muscles rippled as he moved: the thick, corded ones in his back, the flat, taut ones of his abs. Her throat went dry as she looked at him.

Then he was with her, using his weight to shift her on the bed as he stretched out. He rested one warm palm on her belly, steadying her while he kissed her throat. Her collarbone. Lower.

She told herself not to worry, but that didn't stop her from tensing when he dragged a thumb along one thick line of scars. Or when he stroked the pink expanse from the radiation burn.

"Your body is a miracle," he whispered over her skin before he licked a path around her nipple, then sucked gently.

Desire flooded through her, hot and fast, drowning her insecurity in a pool of want. By the time he switched his attention to her other breast, she was so distracted by the heat between her thighs she forgot about anything else.

Jillian snaked her leg around his, holding him against her, rocking her hips into his. She wanted more. Now. The ache of waiting coiled tight inside her.

Fingers flexing against his shoulders, she closed her eyes. She knew she wouldn't last long. Not when the tension was mounting every minute.

He slipped a hand between her legs, touching her just where she needed. The pleasure came so hard and fast she shuddered with it, experiencing waves of sweet, tender release. Clinging to him, she let it roll over her. Through her. When the last spasm hit her, she opened her eyes for a moment—just long enough to see him roll a condom in place.

She unwound her arms and legs from him enough that he could move on top of her and position himself between her thighs. Enter her inch by tantalizing inch.

Raining kisses on his chest, his neck, wherever she could reach, Jillian moved with him, wanting him to feel every bit as fulfilled as she already did. The scent of his aftershave, the taste of his skin, burned into her brain a searing memory she'd never forget. She gave herself over to the joining, back arching so he could capture the taut peak of one breast and then the other again. The feel of his tongue there, loving her body where it had been hurt and neglected for so long, was a potent kind of alchemy.

It changed her somehow. Changed how she felt about her body and sex, so that it all seemed unbearably beautiful. Another orgasm built inside her. When it charged through her, she felt it in every nerve ending, all the way to her toes. She held him tight, and his body tensed before a final thrust put him over the edge in turn.

By then, as the last aftershock faded, Jillian was speechless. Awed. Something wonderful had happened for her. A new acceptance of herself. A new joy in her beleaguered body. And this responsible, practical man of few words had wrought that magic with his hands and his quiet tenderness.

It wasn't supposed to happen this way. Not that she regretted this time with him. But she wasn't ready to have the earth moved and her reality shifted by any man. She had a list of adventures to experience and a promise to herself she would not break.

But with her heart already dancing dizzy pirouettes after their charged encounter, Jillian knew she needed space fast. Distance. She rolled away from him while they each caught their breath.

"Cody—"

"Jillian—"

They started talking at the same time.

"You go first," she offered, not even sure what she would have said. How would she tell him that she needed to get back to LA? That she couldn't afford to stick around Cheyenne and fall for a hot rancher with magic in his hands?

"I have a favor to ask." He reached behind her to drag the duvet around her so she was covered. Warm.

"And how clever of you to ask it when I'm swamped with endorphins and still reeling with physical bliss." She tucked the blanket closer to her chin, rolling over to look in his eyes.

His very serious eyes.

It occurred to her too late that Cody might be concocting a plan to give himself space and distance at the same time she was. Her stomach tightened into a knot.

"You've already gotten my brother's okay to film on his land, and I know that means I could wake up any day and find you gone." He brushed her hair from her face, his touch making her pulse flutter even now.

"I have to show the executives from my company around first. Make sure they're okay with using his ranch instead of the one we really want—Black Creek." She wondered if he would ever budge on that issue.

"I understand." He nodded, but didn't offer his ranch.

"Before you leave Cheyenne, I want you to consider having a blood test."

His words hung in the air between them. Jarring.

She hadn't been expecting anything like that. Hadn't realized he was already making a plan for his life once she was gone.

"A blood test." She repeated the words, unable to make the idea reconcile with what they'd just shared. With everything she'd been feeling.

"Yes. A blood test is sensitive enough to detect pregnancy this early." The reasonable, practical Cody reasserted himsclf. "I think we'll both sleep better once we rule out any chance you've conceived."

The bubble of sensual euphoria burst. At least, she hoped that was the only thing breaking inside her. Because his statement rattled the hell out of her.

A chill crept over her despite the blaze roaring in the hearth at the foot of the bed.

"Of course." She straightened, letting the duvet fall away as she searched for her shirt. "If you'll make the appointment, I'll show up." After punching her fists through the armholes of her blouse, she fastened the bra clasp under the fabric, since the straps were still perched on her shoulders. "I wouldn't want you to lose sleep."

He sat the rest of the way up in bed. "Wait a second. Where are you—"

"I'm sorry. I forgot that one of my bosses is flying in first thing tomorrow." She slid on her jeans and stepped into her boots. "I can't afford to screw up anything else on this job."

Grabbing her purse, she headed for the door.

Eight

After finishing up a meeting with his foreman the following Monday, Cody stalked out of the Black Creek Ranch office. Next month, once renovations were complete, he would move more of the business side of the ranch work to his new facility in town.

A location that would be forever associated in his mind with his passionate first encounter with Jillian.

But for now, Cody's business manager still worked out of an old double-bay garage that had been converted to office space over a decade ago.

Jamming his hat on his head in deference to the noontime sun, Cody headed toward his truck. He needed to get to Cheyenne for the appointment he'd made for Jillian to have a blood test. He'd wanted to drive her there personally, since he hadn't seen her in days—not so much as a glimpse of her after she'd walked out on him at the White Canyon. He'd received a text message in which she'd politely refused his offer of a ride, although she'd agreed to meet him at the assigned appointment time.

Her continued distance stung more than it should have. More even than her walking out on him last week. Clearly, she needed space, something he understood well, since he was the kind of man who needed plenty of space of his own. Yet he'd assumed she would speak to him again. Explain why she'd felt compelled to sprint out the door after the most powerful physical encounter of his life. He knew he hadn't been alone in feeling that way. She'd been right there with him.

Until she wasn't.

He didn't know what he'd done wrong, but after the blood test, he would speak to her. Clear the air and, he hoped, convince her that she didn't need to rush out of town the moment the results came back. How could she ignore the attraction that pulled at him day and night, on his mind even when Jillian was nowhere in sight?

He'd almost reached the truck when he heard the rumble of a four-wheeler coming from the west pasture. Turning, he saw the familiar figure of his father riding toward him.

Cody pocketed his keys and checked the time on his phone. He had a few minutes to spare before he needed to leave. Lifting a hand in greeting, he started toward his dad. A tractor hummed in the distance, haying one of the north fields.

Donovan McNeill had tried his best the last few years to let his sons take over the ranching operations, but Cody knew it wasn't easy for the older man to give up the reins completely. And truth be told, he appreciated his father's input. Whereas his twin butted heads with

Donovan often, Cody's opinions usually aligned with his dad's.

Donovan straightened in the seat as he pulled to a halt and switched off the machine, a cloud of dust spinning around them both. At six feet, he was shorter than his sons, but he shared similar features, including the straight nose and strong jaw. The heavy eyebrows and blue eyes. Even the girls took after him, except for Scarlett, who'd inherited the softer features of her mother.

"You know about this production company that wants to film on our land?" his father began without preamble, as if they'd been in the middle of a conversation.

He didn't look happy. Still, he reached out to pet Morticia when the border collie bounded over to greet him.

"I'm aware. I refused them permission." Cody understood his father would be resistant—he'd never appreciated strangers on McNeill property.

"Then you're also aware that your brother is allowing the whole thing to happen at the Creek Spill?"

"The rest of the family backs him." No surprise there. Carson had been born with a knack for rallying others around him. He'd been the crowd favorite every time he saddled up in their rodeo days.

"Not me. And not Paige." The older man's jaw flexed as he stared out toward the north field, where the haying operation produced a steady mechanical hum. "Your siblings are already flocking around my father like he's the second coming, even though I told them that he's oily as a snake. Now this?" He shook his head. "I'm still a part of this family, damn it."

Cody had known Donovan wouldn't approve of outsiders tromping around the property, but it surprised him that his wife was against the idea, too.

"Paige doesn't want the film crew here?" His stepmother was a quiet woman. She taught yoga classes in town and spent long hours baking, sending healthy, homemade treats to soup kitchens, family and friends. She'd been a good mother to him after his own had died.

Still, she'd never been "Mom." Not to him and not to his brothers. She'd been their babysitter first. Even after she married their father, she'd always been Paige.

"She's adamantly opposed." His father frowned, the lines in his face settling in a natural scowl, as if the unhappiness had long been carved there. "I think she's worried about Scarlett." He shook his head as if that didn't quite add up. "Maybe she's afraid once our baby girl gets a taste of the movie business, she'll leave here for good."

"Scarlett's a grown woman," Cody replied, wondering why Paige would be so upset. She'd never been opposed to much of anything before—let alone adamantly. Her oft-repeated mantra was live and let live.

"You know she left town last week for a trip to the West Coast? She might already be making plans for a move."

Cody hadn't been pleased that she would just drop her responsibilities at the ranch and take off, but she'd hired a temp worker to fill in for her.

"Just because she's a grown woman doesn't mean she's going to make a good decision," Donovan grumbled. "Either way, I know it would mean a lot to your stepmother if we can shut this thing down. I woke up last night and found her doing internet searches for airfare to New Zealand."

"She wants to take a trip?" Cody had never known her to leave Wyoming, let alone the continental United States.

"I'm not sure." His father crossed his arms and knitted his brows. He was troubled, no doubt about it. "She said she's been considering an anniversary trip for us, since we never took a honeymoon."

"Sounds reasonable for a landmark twenty-fifth celebration." The answer seemed clear enough to Cody. Paige was long overdue for a vacation.

"She's never been one for traveling outside the state, let alone across the globe," Donovan growled. "Something doesn't sit right and I don't know what to believe. Just…" He waved at the air, a frustrated gesture, before leaning forward to switch on the ignition of the four-wheeler. "See what you can do." Then he roared off in a new cloud of dust.

Cody pulled his keys from his pocket and stalked to his truck; he didn't want to be late meeting Jillian at the doctor's office. He couldn't puzzle out what was going on in his family. Especially Scarlett's hunger to leave Cheyenne behind and his twin's insistence on opening up the ranch to Hollywood and all the inconveniences and possible dangers sure to come with it.

And now his father and stepmother seemed to be having problems. Problems rooted in that damn movie. The McNeills had been struggling with the reentry of their grandfather in their lives even before Paige started acting funny. But now, with all the stress the film added to the mix, he feared his family was fracturing at the seams.

He had Jillian to thank for that. Not that he would have minded so much if she'd been willing to stick around for the aftermath. To see the project through while his family contended with all the changes it wrought. Instead, she seemed content to turn her back on all of them and proceed onto her next adventure.

Forgetting about him and the incredible time they'd spent together.

Jillian was awaiting her test results at the doctor's office when Cody arrived. He crossed the reception area in no time, his long strides eating up the small space between them.

He dropped his black Stetson on a nearby chair and sat down on the seat beside her. As if they were lovers on good terms instead of...whatever they were.

She hadn't seen him in days. Five and a half, to be exact. Not that she'd expected him to chase after her when she'd left the bungalow at the White Canyon Ranch. But maybe she'd expected more from him after their time together at the rodeo. Their time together afterward. He'd said he wanted to share adventures with her. The rodeo date *had* been his idea.

They hadn't been able to keep their hands off each other. But then after their lovemaking, his primary concern had been obtaining a blood test to assure himself she couldn't possibly be carrying his child. That cold realization had been upsetting to her. It had killed the passion of the moment.

"They've already drawn my blood," she informed him, hoping she sounded detached and indifferent. She would not let him see that he'd hurt her. "The nurse said she could have the results for us in one hour, so I assumed you would want to wait."

"I do." He wore dark jeans and a black button-down

shirt that stretched taut across his shoulders when he leaned forward to flip idly through the magazines on the coffee table. Every one of the publications featured a baby or a pregnant woman. He sat back in the seat again, empty-handed. "And I'm sorry I'm late. My father paid me a visit just as I was ready to get in my truck. He rarely needs to talk about anything, so I found it tough to cut things short."

Some of her irritation eased as she imagined a man even quieter than the brooding cowboy next to her. Donovan McNeill must surely be the strong, silent type. Jillian would rather think about the McNeill men right now than stare at those magazines full of babies she might never have—even with her frozen eggs. And she felt that aching emptiness each time a wriggling baby or pregnant mother passed through the obstetrician's waiting area.

"It's fine." Jillian had planned to use their time before they got the results to gauge where she stood with Cody. She thought it was only fair to tell him when the film would start shooting, since her boss had agreed to her plan B for location shots on *Winning the West*. Now, she only needed to file applications for a few more permits and she could start looking at weather forecasts to ensure the crew arrived on-site at the best time.

What would that mean for her and Cody? Once her job here was over, should she avoid returning to Cheyenne? Was this blood test his way of cutting ties with her?

She glanced at him cautiously. There was a furrow of concern between his brows, and he seemed distracted. At the moment, the waiting area was empty except for the two of them, the big clock on the wall ticking audibly over a children's play area.

"Is everything okay with your family? I hope your father didn't have bad news."

"He's worried about Scarlett. And my stepmother, apparently." Cody turned his gaze to Jillian. She noticed his hand clenching on his knee. "The film shoot has Paige upset and he's not sure why."

Jillian fidgeted with the denim strap of her purse. "I remember the night before the rodeo, when I met Paige, she did seem worried about it. And she definitely didn't want Scarlett to go to LA."

"That's what my dad said." Cody appeared to mull it over. "But I think there's something else going on. Possibly some problems between him and Paige."

"I'm sorry to hear that." Jillian hadn't intended to stir up trouble for the McNeills. "But your siblings are excited for this opportunity, and my company has committed to shooting here. It's happening."

That got his full attention. "Just like that?"

"I spent two days showing my boss around the Creek Spill." She'd been forthright with Cody about this from the start, so she didn't intend to feel guilty now. "She convinced the director that this is the right spot."

The muscle in his jaw flexed. Because he was angry with her? Or with his brother for not siding with him?

She didn't have time to ask as a nurse called her name. "Jillian? The doctor will see you now."

In a flash, her train of thought did a one-eighty. She knew what the doctor would say, and that this visit was a simple formality. It was the last thread tying her and Cody together, one he was all too glad to break. Memories of their last night together—the way it had pulled at her heart and, by contrast, the way he had been able to enjoy the physical release simply for its own sake—forced her to be a realist.

After today, she would have no reason to stay in Cheyenne. The location manager would take over, releasing Jillian from any more work on the site.

Oddly numb, she braced herself for the expected news as she entered the office. Dr. Simmons, a woman of about sixty with long, graying braids, stood to shake hands with both of them before flipping open the file folder on her small oak desk. While she reviewed the papers, Jillian's eye went to the front of the desk, which was completely covered with children's artwork—everything from finger-paint hearts to scribbled coloring book pages.

"It appears I have good news for you." The doctor smiled as she lifted the first sheet out of the file and passed it to Jillian. "Congratulations to you both. You're pregnant, Ms. Ross."

Jillian couldn't take the paper. Couldn't process what she was hearing. Vaguely, she noticed Cody sit forward in his chair beside her.

"Excuse me?" she asked, her voice scratchy and hoarse.

"May I?" Cody reached for the page of test results, since Jillian still couldn't make her hand move.

"The blood test confirms that you're expecting," Dr. Simmons explained, her small brown eyes staying focused on Jillian even as she passed the paper to Cody. "The test is very definitive. Your pregnancy hormone levels are well above normal."

Stunned, Jillian couldn't wrap her brain around the words. Or maybe she was too terrified to do so.

"But I've had cancer." She shook her head, remembering all the things they'd done to her body. All the poisons they'd flooded her with to kill the tumor. She couldn't possibly be pregnant now. "Radiation. Chemo."

She felt Cody's hand on her back. Rubbing. Comforting. He was scanning the results even as he tugged her closer. She couldn't get a full breath of air, her chest constricting.

Dr. Simmons glanced back at her file. The next paper was a brightly colored flyer with an image of a smiling infant. She shuffled through a few more similar pages. "I don't see your medical history, Ms. Ross."

"I was treated in Los Angeles. I've only just cleared the two-year mark since I ended breast cancer treatments." Hot tears leaked out of her eyes. "I'm sure the test is a false positive. I can't possibly be…"

She couldn't even dare to hope for a healthy pregnancy after everything she'd been through. How could her depleted body possibly nurture a tiny life?

Beside her, Cody laid the paper on the doctor's desk, his other hand still stroking Jillian's back. "Is there any risk to the child from those treatments? After two years?"

"That isn't my area of expertise." The doctor was writing a note on a new sheet of paper. "I'm giving you a referral to an obstetrician who specializes in pregnancy and cancer survivors." She passed it to Jillian. "But I can tell you that chemotherapy drugs leave the body within days or weeks. I'm not worried about the health of the baby. But you'll want to speak to your oncologist about any risks of recurrence in your disease, Ms. Ross."

Cody squeezed her shoulder protectively.

Jillian nodded, drinking in the reassurance that her

pregnancy could be healthy despite the treatments. She stared into the doctor's eyes, certain the woman was being forthright.

"I remember reading that doctors recommend waiting two years before trying to become pregnant." How many times had she read all the brochures in her oncologist's office while waiting to see him? "But I thought that didn't apply to me, because I was under the impression I would lose my fertility."

Cody's fingers stilled on her arm. "Is the risk of miscarriage higher?"

The question punctured the small bubble of hope growing inside her, deflating it.

"That's a question for my colleague, Mr. McNeill." Dr. Simmons turned kindly eyes back to Jillian. "But a great deal depends on your medical history. If you sign release forms at the front desk, I'll request your chart, so we can start monitoring the progress of this pregnancy and do everything we can to make sure mother and baby are both healthy."

A baby.

Only then did the idea sink in as a real possibility. She was pregnant. Jillian had never expected her body to return to normal after her treatments, and she thought she'd been prepared to give her fertilized eggs to someone else to carry, down the road in a distant future. But now, just two years after her treatments had ended, a tiny life grew inside her.

Her child. And Cody's.

Only now, while the doctor discussed the more ordinary concerns about pregnancy, did Jillian let herself consider how different her life was going to be if she successfully carried this man's baby to term.

His hand was still splayed along her upper back, filling the space between her shoulder blades. Warm. Reassuring.

Yet with one look at the set of his jaw, the hollow stare of his blue eyes as he studied the literature before him, Jillian could tell that Cody was reeling from the news. He'd been ready to cut ties with her today. Say goodbye forever.

In an instant, their worlds had changed immeasurably. Because no matter how much this independent Wyoming cowboy wanted to remain unfettered and free, Cody's life was now bound to hers through this child they shared.

Nine

A baby.

Cody listened carefully to the doctor's answers to all his questions, knowing he'd think of more once they left. He needed all the information he could get to do everything in his power to make sure Jillian remained healthy.

She looked even more shell-shocked than he felt at the baby news, so he knew that how he handled things going forward was important. He didn't want to upset her. And he needed to stay close to her. As they left Dr. Simmons's office that afternoon, he treaded carefully. Her appointment with the obstetrician specializing in cancer patients in Denver wasn't until tomorrow afternoon, but he wanted to see if they could consult with any other local doctors who might tell them more.

He didn't want to overwhelm her, though.

"Are you all right?" He studied her face in the sunlight, searching for clues to how she was feeling.

Worried? Full of regret? Ready to run? He truly had no idea how she was handling this.

"I'm just so stunned." She hesitated beside the car he recognized as hers, then rested a hand on the fender and closed her eyes for a long moment.

"Would you let me drive you home? Or to my office behind Wrangler's? We could head over there, maybe get something to eat from the bar and bring it in back with us where it's quiet." He liked the plan. They wouldn't see any of his family there. And he didn't think either of them was ready to face outsiders. "I'd like to make a few phone calls to see if we can learn more today. My father is friends with the chief of staff at Cheyenne Regional. I could give him a call and see if there's anyone in oncology who could answer questions for us."

"Sure." She nodded, her eyes unfocused when she opened them. "I would appreciate that. I'd like to call my doctor back home, too. See if I can speak to anyone in the office there."

"Of course." Cody took the papers she held and added them to his stack, then slid a hand around her elbow. "The truck's over here."

She followed him through the parking lot to his pickup. He unlocked the passenger door for her.

"I know we have a lot to talk about," she said, pausing and meeting his gaze directly before stepping into the vehicle. "But I wonder if we could table the discussion until we find out more?"

"I understand." He nodded, recognizing the fear in her voice. "We'll find out all we can and then figure this out."

A baby required their absolute focus and attention, yes. But he understood that Jillian's health could be at risk. And he didn't feel equipped to address her concerns until he knew more about what she'd been through. More about what she might face in the next nine months.

No wonder she was afraid.

As he fired up the truck engine to drive them to his office, he felt his grip on the steering wheel slip a bit. He'd never had sweaty palms in the rodeo arena when he could have been trampled to death on any given night. But right now, thinking about something happening to Jillian or this baby she carried, he was scared as hell.

Scarlett could get used to this life.

She tipped her head back against the seat in the limo. It was shortly after sunset, and the Hollywood lights were already bright. Neon red and blue splashed the bare skin of her calves, filtering through the tinted windows as they slowed for a stop sign. She'd been in Los Angeles for five days, shopping and getting her bearings, sending out a few feelers to friends she'd met at parties over the years.

Confronting Logan King wouldn't be easy when she hadn't seen him in months. She needed trusted intel to figure out where he was going to be and—hopefully—not make it seem like she was seeking him out on purpose. It would undermine her goals if word got back to Logan that she was looking for him. Better for her confrontation to be a surprise.

Though if he happened to hear she was in town, conquering Hollywood and being seen with the hottest celebs of the moment, that was just fine.

The sooner he started eating his heart out, the better. Besides, what kind of actress would she be if she couldn't convince Logan King that he meant nothing to her? Tonight wasn't just about her and Logan, anyway. She was dedicating this performance to every woman who'd ever had a man ignore her. Every woman who'd felt the snub when "I'll call you" actually meant "it's over."

When the limo rolled to a stop in front of Lucerno, the West Hollywood club where Logan was rumored to be this evening for an unofficial wrap party with a handful of other actors, it quickly became the object of side-eye glances from the dozens of people waiting in line for admittance. The vehicle vibrated slightly from the music pouring out the open doors behind the burly bouncer checking a guest list. Pink light glowed from inside the club, the occasional strobe flashing.

Ignoring an attack of nerves, Scarlett squeezed her tiny leather clutch, refusing to give in to an urge to check her makeup. She looked as good as she ever would. She'd painstakingly applied her gold eyeshadow, expertly glued her false eyelashes. She couldn't help the prominent nose, the chin that wasn't quite as strong as she would have liked. That was what highlighting palettes were for.

When the driver opened her door, Scarlett handled the fear the same way she'd handled bronc riding during those years when her father had guilted her into competing to "toughen her up." She charged straight through the heart of it, as fast as possible.

"Scarlett McNeill," she informed the bouncer, not bothering to stand in line.

Chin up. Look like you belong.

She must have fooled a few people, because some of the club-goers waiting in line had pulled out their phones to record her arrival. She hoped her movie studio contact had added her name to that list. The woman was an assistant to a casting director, a friend from a summer theater program Scarlett had joined during her semester abroad in London. While just an elective for her agribusiness degree, the theater work had been the most fun she'd had during her university years. With any luck, Lucie was already inside waiting for her.

"Have a good time," the bouncer told her, moving aside the velvet rope to admit her, not even bothering to check his list.

"Thank you." She gave him a smile and strode down the steps into the sprawling club, where the pink glow got more intense. Would that small victory be an indication of how the rest of the night went? Or would it be her last win?

Heading for the bar across the dance floor, she spotted her friend Lucie, one of the few people in her life besides her sisters who knew what Logan had done to her.

Reed-thin and almost six feet tall, Lucie was easy to spot in a crowd. She could pull anything off a vintage clothing rack and make it look amazing. Tonight she was wearing a sheer floral dress over a tiny jean skirt.

"Darling, you were born to rock those boots," Lucie announced, hugging Scarlett briefly before holding her at arm's length to admire her. "When are you going to leave farm life behind and move here? I can't survive another Hollywood lunch full of fake smiles and air kisses unless I know I can dish about it with you."

She and Lucie had talked about getting an apartment together in LA. While Scarlett could afford her own place with the monthly income from her share of the ranch earnings, she wanted the bohemian experience that she hadn't gotten in college, and to hear industry gossip on a daily basis.

"If *Winning the West* is filmed in my backyard—and it sounds like it will be—I'm going to stay long enough to watch." Her sister had texted her just last night that Carson signed the agreement with the production company. "But after that wraps, there's nothing keeping me in Cheyenne."

Lucie squeezed her arm. "That's what I want to hear. And speaking of *Winning the West*, the future star of that picture is seated at a private table in the Red Room." She pointed to the far wall with a drink in hand, silver bangles sliding down her arm. "Just past that curtain."

Scarlett's heart beat quicker as she anticipated the confrontation. She dreaded it a little, but knew she had to go through with this. A man jostled her from behind, and she turned to see him dart away, a blur of pinstripe jacket and jeans in the strobe lights.

"Then I know where I'm headed." Scarlett's hand went to her hairdo before she could remind herself she wasn't allowed to be self-conscious.

"You're flawless," Lucie insisted, reading her mind the way only a good friend could. "Go tell him what you think of his games." She held out her half-finished beverage. "Bonus points if you toss my drink in his face."

"No need. I've been working on my script." Scarlett had been writing and rewriting her dialogue in her mind for days. Weeks, really, since she'd been dreaming of her revenge speech even before she'd decided to come to Hollywood and face him.

She charged in the direction of the Red Room, a raised nook off the dance floor draped with red curtains to conceal its VIP occupants. Scarlett wasn't going to give this man the satisfaction of seeing her angry. Of thinking he mattered that much.

She expected to see him at a table full of beautiful, young celebutantes, surrounded by expensive champagne bottles and hangers-on. Instead, her first glimpse of Logan King when she entered the room showed him in deep conversation with another man, someone older and dressed more like a banker or a lawyer, his hand on a briefcase under the round table.

Logan was even more attractive than she remembered. Chiseled jaw. Great hair. Wide green eyes with long lashes and heavy, dark eyebrows. Lips made for kissing. He wore a black jacket over a plain gray T-shirt, his excellent physique under wraps. Still, his jacket stretched a bit around his biceps where he bent his arms to rest on the table. Women danced nearby, as if hoping to be noticed by the newly A-list actor with a bottle of seltzer in front of him.

Caught off guard a bit, Scarlett hesitated. She had gone through numerous scenarios in her head. None of them had played out quite like this. She glanced back to the dance floor, wondering if she should make another pass by the table later. But then she heard her name in that familiar voice.

"Scarlett?"

Even now, her brain bursting with her "screw you"

speech, hearing her name on his lips did something funny to her insides. *Damn him.*

Forcing herself to slide into character—a strong woman with a killer sense of self—she squared her shoulders to face him.

"Have we met?" she asked, her heart pounding a mile a minute as she pretended not to know him. That was phase one of her put-down—letting him think he was entirely forgettable, too.

He excused himself from the table and rose to his feet, his eyes on her the whole time.

A waitress passed her with a tray of drinks, and Scarlett stepped sideways to give the woman room. She almost ran into a man—the same guy from the bar wearing the pin-striped jacket with jeans. What was his issue? Had he been following her around the club?

Flustered to be distracted when she had an important job to do, Jillian returned her attention to Logan, who was suddenly standing very close to her. Nearby, the DJ put on a new record, driving more people to the dance floor as the energy kicked into high gear around them. The banker guy Logan had been talking to was gone. A few of the dancing girls slithered back down to the main floor with their sexy moves.

And Logan never took his eyes off her.

"You dropped this." He retrieved a folded sheet of paper from the floor beside her left foot. When he passed it to her, his arm brushed hers. "And I don't blame you for not wanting to remember me. But I sure haven't forgotten you."

Scarlett knew then she would never make it as an actress. All her memorized lines faded from her brain. Words failed her, period. She stared at him like a gaping fish, her jaw hanging open until she at last thought to close it.

"That's not mine," she said finally, glancing down at the folded stationery.

"That guy just handed it to you," Logan insisted, taking her hand and tucking the note into her palm. "And for what it's worth, I'm glad to see you again."

Jamming the paper in her clutch purse, Scarlett got the jolt she needed when she heard those words.

"You're glad to see me?" She could not believe the gall of some men. Especially too-handsome-for-their-own-good actors. "No wonder you're the toast of Hollywood casting directors. That's one hell of an acting job."

She hadn't wanted to show him anger. In her mind, she'd imagined giving him more of a cool, ice princess speech. But apparently, she didn't have enough ice in her veins.

"Scarlett, about that—"

"No." She cut him off, unwilling to listen to lame excuses. She'd flown across four states to tell him exactly what she thought of him. "You made your decision about me long ago. Did it hurt me at the time? Sure it did. But getting some distance from you has helped me see you weren't worth keeping in my life, anyhow. Turns out that sometimes not getting what you want is a wonderful stroke of luck."

She'd cobbled that together from fragments of other speeches she'd memorized. And it felt good to tell him what she thought. Logan shook his head, his brows scrunched as if he couldn't possibly understand that she was telling him off.

"Furthermore," she continued, warming to the task, "the first step to getting what you want in life is getting rid of what you don't want." She smiled tightly. "I know now that you're what I don't want. Goodbye, Logan. And in the future, have the common courtesy of telling a woman that you're not interested in a relationship, instead of just ignoring her texts when you jet off to film your next movie. That's what grown men do."

Turning on her heel, she walked away from him. It wasn't the powerful performance she'd visualized in her daydreams, but it wasn't half bad.

Or so she thought. Right up until Logan called to her.

"That movie I was filming? It was shot on location in the Republic of the Congo."

She wasn't sure what that had to do with her, so Scarlett kept right on walking.

Before she made it back to Lucie, Logan caught up to her, his breath warm in her ear as he said, "One of the worst places on earth for connectivity."

She paused beside a screen broadcasting images of the dancing crowd, the lights and colors swirling and reflecting off her gold dress.

"That may be the worst excuse ever."

"True. But ask yourself, if I was happy about the split, why would I bother to make an excuse?"

Scarlett knew better than to fall for that. Didn't she? In that moment of hesitation, a camera flashed nearby, the streak of light just another headache-inducing strobe across her vision.

Logan took her elbow and swiveled her away from the camera while she struggled to process what was happening.

"Now, like it or not, we're going to be connected in the tabloids." He ushered her toward a back door marked Exit behind the huge screen, skillfully edging his way around people grinding in the shadows of the dance floor. "You can yell at me all you want outside, but I'm unwilling to make a bigger scene than we already have."

Driving back toward the White Canyon Ranch after their evening consultation with the oncologist, Cody knew they couldn't put it off any longer. He'd done his best to honor Jillian's wishes to table the discussion about the baby. But they'd spent the day learning more about her cancer and more about the possible obstacles they faced in this pregnancy. His father's friend at Cheyenne Regional Medical Center had gotten them a meeting with an on-call oncologist, a busy man who'd given them half an hour of his time to talk about their concerns and to review Jillian's medical history.

They would learn more tomorrow when they met with the specialist. But Cody wanted to talk about it tonight, if only to reassure Jillian. To let her know he supported her in whatever happened.

"Would you consider spending the night at the Black Creek?" he asked, as the truck bounced over a pothole. "I can make us something to eat, and we'll have more privacy to talk than at the guest ranch."

"Okay." Her voice was small. Far-off. She sounded different from the determined woman he'd come to know. He glanced across the truck cab to see her staring into the distance out the passenger-side window.

"There's plenty of space. You can have your own room, of course." He didn't mean to make assumptions about their relationship.

"Thank you." She said no more.

He couldn't tell if she was frightened about what a pregnancy could mean for her health, or if she was thinking about what it meant for the two of them as a couple. But she had to be reeling.

"We should talk about this, Jillian." He knew they needed to start thinking about what came next. "I know we agreed to wait until we learned more, but after tonight's meeting—"

"We've known each other for just over a week." She shifted on the leather seat, turning toward him as he steered the truck down a back road. "And I realize this is far more than you ever bargained for when you asked me to dance that night."

The road here was lit only by stars and the two beams of his headlights, but it wasn't nearly as tough to navigate as this conversation.

"I remember asking for a whole lot more than a dance." He had no intention of bowing out of this situation, if that's what she was thinking. "We both did. And we both knew the consequences."

"Honestly, I didn't." She shook her head slowly. In disbelief. "I thought I would be sterile. For years, and maybe forever." She hugged her arms around herself, sitting back in the seat. "You're the only person I've been with since my treatment, because I was having trouble feeling at all desirable."

He reached across the console to rest his hand on her knee, to offer whatever comfort he could. He wanted to wrap her up tight in his arms and keep her safe for the next nine months. Hell, longer than that. Their lives were inextricably entwined now. As the mother of his child, Jillian would come under his protection forever. He'd accepted that fact the moment he'd seen the test results, but he didn't want to overwhelm her with any more than what she was already dealing with today.

"I can't pretend to know what you're going through right now. It's a lot even for me to process, and I know there's far more at stake for you." He couldn't stand the idea of this pregnancy hurting her. What if it triggered her cancer?

The oncologist had insisted there was no definitive proof the hormones from pregnancy could spur a recurrence. He'd cited the most current studies, which showed no difference in recurrence rates between women who got pregnant after breast cancer treatment and women who didn't.

But those studies were very new. And apparently Jillian had only recently stopped her course of hormone blockers. Cody had learned a lot about cancer today, and while he'd found it all scary as hell, he also had renewed appreciation for what she'd gone through in her treatments.

"I've been through every emotion today," she admitted, as he drove the truck under the welcome sign for the ranch. "Happiness and fear, worry and awe. And maybe I should feel guilty for misleading you, but I really thought—"

"You have nothing to feel guilty about." He parked next to the front door, not bothering to put the truck in the garage when he wanted to get her inside and feed her.

"But I assured you there was no chance I could get pregnant. I guess if I'd known it was a possibility, I could have taken contraception after the fact, but I was so certain—"

"You didn't know. You told me the same things your doctors told you. I understand that." He switched off the truck and pocketed the keys. He went around to her side of the pickup to help her down, then led her to the front door of the main house.

She'd been on the property before, but not inside the house. He would never have dreamed these would be the circumstances for her introduction to the place—newly pregnant with his child. The news still staggered him.

He showed her into his home, flipping on light switches as they headed through the living area toward the kitchen.

"Have a seat and I'll make us something to eat. You must be exhausted." He slid a leather-padded stool from the breakfast bar for her, then started pulling ingredients out of the refrigerator. He could have messaged his housekeeper to prepare dinner for them, but he had a strong desire to cook for Jillian himself. To keep his hands busy as an outlet for the fear running through him.

For her. For their child.

Jillian opened the sheaf of papers they'd collected throughout the day—pamphlets from the obstetrician's office and the oncologist. She scanned the contents of one of the sheets while he turned on the gas flame under a cast-iron skillet. Her finger followed the lines of text on the page.

"You realize one of the risks of finding out about a pregnancy this early is that if I miscarry in the first few weeks, we'll both know it was a miscarriage." She glanced up from the paperwork. "Whereas if we'd waited for a missed period, we would have never known about it."

"I thought of that." He hated the knowledge that he might have brought her more pain by insisting on a blood test so soon. He chopped tomatoes and peppers.

"And I'm sorry if it turns out I could have spared you that hurt."

"I'm going to think positively," she insisted. "Last week I thought there was zero chance of getting pregnant, so I've already had good news on that score. Although it does say here that even healthy women have a 10 to 25 percent chance of miscarrying in the early weeks."

He swallowed back the fresh wave of worry for her. How devastated would she be to lose a child after all she'd already been through? He chopped faster, adding mushrooms to the mix as the vegetables started to sizzle in the pan.

"If there's anything at all I can do or offer you to help make sure you stay healthy, I will. Whatever you want or need, it's yours." He cracked eggs on top of the half-cooked veggies. His temples throbbed with thoughts about all the ways this pregnancy could go wrong. Then, after wiping his hands on a kitchen towel, he came around to stand beside her at the breakfast bar and took her hands in his. "But Jillian, if you are worried about the cancer coming back, or if we find out from the specialist that this pregnancy increases your risk of recurrence, I would understand if—"

"No." Shaking her head, she squeezed his hands hard. "This pregnancy is nothing short of a miracle to me. I never expected it, and the timing isn't what I imagined, but after all the nights I've shed tears thinking I might not ever have children, I'll do everything in my power to make sure this is a healthy pregnancy."

Some of the tension inside him eased. But the fear for her still twisted like a knot in his chest. He had watched, helpless, as his mother died. He couldn't let anything happen to Jillian. He would do whatever it took to keep her safe.

"I understand." He wrapped his arms around her, hugging her gently before straightening. "And I want to help in any way I can. For starters, I'd like you to move in with me."

Ten

Jillian let the idea settle in her brain, knowing it was too soon to think long-term, but feeling tempted anyhow. Or maybe it was just the draw of Cody's arms around her that had her considering his proposition for one crazy moment. How often during her treatments had she craved the kind of emotional support he knew how to give?

Cody McNeill would never abandon a woman after surgery to remove a tumor the way her ex-boyfriend had. Honor and responsibility were coded in his very DNA, were a rock-solid part of his character. But Jillian knew that he would offer that support to any woman who carried his child. His suggestion that they live together didn't have anything to do with her. It had everything to do with his baby.

"That's a big step," she told him carefully, not wanting to appear ungrateful. She edged back from his embrace, needing to look into his eyes.

"So is a baby."

She couldn't argue with that. It touched her heart that he would sacrifice his own happiness to provide for her and their child. And at the same time, it hurt to know she'd never be able to differentiate his feelings for her from his sense of duty.

"I just feel like it's too soon. Especially when we agreed to table any discussion until we learned more about my health. More about—" she couldn't bring herself to think about the chance of losing the pregnancy; not when the idea of being a mother was starting to take hold as a possibility for her "—the baby."

She mourned the loss of Cody's touch already. Wished she could have lingered in the circle of his arms, if only to pretend everything was going to be all right. He slid the pan off the stove and turned the burner off.

"Then we'll wait." He nodded brusquely. "We'll see what tomorrow brings and revisit the idea after we speak to the specialist. For now, we can have some dinner, and then I'll let you rest. You deserve a good night's sleep after the day you've had."

They both did. She knew this wasn't easy for him, either. That his life would have been so much simpler if she hadn't gotten pregnant.

"Thank you." She needed to retreat. To try to process this news. To figure out what would be best for her future and her child's.

"After I serve us, I'll show you to your room and make sure you have everything you need," he said, sliding the food onto their plates and setting them on the kitchen counter. He was the perfect host. Attentive. Thoughtful.

She should be thankful he took this news seriously. And she was. But a part of her couldn't help missing the man she'd danced with at Wrangler's that first night. The Cody McNeill who'd been ready to abandon caution, and share life's next adventure with her.

The next afternoon, after her exam, Jillian got dressed and then followed the nurse into Dr. Webster's spacious corner office. Cody was already there; he'd driven her to the appointment, stopped by the White Canyon Ranch to pick up her things and then returned so they could meet with the doctor together. When she entered the room, he waited for her to take a seat in front of the mahogany desk then sat next to her. They didn't have time to speak privately, however, before the doctor arrived.

Cody stood and the two men shook hands. When Cody settled into the chair beside her again, he slid his hand around hers and squeezed. She wondered if he did that without thinking, to seek contact with her, or if it was a conscious attempt to offer her comfort.

Not that it necessarily mattered. It was a kindness either way, and there was no denying his actions touched her. Yet she couldn't help but wonder whether, if she moved in with him, she would ever know what gestures were real and which were a product of his strong sense of responsibility. He already viewed himself as the responsible one in his family—the one who managed the core of the McNeill ranching business while his siblings pursued outside interests like acting or the rodeo.

If a good night's sleep had made Jillian realize only

one thing about this pregnancy, it was that she didn't want to be another person on his list of responsibilities, no matter how seductive his touch was.

"Do you have questions for me?" Dr. Webster was asking, reminding Jillian that she needed to focus on the here and now. She'd missed half of his remarks about her health, but then, the obstetrician had given her his views about her pregnancy prospects when they'd been in the exam room. Up until now, he'd simply been bringing Cody up to speed.

In the obstetrician's opinion, she had as much chance as any woman of carrying a baby to full term. Breast-feeding most likely wouldn't be an option, but he didn't rule that out, either. His patients' experiences with pregnancy and cancer reflected the findings of the recent European study the doctors had mentioned to Jillian and Cody yesterday—that pregnancy hormones did not spur a recurrence of breast cancer.

"You've reviewed Jillian's chart from her medical team in Los Angeles," Cody began, glancing her way a moment before he encircled her shoulders with one arm. "In your opinion, regardless of pregnancy, what is the risk of her disease returning?"

She understood why he needed to ask the question. If she succumbed to a second round of cancer, he would be the sole parent to this child. Cody deserved to know the answer so he could be ready. Still, all the rationalizing in the world didn't lessen the pain that came with those words. The reminder of the shadow cancer cast over her whole life, even now.

It meant the possibility that she would miss out on seeing her child grow up. The stakes were higher than ever. She needed to remain healthy.

"Her risk of contracting breast cancer a second time is slightly higher than the average woman's, but not significantly so. It helps tremendously that her disease isn't hereditary. With no family history working against her, she has every reason to feel more optimistic." The doctor's words echoed those of other medical professionals she'd dealt with during her treatments.

She was lucky that her cancer wasn't hereditary, they'd all agreed two years ago. It had been difficult to feel fortunate, however, when she'd been so ill she'd thought she wouldn't survive the vile drugs they'd given her. When the burns from radiation had reduced her to tears, her skin hurting so badly she couldn't sleep without more powerful drugs. Often, she'd refused the pain medicine, not wanting to introduce even more chemicals to a body overflowing with them.

Cody stroked her arm. Her back. His touch felt familiar. Comforting. She wanted to lean into him, but she couldn't afford to lose her independence now. Not when she had a baby's future to consider.

She regretted that her health concerns gave him far more to grapple with than if she'd been whole. Cancer-free. Yet she couldn't change who she was or what had happened between them. She could only move forward. One foot ahead of the other.

"Where do we go from here?" she asked, focusing on the future. "How often should I be checked?"

The doctor confirmed what she'd read in the literature the night before—that she had to bear in mind that a percentage of all pregnancies ended in miscarriage without the mother even realizing she'd been pregnant. He set up a schedule to monitor her hormone levels over the upcoming weeks, which meant more blood tests.

He also gave them more literature on healthy diet and exercise, stressing the importance of minimizing all other risk factors.

Cody listened carefully, asking more questions, his face carved with lines of worry. His strong shoulders were set in a rigid posture, as if he had to bear all this alone. She understood his fear. She shared it, of course. Yet Jillian was familiar with all the doctor's suggestions. She'd already heard these lectures and read the brochures. She was already doing everything she could to stay healthy. Aside from that glass of wine she'd ordered in the Thirsty Cow the night she met Cody, she'd been a model of good behavior.

But she couldn't stop living because of the disease, or else cancer won. Yes, she would take extra precautions while she was pregnant, since she really did consider it a miracle that she'd conceived at all. Once she'd given birth, though, if she was lucky enough to carry this baby to term, she refused to live in a padded box. She needed to *live*, and that meant continuing to enjoy her list of life adventures. The only way to defy the disease was not just to exist, but to thrive.

As Cody asked the doctor for additional literature on food guidelines and risk factors, Jillian wondered if the responsible father of her child would understand that.

When they emerged from the physician's office half an hour later, a schedule for follow-up visits in hand, Jillian debated how to broach the topic with him. They had known each other so briefly, it was almost impossible to gauge how he might react. But they needed to have some difficult conversations, and soon. From the last time they'd slept together—when the earth had moved for her, but Cody had tried to distance himself from her afterward by asking about the blood test—Jillian knew that he didn't want to date and wasn't interested in furthering a relationship.

So she couldn't afford to let her emotions make the decisions for her.

"We should talk," she told him as he opened the door of his truck for her. She had a lot of things to weigh, and she knew he did, too.

When he didn't answer right away, she peered over at him and saw he'd taken out his phone. She'd noticed last night that it had chimed often, but he'd never checked it once when they'd been discussing the pregnancy. Now, remembering that, along with his concerns about his father and sister, she hesitated before taking her seat.

"Is everything okay with your family?"

He looked up, frowning. "I'm sorry. I was getting so many messages in there, I was worried something serious had happened."

"What is it?"

"See for yourself." He flipped his phone around so she could view a photo of Scarlett and a familiar-looking man filling the screen.

She read the caption aloud, "'Scarlett McNeill, heiress to a cattle ranch fortune, seems to have caught the eye of sought-after playboy Logan King, according to partygoers at a West Hollywood hotspot last night.'" Jillian's gaze flew to Cody's. "This is the actor slated to star in *Winning the West*."

That's why she knew the young man's face—from the director's notes. Logan was handsome enough in a traditional sense—he had, quite literally, movie-star good looks. She couldn't help but compare his style to Cody's more rugged appeal, though. She certainly knew which man she'd choose every time. She guessed Logan King was the actor Scarlett had met. Possibly the same man Paige didn't want her daughter to see.

"Right. So now Carson will get to host a Hollywood playboy looking for an heiress to fund his expensive tastes." Cody jammed the phone into his pocket. "My father will be thrilled," he said drily.

"I'm sure the story is overblown." Jillian hadn't been in the industry long, but she'd seen enough false tabloid reports to know they had no shame when it came to manipulating stories to make a good headline. "Logan King's star is on the rise, and so is the price he commands per film. I doubt he's romancing Scarlett because of her fortune."

Cody shook his head. Only now did Jillian notice the dark circles under his eyes. No doubt he hadn't slept much the night before, between worry about her and worry about his family.

"Damned if I know. But apparently the interest in our family has skyrocketed." He took her hand and eased her into the pickup. "Maddy's been taking reservations for the White Canyon all day, and her website crashed from too much traffic. Brock had to kick out a reporter who was nosing around the barns this morning, so I'm going to look into increasing security before the film crew rolls into town."

Too stunned to argue, Jillian buckled her seat belt while he slid into the driver's side. "I never would have guessed the movie would bring that kind of attention."

"This surge of interest is because of Scarlett, not *Winning the West*." Cody steered the pickup toward the outskirts of town and the Black Creek Ranch, a route she was beginning to know well.

A route that quickly turned rural, and then downright picturesque. The highway leading northwest offered breathtaking views of the Laramie Mountains, with the sky so blue behind them they stood in stark three-dimensional relief. Even the air was different than Southern California, where the ocean breezes could turn heavy with smog. Here, the almost constant wind felt crisp and clean, every day a fresh start.

"Has anyone in your family spoken to Scarlett? What's her take on this?"

"Maisie texted with her briefly this morning, but only enough for Scarlett to say that we're supposed to 'ignore the rumors.' Whatever that means." Cody drummed his thumbs lightly on the steering wheel. "Although to be truthful, I haven't read through all those group messages on my phone. As you know, I have more important things on my mind."

Jillian felt that pull of attraction to him again, less physical this time, and more emotional. She appreciated how he'd handled things so far, even though she recognized they hadn't begun to truly figure out what this baby would mean for them. Yet Cody took the potential complications seriously. And he hadn't pushed her to talk when she wasn't ready.

But would the man who'd asked her to move in with him be able to let her go when the time came?

"I do welcome the break from thinking about our situation, though." She cracked the truck window to let some of that warm summer air flow through her hair and blow away some of the fears. "I went to bed scared last night, and I woke up scared today. So I'm grateful to think about your sister for a few minutes instead."

"Then, if you don't mind—" Cody retrieved his phone

from his pocket and passed it to her, keeping his eyes on the road "—would you mind glancing through the group messages? See if there's anything urgent in there?"

"Are you sure?" She studied his face, but didn't turn on the device. Funny to think she'd slept with him twice yet hesitated to touch his phone.

"There's nothing in there you can't see." His jaw flexed, the slightest hint of emotion crossing his face, an emotion she couldn't read.

"Okay." She switched on the phone. "No password?" She opened his messages easily, seeing the slew of new ones on the same group thread.

"I'm an open book." There was definitely a hint of something defiant in his voice.

"Call me crazy, but I sense a story there." She scanned the messages for him while he turned off the interstate onto the private road that led to the ranch.

"I found out my last girlfriend was cheating when her phone buzzed about fifty times while she was in the shower. I grabbed it to bring to her, thinking the constant messages could be important. But the screen filled with private texts from another guy."

Jillian's finger stilled on the glass surface of the screen. "I'm so sorry."

"Don't be. It's always better to know." His scowl said otherwise, but she wasn't going to argue. "She defended her faithlessness by saying I was too cold to love."

Ouch. The woman must have been blind if she couldn't see the way Cody showed his love for his family by taking on the role of protector and provider. Already Jillian had been swept up into that world now that she was pregnant with his child, landing on the list of people he wouldn't let down.

"Some people go into attack mode when they feel cornered." She flicked the screen on again to finish scrolling. "She probably would have said anything to deflect attention from her own shortcomings."

"What about you?" he asked, glancing Jillian's way. The muscle in his jaw twitched as he frowned. "I hope no one you ever cared about went into attack mode."

She closed her eyes for a moment, remembering old hurts and finding they were nothing compared to all she'd been through since then.

"My ex-boyfriend bailed on me right after my first surgery." She could see now what a pale shadow of a man he'd been, especially in comparison to Cody. Ethan had been interesting enough when their lives were easy, but a crisis had revealed his character. "He said the surgery had been hard enough. He couldn't handle chemo and radiation, too."

"*He* couldn't handle it?" The outrage in Cody's voice was strangely comforting.

"That's a direct quote."

"Good riddance." His grip tightened on the steering wheel, knuckles flexing. "Although I'm sure it didn't seem like it at the time."

"I realized I hadn't really loved him when my main worry after the breakup was how to get to my appointments when I was sick and tired." She'd been so exhausted, and hadn't liked relying on her aging parents, who lived in a small town in Northern California. "But I met a lot of truly lovely Uber drivers during that time in my life."

Cody swore softly and rested a broad, steady hand on her knee for a quick squeeze. "You're never going to have to drive yourself to another appointment again."

The certainty in that promise rattled her, especially when she needed to tell him that Cheyenne couldn't be her forever home. But she wasn't ready yet. Not now. For all they knew, this pregnancy wouldn't last out the month. She would be devastated if she miscarried, but considering the hell her body had been through, she wouldn't be surprised.

As he pulled into the driveway in front of the main house, she was just as glad to sidestep that topic a little longer. Instead, she focused on the text messages from his family.

One that seemed important caught her eye as he slid out of the driver's seat and came around to her side.

"Cody?" She flipped the phone for him to see, hoping she was misunderstanding what she was reading. "It looks like your father is worried that your stepmother has gone missing."

"Impossible." His blue eyes narrowed as he took the device, helping her down with his free hand. "Paige hardly ever leaves the ranch, let alone Cheyenne."

"Maybe she went to see Scarlett?" Jillian remembered the exchange she'd witnessed between mother and daughter the night of the rodeo. Something had seemed off.

"But why?" Cody thumbed through more messages. "Scarlett has enjoyed being the center of attention since she was old enough to talk. Why would her mother worry about her dating some Hollywood dude? It's inconvenient for us, maybe, but I picture Scarlett being thrilled right now."

Jillian didn't have any answers.

"Paige will turn up." He turned off the phone again and slid his arm around her waist. "We've got more pressing matters to think about now. Let me make you dinner and we can figure out what to do if this baby is as stubborn a fighter as his mom."

"His?" She shouldn't allow herself to be charmed by Cody, but felt her heart soften a little anyhow.

"Or hers." He planted a tender kiss on her temple. "If she's as tough as her mom, we're going to need to make some plans for life nine months from now."

Jillian closed her eyes for a moment as they stood there on the front porch. She let herself imagine what it would be like to parent a baby with this honorable, responsible, thoughtful man. To stay in this awe-inspiring part of the country that had captured her imagination so thoroughly she was bringing a whole movie to town to share the beauty of it with the world.

But if ever she needed to be strong, it was right now. Because if this pregnancy lasted and they shared a child, Jillian wouldn't accept a supporting role while Cody McNeill called the shots. No matter how charming he could be, she knew that keeping his child close was going to be his number one priority. She didn't have any intention of giving up all her dreams to be stuck in a loveless relationship.

Cody might not be cold, the way his ex-girlfriend had accused him of being. But he certainly didn't love Jillian. Which meant this conversation he wanted to have was not going to end well.

"Cody, I'm worried about your family." It was the truth, she realized, as the words fell out of her mouth. Yes, she wanted to delay this conversation with him about the future. But she couldn't imagine this strong Wyoming family of his messaging each other twenty times in a day unless something serious was happening. She didn't want the pregnancy news to distract him from something important developing with the rest of the McNeills.

"I don't think we need to worry about Scarlett." His expression was resolute. "Besides, I'm not going to be the one who stops her from living her dreams." He leveled a knowing look at Jillian, reminding her of their argument about personal freedom versus family duty.

"But what about your dad? Your stepmom? Shouldn't you make sure they're okay?" She had barely gotten to know his family, hadn't even met his father or his grandfather.

She'd never had a big, extended family the way he did. And if they one day shared a child who'd be a part of that larger group, she'd want to know them all very well. It wasn't too soon to start making those connections.

And his family would be all the more important to their child if she relapsed. The thought made Jillian's throat dry up.

Stroking his palms over her shoulders, Cody stared down into her eyes. "I will do whatever you want me to, because I don't want you to worry, and I don't want you to have any stress. But first, be honest with me. Is this a stall tactic from talking about us?"

He needed trust between them.

After the way his last relationship had ended, having forthright communication was important to him. And although he'd gotten off on the wrong foot with Jillian when she'd mistaken him for Carson, he'd developed more faith in her character since then. He didn't believe she was the kind of woman who would purposely deceive him.

"Yes and no." Jillian's hazel eyes locked on his. "I'm not ready to move into the ranch for good, but if I promise to stay here for the week, we'll have time to talk about the future. But in the meantime, aren't you a little worried about all the texts going back and forth among your family members today? You don't strike me as the kind of family to spend the afternoon texting each other."

He guessed there was more to it that she wasn't sharing, but maybe that was part of the reason she wanted to delay further discussion. He was new to all of this. And he was trying to navigate it with someone he didn't know well enough.

"We definitely aren't." Cody had worries of his own. If his father was including all the family in his messages—even Carson, with whom he was barely on speaking terms—something was wrong. "If you'll let me get you something to eat first, I'll read all these texts and figure out what's going on. I can ride over to my dad's if it seems necessary."

"I'm perfectly capable of making dinner—"

"Please." He didn't want to argue with her. The only thing he had any control over in this pregnancy was his contribution to Jillian's welfare, and he refused to relinquish that role. "I want to help you stay healthy and get enough rest. Make yourself comfortable and let me feed you, then I promise I'll check in with my family."

At her nod, relief rushed through him. He opened the front door before she changed her mind. His gaze followed her slender figure as she retreated up the stairs to the bedroom where she'd spent the previous night.

His thoughts turned to dinner. The doctor had said maintaining a healthy diet was critical, and Cody intended to make sure she had plenty of variety so she could find foods that would appeal to her. Tomorrow, he'd find a chef who was a certified dietician. Someone more skilled in a kitchen than him. For now, he grabbed some steaks and a couple chicken breasts, then fired up the grill.

Jillian would have every possible advantage to help her through this pregnancy. He would see to it personally. She'd agreed to stay with him for one week. He'd simply find a way to romance her. To get to know her better and make her happy. Above all, to ensure that after their week together was over, she never wanted to leave.

Eleven

When Scarlett touched down in Cheyenne at the tiny private airport outside of town, she was surprised to see her grandfather's limousine waiting nearby. The ground crew retrieved her bags while she walked down the steps of the Learjet. Hopefully, she hadn't kept Malcolm McNeill waiting for his plane.

She lifted her hand to wave at the long, dark Mercedes with tinted windows. It had been a quick flight from LA, too quick because she was dreading facing her family when she got home. Her father hated publicity and the limelight in general, but he especially disliked the superficial kind that came from celebrity stalkers and paparazzi—the kind she'd garnered when she'd been in Hollywood. He'd messaged her a terse command to see him upon her return, and she planned to make his house her first stop so she could get the confrontation over with.

Which reminded her of the last showdown she'd had with a man: Logan King. She had held strong against thinking about him—sort of—last night. But when she woke up to the photos of them together plastered all over the internet, she had weakened. She'd stared at them far too long. Before she knew it, she'd found herself searching for articles about the film shoot in the Congo. Two supporting actors had quit during the grueling months shooting in Africa, a time made more difficult by a demanding director who'd closed the set to "bond" his team. After Logan returned to the United States, he'd said in an interview that it had been the most challenging experience of his life.

What if it wasn't just a sound bite? Frustrated to still be thinking about him, Scarlett focused on her grandfather instead.

Just then, the Mercedes driver got out of the vehicle, hurried around to the back and opened the door to reveal Rose Hanson, Malcolm McNeill's new girlfriend. The woman stepped onto the tarmac, holding a fistful of her long, colorful gauze skirt in one hand to keep it from blowing in the wind. Her long gray hair was in a thick braid draped over one shoulder. She waved at Scarlett while Malcolm emerged from the car behind her, his crisp blue suit making him look every inch the Manhattan business mogul.

"Hello, Granddad. Rose." She hugged them both while the driver pulled their luggage from the trunk. "I hope I didn't keep you waiting. I'm so grateful for the use of the plane."

Malcolm waved aside the thanks. She noticed how his thinning gray hair was perfectly in place despite the breeze. "We timed our arrival so we could see you before we left. I talked to the pilot last night, so I knew your schedule."

"Where are you going?" Scarlett had been under the impression Malcolm would stay in Cheyenne for as long as it took to make peace with his estranged son, her very stubborn father.

"I'm heading to Silicon Valley for a few days to visit my grandson Damon and his wife, Caroline. They have a son that I've yet to meet."

"And my granddaughter, Brianne, will be there visiting with Malcolm's grandson Gabe," Rose added. "So we both get to see grandchildren."

Scarlett had visited Gabe and Brianne and their adorable boy, Jason, on a trip to Martinique last winter. Brianne was just as warmhearted as her grandmother.

"And one shared great-grandchild," Malcolm reminded her, his blue eyes twinkling with mischief as they exchanged smiles.

Rose patted Scarlett's arm. "And one shared great-grandchild. My Brianne loves Gabe's boy like her own. I'm so glad they're coming to the States more now that Damon is in California. They want the cousins to be close."

"That sounds nice," Scarlett admitted, wishing her family would come together the way the rest of Malcolm's heirs had. "I hope we have get-togethers like that one day."

Even among the siblings there were disagreements, with Cody and Carson never seeing eye to eye. Brock coped by keeping them all at arm's length. Since Madeline had started dating Sawyer Calderon, from a rival ranching family, tensions ran even higher.

"Malcolm will win over your dad one of these days."

Rose took his hand in hers and squeezed it. The gesture was so sweet that Scarlett found herself envying them.

"I left the keys to the house for you in the car, if anyone wants to use the place while we're gone." He'd rented a massive hobby ranch in Cheyenne for the year, in the hope of reconciling with Scarlett's father. "I'm sending the plane back up here, too, in case you need it. Take the limo back home, honey, and we'll see you next week." Her grandfather nodded to the driver, who moved to take Scarlett's bags from the ground crew workers who had carted them over.

After a quick goodbye, Scarlett retreated into the back seat of the spacious vehicle. She picked up the envelope with her name on it that contained the keys, and slid it into the back pocket of her purse.

Another piece of paper there caught her eye. She'd forgotten all about the note Logan had handed her at the club the night before. She'd been so distracted, so surprised that he would bother defending himself regarding her unreturned texts six months ago, the mystery note had slipped her mind.

Logan thought the man in the pin-striped jacket had passed it to her. How was that possible? She didn't even know the guy.

Now, as the limousine pulled out of the private airport and onto the deserted the backroads that would lead her home, Scarlett unfolded the heavy parchment.

Inside, there was a brief typed message:

Do you know your mother's true identity? You might be surprised to find out her real name. And to learn her marriage to your father was never legal. I will make trouble for your family if you continue your plan to let *Winning the West* be filmed on McNeill land.

Stunned, Scarlett reread the message two times.

It couldn't possibly be true.

It must be a trick to stir up trouble. Possibly a prelude to blackmail. Her stomach, already in knots after the unsuccessful trip to LA and the public standoff with Logan that had turned into a paparazzi photo op, churned with fear.

Was there any chance her mother hadn't gotten married using her real name? That Paige Samara McNeill had a hidden past? Normally, her mom was unflappable, the anchor of their family. The voice of reason when her father flew off the handle about something. She was stable. Grounded.

But she had seemed a bit anxious ever since the location scout came to town. And especially since Scarlett had mentioned her plan to fly to Los Angeles for a few days. She'd assumed it was because her mother didn't want her to follow dreams that would take Scarlett out of Cheyenne. What if there was more to it than that?

One thing was certain: Scarlett couldn't walk into her father's house and face her mother until she had a plan. Pulling her phone from her purse, she punched in her sister Maisie's number and prayed she would answer.

Maisie would make it all go away with a cynical comment about how gullible Scarlett could be. She'd probably say Scarlett was crazy to put any stock in a note from a stranger.

"Scarlett?" Maisie's voice sounded strained when she answered. "Is that you?"

"Yes." Straightening in her seat, Scarlett got ready to tell her all about the note, but Maisie rushed to fill the pause.

"Honey, get over to Dad's house. Mom is missing."

Too shocked to process much beyond that, Scarlett jammed the note back into her purse while Maisie explained that the whole family was gathering at their father's house right now. That Scarlett needed to be home with them.

The mystery message would have to wait. She needed to be there for her father, who must be going out of his mind. If her mother had a hidden past, what if it did more harm than good to reveal the message to the whole family? What was important was finding her.

Scarlett decided to keep the note to herself a little longer. At least until she could speak to one of her sisters privately and ask what she thought about it. Just until they figured out exactly what was happening.

Alone in her suite at the Black Creek Ranch after dinner, Jillian let her fingers wander over the literature from the obstetrician. Pamphlets about a baby's development. Brochures about maternal health. And yes, special notes for cancer survivors who were expecting a child.

Pulling the throw blanket from the back of the love seat over her lap, Jillian scanned the luxurious bedroom suite, complete with king-size bed near windows that led out onto a balcony overlooking the swimming pool and a courtyard. The sunken sitting area had a gas fireplace, and Cody had carefully placed the TV remote on a table within easy reach for her, along with a pitcher of water, a crystal glass, an ice bucket and her cell phone.

A few feet away, he'd crowded a side table with platters of snacks in case she got hungry while he was gone.
As if that was possible after the huge, multicourse meal
he'd made in short order downstairs. She couldn't possibly eat a strip steak and a whole chicken breast, but
they were both delicious and she'd eaten more than she
thought she would. Vegetables in a rainbow of colors
had filled the rest of her plate; the meal was about as
close to the doctor-recommended guidelines for her
diet as possible.

Cody's every action told her how much he wanted
this baby. How important it was to him to keep her safe.
Healthy. It was important to her, too. But she understood that cancer was indiscriminate. That she could
take every precaution, follow every guideline on those
doctors' lists and still have a recurrence. That was why
she couldn't fall into that trap. She refused to play that
game where she sacrificed her dreams to cater to her
disease's every whim, only to be beaten by the illness
in the end.

Grabbing her cell phone, she punched in the phone
number she already should have called.

"Hello?" On the other end, her boss—the woman
she answered to directly—sounded flustered. Busy.

In the background, Jillian could hear the wail of an
infant. The clatter of dishes and running water.

"Hi, Alyssa, it's Jillian. I hope it's not a bad time."

"Not at all. Just trying to get the kidlets to bed before
Todd gets home from tennis." Alyssa must have put the
phone on speaker because there was some interference,
and the noise on her end got louder. "Guys, what do we
say to Miss Jillian?"

Alyssa's two girls shrieked, "Hi, Miss Jillian!" at

earsplitting volume. A moment later, the baby greeted her with a happy gurgling sound.

"Go to bed for Mom, munchkins, and I'll bring you a prize home from cowboy country." Jillian had gotten to know Alyssa during her chemo treatments. Her boss's eldest son suffered severe rheumatoid arthritis that required chemo, too.

Jack had been fun company during those dark months, his outlook never down in all the times they'd shared a waiting room or a recovery area afterward.

The two little girls squealed some more until Alyssa took the phone off speaker. She must have chased the kids into their beds because it got quiet again.

"How's Jack?" Jillian asked, while Alyssa worked her mom magic with the baby.

In the background, a soft lullaby began playing before her boss responded.

"He's good. Tired from getting back to school after those weeks we had him out with a flare-up, but you know Jack. He keeps going."

"I'm glad he's back at school. I know how much it means to him to feel normal." Jillian remembered what an inspiration the boy had been. He had his own list of life adventures—most of which were far more interesting than hers. She'd laughed so hard when he told her that he was adding Ride a Lawn Mower to School to his list. Thinking about that made her all the more confident in her own decision to keep moving forward. "I'm sorry I didn't check in yesterday. But I think I've got everything in order here for filming to begin. What's my next assignment?"

She took notes while Alyssa reeled off a handful of locations that needed scouting, letting Jillian weigh in on what possibilities sounded the most promising, allowing her to choose her next destination.

Flagstaff or the Pacific Northwest?

She'd never seen the Grand Canyon, and it was on her list. She didn't need to pull it up to know. So, to honor the spirit of adventure that had helped her to conquer cancer the first time, Jillian accepted the Flagstaff scouting job.

After disconnecting the call, the burn in her throat started, the precursor to tears she knew were coming. She didn't want to upset Cody, but she also couldn't afford to stay here and let herself fall the rest of the way in love with him. That last night they'd spent together had rattled her emotions too much already, stirring deep feelings for a man who had looked to her for only a temporary diversion.

She couldn't be another responsibility on his list. This week, they'd hash out a plan for co-parenting. But after that, she needed to move on. Maintaining her independence was more important than ever. If the only legacy she could give her child was the knowledge that she hadn't let cancer keep her down, that she'd chosen to embrace life every moment, that was something Jillian could be proud of.

Cody stood in his parents' small living room, staring out the front window at his siblings' vehicles. Two had arrived on horseback, their animals tied to the front porch rail as if the house was a saloon in some old Western flick. No wonder Jillian thought a movie ought to be shot here.

Behind Brock's quarter horse and Maisie's spirited Appaloosa, their father's ATV sat beside Maddy's brand-new sports car. On the grass in the side field he could see Carson's pickup truck parked beside his own. They'd both bought the same model year—one gray, one black—within days of each other. Seeing the trucks side by side made Cody shake his head. He might scoff at being anything like his twin, but the similarities came out in those kinds of choices.

Proving you didn't escape family.

He glanced across the living room at his twin now, grateful Carson had put in an appearance when their father had asked for them all to be here. Their dad paced in the kitchen, waiting for Scarlett to arrive. Maisie and Maddy were in their mother's bedroom at Dad's request, looking around to see if they noticed anything missing. Cody was anxious to get the family meeting underway because, while he was concerned about his stepmother's whereabouts, his thoughts were preoccupied by Jillian and her pregnancy. They hadn't even scratched the surface of all they needed to discuss. His brain was working a mile a minute thinking through plans. Moving her to Wyoming. Helping her settle in.

Asking her to marry him. He didn't want to rush her, but that had to be a consideration. He didn't plan to have his child come into the world without the security that marriage brought to a family.

"Are you sure we shouldn't call the police?" Brock asked from his corner of the sofa, drawing Cody's attention back to the current situation. His brother was cracking pistachio nuts over a bowl in the far corner of the living room, his eyes on the TV, which was muted and tuned to a baseball game.

Brock had a knack for appearing unconcerned. Unflappable. But Cody knew he did stuff like that—pour the nuts, watch the game—to distract himself from the tense energy that tended to spark at all their family gatherings.

"And say what? My wife didn't make dinner tonight?" Dad quit pacing and filled the coffeepot with water. "I saw her at breakfast this morning, and you know as well as I do they aren't going to do anything until she's been missing at least twenty-four hours."

Cody guessed the real reason he didn't call the police was that he had a long-standing gripe with the local sheriff. But then, their father had never been an easy man to deal with. He had feuds with half of Laramie County.

"Here's Scarlett," Carson announced, getting to his feet as he looked out the window from behind Cody.

Cody watched a Mercedes limo pull up to the house. It had to be their grandfather's car. No one else rode around town in one of those. He hoped his dad wouldn't notice.

Maisie and Maddy emerged from the opposite end of the house. "I don't see anything out of place," Maisie told them. "Her suitcase is still here and there are no clothes or jewelry noticeably gone."

Impatient for their father to fill them in on what the hell was going on, Cody moved to the front door and opened it for Scarlett. Behind her, the limo drove away, its taillights disappearing up the access road.

"Nice ride," he muttered, but he tugged one of her curls as he said it. "Good to have you back."

A few minutes later they were all seated around the living room of what had been the foreman's quarters, a home Donovan had insisted on taking over once he gave the ranch duties to Cody. Brock ran his quarter horse breeding business primarily out of Creek Spill and had a home on the property. Maddy stayed at the White Canyon these days. Scarlett had a house at Black Creek and Maisie had built a tiny cabin for herself down at the creek's edge even though there was more than enough room for her at the main house.

They were a family, yes. But they'd all chosen their own niches, and carefully protected their space. It seemed to work well enough for everyone except Scarlett, who was chafing to move away. And maybe Carson, who was stuck in Cheyenne after his rodeo dreams had ended.

Their father cleared his throat. He was sitting on the edge of an old desk he'd been refurbishing in his spare time.

"I last saw Paige at breakfast this morning. You all know I've been concerned about her researching trips, when she's never expressed a desire to travel." He kept his phone clutched tightly in one hand, the only sign that he was upset. "Paige packed me a lunch, just like always, in case I had work in one of the far fields."

Cody thought about his stepmother's marriage to his father. She was much younger than Donovan, and he had never been an easy man to live with. Could she have decided to leave him?

She didn't have much family. Her parents had died in a car crash when she was a teen and she'd been on her own ever since. She'd been working in a bar in Cheyenne when she met Cody's father and started as a nanny to Cody, Carson and Brock after their mother's death.

"I called her at lunchtime and she didn't answer. She hasn't responded to my text messages all day. The car was gone when I got home for supper. I hoped maybe she forgot to pick up something for dinner and went to the store. But now I'm worried."

"Have you called any of her girlfriends?" Madeline asked. When her father shook his head, she volunteered to do that.

"What about family?" Scarlett asked.

They all stared at her.

"What?" She shrugged, picking at the flowers embroidered on the hem of her black skirt. "Just because she wasn't close with them doesn't mean she couldn't have decided to visit an aunt or an uncle. Do you know where any of her family lives, Dad?"

Cody thought it an odd question. Paige hadn't kept in touch with her extended family. No one had pressed her about it. It was something she had in common with Donovan. They didn't mind leaving the past behind and building a family of their own they could count on, consisting of the group assembled in the living room right now.

"Somewhere in northern Manitoba, I think. But she wouldn't turn to them." He shook his head, certain about that much.

"Have you tried tracking her phone?" Madeline asked. "Do you have any features like that on your plan?"

Their father stared at her blankly.

Cody stood from his seat by the front window, feeling restless. All the anxiety in the room only added to his own fears. "Dad, give Maddy your cell. She can tell if you have a program that shows where other devices on your phone plan are located."

Donovan passed the older model cell to Madeline, but Cody didn't hold out much hope. Neither his father nor stepmother liked their phones, using them mostly as photo albums.

"Are any of her things missing?" Brock asked, shifting to cross his ankles.

"No. Not that I can tell." Their father pursed his lips and looked around the room. The frown lines were etched deep in his tanned face. "Did she text any of you in the last twenty-four hours? Say anything unusual?"

Cody pulled out his phone to double-check, since Jillian had been the one to read through the slew of group messages this afternoon. But there was nothing from Paige.

There was silence for a moment until Scarlett spoke up. "She sent me a note last night telling me to be careful. But that's all."

Their father stared at his youngest daughter for a long moment. "She was worried about this trip. And she didn't like you seeing the actor."

"I didn't go to see Logan," Scarlett protested.

Cody barely grasped what they were talking about. And he only knew as much as he did thanks to Jillian. Funny that he had a better understanding of his family because of her, especially when she hardly knew them. She hadn't even met half of them. But then, maybe that was an indictment of him, and how he'd detached himself from the rest of the McNeills.

Maisie cleared her throat, slanting a glance at Scarlett.

"Okay, I went to see him, but only to tell him exactly what I think of self-important actors." Scarlett crossed her legs, the tulle of her flowered skirt swirling like a dark cloud around her knees.

Carson pinched the bridge of his nose. "Can we focus on Paige? Should we search the ranch?"

A surge of fear jolted Cody. The idea that she might be hurt somewhere on the property hadn't occurred to him. But their mother had died on the ranch.

"Good idea." Cody was already on his feet. "We should divide up the acreage and start looking."

Brock and Carson stood. Someone turned off the TV and Carson pulled up a map on his phone. Maisie was already claiming the terrain she would search on horseback, while Scarlett went to a closet to dig out flashlights. Cody noticed Maddy move to stand beside their father, an arm around his shoulders. The old man—who wasn't all that old—suddenly looked every one of his sixty years. If the thought of something happening to Paige made Cody's gut twist, he could only imagine what it did to his dad.

Once they'd all made a plan to check in with each other, Cody took his phone and his search assignment, then drove Scarlett to the stables, since she didn't have her car. Carson drove behind them. Cody planned to search on horseback, but he would insist that Scarlett take the Gator, so she could use the headlight. It would be safer for her.

"You okay?" he asked her on the way over to the stables near the main house. His gaze went to the bedroom window where Jillian's light was still on.

"I guess." Scarlett seemed nervous. Fidgety and hesitant. She must be really worried. "I just feel bad that Dad thinks Mom disappearing could have anything to do with me, or with my visit to LA. I knew she was worried but…" She shook her head. "Not any more worried than normal, right?"

"You're entitled to follow your dreams," he told her, realizing he meant it even though he'd gotten the idea from Jillian. "Dad and Paige both know that, even if they guilt-trip you about it."

Cody was trying to reassure her, but she still seemed upset. After he parked the truck between the equipment building and the stables, he gave her a hug with one arm.

"She's going to be fine," he told her. "We'll find Paige."

A little while later, as he saddled up his horse to start his search, he hoped that was true. He had thought the most likely scenario was that Paige had left Dad. Maybe they'd had an argument or something that Dad wouldn't own up to. But mounting a search of the property in the dark brought home the reality that something could have happened to her.

The fear in his gut wasn't just about Paige. This night only heightened his sense that Jillian and his child seemed so vulnerable, too. Tomorrow, he would ask Jillian what she needed to be happy in Cheyenne. How he could help her find fulfillment—to pursue her dreams—from Wyoming.

There was nothing more important to him in the world than keeping her and his baby safe.

Twelve

Jillian was awake when Cody returned to the main house at midnight. He'd messaged her earlier to let her know about Paige's disappearance and the search. So when Jillian saw the pickup truck's headlights in the driveway from her window, she rushed downstairs to see if they'd found his stepmother.

She reached the kitchen as he was coming through the front door. His expression was even more somber than usual, and her chest tightened.

"Any word?" she asked, flipping on the light over the oven range to illuminate the kitchen.

"Jillian." His broad shoulders sagged a bit as he saw her. "I didn't want to wake you."

She noticed now that he'd slid off his boots at the door. He padded over to her in his socks, barely making a sound on the hardwood floor.

"I've been worried." She reached to touch him, to offer what comfort she could.

He wrapped her in his arms and kissed her. Fast. Hard. She could feel the tension in him, and the worry. She pressed herself closer, breathing him in. For a span of two heartbeats, she kissed him back, wanting him. Wishing she could lose herself in his touch.

But then, she edged back, knowing they needed to talk.

His gaze held hers for a long moment, his breathing harsh. Then he straightened.

"We halted the search when Paige called Madeline shortly before midnight. She'd decided to drive to Yellowstone to clear her head in the mountains for a few days." Cody edged back to look down at Jillian, his hands rubbing warmth into her upper arms, making her realize she'd forgotten her robe in her rush to get downstairs.

Fresh awareness sparked inside her at his touch.

"Why didn't she answer her cell all day?" Some of the worry slid away at the news that his stepmother was safe, but Jillian wondered why he still seemed so on edge.

She could feel the tension in his shoulders where her hands lingered, and she wanted to ease that away. To curl against him all night long. How was it possible that someone she'd known for such a short amount of time could feel so right beside her?

"She said she forgot it at a rest stop off the highway on the way there. She called from a hotel phone." Frowning, he slid his hand to Jillian's back, gently steering her out of the kitchen. "I'll tell you more once you're in bed. You need your rest."

"Why did she call Madeline and not your father?" she asked, leading him up the stairs toward the room where she'd been sleeping the past two nights.

"I don't know. They didn't talk long, I guess because she was tired. But she told Maddy she'd attended a yoga retreat up there once, and she thought the meditation would be good for her after a stressful week."

"Because of the film shoot?" Jillian couldn't help feeling a twinge of guilt over that. Had the promise of outsiders descending on Paige's home been that upsetting? "I only went ahead with booking the site when your siblings were all on board. It didn't occur to me—"

"It's not your fault. I'm guessing she had a falling out with my father or she would have phoned him." Cody pushed open her bedroom door, accompanying her inside.

The ritual of it, of being in his house, of waiting for him to come home, felt intimate. As did sliding between her sheets when he lifted the blanket for her. Pleasurable shivers chased one another up and down her spine. The heated look in his blue eyes as he pulled the covers up to her chin told her that he was feeling some of those same things.

Attraction, yes. But more than that, connection.

It hadn't been there for him the last time they'd shared a bed, but a hopeful piece of her heart clamored to know—if she lay with him again, would the bond be there this time?

She knew this wasn't the right time to think about those things. He was exhausted from worry. And they'd both had plenty to think about before the news about Paige.

"What did your father have to say?" she asked.

"I didn't see him after Maddy called to update me. I came straight here from the search." Cody shook his head, the weariness evident in his voice as he sat on the edge of the mattress.

"We can talk more in the morning." She lifted her hand to his cheek on impulse, her feelings for this man in a hopeless tangle.

The father of her child.

"Of course." His nod was so automatic, so agreeable, she wondered again if the tenderness was for the baby's sake.

A twinge of hurt forced her hand away, and she reminded herself she would be leaving soon. She'd already committed to her next job, to help ensure she didn't weaken where Cody was concerned. She knew how vulnerable her heart would be to this man if she wasn't careful.

"I need to go to Creek Spill tomorrow afternoon to review a few final details with Carson." She swallowed hard, telling herself it would get easier one day to have a relationship with Cody. A platonic relationship. A functional, co-parenting agreement.

"I'll drive you over there," he offered, his fingers sifting absently through her hair, stirring a hunger for him she couldn't imagine would ever be sated.

The passion that had been there since that first night remained, stronger than ever. But was it fair to lose herself in all that heat when she lost a piece of her heart to him every time?

That was exactly why being around him was so dangerous to her.

"There's no need. I'm just introducing him to the assistant director. And I have a few more questions about storing equipment for the shoot."

Cody lingered another moment, his fingers tracing the line of her jaw as he stared down into her eyes. Her breath caught. Held.

"I want to spend as much time as I can with you while we figure out what's next for us, Jillian. Let me drive you."

She could hardly refuse. If anything, she respected him all the more for his determination to get to know her better. To pave the way for their child's future.

At her nod, he brushed his fingers over her curls one last time, then bade her good-night. Sensation tingled through her scalp long after he left, his touch filtering into her dreams and arousing desire she needed desperately to forget.

Cody couldn't take his eyes off Jillian the next day as she walked around Carson's ranch with the assistant director, Leon Wells. Her laughter floated on the breeze, her joy in simple things infectious as she pointed out patches of ordinary wildflowers or mountain views. It was hard to believe that the movie crew would be shooting at the Creek Spill Ranch as early as next week.

Weather permitting.

It seemed that the assistant director followed the weather like a meteorologist. When they'd all convened at the Creek Spill ranch house earlier this afternoon, the man had asked a dozen questions about Wyoming's climate, and had proceeded to speculate on cloud formation and humidity levels for ten days out, apparently needing as much information as possible to get the shots he wanted.

The discussion around Carson's kitchen table had been more interesting than Cody had anticipated. It also made him realize how long it had been since he'd set foot in his brother's house. The rift between them had grown worse with their grandfather's arrival, but as the weeks dragged on and Malcolm McNeill maintained a presence in Cheyenne, Cody realized he couldn't afford to alienate more members of his family. Especially with a child on the way. He needed to think about building relationships.

Now, while Jillian walked around the yard and outbuildings with Leon Wells, Cody forced his attention away from her and turned to his twin. Carson was bent over the engine of an old pickup truck that had seen better days.

He liked to fix things. Cody had forgotten that about his brother in the years they'd lived apart. From broken televisions to failed sump pumps, Carson was drawn to all things mechanical. He'd never thrown away something that could be fixed with a replacement part bought online, a talent that made him popular among the ranch hands. Cody would bet the truck belonged to one of the local cowboys who couldn't afford to replace it.

"You think Dad and Paige had a falling out?" Cody asked, keeping one eye on Jillian while he bent over the engine by his brother.

"Hard to say. One's about as chatty as the other."

"You're right about that," Cody mused, using a nearby rag to clean up connections on the battery terminal that were caked with rust. "Something's got Paige freaked out."

"The girls know more than they're saying." Carson

passed him a bottle of lemon juice, barely looking up from where he was wrestling with a new timing belt.

"You think?" Cody hadn't gotten that impression. They'd all seemed worried last night. He used the lemon juice on the terminals.

"Just a hunch. Maisie and Scarlett were deep in conversation when I stopped by Maisie's place this morning. But they went quiet when I arrived." Carson tugged the new belt into place and straightened, stretching his forearms from the effort. "Are you going to be okay with this film shoot?"

The question surprised him. "A bit late in the game for me to give my blessing."

"It's happening either way. But I guess I hoped spending time with Jillian was making you more amenable to the idea." Carson's gaze went to her and the assistant director, who were coming toward them.

As Cody watched Jillian, her red hair tipped with gold in the sunlight, he realized how little the film mattered in the big scheme of things. This woman was important to him. The movie, the family drama, even the rift with his grandfather—none of it mattered half as much as Jillian Ross and their child.

All he wanted was for her to stay safe, healthy and with him. Already he could imagine a future of more rodeos. More dances in dive bars. More nights spent with her in his arms.

"She's important to me," he confided to his brother. "So if it makes her happy, I'll have to get on board."

Carson's easy smile was a sight Cody hadn't seen in a while.

"They have a way of changing our priorities in a

hurry, don't they?" He clapped Cody on the back just as Jillian and Leon rejoined them.

"All set?" Cody asked her, ready to take her home. To have her all to himself.

"I am." Her eyes lingered on his, and he realized the heat that had started to burn that first night had only grown hotter.

He wanted to prepare a picnic for supper and drive her out to his favorite spot to view the stars while the weather was mild.

The assistant director, a skinny young man with wire-rimmed glasses, stepped forward, his dress shirt drenched in sweat and clinging to his shoulders in the summer heat.

"It's been nice meeting you." Leon shook Cody's hand and then Carson's, before turning back to Jillian. "And Alyssa told me you've got a fun assignment coming up next. Safe travels to Flagstaff, Jillian."

Cody wondered if he'd just misheard the man.

Of course. He *must* have misheard. Or maybe misunderstood. Because Jillian couldn't be going anywhere.

"Flagstaff?" Cody turned to face Jillian. Leon was already hurrying toward his white rental car. Carson had stalked off, too, his whistle fading as he headed toward the horse barn.

Jillian's face was pale. Her lips pursed. "I was going to talk to you about that."

His stomach fell like a stone.

"About Arizona?" he asked, his brain working overtime to fit pieces together that made no sense. "You're pregnant."

"I know that. But I still have a job to do, Cody. And putting my feet up for nine more months isn't going to ensure a healthy child. If anything, I should stay active and exercise."

He was vaguely aware of Leon's car as the assistant director drove away from Creek Spill. Birds circled overhead, casting shadows on the grass.

"You have a higher risk for recurrence." He'd read and reread his copies of the literature from all the doctors they'd seen. "You need to be careful. We can stack the odds in your favor with a more relaxed lifestyle. Less stress."

Maybe he wasn't fighting fair to remind her of those things. But damn it. She couldn't leave. Not now.

"The baby is not at risk," she reminded him, her voice steely.

As if that was all that mattered to him.

"But you are," he repeated, his heart pounding. Fear chilled the sweat on his skin. How could she even consider walking away? "Jillian, why not do everything in our power to ensure you stay healthy?"

They weren't the romantic words he wanted to give her. But she'd forced his hand. Hadn't given him enough time to woo her. To win her forever.

"I will." She laid a hand on his chest, her touch stirring desire despite the way things were falling apart all around them. "I promise you, I will. But I can't stop living just because there's a chance cancer will come back. I won't spend my life cowering in fear of what-ifs that are out of my control."

Something in those beautiful hazel eyes told him that her mind was made up. He felt like the ground had just given way beneath him.

"How long have you known you're leaving?" He

couldn't catch his breath, the sense of betrayal rising right alongside the fear.

They'd only just started to really know each other. To build something on top of all that heat and passion.

"I've been prepared to spend the whole week here so we can come up with a plan for co-parenting—"

"Is that what this week was going to be about for you?" He thought about all the plans he'd made. The picnic under the stars. A drive up to Yellowstone to show her the sights, followed by a candlelight dinner.

None of his ideas had involved a co-parenting plan. They were all about *her*. Even now, he wanted to haul her into his arms and kiss her. Remind her how good they were together.

"How long have you known you're leaving?" He repeated the question because he needed an answer.

He had to know how long she'd been plotting her getaway while he charted out a future together. A future she didn't want any part of.

"I just committed to the assignment last night." Her palm fell away from his chest.

He missed her touch already. But damn it, her hand wasn't the only thing slipping away.

"Jillian, don't do this. Don't shut me out." He reached for anything to make her stay, caught on his worst fear. "What if something happens to you? How will I raise this child by myself?" He couldn't afford to lose her. The idea cracked open an ache inside him, one that no amount of words could soothe.

"I hope you won't have to." Her eyes glittered in the sunlight, and he knew she was hurting, too. "But if it came to that, I know you could."

So that was it?

They stared at each other under the cloudless blue sky. Cody couldn't imagine a worse pain than that. He had lost his own mother as a child. He knew exactly how big a scar it left. Anger stirred.

"I can't believe you would choose some superficial adventures over this—the chance to be a family." He'd thought family was more important to her than that. She'd said she envied his.

She huffed out an exasperated sigh.

"It's not about that. We hardly know each other. We can't force ourselves to be a family when we're not ready. I won't be another responsibility weighing you down."

The gulf between them widened. And Cody didn't have a single idea how to bridge it.

While hope dried up to nothing, he became aware of his brother running toward them.

Running?

Jillian turned toward Carson, too. He was just fifteen yards away, waving a hand over his head, flagging their attention.

"We need to get to the hospital," he called to them, his cell phone in one hand while he pulled his keys from his jeans pocket. "Paige has been in an accident."

Thirteen

Scarlett couldn't catch her breath.

A panic attack was coming and she couldn't stop it as she paced around the women's bathroom at Eastern Idaho Regional Medical Center, clutching her phone and waiting for word on her mother's condition following emergency surgery. According to the report from the emergency techs who brought her in, a sudden rainstorm had created dangerous conditions on a trail where Paige had been hiking that morning, and she'd slipped down a mountainside. She had to be rescued by horseback and then airlifted to the nearest trauma center with a fractured hip and tibia.

The last few hours had been a blur, but at least they'd all made it to the hospital as fast as possible. It would have been nine hours away by car, but because Malcolm McNeill had sent his plane back to the private airfield outside Cheyenne, Scarlett and her family were able to fly. They'd been in the air for only an hour, but it had seemed endless. Brock had stayed behind to tend to some business at the White Canyon Ranch for Madeline so she could be with Paige. But all the other siblings had come.

Maisie plowed through the swinging bathroom door.

"I got your text…" She rushed over as soon as she got a look at Scarlett. "Are you okay?"

Scarlett shook her head. "I think—" she breathed faster "—I'm hyperventilating."

Maisie squeezed her. "You're okay." She spoke slowly. "I want you to hold your breath, honey. Just clamp down and hold it."

Scarlett sucked in air and tried not to breathe out, watching her sister. Keeping her eyes on Maisie, who always knew what to do. Those deep blue eyes grounded her. Helped her.

When the air rushed out again, Maisie nodded. "That's okay. This time purse your lips. Like this." She scrunched her lips tight. "That way you can slow the exhale, okay?"

Scarlett followed instructions. She could feel her heart rate slowing. She was calming down. Oxygen was flowing to her brain again. She nodded.

"I'm okay," she said finally. "Thanks for coming in. I just got in a panic thinking about that note. How am I ever going to tell everyone about it?"

She'd shown it to Maisie last night during the search for their mother. Scarlett had been ready to show it to her whole family. But once they'd learned Paige was safe, Maisie had told her it would be okay to sit on the note until they could show it to their mom. Give her a chance to respond before getting their father involved, just in case the message was something that could hurt their marriage.

"You haven't done anything wrong." Maisie combed her fingers through Scarlett's hair before tugging her toward the mirror. "Come here." She wet a paper towel.

"Dad and Cody will say I should have told them last night." Scarlett peered into the mirror at her smeared mascara. Her eyes were bloodshot from lack of sleep.

"Coulda, shoulda, woulda," Maisie chanted as she dabbed away the mascara streaks, meeting Scarlett's eyes in the mirror. "Doesn't matter now. Just go out there and share it. Let them weigh in. This is not your burden alone, okay? They deserve to know so they can help figure out what to do."

"Right." Scarlett nodded. "How would anyone who doesn't know our family know that I was in LA? I just keep wondering how that guy knew where to find me."

"Your friend Lucie knew you were going. She could have told someone." Maisie rubbed her cheek hard to get a spot off. "Logan could have heard you'd be there. And he's the one who actually handed it to you."

Scarlett's heart sank. "No."

"He's involved with the film, too," Maisie insisted, making perfect, logical sense. "And don't forget the note isn't just about Mom. Someone clearly doesn't want *Winning the West* to be filmed in Cheyenne."

But it couldn't be Logan. That theory would make more sense if he was trying to avoid Scarlett. But based on what he'd said when he'd followed her out of the club, he hadn't meant to break things off with her in the first place. She couldn't deny a tiny piece of her wished those words were true. For her family's sake, though, she wouldn't take chances.

"All the more reason to be on my guard when the film starts shooting." Taking the paper towel from her sister, Scarlett finished cleaning up her face. "I'm ready. I need to go tell them."

Jillian's head throbbed with worry as she sat next to Cody in the busy trauma center's waiting room. Donovan McNeill paced near a window, pausing now and again to drum his fist gently on the glass or to slouch in a seat nearby. Cody and Carson sat on opposite sides of the room, their tense shoulders and jutting jaws like matching bookends of worry.

The hospital had to bring up tough feelings for them both. They'd lost their own mother to her injuries from the bull.

Jillian had never questioned whether she would make the trip with him or not. Although now, looking back at the last few frightening hours, she wondered if that had been the right decision. Maybe she didn't belong here.

Yet even while things were falling apart between her and Cody, she couldn't turn her back on the McNeills. Not when she carried Cody's heir. Not after seeing the way they pulled together, even when it hurt. When Paige had been missing, Cody and Carson had even set aside their differences to search for her.

Donovan McNeill hadn't thought twice about accepting his father's plane when it meant getting to his wife's bedside, and from what Jillian could gather, he hadn't spoken to Malcolm in over twenty-five years. It was moments like this that brought people together and made crystal clear what was really important in life.

And for Jillian, she couldn't imagine being anywhere else right now. Everything she'd spouted to Cody about pursuing dreams paled in comparison to being beside him when he needed her. She wanted to be right here. With him. With her child's family.

The institutional clock on the wall ticked audibly, even over the hum of activity all around them. The nurses' station monitors beeped at regular intervals. The steady sound of machinery helping struggling human bodies to function was strangely reassuring.

Maisie and Scarlett were just returning from the bathroom. Had Scarlett been crying? Her face looked puffy and red.

"Family of Paige McNeill?" a gray-haired doctor in green scrubs called out as he exited one of the doors marked Do Not Enter.

As one, seven people tensed.

The siblings seemed to realize it was their father's right to speak to the doctor, so they waited while Donovan strode over to him first. But Jillian and Cody were close enough to overhear the conversation. And the others crowded closer, behind their father.

"The surgery went well," the doctor assured him. "I was worried about the hip, but I'm pleased with how well the fracture set. The tibia gave us no trouble. We might find more damage in her left arm that needs attention, but we've splinted it and want her to heal from the trauma of the fall before we work on anything else."

A sigh of relief echoed around the group.

"Can we see her?" Donovan asked, raking a hand through his salt-and-pepper hair.

"She won't come out of the anesthesia for a while, but you're welcome to sit with her in the recovery room.

Only one at a time, though, I'm afraid." His gray eyebrows swooped down. "Her condition is still critical."

Donovan nodded. Cody rose and interjected, "Doctor, what about her head? Did she hit it in the fall?"

The surgeon nodded in turn, as if the question was expected. "There is very little external damage and her scans look clear, but she definitely hit her temple, so we'll be monitoring her closely for problems. She's on a ventilator and she's been sedated because of the trauma. She might not be able to communicate much even after the anesthesia wears off." Excusing himself, the doctor left, pointing them toward a small vestibule outside the recovery area.

Donovan turned to Madeline, clapping a hand on her shoulder. "We can trade off sitting with her once she wakes up, but I'd like to go in there first."

No one argued with him as the rest of the family relocated to the quieter waiting area.

"It's good news, though, right?" Madeline asked.

When no one else said anything, Jillian gave her shoulders a hug. "I think so."

Jillian had barely settled in her seat next to Cody when Maisie leaned forward in her chair.

"I know we're all worried about Mom. But now that Dad's gone, Scarlett has something to share." She leveled a stare at her sister.

Cody straightened in his seat. Jillian found herself reaching for him. Her fingers threading through his on instinct.

Scarlett's cheeks went pink. "With all that was going on, I didn't know when to bring this up." She reached into her purse and withdrew a folded piece of paper. Her hands were unsteady as she smoothed the wrinkles and flattened it with her hand before continuing.

"When I was in Hollywood, some guy I never met before tried to hand me this note." She kept her voice quiet even though there was no one else around in the waiting area.

She passed the note to Cody first.

As she read it over his shoulder, Jillian's gut clenched. For Cody. For Paige. For all of them. And what did her film have to do with any of it?

Cody swore softly as he read and quickly passed the note to Carson. Madeline moved closer to read it with him. Maisie had obviously already seen it.

"Why the hell didn't you tell us about this last night when Paige went missing?" Cody demanded. Anger had crept into his voice, though he didn't raise it.

Jillian wondered the same thing.

"Scarlett told me," Maisie retorted, her posture defensive as she moved to shield her sister. "And we were about to bring it to Dad when Mom called home. We had hoped to ask her about it first."

Cody took a deep breath and changed his approach. "I get it. You were worried your mother had good reason for hiding something about her past from Dad. But what if the person who gave you this note intends to hurt her? What if someone already did?"

Scarlett leaned forward in her chair. "It doesn't read like a physical threat. And blackmail isn't usually that kind of crime."

"Do you think this is blackmail?" Jillian asked, trying to make sense of it.

At the same time, Carson said, "Would you recognize the guy who gave this to you if you saw him again?"

"I wouldn't recognize him." Scarlett shook her head, her long dark curls drooping. All the McNeills looked the worse for wear after the hours of uncertainty, but Scarlett seemed even more bedraggled. Maybe she hadn't slept well with the weight of the letter on her mind.

"Your friend might," Maisie said, turning to the rest of the family. "Scarlett was with Logan when it happened. He saw the guy, too."

"Should we tell Dad?" Scarlett asked. "I just don't want to pile too much on him now."

Cody was the first to answer. "We tell him as soon as she wakes up."

Beside him, Carson nodded, cementing the decision.

"If someone is trying to make trouble for us, we all need to be on guard," Carson added. "I wouldn't have agreed to the film if I'd known."

Scarlett looked miserable. "I didn't get this until afterward."

Maisie jumped to her little sister's defense again, and while she explained to Carson all the reasons this was a difficult position for Scarlett, Cody leaned over to speak in Jillian's ear.

"Walk with me?"

It was a question, but he was already pulling her to her feet. Grateful for the suggestion, Jillian followed him.

"We'll be back in ten," Cody announced over his shoulder. He placed a hand on the small of her back, guiding her out the door of the private waiting room and back into the frenzy of the trauma floor.

But a few moments later, they were walking down a long corridor toward a door with a small green sign pointing the way to the meditation garden. It was sponsored by a local nursery.

"I needed some air." His voice rasped with exhaustion even though it was only eight o'clock.

Neither of them had slept much the night before.

"Me, too." She stepped out into a sweet-smelling garden half covered with a white pergola. Jasmine hung over the arches, the fragrance heavy in the fresh air.

Cody guided them toward a bench near a bubbling fountain with a statue of a little girl reaching into a stream of running water. The sun had just set, but landscape lights and the moon made it easy to see.

"How are you feeling?" He led her to the bench and they sat down side by side.

The sound of water rushing from the fountain into a small pond soothed her.

Or maybe it was the presence of the man beside her. A man who meant more to her with each passing hour. Their lives had become intertwined so fast, fueled by the adrenaline of their life circumstances—her illness, his family. And somehow, they'd found something special.

Something she wasn't ready to turn her back on.

"Physically, I'm fine." She turned and glanced up at him. "Emotionally drained, as I'm sure you are, too." She put her hand on his knee. "I hope it wasn't presumptuous of me to make the trip here with your family."

"I'm glad you're here, Jillian." He slid his fingers around hers, his touch warming her as it had from that first night when they'd danced. "If it was up to me, you'd be staying in Cheyenne." He looked up at the stars for a long moment before his eyes locked on hers. "Spending time with me and my family. Giving us a chance to grow on you."

Her throat burned at the picture he painted. As if it was that simple. She picked at a tendril of jasmine that curled around the arm of the bench, traced the veins in one green leaf.

"Cody, I know how fast you'd all grow on me if I stay in Cheyenne." But she'd given her love to someone before, only to discover at the cruelest possible moment how much it could hurt to find that love was one-sided.

Cody was too honorable a man to pretend a devotion he didn't feel. But Jillian would never know if his tender concern was all for the sake of his child. His heir.

The tiny life that had only just begun to grow.

"Then why won't you?" The hurt and confusion in his voice forced her to be honest.

To share her hurts, too.

She let go of the jasmine and looked him in the eye. "Because I can't bear to fall in love with you and know you only wanted me here for the sake of this baby."

His eyes closed as if she'd dealt him a blow. When he opened them, they were clearer. Determined.

"You faced cancer alone. You scrapped the whole direction of your life to start over again. You got a dream job by sheer force of will. And you waltzed into Cheyenne and took on the most formidable McNeill in town to get what you wanted." He lifted her hands in both of his as he stared into her eyes. "Don't you dare tell me you're too scared to fall in love with me."

A shocked laugh escaped her. Or maybe it was a little bit of hysteria edging through after the upheaval of the last few days.

"A woman has her limits." She felt tears bubbling up, but didn't want to shed them. "There's so much out of my control—"

"But you can control this? Us?" He brought her hand to his face and laid it along his jaw, kissing the palm. "That's the worst thing to try to dictate. You can't tell your heart what to feel."

The breeze stirred a flag over their heads, the fabric snapping in the wind. She struggled to keep her wits about her. To look at this relationship rationally and not through the eyes of a woman in love. She couldn't afford that kind of weakness now.

"I can try to protect it," she argued weakly, feeling her defenses slide away and helpless to resurrect them.

He shook his head, sadness and regret in his eyes. "Can I tell you a secret? It's going to sound awful to say, but my father has been protecting his heart ever since my mother died."

Jillian blinked in surprise. An older couple strolled past them, arm in arm, and disappeared into the grounds beyond the garden.

"What about Paige?" She couldn't imagine putting her heart in Cody's hands if she wasn't certain he would give her his in return. But maybe some women could love that way.

"A marriage of convenience. I always knew why my father chose her—she took care of his kids, no questions asked. But until I read that note Scarlett showed us, it never occurred to me Paige might have been running from demons of her own when she agreed to marry Dad."

Jillian shivered. "I couldn't bear a lifetime of loneliness like that."

"There's still time for them." Cody glanced toward the hospital. "I sure as hell hope so, anyway." He turned to her again. "But my point is this. Protecting your heart is what leads to the real hurt. To the emptiness of never really connecting with people."

"So your advice to me is that I should open my heart to you."

"Obviously." He grinned, and for a moment it was that same easy grin as his brother's, the smile that had captivated her that first night at the bar. Except it was all his. Uniquely Cody. "But what I'm really trying to say is that I would never trap either one of us in that kind of relationship. If it doesn't work, we'll find a way to love our child as equals and friends."

Her heart hurt at the idea of walking away. Of trying at love and failing.

On the far side of the hospital, an ambulance siren blared, a surge of urgency sounding through the otherwise peaceful retreat.

"I want more than that for this baby." Her hand crept to her flat belly, where she prayed their child would grow.

"So do I." He tipped his forehead to hers. "Family means everything to me, Jillian."

"I don't want you to force yourself to love me."

"You wouldn't be forcing me." He shook his head, certainty in his eyes. "My feelings for you are so real, I can't imagine a life without you. And I don't know how that happened so fast, but it did."

She blinked, struggling to follow what he was saying. "Do you mean—"

"Wait." He pressed a finger to her lips. Gently. "Let me get this out while I can. I don't want to rush you, Jillian. But I love you, and I don't want you to leave."

Her heart melted. Or maybe it was all her doubts that slid away at his words—words he would never utter unless he meant them. Happiness unfurled like a spring bloom, but before she could answer, he rushed on, continuing, "And we can date first, you know, if you aren't ready for more. Take it one day at a time. But we can only do that if we're in the same state."

"You don't want me to go to Flagstaff." She understood what he was asking. Recognized the practical limitations of being a rancher. He was tied to the land.

"I didn't say that. If you go, I go with you." He kissed her cheek.

Then the other.

Her pulse rate doubled as she thought through his words, felt the rasp of his unshaved face against her skin.

"You would do that for me?" That alone told her so much about his commitment to her. To this love.

"Without a moment's hesitation." He wasn't a man to tease. And he sure wouldn't lie about something like that.

But she had to think of his wants, as well. "I love you, Cody. And I love that you would do that for me. But you're a rancher. How could you leave the ranch?"

She appreciated that earthiness about him. The way he embraced the land and wasn't pretentious in spite of his vast fortune. She didn't want to change him.

"I like to think of myself as a rancher, Jillian. But first and foremost, I am a McNeill." He said it like that explained everything. But even though she'd researched his lands for the film, she'd never read much about his family's assets or wealth.

"I know your grandfather is rich," she began, think-

ing through what he was saying. "He's the head of Mc-
Neill Resorts."

"Yes. And my father has spent his whole life trying to outshine his old man because of an old feud that
stopped mattering a long time ago. While I prefer to
live off what I earn on the ranch, I have enough other
holdings that I could take some time away from Cheyenne while we see the world. Check off some of those
adventures on your list." He leaned in to kiss her lips
with infinite tenderness. "Together."

She couldn't have been more stunned.

Biting her lip, she tasted his kiss on her mouth. She
hardly dared to believe what he was offering her.

"That would be amazing." She felt light. Free.

Loved.

Her heart soared high and she didn't try to stop it.
She simply let the joy fill her up.

"You have to let me take care of you, though. Good
food. Enough rest." He kissed her again, lingering this
time until her body heated with awareness. "And if I
opt to spend the day in bed with you, you have to tell
me if I wear you out."

She leaned back long enough to see the wicked gleam
in his eyes. She nipped his ear in retaliation before she
whispered, "I bet I'll wear you out first."

"Are we really going to do this, Jillian? Conquer the
world and that list of adventures together?" His eyes
were serious again. "Hearing about Paige today, knowing how fragile life can be—" He swallowed hard and
kissed her again. "I don't want to waste a day being
away from you."

With all her heart, Jillian hoped she could fulfill this
man's dreams. But if nothing else, she was going to try

to make him happy for as much time as they had together. And yes, she was going to let herself fall head over heels for him.

She guessed the woozy feeling she had meant it was already happening.

"I won't waste a minute," she promised.

And kissed him with abandon, treasuring the promise of tomorrow with the worthiest man she'd ever met.

* * * * *

COMING SOON!

We really hope you enjoyed reading this book. If you're looking for more romance, be sure to head to the shops when new books are available on

Thursday
12th July

MILLS & BOON

LET'S TALK
Romance

For exclusive extracts, competitions
and special offers, find us online:

Or get in touch on 0844 844 1351*

For all the latest titles coming soon, visit
millsandboon.co.uk/nextmonth